SNOWDRIFT

Books by Helene Tursten

THE IRENE HUSS INVESTIGATIONS
Detective Inspector Huss
Night Rounds
The Torso
The Glass Devil
The Golden Calf
The Fire Dance
The Beige Man
The Treacherous Net
Who Watcheth
Protected by the Shadows

THE EMBLA NYSTRÖM INVESTIGATIONS
Hunting Game
Winter Grave
Snowdrift

An Elderly Lady Is Up to No Good: Stories
An Elderly Lady Must Not Be Crossed: Stories

SNOWDRIFT
HELENE TURSTEN

Translated from the Swedish by Marlaine Delargy

First English translation published in 2020 by
Soho Press
227 W 17th Street
New York, NY 10011

Library of Congress Cataloging-in-Publication Data

Names: Tursten, Helene, 1954– author. | Delargy, Marlaine, translator.
Title: Snowdrift / Helene Tursten
translated from the Swedish by Marlaine Delargy.
Other titles: Snödrev. English
Description: New York, NY : Soho Crime, 2020.
Series: The Embla Nystrom investigations; book 3
Identifiers: LCCN 2020012354

ISBN 978-1-64129-308-2
eISBN 978-1-64129-161-3

Subjects: GSAFD: Mystery fiction.
Classification: LCC PT9876.3.U55 S6613 2020 | DDC 839.73/74—dc23
LC record available at https://lccn.loc.gov/2020012354

Printed in the United States of America

10 9 8 7 6 5 4 3 2 1

To Hilmer,
with all my love.
You have always been there for me.

THE FRONT DOOR slowly opened a fraction of an inch. After a while, a head cautiously peeped out. Everything seemed quiet, and a man stepped onto the small porch. Taking his time, he tucked a gun into the waistband of his pants, and slipped a cell phone into his pocket. Then he zipped his leather jacket, adjusted his night-vision glasses, and pulled up the hood of the sweatshirt he was wearing under his jacket.

Large fields extended on both sides of the house. This was an advantage; there was no one nearby to see or hear him. But just to be safe, he reached around the doorframe and turned off the external light. He also removed the key from the inside, pushed the door shut with his hip, and locked it. Then he turned around and, with a flick of his wrist, he tossed the key into the darkness. Carefully he made his way down the slippery steps and was swallowed up by the night in seconds.

The blizzard came sweeping in from the west. The strong wind whipped up the snow that had fallen earlier in the week, and, within minutes, visibility was virtually down to zero.

THE FLOOR NO longer felt solid, and her feet sank deeper with each step. She mustn't stop or she would get stuck. Keep going, keep going! There was no time to waste! I'm coming, Lollo! The light got closer, and she thought she could hear voices through the pounding in her ears. She could just make out three large shadows up ahead. They were bending over a small curled-up figure; she knew it was Lollo. Please, God, don't let it be too late! I promise I'll never . . . If you just help us, God! She tried to call out, but nothing passed her lips; they merely moved in silence.

One of the shadows suddenly turned toward her, and she realized she'd been spotted. At first she froze in fear, then she tried to run. But that moment of hesitation had been enough. Her feet were stuck. The menacing shadow was approaching, but she couldn't move. He reached her and she felt him grasp her by the throat.

"If you say a word to anyone, you're dead! We know who you are and where you live," he hissed.

Somehow she managed to speak: "Lollo, Lol . . ."

"Forget her!"

He pushed her to the floor. The walls around her collapsed, and she sank into the ice-cold sludge; it filled her nostrils and her mouth. Breathe . . . she couldn't breathe! Beneath her the ground began to shake.

EMBLA WOKE TO find herself sitting bolt upright in bed, terrified and gasping for air as sweat trickled between her breasts. Her T-shirt stuck to her back. It was usually the same when she had the recurring nightmare: she woke up because she couldn't breathe. But this time something was different. The ground was shaking. Why was the ground shaking? And where was she?

Slowly she began to gather her wits and realized the bed was moving.

Uncle Nisse's guest room was small, but there was just enough space for a camp bed at the foot of hers. That was where the movement was coming from. A halo of tousled brown hair appeared with a pair of wide-awake eyes sparkling beneath the curls. Elliot was impatiently shaking the rail at the bottom of Embla's bed.

"Come on, Embla—we're going hunting today!"

He leaped up and onto her bedspread.

"Hunting! Hunting! Hunting!"

He warbled away happily as he bounced up and down; Embla couldn't help laughing. He was always full of energy, but right now the dial was turned up to maximum.

"Okay—off you go to the bathroom, then put on the clothes I've left on the chair in the hallw . . ."

She didn't get any further; he was already on his way to the tiny en suite bathroom.

Elliot was the best thing to come out of Embla's relationship with Jason Abbot, a jazz musician. They'd split up almost five years ago after a series of excoriating rows about Jason's inability to remain faithful, but a deep bond had grown between Embla and Jason's son, Elliot, which his father had sensibly chosen to nurture. Needless to say, he had seen the value of having an adult around who was willing to help out. Elliot's mother had died before he was one year old, and the boy's only close relations in Sweden were a divorced maternal aunt and her three children, but she already had her hands full.

Embla stayed under the covers for a little longer, trying to shake off the fear that still sat in the middle of her chest like a hard knot. Over the past week, the nightmare had haunted her every night. The reason was obvious. Her childhood best friend, Louise, who went by Lollo and had disappeared fourteen and a half years ago, had suddenly gotten in touch.

Late on Friday night—eight days ago—Embla's phone had trilled the opening bars of the original 1977 *Star Wars* soundtrack. She'd been annoyed, because she'd just broken up with Nadir and assumed it was him calling. Warily she'd answered: "Embla Nyström."

No one said anything, but she could hear shallow breathing and a faint rushing in the background as if the person on the other end was far away, or standing by the sea.

"Hello? Who is this?"

There was a sharp intake of breath, then a female voice whispered, "Å . . . Åsa? Is that Åsa?"

The hairs on the back of her neck had stood on end. Nobody had called her Åsa in years. Everyone called her Embla these days, which was her given name, but when she was little she'd hated it because it was so unusual, and she had persuaded all her friends and teachers to use her middle name, Åsa. As an adult she'd started to prefer Embla and had switched back. But someone who hadn't seen her since she was a teenager couldn't possibly know that. And the person on the other end of the phone hadn't seen her for fourteen and a half years. She was certain of that because she recognized the voice.

"Lo . . . Lollo!" she managed eventually.

There was a gasp, and the connection was broken.

Her initial reaction had been shock, but after a while she had pulled herself together and began to process the realization that her friend was still alive. So many questions whirled around in her mind: Where was Lollo? Was she in danger? Would she get in touch again? Why had she called?

Embla had decided to finally tell someone everything she knew about that night. There was only one person she could bring herself to share her trauma with: her former boss, Superintendent Göran Krantz, head of the technical department at Police HQ in Gothenburg. She'd called him and told him the whole story. Her best friend had disappeared one night when they were both fourteen years old. Embla had gotten seriously drunk for the first—and only—time. The only thing she remembered was the scene that constantly replayed in her nightmare: the three men bending over Lollo. The grip on her throat. The death threat. The sense of impotence. The guilt.

As Embla and Elliot planned to travel to Dalsland the following morning for the school break, she and Göran had agreed to meet up as soon as she returned to Gothenburg. While she was away, he would try to take a closer look at the case notes surrounding Louise's disappearance if time allowed. If Louise got in touch again, Embla was to contact Göran right away, and he would do his best to trace the call.

Embla was glad she'd spoken to him. It had felt good

to know that he'd taken her seriously and was going to help her find out what had really happened to Lollo.

Ever since that phone call, Embla had gone over and over what she remembered. Sometimes she felt as if her head were about to explode. It was only when she was with Elliot and Nisse that she was able to relax for a while.

Within minutes the bathroom door flew open and Elliot shot into the hallway, still singing his hunting song to the accompaniment of the toilet flush. The melody was catchy, but the lyrics were a little monotonous, as they still consisted of just one word: hunting. He used different stresses and tones; he had clearly inherited his father's musicality and knew how to perform, but it was starting to get tiresome. This had been going on for several days, ever since Embla had given in to his pleas and Nisse's assertion that she ought to let the boy find out what it's like to go hunting.

Embla still wasn't sure it was a good idea to take a nine-year-old on a fox hunt. She had been fifteen when she first went out and had kept putting this forward as a reason to wait. Nisse had objected on the grounds that he'd been the same age as Elliot when his father had taken *him* hunting for the first time. But Embla knew the two situations weren't the same. The tradition had been in her family's blood for generations, but that wasn't the case in Elliot's family.

Familiar sounds from downstairs penetrated her consciousness: the hiss of the coffee machine, the clink of plates and bowls, footsteps crossing the creaking floor, the low hum of voices on the radio. Her uncle Nisse was making breakfast.

As usual he was up first. He'd always been an early

riser. That's what happens when you own a small farm. The animals have to be fed and stalls mucked out first, before you move on to the job that provides you with a regular income. Nisse had worked at the sawmill for nearly all of his adult life. He had just retired two years ago, and unfortunately he was now a widower. He and Aunt Ann-Sofi had no children, but Embla had always spent a lot of time with them. She loved the countryside, the forest, and the animals. Maybe she'd always felt more at home here than with her large family in the middle of Gothenburg, she reflected.

She was a late arrival, the child no one could really be bothered with. Her three older brothers had, each in their own way, taken up a lot of space. All three had already started school by the time she was born. Her strongest recollection from her childhood was loneliness. Fortunately she'd had Lollo . . .

At the thought of her friend she gave a start; she was suddenly wide awake.

"Breakfast!" Nisse shouted up the stairs.

Embla yawned and stretched before reluctantly clambering out of bed. She opened the roller blind, then stood gazing out the window. Much to her surprise, heavy snow had fallen overnight. Around six inches had come down earlier in the week, but now at least eighteen inches had accumulated. Another reason not to go hunting today. And it was cold. The thermometer outside her window read twelve degrees Fahrenheit, and a strong wind was still blowing.

"Hurry up, Embla!" Elliot shouted impatiently. He had to go back to school in two days, after the February break. He couldn't wait to tell his open-mouthed classmates about going hunting; a charter holiday in Gran Canaria or a ski trip to Åre didn't even come close.

ELLIOT COULD HARDLY sit still; his whole body was quivering with excitement.

"I can have a gun, too, can't I? Like, a little one? It doesn't have to be loaded. Or maybe a bit, just in case a bear comes along."

"Elliot, there won't be any bears. They're asleep in their dens during the winter. We're only going out to see if we can spot a fox," Nisse said.

"A fox? But I need a gun in case a wolf turns up! We'll shoot him dead! BANG!" He aimed at an imaginary animal in the hallway, his body jerking with each shot he fired. "POW! POW! BANG!"

"That's a powerful recoil you have there," Nisse commented, winking at Embla.

She smiled at him, but she still wasn't sure taking the boy hunting was a good idea. The snow, the cold, the fact that he was only nine . . .

"And Seppo has to come, too!" Elliot exclaimed, pointing to the sturdy elkhound lying by the fire.

When the dog heard his name, he opened one eye and pricked up his ears. But when he realized it wasn't time for food, he closed his eye and went back to sleep.

"No, Seppo isn't the kind of dog we use for hunting foxes. He's trained to deal with moose and deer," Nisse explained patiently.

"So what kind of dogs hunt foxes?"

"Smaller dogs, often terriers. For example—"

The ringing of the landline interrupted him. Nisse went over to the phone on the wall by the door.

"Good morning! How's life out there in Herremark?" he asked cheerfully.

Embla immediately knew who it was: Harald Fäldt, her mother and Uncle Nisse's cousin. Nisse had spent quite a lot of time with Harald and his wife over the years, but Embla hadn't seen them for ages. She could hardly remember when they'd last seen each other . . . Oh yes, Harald and Monika had thrown a big party at the guesthouse they ran. A summer party—midsummer, perhaps? She wasn't sure; she must have been seven or eight years old.

"Did you use a little gun when you were my age? Do you still have it? Can I borrow it? Please?"

"No, Elliot. There are no children's guns. And I didn't get a gun of my own until I was eighteen, and I'd passed my hunting exam," Embla explained.

Elliot frowned, looking confused. "Your what?"

"My hunting exam."

"What's that?"

"Well, it's kind of like school."

He thought for a moment, then his face lit up. "Did you learn stuff about guns?"

"Yes, but you also have to learn a lot about animals, and about the rules and regulations. Guns are very, very dangerous; you could easily shoot a person if you're not careful."

Elliot nodded, his expression serious. It didn't last. "So after you've been to this school, you're allowed to fire guns?"

"Yes. But you have to be eighteen."

He rolled his big hazel eyes and let out a huge sigh.

Nisse turned to Embla. "Could you have a word with Harald? There's a problem in Herremark."

Embla stood up and took the receiver from her uncle.

"Hi, it's Embla," she said. She wasn't sure what to expect.

"Good morning—cousin Harald here. Well, not your cousin, Sonja's and Nisse's. Although we are related."

He sounded stressed. He could obviously hear it for himself because he took a couple of deep breaths in an attempt to steady himself.

"It's been a long time, Embla. But Nisse told me you and the boy were coming up this week, and I know you're a police officer. You investigate homicides, don't you? Well, something's happened. One of our guests has been murdered during the night. We found him this morning," he said, making an effort to remain calm.

It was hard to imagine people killing one another in the peaceful surroundings of Herremark, but after her years with the Västra Götaland County Bureau of Investigation's Mobile Unit, known as VGM, Embla was well aware that violent crimes were committed even in the most idyllic pastoral settings. But she was still taken by surprise.

"Murdered? No chance it could be suicide?" she asked quietly so that Elliot wouldn't hear. It was an unnecessary precaution; a boring phone call didn't interest him at all. He was busy outlining his strategy for the hunt, while Nisse nodded in agreement.

"He's lying in his bed. Shot in the head," Harald informed her, his voice shaking.

Embla remained silent for a moment, thinking fast. Murder, suicide, sometimes it was difficult to establish which it was. Shooting oneself in the head was often a preferred method for those who'd decided to end their life using a gun.

"Where is he?"

"In one of the cottages we rent out."

Then she asked the most obvious question.

"Have you called the police?"

"Yes, but because it's Saturday, only the police in Åmål are on duty, and they're busy with another murder that happened last night—just a few kilometers from here, in fact. A young lad was stabbed at the indoor bandy club's party."

"Okay, but the police in Bengtsfors . . ." Embla ventured.

"As I said, the police station isn't open on the weekends. I've heard they're closing it down for good. That's what Monika told me."

A violent coughing fit interrupted Harald's account. "The Åmål cops said it would be a while before they can get over here," he continued. "So I was wondering if you could come and take a look? It would make us feel better."

Embla glanced at Elliot. He was so excited, his eyes shone with anticipation. Postponing the hunt wasn't an option. He'd been talking about nothing else since they arrived at Nisse's the previous weekend.

"Listen, can I call you back in a few minutes? I just need to have a word with Nisse. We've made a promise to Elliot, and Nisse's going to have to take over if I come to Herremark." She hung up, her eyes fixed on Elliot.

"You go—I'll take the boy out," Nisse said before she had a chance to explain. "I'm sure we can manage to shoot a fox on our own."

He winked at Elliot, who responded with a beaming smile.

The strong wind had packed the snow into solid drifts, and at any moment a swirl of fine snow, known as "snow smoke," could hide the way ahead completely. Luckily the 172 had been cleared pretty well, so it didn't take Embla very long to cover the thirty kilometers. When she saw a sign for Herremark Guesthouse, she turned off the main road, following the arrow. It wasn't easy to cover the last few hundred meters, even though her car had good winter tires. She had borrowed a Kia Sportage from her friend Bella, who'd gone to New York to spend a year working for a bank. Embla's own vintage Volvo 245 was due for a tune-up at some point during the spring.

As she slid to a halt in front of the guesthouse, the carved double doors opened and Harald and Monika came out to greet her.

"Embla—thank you so much for coming! This is just dreadful!" Monika exclaimed. She was shaking as she took Embla's outstretched hand between her own. Her grip was unexpectedly firm, as if she were clinging to a life buoy. Harald's anxiety showed itself in his inability to stand still. He kept shifting from one foot to the other, which made him sway slightly.

Monika was small and neat, with thick steel-gray hair cut into a short bob. She was wearing black pants and a pretty traditional Norwegian sweater in shades of blue. Harald was tall and had grown a little rotund over the years. Like Nisse, he'd lost most of his hair, and, also like his cousin, he'd chosen to shave off the few remaining strands. When they were young, Harald, Nisse, and Embla's mother, Sonja, had all had flaming dark-red hair. Only Embla and her youngest brother, Kolbjörn, had inherited the family color; the two older brothers had dark hair like their father.

Harald was wearing a red checked flannel shirt and dark-blue chinos with a pair of neon-green Crocs. In spite of the cold, his forehead and upper lip were beaded with sweat.

Before Embla left, Nisse had told her something about the history of the guesthouse. It dated from the mid-nineteenth century, a prosperous manor house with plenty of agricultural land and forest. Unfortunately, subsequent generations had failed to manage the property responsibly. The last impoverished owner had sold the whole lot to Monika and Harald, and together they had built up the business over the past forty years. Today they were able to offer their guests five-star food in a restaurant with an excellent reputation, along with comfortable overnight accommodation. Behind the main guesthouse a field sloped down toward a large lake, and this was where Harald had had a number of cabins built, all expertly finished. Many visitors returned year after year, booking several weeks during the summer, when renting canoes to explore the region's rivers and lakes was a popular activity.

The place was usually fully booked in the winter, too. Only a few kilometers away there was a slalom run with a drag lift, which families with children enjoyed, but most people came for the outstanding cross-country skiing. The tracks were well marked and maintained throughout the season. The restaurant was also highly regarded; you had to make a reservation weeks in advance. The specialty was game, often provided by Harald himself. Monika ran the kitchen, and had managed to attract a number of skilled chefs.

The couple were approaching retirement age now, and Nisse had told Embla that they were already negotiating with a possible successor. It was clear that the discovery of a body in one of their cabins had shocked them, and of course there were also implications for the guesthouse's reputation.

"Come on in—you'll freeze to death out here," Monika said, drawing Embla inside. Only then did she release her grip on Embla's hand. She gave her a warm hug, and Embla realized Monika's cheek was damp with tears. Embla hugged her warmly in return as Harald followed them in and closed the heavy doors. The small lobby was welcoming, with several armchairs arranged around a crackling open fire.

"Let's go upstairs," Harald said, leading the way to a door marked PRIVATE. He held it open politely for the two ladies. Embla took off her boots and hung up her jacket on one of the hand-forged iron hooks in the hallway. Then they headed up the stairs, Harald bringing up the rear with a heavy tread. The large, airy room was lined with bookshelves. The windows provided a fantastic view of the lake. There was a cane sofa and chairs with soft blue-and-white-striped cushions, and the rag rug on the floor was perfect, in different shades of blue.

"Please sit down," Monika said.

Embla chose one of the chairs, while Harald and Monika sat close together on the sofa, unconsciously seeking each other's hands. The cane creaked alarmingly beneath their combined weight.

No time for small talk—best get on with it, Embla thought.

"Are you absolutely certain the man is dead?" she began, looking at Harald.

"Definitely. All the blood . . . the head . . ." He broke off, fighting back the nausea.

He's a huntsman. I'm sure he knows a fatal bullet wound when he sees one, Embla thought.

"When did he arrive?" she asked.

After a quick glance at her husband, who was still swallowing hard, Monika answered. "Yesterday afternoon. He signed in as Jan Müller, which was the name he'd used when he booked. And he said he didn't want to be disturbed, so he requested the accommodation that was farthest away."

Embla frowned. "Farthest away? But they're all pretty close together along the slope, aren't they?"

"It's not one of the cabins by the lake—we have three newly built cottages on the road leading down to Klevskog—the nature reserve."

Embla knew nothing about the nature reserve or the cottages, but decided to keep that to herself. "Are all three cottages currently occupied?"

The couple shook their heads, then Harald got to his feet with a mumbled apology. He looked terrible. He quickly walked over to a closed door, opened it, and disappeared. Monika watched him go with a concerned expression, then turned back to Embla.

"No. Our winter guests usually stay in the cabins by the lake. It was only Jan Müller who specifically asked to be by the nature reserve."

"So how far away are these cottages?"

Monika frowned. "Let me think . . . The turnoff is about a hundred and fifty meters from here, then it's maybe a hundred meters to the first cottage. They're twenty meters apart—I remember that from the architect's drawings."

So the man had chosen to be as far away as possible from the main guesthouse, which might suggest that he'd been intending to take his own life, and didn't want to risk being disturbed.

The door opened and Harald reappeared. His face was still flushed, but he looked calmer. He sank down on the sofa, which complained loudly.

"Sorry—I just needed a glass of water."

Monika took his hand and squeezed it, while Embla gave him an encouraging smile.

"I assume Müller had a car."

"Yes, an SUV—an Audi. And it was new—I remember him telling me he was breaking it in."

"What color?"

"White."

"Has the road to the cottages been cleared?"

"Yes—the snowplow goes all the way to the reserve."

"Müller . . . Is he German?"

Harald frowned. "I don't think so. He spoke Swedish; he sounded as if he came from Gothenburg. He did have a slight accent, but we have a lot of German guests and they don't sound like that. Hard to say where he came from, really."

Monika nodded in agreement.

"What did he look like? How old was he? Any distinguishing features?" Embla continued.

Harald nodded to his wife to take over.

"Average height or slightly below, but powerfully built. I'd say he was between forty-five and fifty. Dark hair peppered with gray, a small bald patch that he was trying to hide with a comb-over. He was in a smart suit and a blue overcoat when he arrived, and he was also well-dressed at dinner last night. I remember he was wearing a pretty strong fragrance, and he had an enormous gold watch on his wrist. I noticed it when he checked in."

"When did he make the reservation?"

"Early yesterday morning, and he immediately asked if any of the cottages by the nature reserve were available. When I told him all three were empty, he asked for the one farthest away."

So he must have been familiar with the three cottages. Then again, no doubt the information was on the guesthouse's website; Embla had taken a quick look before she set off for Herremark, although she'd missed the cottages.

"How long was he planning to stay?"

Harald took over. "Just the one night. He booked a table for dinner on Friday and breakfast on Saturday. He said he was an early riser, so he ordered breakfast for seven o'clock sharp. He mentioned it more than once, so when he didn't appear this morning, I called the cottage. It was just before seven-thirty. There was no answer, which worried me; I thought he might have come down with something. It's pretty isolated when the other cottages are empty."

"When did you go to check on him?"

"At about quarter to eight. I took the car."

Embla stood up. "Okay, I'll go and take a look. Can you give me your cell phone numbers and a key? Plus I'll need directions."

"I don't think I locked the door when I left, but here's one of our spare keys."

Harald produced a key from his pocket and passed it over to Embla.

"Was the place locked up when you got there?"

"Yes, but the key wasn't inside."

A detail that could be important.

"Is it possible that someone got a hold of a spare key?"

Harald shook his head. "No," he said firmly. "There are four keys to each cottage. I gave one to Müller, and the other three are in our locked key cabinet. I noticed when I took out that one this morning." His finger was trembling as he pointed to the key in Embla's hand.

According to Harald's directions, she was to drive approximately one hundred and fifty meters heading north on the 172 before turning off when she saw the sign for Klevskog Nature Reserve. Just as Harald had said, the road had been cleared. Through the snow-mist she could see the three cottages in a row.

Large fields extended on both sides of the road. Dense snow smoke whirled across the landscape in the strong wind. Embla could see majestic fir trees beyond the cottages, where the nature reserve began. Harald had given her a quick rundown before she left.

Klevskog was famous for being home to a variety of species, particularly birds. In the middle of the reserve lay a shallow lake, ideal for waders and seabirds. There were no houses inside the reserve. The cottages had been built with birdwatchers in mind, but because the standard was so high, they also attracted visitors who weren't particularly keen on birds. According to Harald, the project had been a very good investment. However, they weren't rented out as much from November to March, when tourists preferred to be closer to the guesthouse.

Why had Jan Müller specifically asked for the cottage that was the farthest away? He must have known the area—had he been there before? Was he an ornithologist? However, neither the time of year nor Monika's description of his clothing suggested this was the case—a smart suit and a gold watch. Then there was the SUV—a brand-new Audi. Expensive and exclusive.

As Embla drew closer to the cottage, she saw a huge pile of snow covering the car. She parked her Kia behind the pile, where Harald's tire tracks stopped. After turning off the engine she stayed put for a little while, observing her surroundings. The virgin snow in front of the cottage was marked only by a set of footprints leading to the steps, and another slightly different set leading away; clearly Harald had run back to his car.

The blizzard had abated, but there was no sign of the wind dropping. According to the forecast, more snow was expected during the day. Embla took out her phone and checked the weather for the previous night. The snow had begun to fall at around 1:00 A.M. and stopped at about 5:30. It seemed likely that whatever had gone on in the cottage had happened shortly before or early on within that period. Snow and wind can obliterate any traces very quickly. However, as a matter of routine she would check for any possible evidence before she went inside; she was first on the scene, apart from Harald. She put on a pair of latex gloves, slipped on her thick mittens, and got out of the car.

The full force of the wind hit her immediately, making her bend forward. The sharp snowflakes struck her face like tiny needles. She consoled herself with the thought that Elliot and Nisse wouldn't want to be out in the cold for too long. They'd go home for hot chocolate and Uncle Nisse's delicious cinnamon buns. That would be enough for Elliot; at least he'd participated in his very first hunting trip.

She set off toward the cottage, stepping in Harald's tracks. She stopped several times, pulling off her mittens and photographing the ground with the camera on her phone. She couldn't see anything out of the ordinary, but it was important to document Harald's tracks.

Harald was right—he hadn't locked the door behind him. Cautiously she pushed it open. The first thing she noticed was a distinct male fragrance. A bit too strong, in fact. She closed the door behind her, then flicked the switch on the doorframe, and two lights came on—one above the kitchen area and one in the center of the small room. She pushed back her fur-lined hood—the fur came from a fox she'd shot herself—and quickly scanned the interior of the cottage. A wall to her left, with a coatrack and a small closet. There was a dark-blue overcoat hanging on the rack and a neatly folded checked wool scarf on the shelf above, along with a pair of black leather gloves. A pair of black shoes was on the floor—definitely not suitable for the current weather conditions. The walls were covered in white-painted tongue-and-groove paneling, and the floor was pale varnished wood. The kitchenette was modern; there were no dishes in the draining board, and Embla made a mental note to check the dishwasher. By the window was a table and four chairs, and the space was brightened by green-and-white rag rugs. The living room was furnished with a sofa and two armchairs facing a TV on the wall, with an impressive soapstone stove next to the sofa. The plaited-iron basket was filled with logs; it didn't look like the man had lit a fire.

As Embla was on vacation, she didn't have her crime-scene kit in the car, but she had brought a couple of plastic bags from Nisse's. She slipped them over her shoes before moving into the living room. One of the two doors was ajar, and through the gap she could see reflections in the glass of a medicine cabinet. The other door, leading to the bedroom, was wide open.

She decided to check out the bathroom first. She switched on the light, revealing a fully tiled room with a toilet, washbasin, and shower. The smell of male fragrance was strong, almost nauseating. She noticed a black toilet bag on a hook, a thick white bath towel, and a hand towel. Everything seemed fresh and new.

She closed the door and headed for the bedroom. She reached inside, switched on the light, and remained in the doorway, taking in the scene before her.

The raw smell of blood mingled with cologne and alcohol was striking. A double bed dominated the room and had a nightstand on each side. On the one nearest the door stood an empty vodka bottle and a glass. There was a double wardrobe along one wall. On a neat bench below the window lay a closed black carry-on suitcase—an ultra-light, ultra-expensive Samsonite. She turned her attention to the man in the bed.

She understood why Harald had been shocked; it was a horrific sight.

He was lying on his back, his large hands folded on top of the duvet, which created an oddly peaceful impression. He was wearing a gold signet ring with a polished green stone on the pinky of his right hand. She could see a pistol beneath his hands. To her surprise, he appeared to be wearing dark-blue silk pajamas. Who wears silk pajamas in a cottage in the country in the middle of winter? The man in the bed, obviously . . .

The hole between his eyebrows was pretty big. Large caliber. The pillow was sodden with blood, indicating a significant exit wound. Presumably the back of his head had been blown off. Embla stood on tiptoe to get a better look, which wasn't easy in her heavy boots. Then she saw a bloodstain on the duvet in the vicinity of his heart. Two shots, then. His face had taken on a grayish tone, which suggested that he'd been dead for quite some time.

Given the two bullet wounds from a large-caliber gun, this definitely wasn't suicide. You can't fold your hands neatly after you've shot yourself in the head *and* the heart.

The victim was powerfully built, but not overweight. Even though Embla was three meters from the bed, she thought there was something familiar about his features: the bushy eyebrows, the dominant chin, the thinning hair peppered with gray.

She got the shock of her life when she realized who he was.

Milo Stavic, the man in the recurring nightmares that had plagued her for almost fifteen years. The man who, together with his two brothers, had abducted Lollo. The man who had threatened to kill Embla if she told anyone what had happened that night.

Instinctively she took a step back.

"No! That's . . . crazy!" she said out loud.

Her voice was shaking and she took a deep breath, her heart racing.

"Crazy?"

The male voice behind her was deep, and she didn't recognize it.

EMBLA'S REFLEXES KICKED in. It was part of her DNA now. She spun around, half-crouching, fists clenched and raised in the defensive position, and stepped into the other room.

The man was tall, his cap almost touching the ceiling. A police uniform cap, she noted. Beneath his bulky jacket she could see a dark-blue sweater, and he was wearing uniform pants. He was about the same age as her, and he was standing in the middle of the room, his right hand resting on his holster.

She should have been relieved, but instead her fear turned to anger as she straightened up and glared at him.

"What the hell are you doing here?" she snapped.

"I was about to ask you the same question," he replied calmly. He seemed relaxed, but Embla was aware that every muscle was tensed and ready to act if necessary. As a boxer she was sensitive to her opponent's body language.

"Detective Inspector Embla Nyström. I'm with the Violent Crimes Unit in Gothenburg," she informed him brusquely.

"Can I see your ID?"

Fuck! It was in her wallet, which she'd left behind at

Nisse's. She realized she'd also driven over here without her driver's license.

"The thing is . . . I'm staying with my uncle for a few days. This morning we had a call from Harald Fäldt, who owns the guesthouse. He's my uncle's cousin, and he knew I was visiting. He told us he'd found a body in one of his rental cottages—this one—and he was certain the man had been murdered. He asked me to come over because the local police were busy with another homicide that had taken place last night. In the rush I forgot my wallet. And right now you're contaminating a crime scene!"

She pointed an accusatory finger at his great big boots; pools of water were already forming around his feet in the warmth of the cottage. He raised his eyebrows at the plastic bags knotted around her own boots.

"They work!" she said before he could come out with some smart remark. She was on a roll now. "I know who this man is," she continued. "His name is Milo Stavic, and he's one of Gothenburg's biggest gangster bosses. Which means this investigation falls under the jurisdiction of the Gothenburg police."

Once again he raised his eyebrows. "You still haven't provided any ID."

He had a point.

"As I said, I left my wallet at my uncle's house."

It sounded defensive and not entirely convincing. Desperately she tried to work out how she could confirm her identity.

Got it!

"Do you have a cell phone?" she asked.

He nodded, his face expressionless.

"Google 'Embla Nyström.' Or go on Facebook. You'll find pictures of me. I'm a boxer. And a cop."

He shook his head, but produced a phone from his pocket, keeping an eye on her as he tapped the screen.

"So there's a dead guy in the bedroom?" he asked while he waited for the search results.

"Yes. And he's been murdered. Shot." Embla stepped aside and waved her hand. "See for yourself."

With the phone in his left hand and his right hand still hovering over his gun, he moved toward the door.

"Don't go into the room," Embla warned him. Much to her surprise, he cooperated. He stood perfectly still, taking in the macabre scene. When he turned to face her, she saw that he was several shades paler.

"Fucking hell," he said quietly, with real emotion in every syllable.

"That's what I said."

"No, you said it was crazy."

How irritating was this guy? Singling out what she'd said at a crime scene where a murder had been committed!

"And that's exactly what it is—crazy. You might expect a gangster like this to be gunned down on the street in Gothenburg or taken out by a sniper near his home or in his top-of-the-line car. You wouldn't expect to find him in bed in the middle of nowhere," she pointed out irritably.

"So what was he doing here?"

"I don't know. I'm going to call my boss and tell him what's happened. As I said, this is a case for the Gothenburg police."

She thought for a moment; who should she contact?

Chief Inspector Tommy Persson in the Violent Crimes Unit was her boss these days, but Göran Krantz had been her boss during her time with the VGM. They'd grown close, and she knew him better than Tommy. Plus Göran was the only person she'd told about the circumstances surrounding Lollo's disappearance, which meant he was the only one who knew about Milo Stavic's role in the events of that night.

She decided to call Göran and reached into her pocket for her phone. Just as she got a hold of it she heard her colleague's voice again, but this time his tone was sharp and authoritative.

"Stop right there! Keep your hands out of your pockets!"

For fuck's sake, she thought. But when she looked up at him to speak her mind, she saw that he'd drawn his Sig Sauer and was pointing it straight at her. He was certainly fast. She realized it would be best not to make any sudden movements. The whole situation was completely surreal.

"By the way, I haven't seen your ID either," she said.

"That's not necessary. I found you at the crime scene with no ID. You claim you're a police officer, but for all I know you could be the perp."

She picked up a slight tremor in his voice that hadn't been there before. Of course he was shaken; she hadn't thought of that. She was pretty used to seeing dead bodies during the course of her work with the Violent Crimes Unit, but a young officer outside the big city probably hadn't encountered many homicide victims, if any.

In addition to being a skilled boxer, she was also a good Thai boxer. She would easily be able to kick his wrist—hard, if he managed to pull the trigger. The bullet would hit the ceiling, and when the nerve paralysis took over he would inevitably drop the gun. It would be an easy victory, but it wouldn't do much to improve their already-strained relationship. She decided not to go for the kick.

"Can we calm things down? If you take a closer look, you'll see from the color of his skin that he's been dead for several hours. No murderer is dumb enough to hang around after shooting someone."

Slowly she raised her hands above her head.

"Can you get my phone out of my pocket? I have to call this in. The clock's ticking, and our perp already has a head start."

He hesitated, then took a single long stride toward her, his pistol still drawn. She turned slightly to make it easier for him to reach into her pocket. He grabbed her phone, but before he gave it to her he checked the other pocket.

"Just tissues," she said, sniffing demonstratively.

Without a word he handed her the phone, then to her relief he slipped the gun back in its holster.

"Okay, so I'm calling Superintendent Göran Krantz. I'll put him on speakerphone." She scrolled down her contacts list and selected his name.

"Hi, Embla," he answered right away. The familiar voice of her former boss immediately made her feel better.

"Hi, Göran. Sorry to disturb you on the weekend, but something's happened up here in Dalsland."

"Okay . . . How's your vacation going?"

"It's been fine until now, but my uncle Nisse's cousin Harald Fäldt called a few hours ago and asked me to come over to Herremark, where he and his wife run the guesthouse."

She tried to explain the situation as clearly and concisely as possible. When she said that she was sure the victim was Milo Stavic, she heard a sharp intake of breath from the superintendent, but he didn't interrupt her. She told him about the two bullet wounds and the pistol carefully placed beneath the folded hands.

"It has to be a homicide," Göran agreed.

When she revealed that her colleague at the scene was so suspicious of her that he'd actually drawn his gun on her, Göran burst out laughing.

"I guess he didn't realize how dangerous that could be for him," he said.

The young officer had grasped that Embla and the man she was talking to really were detectives, but the superintendent's comment left him totally bewildered. Embla had no intention of enlightening him. The fact was that her former colleagues with VGM, Göran and Detective Inspector Hampus Stahre, used to tease her and call her their pit bull, particularly in situations where her temper gained the upper hand.

Before she could come up with a cutting response, Göran continued, "That's remarkable, given what you've told me about Milo Stavic."

Embla involuntarily took a deep, ragged breath. With a huge effort, she managed not to look at either the dead man or the living man in the room, instead focusing her attention on a small picture on the wall of a brightly colored bird perched on a branch laden with apple blossoms. Or some other kind of blossoms.

"It was a shock when I recognized him," she admitted, fighting to keep her voice steady.

"I can understand that. And you're absolutely certain it's Stavic?"

"Yes."

"Okay. In that case I'll come up and take a look. I'm in Trollhättan at the moment, but I was intending to go home anyway. Paula's ex-husband is going to a fiftieth birthday party, so she's having the kids over here tonight."

"Thanks—that makes me feel so much better!"

"I'll call the Dalsland area chief of police and outline the situation, then I'll send some of my CSIs. They can get to work straightaway," Göran added.

"And I'll stay here and secure the cottage."

Embla felt as if a great weight had been lifted from her shoulders, and she caught herself smiling when the call was over.

A discreet cough behind her made her jump. She'd forgotten about the uniformed officer.

"There's no need for you to hang around, but give me your name before you leave," she said.

He immediately straightened his shoulders and gave her a perfect salute. "Inspector Olle Tillman, Åmål police."

"Åmål? So what are you doing here?"

"Ours is the only station that's manned on weekends."

"So you were called out to the stabbing."

"Yes—how do you know about that?"

"Harald—the relative who contacted me—told me the Åmål police couldn't get here right away."

She jerked her head in the direction of the bed. Olle Tillman automatically glanced at the dead man, but quickly looked away.

"There are only five of us on duty," he said, "but two detectives from Trollhättan are coming over later. My boss thought it would be a good idea if I checked out the situation. And what did I find? A total stranger in the same room as the body. She claims to be a cop, but can't provide any ID. Clearly a person of interest."

This was obviously meant as an explanation and an apology for drawing his gun.

"So you've been on duty all night?" Embla said, trying to sound a little more friendly.

"Yes. My shift started at six yesterday evening."

Which meant he'd been working for almost sixteen hours.

"I really think you ought to go home and—"

"I'm not going to get any sleep today. We tried to question a number of witnesses during the night, but we didn't get very far. Most of them were drunk and very shaken up, so we'll have to try again today. And tomorrow and the next day."

"How many witnesses are involved?"

The answer came with no hesitation. "Sixty-two."

"That's going to take some time," Embla said.

"Yes, but the organizers have given me a list of those who were at the party, which helps. We'll divide up the names among us, and, as I said, we're expecting two detectives from Trollhättan."

Embla looked around the room. "Listen, I think we'd better get out of here before the CSIs arrive. They won't be happy when they find out we've contaminated the crime scene. We'll have to give a DNA sample, and they'll want to take our footprints. Well, yours, anyway."

She gave his size forty-six boots a meaningful glance.

Olle Tillman didn't seem too concerned. It occurred to Embla that Harald might also have gone into the bedroom; she hadn't asked him. Hopefully he hadn't crossed the threshold after seeing the bloodbath in the bed.

The windows were almost covered by deep snowdrifts. The wind was howling around the cottage, rattling the panes.

"We can't go outside," Olle pointed out.

"No. We'll go and sit at the kitchen table and wait for Göran and the CSIs."

"Okay."

He gave her a grateful look. It had been a long shift. They sat down and undid their jackets; it was pretty warm in spite of the weather outside. Olle took off his cap. His fair hair was unusually long; most male police officers either shaved their heads or had very short hair, partly because it was easy to look after, and partly because it doesn't give an attacker anything to grab. On the other hand, many of Embla's coworkers had started cultivating impressive beards, which carried the same risk. She thought Olle was sporting three-day stubble rather than the beginnings of a beard.

He hid a yawn behind one hand and rubbed his eyes with the other. Maybe tiredness was the main reason why he was in no hurry to rejoin his team.

"It'll be a while before Göran gets here," Embla said. "Tell me about the boy who was murdered—what happened?"

Olle blinked several times before he began to talk.

"The local indoor bandy team, Herremarks IBK, had arranged a party to celebrate the club's twentieth anniversary. We got the call about a stabbing at twelve-forty."

"Sorry to interrupt, but was it snowing when you got there?"

"Yes, it had just started to come down when we arrived. There were lots of cars around because most of the kids had contacted parents or friends and asked to be picked up. A lot of them were crying—and very drunk. No one was prepared to talk to us; they probably didn't want their parents to find out how much they'd had to drink."

"But the parents were once teenagers themselves."

"Exactly." Olle smiled again, and this time he seemed more present. He was a good-looking guy, with attractive blue-gray eyes. Embla's thoughts were interrupted as he continued with his account.

". . . a place called the Lodge. It's a converted barn, and these days it's used for parties, auctions, and all kinds of things. A boy was stabbed outside the Lodge at around half past midnight. He died in the ambulance on the way to the hospital. It had arrived at five to one; we got there about fifteen minutes later, by which time the ambulance had already gone. As I said, it was snowing, and the wind was blowing hard."

"Did the victim say anything?" she asked.

"Not according to those we've questioned so far."

"Who was he?"

"His name is Robin Pettersson. He was eighteen years old and in his final year of high school. According to one of the club leaders, he was the star of the bandy team. Apparently his family moved to Åmål a month ago, and he was due to transfer to another team in Säffle after the party."

"Any information on the perpetrator?"

"Not a thing. No witnesses have come forward—not yet, anyway."

Embla thought about what he'd told her, then asked, "How far is it from here to the Lodge?"

"Two kilometers."

Closer than she'd thought, which meant there'd been plenty of cars on the move from about 12:45 until at least 2:00. Someone might have seen a car or a person they didn't recognize, or noticed something unusual, something that might be connected to the death of Milo Stavic. The snowstorm was a problem because it would have reduced visibility.

Olle Tillman was looking at her and frowning. "So do you think these two murders are connected?" he asked eventually.

She didn't answer right away. "I can't imagine that an eighteen-year-old boy at the high school in Åmål was stabbed by the same perp who shot Stavic. That seems unlikely."

"But you can't rule it out?"

Once again, Embla considered her response. "I think I probably can, if we look at the victims. Milo Stavic has been a top-level gangster in Gothenburg for many years. He owns several restaurants, hotels, nightclubs and casinos, which he uses to launder the money he makes from smuggling drugs and arms, human trafficking, prostitution—you name it, he's into it."

Olle nodded. "My boss, Chief Inspector Johnzén— with a z—thought this was just some nutjob who'd decided to end it all. But I guess he was wrong," he said.

"He was. My first thought was suicide, too, but this was definitely a homicide. You can't shoot yourself in the head and the heart, then settle down with your hands neatly folded on your chest. I'm certain the gun was placed there after he was killed."

Olle glanced toward the bedroom door; Embla knew he couldn't see the bed from where he stood.

"What was a guy like that doing here?" he said.

"Good question. I have no idea."

Embla picked up her phone and called Harald Fäldt, who answered almost immediately.

"Hi, it's Embla. Sorry I haven't been in touch until now, but . . . yes, it's definitely a homicide . . . I've contacted my colleagues in Gothenburg, and they'll be here at any moment to take over the investigation . . . No, it doesn't have anything to do with the police in Åmål because the victim is from Gothenburg . . . I recognized him. He's come up in a couple of my department's investigations."

Harald asked a few more questions, which Embla did her best to answer without giving too much away.

"You and your colleagues are welcome to come here for lunch when you're done," Harald offered.

"That's very kind of you—I'll pass it on."

Olle brightened up when she relayed Harald's invitation, but one look at his weary face made her wonder if he'd manage to stay awake until lunchtime.

Superintendent Göran Krantz knocked before entering the cottage. As Embla had expected, he stopped just inside the door and quickly scanned the interior. He nodded to the two officers at the kitchen table.

"Good morning! So you're sitting here shedding DNA." He smiled at them to take the sting out of his words.

Embla gave Olle Tillman a meaningful glance and whispered loudly, "What did I tell you? We're in trouble for staying indoors and contaminating the crime scene."

Göran put on plastic shoe covers before coming over to join them. Olle got to his feet and held out his hand.

"Olle Tillman—I'm a detective inspector from Åmål."

"Göran Krantz, superintendent with the technical department in Gothenburg. Good to meet you, even if it's not under the best circumstances."

"Yes—this is all pretty overwhelming," Olle replied with a pale attempt at a smile.

"Olle came over because there was another murder last night, only two kilometers from here. He and his colleagues are investigating," Embla explained.

Any hint of joviality disappeared from Göran's face.

"Another murder? And was the victim also shot?" he demanded sharply.

"No, an eighteen-year-old high school student was stabbed. The local indoor bandy team was having a party, and something went wrong," Embla said.

Göran nodded and muttered something.

He pulled on a pair of latex gloves. "My team will be here in about an hour. I'd like to take a look at the scene of the crime, then we can talk."

"We won't be able to do much once the CSIs arrive— I suggest we go over to the guesthouse. Harald has offered to provide lunch," Embla said.

Olle's phone rang. He took it out of his pocket, glanced at the display, and sighed. "Tillman."

He wasn't on speakerphone, but Embla could hear a male voice speaking sharply on the other end of the line.

"Yes, but it's not a suicide. He was murd—"

Another torrent of words interrupted Olle's attempt to clarify the situation.

"I know it's not my call, but Superintendent Göran Krantz and Detective Inspector Embla Nyström from Gothenburg are also here. They've checked out the body and they think we're looking at homicide."

That wasn't strictly true, because Göran hadn't yet seen the dead man, but it was clear from Olle's tone that he was annoyed with his boss. Maybe it was due to tiredness, given how many hours he'd been on duty, but Embla got the feeling that he was pretty sick of Chief Inspector Johnzén, who barked out a brief question.

"Shot in the head. The CSIs from Gothenburg will be here in—"

The roar at the other end of the phone made Olle hold it away from his ear.

" . . . the fuck has it got to do with them?"

Both Embla and Göran heard every word. Göran held out his hand, and a smile of pure joy spread across Olle's face as he passed over the phone.

"Good morning. Superintendent Göran Krantz from the technical department in Gothenburg. My colleague Detective Inspector Embla Nyström was called to the scene by a relative who rents out this cottage. It was this relative who found the body this morning. DI Nyström immediately realized that the victim had been murdered and called me. I happened to be in Trollhättan and was able to get here quickly."

Once again Embla heard a sharp comment. Göran rolled his eyes, but kept his tone perfectly civil as he answered.

"No, we don't have too little to do, but the victim is ours. Formal identification has yet to take place, but we're pretty sure he's a major criminal from Gothenburg who features in several of our ongoing investigations. That's why the case falls under our jurisdiction. I believe you have another homicide to deal with."

Another irate comment came through the ether. Göran winked at his audience and said pleasantly, "I'll pass that on."

He ended the call and handed the phone back to Olle.

"Your esteemed boss wants me to tell you, and I quote, to get your ass back there right now."

"He could do with signing up for a course on how to treat colleagues," Olle replied with a sigh.

"Absolutely. I'm sure there's a college course worth

two hundred points on sense and sensibility that we could enroll him in," Göran said with a smile. "Okay, time I took a look at our victim. For real, this time."

Olle pulled on his cap, headed for the front door, and opened it. A gust of icy wind blew snow all over the rubber doormat.

"When you and your colleagues are questioning witnesses who were at the Lodge or who came along later, could you ask if they saw a car or a person they didn't recognize? I'm thinking of our murderer," Embla said quickly.

"No problem," Olle said. He closed the door behind him and stepped out into the whirling snow.

GÖRAN STOOD IN the bedroom doorway in silence for quite some time, taking in the scene before him. Embla knew from past experience that very little escaped him. She admired him above all for his competence and sharp mind, plus he was an absolute genius when it came to computers. Göran was someone she trusted and respected, which was why she had confided in him just over a week ago.

Göran returned to the table and sat down. He clasped his hands and looked at her; it was hard to read his expression.

"You didn't put a bullet through his brain, did you?" he asked. There was a hint of a smile at one corner of his mouth, but there was an element of seriousness in his eyes.

"What the . . . Are you crazy?" she exclaimed. "If I were going to kill Milo Stavic I wouldn't do it here—the sensible option would be to shoot him in Gothenburg. And nobody would find me anywhere near the body, I can promise you that. He's got plenty of enemies down there, whereas here . . ."

"He only has one. You."

"Obviously not, as he's lying dead ten meters from where we're sitting! And I was fast asleep in my bed at Nisse's all night. Elliot was in the same room—he would have woken up if I'd left."

That wasn't necessarily true; the boy slept like the dead once he'd nodded off.

Göran leaned back in the chair, which creaked in protest, and waved his hands dismissively. "Calm down— I had to ask. You must admit it's an odd coincidence for him to be murdered here, when you're only a few kilometers away."

"Okay, I get that."

Embla summoned every scrap of self-control to suppress her anger, but at the same time she had to admit that Göran was right—it was weird.

"We've got some time before the CSIs arrive. Remind me about your friend's disappearance."

Embla nodded. Her guts began to writhe around like a nest of snakes; she didn't want to go back to that terrible night, but she knew she had to confront her demons at some point.

She began by describing the nightmare that had plagued her for so long. Göran listened attentively, without interrupting.

"I've had this nightmare for fourteen and a half years about what happened when Lollo went missing. I saw three men bending over her at the end of a hallway. The man who grabbed me by the throat and threatened to kill me if I told anyone was Milo Stavic.

The other two were probably his brothers, Kador and Luca."

Göran nodded. "I hear you scream in the middle of the night sometimes on work trips. In the past you said you've had nightmares ever since you were a little girl, and no one knew why—but now you're telling me they started after your friend disappeared. Exactly how old were you then?"

"It was the end of August—the last weekend of the summer vacation. My birthday is in July, so I'd just turned fourteen. Lollo was fourteen, too, but she was going to be fifteen in September. She was a year ahead of me in school, but we'd been best friends ever since we used to play in the sandbox."

"How did you get to know each other?"

"We lived in the same apartment building when we were young; our parents socialized. We went to the same school, and we were together almost all the time, except for a few weeks in the summer when I would come up here to stay with Nisse and Ann-Sofi. When she was twelve, her parents split up. Her father had met someone else—she was already pregnant, and he joined her in London. Lollo's mother was a children's book illustrator and worked from home. After a year they moved to a smaller apartment in Högsbo, on Axel Dahlström Square. Lollo didn't want to change schools; she caught the tram to Nordhem. She said she was afraid we'd lose touch, and I felt the same. We saw each other almost every day, and hung out together in our free time. She usually came to our place for dinner, and she often stayed over."

"What was she like?"

Embla thought for a moment. "Lively. Full of ideas.

Adventurous. But she could get very low sometimes. Up and down, really."

"Any idea why?"

"I think there were several reasons. It hit her pretty hard when her father ran off. And I eventually realized that her mother was drinking heavily before . . . before Lollo went missing. Afterward she just drank all the time. She couldn't work, couldn't do anything. She killed herself a year to the day after Lollo's disappearance."

Embla had to pause to try to get rid of the lump in her throat. Lollo's mother's suicide was a big reason she still felt so guilty. She knew she should have acted differently; if only she'd had the courage to tell the truth, the police would have had a better chance of finding Lollo, and her mother might still be alive.

"I think you said you were going to a disco at Frölunda Kulturhus—what happened?"

The lump was still there; Embla swallowed several times before she was able to continue.

"We lied."

Göran nodded, his eyes never leaving her face. "Yes, I remember you telling me you'd both lied to your parents. Lollo said she was staying over with you, and vice versa. Did your mom and dad know Lollo's mother had a drinking problem?"

"No. I told them Lollo's mom would be home, but she'd gone to stay with a friend for a couple of days. We were alone."

She paused to compose herself before continuing.

"Lollo opened a box of white wine. I didn't want to look pathetic, so I joined in. She kept refilling my glass.

I wasn't allowed to drink at all at home. My otherwise oh-so-liberal parents were adamant that none of us touch alcohol until we were eighteen. Needless to say, I was drunk in no time. Lollo decided we should go into town to meet up with the guy she was in love with. She wouldn't tell me his name because things were 'a little tricky.' I was really curious, so I went along with it. The apartment wasn't far from the tram stop, and we managed to get there somehow. I don't remember much about the trip."

It was so hard to revisit that night, to see the images she'd suppressed forcing their way to the front of her mind. Lollo, tottering along in her white high-heeled sandals. The pale-blue dress fluttering around her friend's slim, tan thighs. The stench of vomit in the bathroom. The embarrassment of not being able to hold her drink. Feeling sick on the tram. The panic that she might throw up again . . .

"So you took the tram," Göran prompted her gently.

"Yes. When we reached the Avenue Lollo dragged me off and took me to a nightclub somewhere along the boulevard. She just sailed past the long line of people waiting to get in. The doormen said hi; they seemed to recognize her."

"So it wasn't the first time she'd been there."

"No, definitely not. The place was packed, and we got separated. I was scared, but then I saw her standing at the bar, talking to a hot guy. Later on I realized that was Luca Stavic. I could understand why she was head over heels in love—he was quite something. I was on my way to join them when a drunk started coming on to me, and I had to fight him off. Unfortunately, I hadn't started boxing back then!"

She often thought that if that idiot hadn't started pawing at her, she'd have reached Lollo and they wouldn't have been able to take her.

"So you were held up by the drunk."

"Yes. By the time I'd shaken him off, both Lollo and Luca had disappeared. I was even more panic-stricken then, but suddenly I caught a glimpse of her blue dress before it disappeared through a door marked STAFF ONLY. I managed to fight my way across the room, and my recurring nightmare is all about what happened next."

Göran gazed pensively at the snow-covered window. The wind howled down the chimney like a despairing ghost, and Embla shuddered. Her grandmother always used to say, "Someone just walked over my grave" when she felt a shiver run down her spine.

"And you never told anyone the truth," Göran said eventually.

"No, I didn't dare. Milo had threatened to kill me if I said a word to anyone. I said we'd had an argument on the way into town, and Lollo had gone off on her own to meet some guy. I headed back to the apartment to wait for her; she'd given me a key before we went out, in case we got separated."

She broke off; should she reveal the thought that had often occurred to her? She'd promised herself that she'd be totally honest with Göran.

"Sometimes it seems to me that she already knew I'd need a key. That she already knew she wouldn't be coming home."

"Did she take a bag with her?"

"No."

"Not even a purse?"

"A tiny shoulder purse. There was just room for her wallet, her key, and her mascara."

Göran nodded, narrowing his eyes as he asked, "No one remembered you from the nightclub? No one realized you'd arrived together?"

"No. I was interviewed more than once, but no one ever questioned what I said. Nobody from the club came forward, so the police never even found out we'd been there. The place was packed; I guess they didn't notice me or Lollo. And in hindsight I suspect alcohol wasn't the only substance being consumed."

"You mean any possible witnesses wouldn't want to contact the police because they'd been under the influence of drugs. Given what we know about the activities of the Stavic brothers, I assume all kinds of stuff was readily available." He fell silent for a moment. "How long had Lollo known Luca Stavic?"

Embla had often wondered exactly that over the years, so she didn't need to think about her answer.

"Six or seven weeks, I'd say. She never mentioned him before I went off to Dalsland to stay with Nisse, but they could have met around midsummer. My dad's cousin and his family came over from the USA to visit us; one of the kids is about the same age as me, and I had to go on various outings with them. They stayed for ten days. When I met up with Lollo afterward and asked her what she'd been doing, she said she'd hung out with some of her classmates and been partying."

"Partying? Did she say where they'd gone?"

"No, and I didn't want to ask. Didn't want her to see how envious I was. Maybe that's when she met Luca."

"So you didn't see much of her after midsummer?"

"No. I came up here for five weeks."

Göran nodded, then he leaned across the table and said softly, "How did you feel as the days passed and she didn't come back?"

This was the hardest thing to talk about. She couldn't meet his gaze.

"Of course I was worried, but at the same time I was relieved—I thought I'd gotten away with it. My emotions were so mixed up—shame, guilt, anxiety, relief. I've often wished that someone had seen through me, started searching for Lollo right away. But I didn't dare say anything."

She pointed to the bedroom.

"The man in there threatened to kill me if I told anyone, and I believed him. He said he knew my name and where I lived."

Göran caught her gaze and held it. "I understand," he said, "but bearing in mind what we know about him, I'm surprised they didn't take you, too. Or get rid of you on the spot to make sure you could never talk."

That thought had never occurred to Embla, but now she realized Göran was right. The Stavic brothers had taken a huge risk.

"Now that you mention it . . . why *didn't* he make sure I kept quiet?"

"I have no idea. He's the only one who knows the answer. There are lots of questions about Milo Stavic that will never be resolved, but I'd really like to know what he was doing up here in the middle of winter."

Another memory pushed its way forward in Embla's mind. "But, Göran, we've seen him before!"

"Have we?"

"Yes. No. Not here—in Mellerud. Back in the fall, when we were having lunch at that Thai restaurant. During the investigation into the disappearance of Beehn and Cahneborg. During the moose hunt . . ."

He interrupted her. "Oh, was that him? I remember a big guy, smartly dressed, but above all I remember his car. It was a top-of-the-line Mercedes; I'd never seen anything like it in Sweden."

"Exactly—that was Milo."

Instinctively they glanced at the open bedroom door, both wondering the same thing: What had Milo been doing in Mellerud, and why was he back here now?

"That was only four months ago. I'm guessing he was coming from the north and traveling down to Gothenburg," Göran speculated.

"Yes, and I've just remembered something else. Milo had a gold watch the size of an American cupcake. Harald and Monika noticed a watch like that when he checked in. Did you see it in there?"

"Not on his wrist or on the nightstand. There's a pair of reading glasses by the bed, plus an empty spirits bottle and an empty glass. There's also a charger for an iPhone or iPad."

Sometimes Embla found Göran's photographic memory kind of creepy.

"If we don't find the watch, we can probably assume that the killer took it, along with his phone and possibly a laptop. We'll ask for any traffic on his cell phone to be monitored," he added.

They both heard the sound of an approaching engine. Göran stood up and peered out through the remaining gap in the snow-covered window.

"The cavalry has arrived. Time for us to leave."

"In that case let's go to the guesthouse," Embla suggested.

They waited until the two CSIs appeared, already dressed in full protective clothing. They stamped the snow off their shoes before coming in. The female technician, who Embla knew was named Linda, came over to the table to say hello. Her male colleague stopped in the doorway with camera equipment and lamps.

"Is it just the two of you?" Göran asked.

"Yes, the others are busy with a fatal shooting in Hisingen. A guy who belongs to some criminal gang, as far as I know. It was reported at about six o'clock this morning. Bengan and I were called in when dispatch realized who your victim was," Linda explained, glancing around the cottage.

"Those gangland murders swallow up our already-minimal resources," Göran said with a sigh.

"Too right."

Bengan pointed to the bedroom. "In there?"

"Yes. We'll leave you to work in peace. Call me if you need me," Göran said, getting to his feet.

"Will do. We've requested transportation for the body. We can't get a hold of a forensic pathologist up here, so we're taking him to Gothenburg."

"Good. We're going to the guesthouse for lunch; come over for something to eat when you're done, and we can have a chat. You're bound to discover things we haven't been able to see; nobody's actually entered the room; we've only taken a look from the doorway."

Embla thought of something important.

"Two other people have been in here today—apart from the killer. Olle Tillman, a police officer who works in Åmål, and Harald Fäldt, the owner of the cottage. He's the one who found the body. I don't think he went into the bedroom, but I'm not sure. I guess you might need their DNA?"

"We will—thanks for letting us know. You're already on the register, and I assume Tillman is, too," Linda said from behind her mask.

Embla and Göran certainly did justice to the oven-baked salmon stuffed with horseradish and herbs. The fish was served with new potatoes cooked in dill, and a lemon sauce. There was also a dish of freshly grated horseradish for anyone who wanted to intensify the flavor. Göran heaped a generous amount on top of his salmon, and Embla was a little worried about how his stomach would react. Then again, it was well used to such onslaughts. Maybe he'd try to lose some weight now that he was with Paula Nilsson, a colleague from Trollhättan. He looked good, with thick blond hair that had just started to recede at his temples, and kind blue eyes.

"I'm going to get myself a cup of coffee and a few raspberry cookies. Can I tempt you?" he said.

"Just a cup of tea, thanks."

Göran went over to the table where hot drinks and cookies had been set out. As Embla watched him go, she felt a pang of regret that they were no longer working together. He was the best boss anyone could wish for, and she was genuinely sorry that VGM had been disbanded as a result of reorganization within the police force. The country's twenty-one police districts had been brought together into seven regions, with a number of national departments and a head office based in Stockholm. One effect of this restructuring was that many experienced and skilled officers had taken early retirement. Units that had worked well for many years were broken up, including VGM.

The situation in many districts today is pretty chaotic. The police don't have the resources to investigate all the crimes that are reported; cases pile up, or are immediately written off. Sweden is around one thousand five hundred kilometers long and has significant regional variations when it comes to both climate and population. Sometimes police had to cover vast distances, particularly in the far north. The only advantage was that it was now possible to coordinate investigations across the whole country; this hadn't worked well when there were twenty-one separate districts.

The sound of Göran's phone cut into her thoughts. He put his tray down on the table and fished his phone out of the pocket of his jacket, which was draped over the chair. He answered as he sat down, then listened in silence. Judging by the look on his face, it wasn't good news. After a minute or so he thanked the caller and hung up. Slowly he shook his head, then met Embla's gaze.

"That was Sabina Amir, my new deputy. She was calling about Milo's younger brother."

Embla had met Sabina; Göran had introduced the two of them at the beginning of the previous month, but he'd clearly forgotten.

"Which one? Kador or Luca?"

"Luca. He was found at six o'clock this morning. That was the shooting Linda mentioned."

Embla's brain refused to work. This morning had already brought a number of surprises that had reawakened powerful emotions. Eventually she managed to process what Göran had just said: Two of the Stavic brothers were dead. Murdered. She couldn't speak.

"He was lying on the ground by his car," Göran continued, watching Embla's face closely. "He was behind other parked cars, so several hours passed before his body was discovered. They think he's been there since last night."

Embla tried to pull herself together. She was confused. "Does anyone know when he left La Dolce Vita?" she asked.

That was the club from which Lollo had disappeared; as far as Embla knew, Luca still worked there.

"Yes, there's a camera by the staff entrance; he left just after seven-thirty. Unfortunately there are no cameras in the parking garage where he was shot. Sorry—there is one by the entry ramp, but it's broken."

Over the years Embla had tried to keep herself up to speed on the Stavic brothers, but she'd mostly relied on what was in the media. She didn't have access to the police database, but she did remember an incident that had made headlines a few years ago. She cleared her throat a couple of times before she was able to trust her voice again.

"Four years ago, Luca and one of the doormen were shot outside the club. Luca survived, but the other guy died. Then nothing else happened—or did it?"

"You mean was the gunman arrested, or did the cops know for sure who he was? As in most cases involving gang-related violence, the answer is no. But this isn't just some suburban crew—this is the Stavic brothers. All I know is that a body was found floating in the water below the Opera House a month or so later. The man was from one of the Balkan countries, and had arrived in Gothenburg the day before the shootings. Rumor had it that he belonged to a rival gang."

A power struggle between two gangs would explain a great deal.

"And was that the case?"

Göran shrugged. "I have no idea. There's been no more trouble since then, but now everything's kicking off. Two brothers, murdered within a few hours. And the two crime scenes were only about two hundred kilometers apart."

"Where's Kador—the third brother?"

"The last I heard, he'd moved to Croatia. He'd already been there for ten years when Luca and the doorman were shot. I'll check him out; killings like this are often internal affairs. He's definitely a person of interest."

Embla was beginning to feel exhausted. For almost fifteen years she'd wanted to find out what had really happened on that warm August night. She'd been keen to investigate the brothers thoroughly, but at the same time she had been terrified to get too close to them. But now, with Milo and Luca dead, locating Kador was crucial.

IT WOULD BE a few hours before the CSIs were finished with the cottage, so Göran decided to go up to the room Harald had reserved for him in the main guesthouse. He wanted to check the police database for the latest information on the Stavic brothers. Embla had also been given a room. At first she'd thought it unnecessary, because she was staying with Nisse, but she knew things would be easier if she and Göran were in the same place. As all police officers know, the first forty-eight hours of an investigation are critical.

SHE DECIDED TO look into the murder of the teenager at the Lodge. She kept thinking about the fact that the timing of both homicides seemed to coincide. Someone could have seen something relevant to the death of Milo Stavic. It was a long shot, but it might just pay off, and at the moment, she couldn't think of a better way of starting the Stavic case. She didn't know anyone in this part of Dalsland, and she wasn't familiar with the area. There was no point in embarking on door-to-door inquiries because there were no inhabited buildings anywhere near the scene of the crime.

TWO POLICE CARS were parked outside the party venue, a standard Volvo V70 and a V70 Cross Country. The latter was the CSIs' vehicle. The door of the Lodge was open, and the technicians were just coming out. They were from the Trollhättan district and said hi to Embla because they recognized her from the homicide investigation during the previous year's moose hunt. She was about to go inside when Olle Tillman appeared. His face lit up when he saw her.

"Hi. We're done here," he said.

Embla nodded in the direction of the CSIs. "So I see."

"Have your technicians arrived?"

"Yes, they're hard at work, so I thought I'd ask if you've got time to show me this crime scene so I can get a feeling for the place. I can't help hoping that someone who was here last night might have seen something connected to Stavic's murder."

"Of course, if you think it will help."

He turned and waved her into the Lodge.

From the outside, the building looked like a large barn, well-maintained and with decent doors and windows. Once they stepped inside, any resemblance to a barn disappeared. It was a spacious, airy hallway with plenty of hooks and shelves for outdoor clothing. The temperature was pleasantly warm. Olle opened a double door, and they entered a generous venue with white-painted walls. The windows were new, but made to look old-fashioned. There was a small stage at the front, and the floor was clear of chairs and tables, which were stacked along the walls. Black plastic garbage bags were dotted around, filled with plastic plates and tumblers. The tables and floor were sticky with spilled drinks and food. Embla picked up the faint aroma of familiar spices.

"The club put up a taco buffet," Olle said. "The invited guests were trainers and players from the men's and women's teams in Herremarks IBK, and each person was allowed to bring one guest."

"Does the club often throw parties?"

"I don't know. This was to celebrate their twentieth anniversary."

"Did they provide the drinks, too?"

"No, everyone brought their own. The kids had put away quite a lot. Most of them were drunk, some virtually incapacitated, but, according to those we've spoken to, the atmosphere was good."

Embla looked around. "I guess there was dancing?"

"Yes, a local DJ from Bengtsfors started his set at about eleven o'clock."

Embla nodded. A fun party, with teenagers and a few older leaders dancing and having a good time. And yet a boy had been stabbed.

"No trouble?"

Olle frowned. "Well, one of the girls . . . Mikaela . . . said she was with the victim. She found him; she was completely hysterical when we got here. She said something along the lines of, 'It's that little fucker Ida! She couldn't cope with being dumped by him!'"

He rolled his eyes, his voice rising to a falsetto as he imitated the girl. Embla couldn't help smiling. Even though he was exhausted, Olle could still manage to be funny, which was a point in his favor.

"Did she or anyone else say anything interesting?"

"She didn't; the only other person I spoke to was

Wille. He was covered in blood; he'd rushed over and tried to stop the bleeding. At first I didn't think it was worth questioning him because he was so drunk, but then he said something strange. He was pretty aggressive and claimed it was Robin's own fault he'd been stabbed. I asked what he meant, and he almost yelled at me that Robin was 'so fucking cocky.' When I asked him to explain, he clammed up on me."

"You need to talk to him right away," Embla said.

"Absolutely."

"Remind me of the victim's surname?"

"Pettersson," he said, trying to suppress a yawn.

Embla was becoming increasingly certain that the two homicides were unconnected. The victims were too different in every way.

"Tell me what you know about the course of events leading up to the stabbing."

Olle reached into his breast pocket and took out his notebook. He found the page he was looking for, then glanced through what he'd written. A smile spread across his tired face.

"That's it—Mikaela Malm is the girl who said she and Robin were together. And the boy who said it was Robin's fault is Wille Andersson."

"You need to talk to both of them," Embla reminded him.

"Of course—tomorrow. We've already got people interviewing those who were at the party; we've divided the list of names between us, and those two are mine. Along with a few more."

"So what happened last night?"

Olle turned the page, unconsciously clearing his throat before he began to read.

"Witnesses saw Robin leave through the back door of the kitchen shortly before twelve-thirty. Apparently the boys often go out that way to pee."

"Was he alone?"

"Yes, but people were coming and going through that door the whole time. Most of them were far from sober, so it would have been possible to slip out without anyone noticing. And of course someone could have left by the main door at the front and crept around the back. Or the killer could have been out there waiting for Robin; he was bound to appear sooner or later."

"Okay, so Robin went out for a pee at about twelve twenty-five. What next?"

"No one missed him at first, but after a few minutes Mikaela Malm started looking for him. She said it was pitch dark at the back of the Lodge; apparently the external light is broken. She eventually found him twenty meters from the back door. He was curled up on the ground, unconscious and bleeding heavily. She ran back inside, screaming for help. It was all pretty chaotic, but one of the leaders realized that something serious had happened and went outside with Mikaela. He could see that Robin was badly injured; Wille Andersson was trying to stop the bleeding, along with another guy named . . . let me see . . . Gustav. The leader called an ambulance, which took around twenty-five minutes to arrive. Robin was showing no signs of life by this stage and was pronounced dead in the ambulance. We got here fifteen minutes later."

"Do you know what injuries he'd sustained?"

"Yes—several deep stab wounds to the chest and abdomen, inflicted with a large knife. The blade was long and wide—longer and wider than a Mora knife.

According to the doctor, one or more arteries had been severed."

"So you already have the report?" Embla said in surprise. *That was quick.*

"Only the preliminary, so we know what weapon we're looking for."

"You haven't found a knife that matches the description?"

"Not yet."

"Good."

Olle raised his eyebrows. "Good? Why is that good?"

"Because something tells me you're not looking for a professional hitman here. A person who kills for the first time usually makes mistakes. A cardinal error is holding on to the weapon. Search for a large kitchen knife or hunting knife in the homes of those you eventually identify as suspects."

He looked at her thoughtfully, then nodded. Suddenly his expression darkened. "We do have one problem," he said. "Johnzén."

"Your boss? Why is he a problem?"

To be fair, she'd already concluded as much from Johnzén's phone conversation with Olle and then with Göran.

"He's got it into his head that one of the boys from the residential care home is our perp," Olle said with a sigh.

This was news to Embla.

"Where's this home?"

"About three kilometers from here. It's an old school that's been converted into a home for unaccompanied refugee children. At the moment eight boys from Syria and Afghanistan are living there, but they're going to be relocated since the place is closing."

"Were any of them seen around the Lodge last night?"

"Not as far as we know."

"But Johnzén is sticking to his theory."

Olle nodded, then closed his notebook and slipped it in his pocket.

"Okay—I'm going home to Tore," he said firmly.

His son? Or partner?

"So poor Tore's been all alone since yesterday evening?" Embla said casually.

"No, my sister has him when I'm working. But they're going out tonight, so I need to get back."

Not a partner, then. A son?

"It's a shame if he doesn't get to see you on a Saturday when he's free," she said in the same tone.

"Tore's always free, except when he's training. Then he works very hard."

Training? Works very hard? Given Olle's age, his son couldn't be much more than five or six. Why would he drive a little boy so hard?

"How old is he?"

"Almost two."

Almost two—that's crazy! She had to make a real effort not to show what she was thinking.

"So what kind of training is he doing?" She couldn't quite keep the sharpness out of her voice.

Olle spread his hands wide. "It varies. Obedience, seek and find, narcotics . . ."

A dog.

"What breed is he?"

"A Belgian shepherd. He's passed the aptitude test to become a police dog, and he's done particularly well in the assessment for sniffing out drugs. I've done the dog handling course, and we've applied to the center in Karlsborg to do our basic training. It starts in two months; I should hear pretty soon."

"So you're going to be a dog handler."

"I hope so. There are plenty of vacancies; far too many dog teams were scrapped when the service was reorganized, so now new ones have to be trained."

Embla knew that dog teams were vital when people went missing in the vast forests. During her time with VGM she had been involved in a number of searches where the dogs had played a key role.

She thanked Olle for the information he'd given her, then they said goodbye and jumped in their respective cars.

EMBLA DROVE BACK to the guesthouse to see if Göran had heard from the CSIs at the cottage. Just as she'd suspected, he was still hunched over the computer in his room. The CSIs had been in touch, but only to say they wouldn't be joining him for a few hours.

"In that case I'll go over to Nisse's and pick up my things," Embla said.

"Good idea. If we meet here at six, that gives us an hour before dinner. I should have something from Linda and Bengan by then. The body's on its way to the pathologist, and we've been promised a preliminary report by tomorrow. I've also spoken to the district chief of police, Marjatta Svensson. She's happy that we've made a start at the crime scene and that we'll continue the investigation in Gothenburg. She used to be an inspector with Narcotics, so she's familiar with the Stavic brothers."

He turned away and was immediately absorbed in the text on the screen once more.

When Embla pulled up on the drive in front of Nisse's house, the first thing that caught her attention was a fox's pelt nailed to the wall of the woodshed. It was a big one, with thick, reddish-brown shimmering fur. A successful hunt, then. Nisse and Elliot must be pleased.

As soon as she stepped inside she sensed that something was wrong. There was silence downstairs; the only sign of life was from Seppo, who leaped up from his place by the stove to welcome her. He hurried over, wanting to be petted.

"There's a good boy! What have you done with your master?"

The dog understood the word "master" and let out a bark before going to the foot of the stairs. He turned his head and looked back at her, then stopped wagging his tail and allowed it to droop. Embla joined him and scratched behind his ears. She heard the sound of sobbing from the bedroom, accompanied by the low hum of Nisse's voice.

She took the stairs in a few strides; the door of the guestroom was ajar. She tapped gently before she went in.

"Hello, you two! Congratulations on a good day's hunting!" she said with excessive cheerfulness.

Elliot was lying on his stomach with his face buried in the pillow. Nisse was perched on the bed beside him, clumsily stroking the boy's back. When he heard Embla's voice he turned and shook his head, but it was too late. Elliot raised his head, his eyes red from weeping. She hurried over, crouched down, and gently placed her hand on his shoulder.

"Oh, Elliot . . ."

"I didn't want it to DIE!"

Tears poured down his cheeks, and he buried his face once more. Nisse exchanged a helpless look with his niece, who was equally at a loss.

"What happened?" she asked.

"I'm sure you can work it out," Nisse said with a deep sigh.

"You shot a fox. I saw the pelt on the—"

Loud sobs interrupted her. Nisse made a gesture indicating that she should stop talking about the unfortunate fox.

It was exactly as she'd feared: Elliot wasn't mature enough to cope with the hunt. He had no relationship with the tradition of hunting; his father only went after women, Embla thought sourly. The closest Elliot had come was people chasing and shooting one another in movies and computer games, where death is an abstract concept that affects no one because everyone knows it's only pretend. However, if he saw an animal die in a nature documentary, he would sob as if his heart was breaking. And now he'd seen it for real.

Killing an animal during the hunt demands respect for nature and for the animal itself, along with knowledge and good judgment. Because death is irrevocable. Embla often felt sad when she shot a fox or a moose, but hunting was necessary. How could she explain that to a devastated child?

She decided to try, and signaled to Nisse to swap places. His relief was unmistakable as he stood up and made room for her.

She stroked the boy's curls and spoke softly.

"Listen, sweetheart. I know this is hard, but it's really important that we—"

"There's no need to kill animals!" The sentiment was somewhat muffled as he was shouting into the pillow.

"Actually, there is. You remember those little fawns we saw when we were here last summer?"

He didn't reply, but he didn't move either, which suggested that he was listening. Good. Now it was just a matter of saying the right thing.

"You remember how sweet they were, scampering around in the meadow? They were only a few days old."

"I took lots of photos of them."

"You did. Your pictures of the mother deer with her two fawns were fantastic."

He turned his head and looked at her with his puffy eyes.

"I kept them on my phone. Everybody in my class has s-s-seen them." He hiccupped.

He sat up and grabbed his phone from the nightstand. In seconds he'd found the images of the little family.

"Look! That one's Bambi, and this one's Prancer," he said.

"So sweet," Embla said. *Okay, time to go for it.* "Do you know who Bambi and Prancer's worst enemy is? Who kills the most fawns?"

He glanced up at her, and she could see the anxiety in his eyes.

"No . . . a hunter, maybe?"

"Hunters aren't interested in fawns. They're too small. It's someone else."

"Who?"

"The fox."

A long silence followed. "But . . . foxes aren't very big. They can't . . ." His voice was shaking.

"Yes, they can. They love to take baby deer. Yum yum!"

Elliot stared down at the deer, playing in the sun-drenched meadow on a beautiful summer's day.

"That's why we have to control the number of predators," Embla continued. "If we don't, there won't be any deer left. It's all about maintaining balance in nature."

She realized he wasn't listening. He wiped away a tear with the back of his hand. *He needs a distraction*, Embla thought.

"Nisse, can you call Karin and check if it was this evening she wanted Elliot to come over? I think she mentioned tea and computer games." She winked to make sure he understood; he smiled and nodded.

"I think it was, but I'll give her a call just to be on the safe side."

He looked much happier as he left the room to contact his other niece.

Karin was seven years older than Embla, but the cousins had always been close. They both had older brothers and no sisters, and they were both members of the local hunting club. Karin had qualified as a nurse, then returned to her home village to marry Björn. She'd been working as a district nurse for many years now. They had three children: two girls, ages thirteen and ten, and a four-year-old boy. Both girls had a knack for computer games, and Elliot loved playing with them.

After a couple of minutes Nisse was back. He looked positively cheerful as he stuck his head around the door.

"You're right, it is this evening. Karin's cooking moose meatballs with cream sauce and lingonberries for dinner."

Elliot's favorite. Thank God for Karin, fixing that up at such short notice. As long as no one mentioned where the moose meat had come from . . .

"Yesss!"

Elliot leaped to his feet and ran into the bathroom to blow his nose and wash his face. For the time being, the fox was forgotten.

"Go take down that pelt and put it somewhere out of sight," Embla whispered to her uncle.

"I will. And tomorrow I'll drive him back to his father in Gothenburg."

"Okay, in that case I'll take him to Karin's. That will give us a little time together before I head back to Herremark. It doesn't feel right to leave him without giving him an explanation."

"I understand. Karin's invited me over as well, so I'll be there around six. We thought it would be good if the kids had a chance to play before dinner."

"Fantastic! You're the best uncle in the whole wide world!"

She gave him a big hug, which brought a contented smile to his face.

EMBLA HAD CALLED to warn Göran that she was going to be late, so they'd arranged to meet in the restaurant at the guesthouse.

Monika welcomed her at reception. When she handed over Embla's room key, she leaned across the desk and said quietly, "The CSIs came in to eat about an hour ago. The cottage is still cordoned off in case they need to come back, although they said that probably wouldn't be necessary. If you or Superintendent Krantz want to take another look, just let me know and I'll give you the key. I checked with the technicians, and they said that would be fine."

"Thanks, Monika," Embla said before running up the creaking stairs. There were only four guest rooms in the main building these days; most visitors preferred the cabins. Embla was grateful that Harald had reserved two for her and Göran.

Her room was very pleasant, with thick cream-colored cotton curtains and a matching bedspread. In the middle of the polished wooden floor lay a bright rug. There were potted plants in both windows, illuminated by small lamps with frosted glass shades. On the neat desk and the two nightstands, more lamps gave a soft glow. A comfortable-looking leather armchair was by one of the windows, along with an old-fashioned standard lamp, complete with a parchment shade that had a brown fringe around the bottom. She also had her own en suite bathroom; she knew the other guests had to share the bathroom in the hallway.

She took off her coat and changed into her high-heeled boots. Combined with her black jeans and emerald-green jersey top, she was dressed smart enough for dinner. She let down her long hair and brushed it until it shone, then applied a quick application of mascara and a slick of lipstick.

The restaurant occupied most of the ground floor and had a large glass veranda with a magnificent view over the lake. The décor was rustic, adding to the cozy, welcoming atmosphere. An open fire was crackling in one corner.

A female maître d' guided her to Göran's table, at the back of the room. As Embla sat down she glanced outside. The wind had dropped and it was no longer snowing. The clouds were beginning to disperse, and as a result the temperature was falling. A full moon spread its ice-cold light over the snow-covered surface of the lake, making it sparkle like a diamond bedspread. Far away on the horizon, a faint yellowish-green shimmer suggested that the northern lights were putting on a show.

"The CSIs were here about an hour ago and gave me their preliminary report," Göran said, getting straight to the point.

"Did they find anything?"

"The most interesting thing is what they didn't find—no phone, no laptop. And no big gold watch. However, there was a charger for an iPhone or iPad, which means—"

He broke off, looking up at a point above Embla's shoulder. When he smiled, she realized there was someone behind her.

"Are you ready to order?" their waitress asked.

"We need a couple more minutes, but I'd like a beer to start with. Embla?"

"Cider, please."

"Coming right up," the waitress said, tip-tapping away across the wooden floor on her high heels.

"I guess we'd better see what they have," Göran said, opening up the menu. The folders were made of tanned moose hide, and Embla knew that Harald had shot the animal himself. The menu itself was printed on thick cream-colored paper. As usual there was a choice of two starters and main courses, plus a vegetarian option. Embla chose homemade tomato soup followed by a hare casserole. Göran went for smoked moose heart with a salad to start with, then decided to try the hare, on Embla's recommendation. After all, the restaurant was famous for the quality of its game dishes.

"You can eat fried alpine char at home," Embla pointed out.

Dessert was a dark chocolate mousse with raspberry sauce and a Florentine. Her mouth was already watering, and she suddenly realized how hungry she was.

The waitress returned with their drinks, a basket of home-baked bread, and a dish of whipped butter. The bread was still warm and smelled amazing. Against her strict principles, Embla took two pieces as soon as the waitress had taken their order.

The restaurant was busy, but three families with small children were just about to leave. After the large group had gone, the noise level dropped significantly. It didn't make any difference to the two police officers. There was no one close enough to their table to hear what they were saying, but they still instinctively spoke in hushed tones.

"The body has been transported to the forensic pathologist. According to Linda, Milo Stavic had been shot in the head and heart at close range with a large-caliber weapon. That fits with the gun beneath his hands—a Beretta M9. They couldn't see any signs of a struggle, or any indication that he'd tried to defend himself. All the evidence suggests that he was shot in his sleep."

Göran started searching the pockets of his jacket, which was draped over the back of the chair. Eventually he found his notebook, licked his index finger, and leafed through the pages until he came to the right place. His face lit up.

"Okay, so . . . No dirty dishes, the dishwasher was empty. An empty wine bottle in the trash can. An unopened bottle of Slivovitz in the closet, plus a bottle of Croatian red wine. A packet of mixed salted nuts and a bag of potato chips, along with an empty box that had contained handmade chocolates from Bräutigams. But no food—he'd booked his meals here in the restaurant. They also found an expensive-looking suit and two shirts. The shirts were handmade in London. There was a wool overcoat hanging up in the hallway. A large bag in the closet contained a winter jacket with matching pants, thick socks, lined gloves, and a pair of long underwear. All from Peak Performance. There was a pair of heavy winter boots, still in their box. Everything brand-new and unused."

He fell silent and looked at her over the top of his reading glasses. Why did Milo need an entire set of new clothes suitable for winter conditions? There was nothing to indicate that he'd had the slightest interest in outdoor activities in the past. And since Milo Stavic was involved, this was no impulse buy. He was a man who always knew what he was doing.

Before Embla could speak, the waitress brought their starters.

There's tomato soup, and then there's homemade Italian tomato soup. It was delicious, and Embla caught herself shoveling it down way too fast. So fast that she scalded the roof of her mouth, but it was worth it. She glanced up when she heard a groan of pleasure from the other side of the table.

"Oh my God! Smoked moose heart with pickled chanterelles and salad—amazing!" Göran said, rolling his eyes.

The restaurant had more than lived up to its reputation and their expectations. The service was also outstanding; as soon as they'd finished, their plates were whisked away.

The French cider was dry and cold, the alcohol content probably higher than in Swedish varieties. As the sparkling liquid cooled her palate, Embla felt the tension in her shoulders ease. It had been quite a day; she hadn't had the chance to process everything that had happened, but now the snow had eased, and she and Göran were sitting in the cozy restaurant enjoying their meal. Her brain felt clearer, and she was sure they could make some progress in the investigation, even if the information they had so far was a little sparse.

"How did the perpetrator get in?" she asked.

"Through the door. There are fresh marks on the lock. Forced."

"Wouldn't Milo have heard him?"

"Not necessarily. The Slivovitz bottle on the nightstand was empty, as was another red wine bottle on the floor by the bed. I think we can assume he was in the habit of drinking quite a lot; he was probably comatose when the killer entered the cottage."

"Isn't that a bit strange?" Embla objected.

"Why?"

"I'm surprised he dared to drink so much, given the effect it has."

"True, but doesn't that tell us something important?" Göran held up his index finger to stress just how important that something was. "Milo felt safe in the cottage. He wasn't expecting any trouble. However . . . the bag containing the new winter clothes had a false bottom, and in the secret compartment was a significant amount of ammunition—9 x 19mm Parabellum, which fits the Beretta. And I've checked—Milo had a license to carry a Beretta M9, so that could well be the gun that was found on the body."

"So he was shot with his own gun. I've been thinking about the fact that he came alone," Embla said.

Göran nodded. "You mean you'd expect him to bring one or more bodyguards. Which reinforces what I said before: he didn't feel threatened."

The waitress appeared with their main courses. The hare casserole gave off a wonderful aroma of garlic, spices, and red wine. It was served with Hasselback potatoes and fried apple slices. They ate in respectful silence, then decided to wait a little while before moving on to dessert.

"Did I tell you that Milo's car is being taken down to our lab in Gothenburg first thing tomorrow morning?" Göran asked.

Embla shook her head. She'd been wondering about Milo's new car.

"Why buy a great big Audi SUV when you've already got a top-of-the-line Merc?" she asked.

Göran took a swig of his beer before he answered. "I've checked out the Audi, and it's a company car, registered to a brand-new firm, STAV Property Ltd. All three brothers are listed as owners. The company has just bought up a number of buildings in Vasastan. Big business. I'll take a closer look when I have time. There's also another Audi—an A6—registered to STAV Property."

It would take a while to disentangle the Stavic brothers' affairs, while investigating the homicides of two of them. The questions were piling up, but the biggest puzzle was still what the hell he'd been doing in Herremark.

Göran turned a page in his notebook. "I've been looking into Milo's history, and I found out a couple of things I didn't know before. For example, he's actually Kador and Luca's half-brother. Those two are full brothers."

"I didn't know that either," Embla said in surprise.

"Milo was forty-five years old. He was born in Dubrovnik; his mother, Maria, was a Croat, and his father, Milan, was a Serb. When Milo was six, his father drowned in a boating accident. Two years later Maria married Ivan Stavic, a fellow Croat, and they moved to Gothenburg. She must have been pregnant on her wedding day, because Kador was born six months later."

"Was that when the Bosnian War broke out?"

"No, this was several years before the war."

"So why did they move?"

"I have no idea. Luca arrived three years later, so the two youngest were born in Sweden."

Göran turned another page and quickly scanned the text. "Ivan Stavic started working at a pizzeria and kebab shop in the city center. After a year the owner died of cancer, and Ivan took over. Soon he acquired two more places, and Milo joined him in the business as soon as he left school. Together, they picked up more and more establishments—restaurants, nightclubs, pizzerias and bars, casinos. Even back then they were laundering money for various gangs in the city, but the police never managed to prove anything. Ivan died of a heart attack twenty-three years ago. By then Milo was more than capable of running things on his own. Today he's regarded as one of Gothenburg's—one of Sweden's—most powerful mafia bosses. Needless to say he's well-paid for laundering money; his latest 'client' is a luxury hotel in the city. Apparently it's all going very well."

Göran paused to catch his breath, and Embla took the opportunity to ask a couple of questions.

"It sounds to me as if Ivan knew what he was doing—it didn't take him long to become a player. Did he have contacts in Gothenburg before he came here? Was the owner of the first pizzeria a relative?"

"I have no idea."

"And the police have never managed to pin anything on Milo?"

"No—apart from tax infringement, for which he was fined."

"Ivan must have taught him well."

"Yes, and Milo was a willing student. Street smart, intelligent, tough, ruthless. Ivan must have seen those qualities in his stepson."

Embla thought for a moment before she responded.

"So he earmarked Milo as his successor, not Kador or Luca."

"Exactly—they were probably too young. Kador was fourteen and Luca was only eleven when their father died. But Milo has always taken care of his half-brothers, and they've worked well together over the years."

It was a lot of new information.

"Come to think of it, I haven't heard anything about Kador since I started monitoring the Stavic brothers," Embla said after a while.

"That's hardly surprising. He's lived in Split for a long time. He's married to a Finnish woman and they have three children. According to our colleagues dealing with organized crime in Gothenburg, he's responsible for smuggling prostitutes, drugs, and guns from the Balkans. Access to illegal weapons has increased significantly in Sweden in the recent past. They're pretty sure Milo is a major player when it comes to bringing arms into the south and west, and Kador is Milo's man in the Balkans. The Stavic brothers are also heavily involved with human trafficking. The victims are moved around and distributed in a steady stream all over Europe. We're talking about vast amounts of money—which also have to be laundered."

"So we're looking at a huge international organization?"

"Absolutely. Globalization works to the advantage of many, especially criminal networks."

Embla hadn't been aware of the scale of the operation until now. To be honest, she'd concentrated on Milo and Luca and their activities in Gothenburg, and they didn't often feature in the media. Except when Luca got shot outside the nightclub.

"So Kador is married and has children. How about Milo?"

"No children, but he was married to a Swede for almost eight years. Her maiden name was Carolina Karlsson. They parted as friends, and the divorce settlement was very generous. She doesn't live in Sweden anymore; she runs a restaurant in London with her new husband. They have two kids."

"So does Milo pay alimony even though she's remarried?"

"Apparently."

Göran looked up from his notes and gave her a sly smile.

"I guess she knows too much."

"You could be right," Embla said, smiling back.

Deep down, she wasn't sure. If she was right about Milo, he wouldn't have hesitated to get rid of Carolina if she'd tried to blackmail him when they split up. A man like Milo never pays up without good reason. He must have thought she was worth more to him alive than dead.

"How old were they when they got married?" she asked, mainly out of curiosity.

Göran switched on his tablet and searched online. Within a very short time he nodded, looking very pleased with himself.

"Okay, so Carolina was twenty-one and Milo was

twenty-nine. Married for eight years, as I said, so she was twenty-nine and he was thirty-seven when they divorced."

"That's a long time ago. No new woman or live-in partner?"

"Plenty of women and aspiring partners, but he never let any of them move in."

More information to absorb. Embla was beginning to feel as if her hard drive was full.

"Have you found anything about Luca?" she asked.

"Not much. He'd just turned thirty-four when he was shot yesterday morning; his birthday is February tenth. No criminal record, apart from speeding tickets fifteen years ago and twelve years ago. Nothing else in our database until the shooting outside La Dolce Vita. The investigating officers at the time thought the doorman who was killed was the actual target. He'd refused to let a group of young men in earlier in the evening, and there had been some trouble. It was assumed that the perpetrator was in that group, but they all had watertight alibis. No one was ever charged with the homicide."

"No other suspects?"

"No. But as I said, there was a rumor that it could be a rival gang wanting to take over the Stavic brothers' lucrative operation. That rumor was strengthened when they fished that body out of the river down below the Opera House, the one I mentioned before. He turned out to be a Serbian citizen, Damian Pacić. According to the Serbian police, he had an extensive criminal record, and was a professional hit man."

"In which case he wouldn't have missed," Embla pointed out.

"Not everyone is as accurate as you. But the theory is that Pacić made a mistake. Luca and the doorman were pretty similar. Same height and age, same dark hair cut in the same style. The doorman came out first, closely followed by Luca. When the shot that killed the doorman was fired, Luca had just enough time to throw himself backward. He was hit, but it was only a superficial wound; the bullet didn't enter his body. His guardian angel was watching over him that night."

"I guess the doorman's and the Serb's guardian angels were off duty," Embla said dryly.

Göran didn't answer right away. He seemed to be sizing her up, then he made a decision.

"There was another rumor circulating at the time. A suggestion that Luca and the doorman were together. That they were a couple."

Embla was surprised. The idea that Luca was gay didn't fit with her theory; she was convinced he was the guy Lollo had fallen in love with. Of course he could have pretended to like her, or he could have been bisexual. Suddenly her head was full of fresh questions.

"However, that was just a rumor in the immediate aftermath of the shooting," Göran added.

"I expect we'll find out more in the course of the investigation into his murder."

"I'm sure we will. I plan to be hands-on, and I'll be bringing you down to Gothenburg when the time is right. I'll speak to Tommy Persson; I should think quite a few of your colleagues will be involved. However, right now you're needed up here in case anything new turns up."

"Okay, but I'm confused. Are you going to be my boss, or is Tommy Persson?"

"Good question. Since you and I have already started looking into Milo's murder, it makes sense for us to carry on together. Tommy will be leading the investigation into the shooting of Luca Stavic. We'll obviously be sharing information, because it seems more than likely that the two deaths are connected. I'll speak to Tommy in the morning and let you know how things are going to work."

Göran's tablet pinged, and he couldn't hide his surprise as he read the message.

"There's an international alert out for Kador Stavic. Let's see . . . He's been missing for almost two weeks. So he's not a suspect—they think he might be the victim of a crime. Must be unusual for him. No indication that he had any reason to disappear. His relatives are concerned." He looked up at Embla. "With good reason, I'd say, given what's happened to his brothers."

"Missing for almost two weeks . . . Could he be in Sweden?" Embla wondered.

"Anything's possible. I'll contact our colleagues in Split right away. Officially Kador runs a number of restaurants and nightclubs over there—and a couple of hotels, I think. But the Croatian police might know more. Something that could be useful to us."

It was essential to act fast before the media picked up on the murders and any possible trail went cold. Speaking of cold . . . Embla looked out at the moonlit landscape. Nothing was moving, and the stars were twinkling in a clear sky. According to the forecast, the temperature was due to drop to minus four degrees Fahrenheit during the night. She shivered and turned back to Göran.

"I need to make a couple of calls."

"No problem. I'll see you at breakfast."

On the way up to her room, Embla realized they'd forgotten dessert.

HER FIRST CALL was to Elliot's father, Jason, to explain what had happened during and after the unfortunate hunting expedition. She wasn't looking forward to the conversation, but it was best to get it out of the way. As she'd expected, he was furious that she'd even considered taking his son hunting.

"He's only nine years old! Are you crazy?" he yelled.

"I know, and I was against the idea, but he really wanted to go," she said feebly.

"That's irrelevant—he's only nine years old!"

"I'm well aware of that, but he's been nagging me for weeks, and Nisse thought—"

"Don't blame your senile uncle! You're the one who's responsible for Elliot!"

Making a huge effort to remain calm, Embla replied, "I know that, too, and I take full responsibility for the decision. I wasn't actually there. My mother's cousin called; he rents out cottages to tourists, and he found a dead man in one of them."

That silenced Jason, but not for long.

"You are fucking unbelievable! You're supposed to be looking after my son, but instead you hand him over to an old man, who takes the kid hunting while you go chasing after a murderer!"

Enough.

"And what have you been doing this week?" she asked, shards of ice clinking in her voice.

This time the silence was considerably longer.

Presumably he wasn't sure how much she knew, whether he dared to lie. In fact she knew everything; Elliot had spilled.

During the drive up to Dalsland, he'd suddenly said: "Do you think I call too often?"

He sounded a little down, but she couldn't work out why.

"No. Sometimes maybe . . . No. Why do you ask?"

"Dad said I wasn't to call him so much this week."

"Why not?"

"He and . . . Tanya, I think her name is . . . are going away somewhere," he said with a deep sigh.

Embla got the picture. Jason didn't want to be disturbed by phone calls from his son while he was enjoying himself with his new girlfriend. *Same old, same old, in other words*, she thought, unconsciously pursing her lips as she waited for Jason's response.

"That's none of your business. My concern is the lasting damage this experience has inflicted on my son . . ." He was doing his best to recapture his initial outrage.

"There is no lasting damage. Right now he's at Karin's, playing computer games with her two daughters. She cooked him his favorite dinner, which he really enjoyed. He's as happy as can be. He's with people who care about him; it's good for him to experience the security and love of a family environment."

The last comment was a deliberate jab; Embla knew exactly what she was doing.

"If you're insinuating that I don't love Elliot . . ."

"I'm sure you do. In your own way. But some people might wonder why you didn't take him away for the spring vacation."

"Because you and he had already decided you were

going up to Nisse's. The two of you always spend the February break with him."

"That's very convenient for you. I guess you were able to devote yourself wholeheartedly to your new girlfriend. Everyone's happy!"

It was all spiraling out of control, as their quarrels always did, but Jason was bright enough to realize where this could end up. If he pushed any further, he would have to stop Embla from taking care of Elliot. That would cause huge problems, both for him and the boy. As a jazz musician he toured a great deal, and Embla always tried to step up. Jason valued the opportunity to live his life without having to bother about his son from time to time.

Time for a tactical retreat.

"Okay, so I'm not happy that Elliot had such an upsetting experience, but let's draw a line under it now. We'll need to keep an eye on him. I'm sure he'll get over it, as you said, but I don't want him going hunting again."

"You have my word—at least not without asking you first. And to be honest, I don't think he'll want to go."

"Sounds good. By the way, did you say Nisse's bringing him home?"

"Yes. They're leaving straight after breakfast tomorrow."

"Okay. And Embla"—he cleared his throat a couple of times—"thanks for being there for him."

"No problem," she said, ending the call.

Relief flooded her body. The conversation had been tricky, but it was clear that Jason relied on her to be around and to take care of his son. For the first time she wondered what would happen in the future, as Elliot grew up. Would Jason take more responsibility, or would he continue to dodge his obligations?

IN SPITE OF everything that had happened on Saturday, Embla slept deeply, with no bad dreams. The alarm on her phone woke her at seven-thirty the following morning, and she was astonished to realize that she'd slept for almost nine hours. That was unheard of. Was it because Milo was dead, because she felt safe now that he could no longer threaten or hurt her? And Luca was out of the picture, too. Now there was only Kador to worry about. Where could he be? Two weeks is a long time to be missing. Was he in Sweden? Had he murdered his brothers? Even though such a course of action would give him greater power in the organization, she didn't think it was very likely. The network was too extensive for one man to lead. Then again, maybe Kador had a different view of power and leadership.

She still didn't feel she was in any real danger from him. If he was in the country, then no doubt he had his hands full with other matters.

Her thoughts returned to Lollo. Where was she? She'd contacted Embla after almost fifteen years, but the call had ended abruptly. Had it been a cry for help? For the first time in many years she was filled with hope that they would find Lollo alive.

She stretched out in the comfortable bed. The radiator made a ticking noise; it was doing a wonderful job of warming the room. The windows were still covered in snow and ice; she hadn't pulled down the blinds. It was cold outside, just as the weather forecast had promised.

THE WOODEN FLOORBOARDS creaked as she made her way along the hallway. A stern gentleman was staring down at her from an old, dark oil painting; his eyes seemed to follow her. A small brass plaque on the frame informed her it was Baron Gustaf Adolf Holze af Falkeclou (1795–1866). He could well be the original owner of the manor house, Embla thought.

To her surprise there were only a few guests at the tables laid for breakfast. Monika came hurrying over with a steaming pot of coffee.

"Good morning! Not many people up yet, I see," Embla said.

"Morning! No, most prefer to have breakfast in their cabins. About half come in for lunch, and almost everyone for dinner," Monika explained.

"So they don't have to book half or full board?"

"Not at all, but as I said, most book dinner. It's an important part of the Herremark experience."

Embla asked Monika about something that had occurred to her the previous day. "Are the cottages cleaned while the guests are here?"

"No—not until they've left."

"And Jan Müller had booked for one night?"

"Yes."

"So the cottage would have been cleaned yesterday?"

"No. On weekends our cleaners come on the Sunday,

which is when most people check out. No one was sched-
uled to check in to Müller's cottage right away, so it was
on the list for today."

"Had he paid the full amount in advance?"

"Yes—accommodation for one night, plus dinner on
Friday and breakfast on Saturday."

It was pure luck that Milo Stavic had requested an
early breakfast and stressed that he wanted to eat at
seven. The murderer wouldn't have expected the body to
be discovered so soon.

She saw that Göran had claimed the same table they'd
sat at yesterday evening. He was absorbed in something
on his laptop. On her way over, Embla helped herself to
a glass of orange juice, a cup of tea, a bowl of porridge,
and cheese and tomato on crispbread from the buffet. As
usual Göran gave her breakfast a disapproving glance. He
had gone for several slices of toast with apricot jelly,
warm croissants with a generous dollop of Nutella, plus a
pot of coffee. He was drinking the coffee from a large cup,
having added four sugar cubes. The perfect start to the
day, according to the superintendent.

"Morning! Good news—I just heard that Milo's Audi
is on its way to the lab. I've also found out that he picked
up both cars only ten days ago. And according to the
national vehicle register, he still owns the Mercedes we
saw back in the fall. He bought it in June last year, so it's
not even a year old."

He paused to attack his toast and have a mouthful of
the sweet coffee. Embla nodded and made a start on her
porridge; she was hungry.

Strengthened by the fast carbs, Göran continued. "I'm
driving down to Gothenburg as soon as I've eaten, but I'd

like you to stay on for a while, check if anyone saw anything on Friday night. Not a single witness has come forward. The press said a man was found shot dead up here, but we've managed to keep his real identity quiet. The media circus hasn't arrived yet, but it's only a matter of time."

He grimaced; Embla knew everything would kick off as soon as Milo Stavic's name was released.

AFTER BREAKFAST SHE decided to take another look at the cottage. The temperature was around three degrees Fahrenheit, but the wind had dropped. She paused on the steps of the guesthouse and gazed at the cabins, dotted across the land leading down to the lake. A pale sun had begun to peek above the horizon, spreading a faint pink glow over the sparkling snow. The phenomenon lasted only a few minutes, but it was beautiful. It was going to be a clear but chilly day. She didn't mind the cold, as long as the wind and snow stayed away.

Monika had given her the key to the cottage. Embla didn't think the CSIs would have missed anything; she just wanted to make sure that she herself hadn't overlooked something vital. If her trigger-happy colleague hadn't come stomping in and disturbed her, she might have been more focused.

Olle Tillman. She needed to contact him, ask if she could sit in on his interviews with the partygoers on his list. She was interested in the results of the door-to-door inquiries currently underway in the area around the Lodge.

Her phone rang. She pulled off her mittens and

reached into her pocket. The display showed only a number, no name.

"Embla Nyström," she said warily.

"Hi, it's Olle Tillman. The cop from Åmål, if you recall."

She could have acidly pointed out that she usually remembered people who'd pointed a gun at her, but instead she simply replied, "Hi. I was just about to call you."

"In that case I'm guessing we're on the same page. I thought you'd like to sit in on my interviews."

"Yes."

"I'll be leaving Åmål in a little while; see you at the Lodge in an hour and a half?"

"Sounds good. But surely it's only sixty or seventy kilometers? It doesn't take ninety minutes to cover that distance."

"It does if you have a dog. I have to take Tore out first," he said with a laugh.

"Okay. See you at the Lodge."

A LARGE RECTANGULAR hollow in the snow showed where the Audi had been. Embla stared at it for a while, along with tire tracks of the tow truck that had taken it away.

Why had Milo bought a car like that? It didn't fit with his lifestyle at all. And neither did renting a cottage in the middle of nowhere, almost two hundred kilometers from Gothenburg. She couldn't think of any reason why he would come up here. All his business could be done from his exclusive office in the newly built block in Gårda.

He must have been aware that Kador had gone missing in Croatia, and yet he had left the security of the city, where he was surrounded by his heavies. Apparently his brother's disappearance hadn't worried him too much—or else Milo knew where Kador was. Maybe Kador had been forced to go underground and remain hidden; a man like that could easily have several reasons to stay out of the way.

So Milo had come alone to the cottage in Herremark. Presumably he'd felt safe with his gun for protection. He had a license for the 9mm Beretta M9. Embla knew that a special version of this model, the Beretta 92FS, was used by the US Marine Corps. It was regarded as one of the best handguns around.

She herself had used only the standard M9 during her training. She was a good shot, but a rifle was her weapon of choice. The police pistol shooting team had tried to persuade her to join, but she just couldn't fit it into her crowded schedule: a full-time job with a lot of overtime, boxing, hunting, friends and family—including Elliot. However, following the injury she'd sustained during the investigation into the murders of two hunters during the previous year's moose hunt, doctors had told her she would never be able to box at national level again since the risk of permanent brain damage was too great. So maybe she would take up competitive shooting.

But now she had to concentrate on Milo's Beretta M9. Had he been shot with his own gun? If so, then it must have been lying on the nightstand, already loaded, because he'd been killed while he was asleep. After the murder, the perpetrator had placed it beneath his folded hands and taken Milo's iPhone or iPad or both. And probably the expensive watch Harald had noticed when Milo checked in, but not the ring on Milo's little finger. According to Linda, the CSI, it would have been difficult to remove. They hadn't found any house or apartment keys, only car keys. Could this be a simple robbery? No, because Milo's wallet had been in the inside pocket of his jacket, its contents untouched.

The strong wind might have dropped, but the odd icy blast lashed her face. Her nose and cheeks were beginning to feel tight. Her feet were freezing. Time to go into the cottage.

The metallic smell of blood, mixed with that powerful male cologne, struck her as soon as she walked in. The heat hadn't been turned down; it was still something like seventy degrees indoors. There was no reason to take off her boots; the CSIs were unlikely to return, and the whole place would be thoroughly cleaned over the next few days.

The outdoor clothes that had been on the rack had disappeared. That was only to be expected; the CSIs would have taken any personal items that might carry traces of DNA. She moved on to the bedroom; the bed linen was also gone. She took a good look around. There were bloodstains on the wall above the headboard, and a pool of rusty-red coagulated blood on the floor; Milo had bled profusely through the hole in the pillow and the mattress. The drawers in the nightstands were empty. The closet doors were open, revealing only a few hangers. The expensive Samsonite cabin suitcase was also gone, removed for forensic examination down in Gothenburg.

The guest in this cottage had checked out for good.

So the killer had picked the lock and crept in. It must

have been pitch dark. If he was here before the snow-storm began, then maybe the external lighting would have provided a faint glow. However, conditions had quickly deteriorated, and the snow later covered the window.

She positioned herself in the middle of the room, closed her eyes, and tried to think like the hunter she was.

My task is to kill Milo Stavic. Somehow I've found out that he's coming up here alone, to this isolated cottage. A dream scenario, as far as I'm concerned. How do I proceed? Needless to say, I carry out a detailed reconnaissance in advance to familiarize myself with the surroundings. When I return during the night, I have to be able to see in the dark. Night-vision glasses are the natural solution to this problem. I have my own gun with me. I know that Milo will have his Beretta nearby, and I have to allow for the possibility that he will wake up and grab it. When I've done what I came to do, I must have a car so that I can make a quick getaway.

She opened her eyes and stared at the picture of the bird perched on the blossom-laden branch without really seeing it.

Her brain was working at top speed. How could the killer get into the bedroom without waking Milo? One thing was clear: he must have known that his victim would be heavily under the influence of alcohol. Milo had probably drunk wine with dinner at the guesthouse, in addition to the bottles of red wine and Slivovitz in the cottage. She must remember to check his bill. Maybe he was in the habit of knocking back a fair amount of booze in order to sleep. If the killer was aware of this, did that mean they knew each other? And why had Milo drunk so much when he was intending to get up early the next day? He must have realized he'd have one hell of a hangover.

She couldn't get any further; this was just wild speculation.

She shuddered, suddenly feeling as if Milo were in the room, about to grab her by the throat and hiss: *"If you say a word to anyone, you're dead!"*

Her heart started pounding and panic sank its sharp claws into her breast. *Calm down, he's dead. Dead! Pull yourself together!* She forced herself to take deep breaths, but to no avail. Time to move on.

Fortunately her phone rang at that moment: Olle Tillman.

"Hi—we'll be at the Lodge in about fifteen minutes."

"Great—see you there."

As she ended the call she smiled. He'd said "we"— apparently they would be working with a future police dog today.

IT WAS A wide-awake and clear-eyed Olle who met her at the party venue, with Tore by his side. The dog was similar to a German shepherd, but slimmer and with longer legs. His fur was reddish brown with black patches, mainly around the head. His entire body was quivering with excitement.

"Hi. This is Tore," Olle said, pointing proudly to his companion.

Embla held out her hand and Tore gave it a good sniff. He allowed her to pat his back gently, then decided that was enough. He took a few steps away from her and turned his back on her. She had been classified as uninteresting. Olle looked slightly embarrassed.

"Belgian shepherds tend to be a one-man dog. He's like this with everyone except me."

"No problem. At least he's accepted me; I'd prefer not to be bitten by a colleague in training," Embla responded with a smile.

"He thinks you're okay, otherwise you'd know about it," Olle said with a wry smile.

She didn't doubt that for a second. There was something about Tore's body language that told her he didn't miss much. His ears and nose were twitching, and he was constantly moving his head, all his sharp senses on full alert.

"Do you always bring him to work?"

"No, my mom or my sister usually have him, but things didn't work out today. The whole of my sister's family has come down with the flu, and Mom's gone to Tenerife with some friends. So Tore is with me, but it's no problem. He loves being in the car."

Tore turned and looked up at his master's face, as if he realized they were talking about him.

"Shall we take the squad car, or mine?" Embla asked.

After a critical glance at the Kia, Olle shook his head.

"The Volvo—Tore has to be in his cage in the back."

They went over to the squad car and he opened the trunk. Embla saw a flash of reddish brown as Tore leaped into his cage. *Impressive*, she thought.

Out of sheer habit she moved toward the driver's side, then remembered and headed for the passenger seat. She usually drove when she was out on a case with VGM, but this was Olle's investigation and Olle's car, not hers.

"Okay, I thought we'd speak to Wille Andersson first, as you suggested," Olle said. "He was the one who told me it was Robin's own fault that he'd been stabbed."

"Because he was 'so fucking cocky.'"

"Yes. And Wille was first on the scene, and he was covered in blood. He has a lot of questions to answer."

"Absolutely."

"His younger sister, Ida, was at the party, too; Robin had just dumped her. I'd like to have a chat with her as well."

They sat in silence for a while, then Embla said, "These interviews are going to take quite some time."

Olle glanced at her out of the corner of his eye as he pulled onto the main road. "Yes, but we've got reinforcements—two officers from Trollhättan."

"Do you know their names?"

"No, but my boss thinks it's a total waste of time. He's interviewing the refugees at the residential care home, although I believe there's something of a language barrier."

A contented grin spread across his face. Olle certainly wasn't fond of his boss, and from the little she'd heard about Chief Inspector Johnzén, she could understand why.

AT THE TOP of the hill lay three newly built wooden houses. The Anderssons' pale-gray home was the largest. The window frames, eaves, and the front door were painted cornflower blue. On the drive stood a black Renault van that had been cleared of snow. On the sides and back doors, ANDERSSON ELECTRICAL SERVICES was printed in large letters. So Embla and Olle knew what Wille and Ida's father did for a living. Beside the van was the impression of a car that had been pushed forward, then driven away.

They parked behind the Renault and got out. A curtain fluttered at one of the windows, and Embla caught a glimpse of a pale face.

They rang the bell, and a long time passed before they heard heavy footsteps and the entire doorway was filled with a huge man. He was about the same height as Olle, but considerably wider. His thin, sandy hair was standing on end, and his red-rimmed eyes suggested that he hadn't slept well. His red checked shirt and jeans looked as if he'd slept in them. He held on to the door handle with one meaty fist, the other resting on the frame. He might as well have yelled: "No you can't fucking come in!"

Olle introduced himself and Embla, then asked to speak to Wille and Ida. The man simply stared at them, without even giving his name. After a few seconds, Olle tried again.

"Could we come in and have a word with them? We just have one or two questions . . ."

"No." The man wasn't about to move.

"Can I ask why not?"

"Wille's at a friend's. Ida's sick."

This was a blow, but Olle had no intention of giving up.

"So where does this friend live?"

The man gave an almost imperceptible shrug. "Somewhere near Mellerud."

"Okay, and what's his name?"

Olle was clearly starting to get annoyed. Embla could only admire his calmness in the face of such intransigence.

"Micke. That's all I know."

"And why has Wille gone to see this friend? I spoke to him myself last night, after Robin was murdered. He knew I was coming." Olle had stopped trying to hide his irritation.

"I don't know anything about that, but the boys usually travel to college together. In Wille's car."

The look he gave Olle was provocative. Andersson clearly thought he had the upper hand in the battle with this upstart young cop.

"College? What college?" Olle persisted.

"The agricultural college in Nuntorp."

Embla knew where that was, just south of Brålanda. At least eighty kilometers away, maybe more.

"When will he be home?"

"Next weekend."

A major setback. For the first time Embla spoke up. She turned to Olle and said, "I can take that interview when I go back down to Gothenburg tomorrow."

"Good."

She could hear the relief in Olle's voice; he hadn't lost face in front of Andersson.

"In that case we'd like to speak to Ida," he said.

"You can't," her father said firmly.

"Why not?"

"Like I said, she's sick. She's got a temperature."

At that moment Embla heard a sound from inside the house. Someone was crying, while another voice spoke softly and reassuringly. Andersson must have heard it, too, because he said, "She's very upset by what happened. Imagine seeing your boyfriend murdered. Something like that would be hard for anyone to bear, and she's only sixteen."

Embla had the feeling that they'd come close to something he didn't want to reveal. She adopted a stern expression and her most authoritative tone of voice. "Okay, listen to me. I'm a detective inspector with the Violent Crimes Unit in Gothenburg. I deal mainly with homicide investigations. This is serious. A young man has been stabbed to death. Your children were at the party, and we need to interview them and everyone else who was there. And I mean everyone! It's essential to give us a clear picture of the course of events. I would find it *very* strange if your son and daughter didn't wish to help us solve the murder of their friend Robin."

She held his gaze; it was clear that he hadn't been

prepared for the little red-haired girlie to speak up. And in that tone. *Detective inspector. Homicide investigations. Fucking hell!* He glared back at her, then looked away. Embla saw a flash of fear in his eyes, reinforcing the impression that he was trying to hide something.

"We'll be back tomorrow morning at nine o'clock," she informed him.

Olle raised an eyebrow, but quickly joined in.

"Nine o'clock—on the dot."

They felt the draft as the door was slammed in their faces.

AFTER LEAVING THE Andersson house they sat in the car, thinking about what had just happened. Eventually Embla broke the silence.

"You said Mikaela Malm accused Ida Andersson of having killed Robin."

"That's right. According to Mikaela, Ida wanted revenge because Robin had dumped her."

"So what if Mikaela's right? Ida's father seems determined to make sure that we . . . you don't get the chance to talk to her."

"He made that crystal clear," Olle replied.

"Worth considering."

"Absolutely."

In pensive silence they set off to find the next person on Olle's list: Anton Åkesson.

THE SNOW WAS piled a meter high along the sides of the road leading to the beautifully restored farmhouse. A large truck was parked in the yard; it was clearly in the process of being loaded, because the back doors were wide open and a loading ramp was in place. Diggers and snowplows could be seen inside a huge storage shed with a sign on the wall that said JOHN'S DIGGERS LTD. The truck was marked with a different name—ÅKESSON'S TRANSPORT. Embla knew that those who lived in rural communities often had to wear several different hats. Most of her relatives and friends in Dalsland had at least two—often more—enterprises going to make ends meet.

Before they had time to get out of the car, the front door of the farmhouse opened and a woman emerged. She was trying to push her arms into a black padded jacket and close the door at the same time. *Someone else who doesn't want to let us in*, Embla thought. The woman made her way cautiously down the steps, which had been swept. She was small and slim, and her medium-length blonde hair was tied back in a messy ponytail. She was wearing heavy boots, which weren't laced up. Presumably she'd shoved her feet in the first pair she found; they were way too big for her. As she came closer they could see she'd been crying; her face was swollen and her eyes were bloodshot.

"Good morning. Olle Tillman, Åmål police," Olle said with a little too much enthusiasm. He gave her a warm smile.

She recoiled as if he'd slapped her across the face, and tears sprang to her eyes once more.

"We'd like a word with Anton," he added quickly.

"Do you have to? Really?"

The words came out like a protracted sob. She gazed pleadingly at the two officers, her hands shaking as she pulled the coat around her. When she breathed in, they heard a whistling sound, as if she was having an asthma attack.

"It's not . . . possible," she gasped.

Not again, Embla thought.

"Why not?" Olle asked in a calm, friendly tone.

"He's not here."

Déjà fucking vu.

The woman, who was presumably fru Åkesson, looked away. It was obvious that she was either lying or hiding something, but they had no grounds for forcing their way into the house. They had to accept what she said, even if she was lying.

"So where is he?"

"He and John—his father—have gone . . . out. They've gone to fetch . . . something."

"Something? Could you be a little more specific?" Olle was losing patience.

She merely shrugged; she still couldn't look him in the eye. *Talk about a crap liar.* Embla almost felt sorry for her.

"In that case, please tell Anton that he needs to be at home at ten o'clock tomorrow morning. If he's not here, he'll be required to go to the Trollhättan police station for an interview—and I mean a formal interview, not just a chat," Olle said sternly.

Embla suppressed a smile. Trollhättan police station was a nice touch—it definitely sounded more alarming than Åmål.

One look at Anton's mother made her wonder what was actually going on. Every scrap of color had drained from the woman's face, and her hands were shaking even more now. Was she having a stroke or a heart attack?

"I'll t-t-t-tell h-h-him," she stammered.

"Thank you," Olle replied, turning away.

Anton's mother headed back to the warmth and safety of the house in her oversized boots; she looked like a penguin as she shuffled across the yard and up the steps. Embla hoped she realized she was anything but safe. *We're going to cling on like leeches!* she thought. Then again, why "we"? This was Olle's case. Of course she hoped that someone had seen something relevant to her investigation, but she was beginning to find it interesting that no one seemed willing to talk to the police about Robin's murder. Strange, and pretty shocking, given that such a young man had been brutally stabbed. Presumably her instincts as a cop were kicking in, along with a generous portion of good old curiosity.

Just as she and Olle were about to get in the car, Tore started whimpering.

"He needs a comfort break," Olle explained. He opened up the back door and the cage, and Tore was out in a flash. Olle grabbed his leash and shouted: "Tore! Here!"

Suddenly the dog's acute sense of hearing didn't seem to be working. He raced up the bank of snow piled against the storage shed and released an impressive stream of urine against the wall. If Olle thought he would come trotting back obediently, he was mistaken. Tore disappeared around the corner of the building.

"Tore! What the hell is wrong with you? Here! Now!"

Both he and Embla ran after the dog.

"Was it obedience training you were focusing on?" Embla couldn't help asking.

"Seek and find," Olle informed her through gritted teeth.

Tore still has a lot to learn, Embla thought, but wisely refrained from actually saying so.

As if he'd read her mind, Olle said, "He's only twenty-two months old. Right in the middle of puberty."

Was that supposed to be an excuse? When Embla glanced back over her shoulder, she saw that Anton's mother had reappeared and was standing on the top step, moving her feet up and down. She seemed terribly anxious.

The realization made Embla speed up. She raced up the bank of snow and saw Tore bouncing around, yelping with excitement. She suddenly stopped, and Olle ran straight into her.

"What the . . . !"

Then he, too, stopped.

The dog had found a car. The roof was badly dented, the windows smashed. It was bright red and looked like a sports model.

"A Toyota," Olle said.

The yard had been cleared and the snow piled up after the car had been dumped here. Was it a deliberate attempt to hide it? Tore was sniffing eagerly around the broken window on the passenger side.

"Tore! Come here! You might cut yourself . . . For fuck's sake!"

Olle set off toward the dog with determination. Suddenly Tore's body language changed. He stiffened, his nose pointing at the window, ears forward as if he were listening. However, he wasn't completely motionless; his muscles trembled with tension and his tail was slowly wagging. Then he began to scratch at the door, whimpering and yelping. His tail was going like a propeller now.

His master's attitude changed, too. Olle stopped and said quietly: "He's found something."

He edged closer and clipped the leash onto Tore's collar.

"Good boy," he said reassuringly.

Tore ignored him and continued to mark, as he'd been taught. Olle handed the leash to Embla.

"Can you hold on to him while I take a closer look?"

He leaned forward and peered into the car.

"There's a lot of fresh blood—that's what Tore was reacting to. Both airbags have deployed and—"

"Hey, what are you doing up there? You've got no business poking around!" came fru Åkesson's shaky voice.

"The dog needed to pee, and he ran off when we let him out. We've found a car that's clearly been in a crash," Embla yelled back, even though she suspected that the woman was well aware of the car's presence.

Olle was still examining the vehicle, clicking away with the camera on his phone.

"What's it doing here?" Embla shouted to fru Åkesson. There was no answer at first; the eventual response was almost inaudible.

"John's going to take it to the scrapyard."

Embla handed the leash back to Olle; the dog had no intention of going anywhere. She followed her own footprints back down to the bottom of the bank of snow and stamped her feet.

"Who does the car belong to?" she demanded.

Fru Åkesson stared at her, eyes wide and filled with tears in a pale, sickly face. She swayed where she stood.

"A . . . a customer. It's . . . not fit to drive," she whispered.

This was an unnecessary piece of information for anyone who'd seen the vehicle, but Embla realized there was no point in upsetting her even more.

"When was it brought here?" she asked in a gentler tone.

Fru Åkesson merely shook her head. Olle slithered down the bank of snow with Tore, still excited but now on the leash.

"Was anyone hurt in the accident?" Olle asked when he'd brushed the snow off himself and the dog.

"Not . . . not as far as I know." Her eyes darted from one officer to the other as if she were watching a game of table tennis.

"And when did the accident happen?"

"I don't . . . I don't know."

With that she clamped her lips together, turned around, and shuffled back to the house as quickly as her oversized boots would allow. Embla and Olle exchanged a surprised glance, then shrugged. They knew where she was if they wanted to speak to her again.

After they'd put Tore in his cage and got into the car, Olle's phone rang. The look on his face told Embla exactly who it was before he answered. Just as before, she could hear most of what Chief Inspector Johnzén had to say.

"Some old woman called—she claims she heard something around the time of the murder! Get over there and talk to her!"

Some people speak as if there's an exclamation point at the end of every sentence. Chief Inspector Johnzén was one of them. Tiresome! With an exclamation point.

He gave Olle the woman's contact details and ended the call. Olle sighed and started the car.

"He's a real charmer, isn't he?" Embla said.

"He sure is."

Tore hadn't settled, and started to whimper.

"What's the matter with him?" Embla asked.

"I have no idea."

"Wait—what did you say you'd been concentrating on in his training?"

"Seek and find."

"But what's he supposed to find?"

"Drugs, but we've also done some work on searching for people—"

"Stop the car!"

He looked at her in surprise, but braked immediately.

"I just want to check something," she said. Without further explanation she opened the door and jumped out. They hadn't gone far, and she ran back to the bank of snow and took out her flashlight.

The car was buried so deep that it was impossible to open the doors. Cautiously she reached in through the broken window and turned on the flashlight. As Olle had said, both airbags had deployed. There were large blood-stains on the seats and the dashboard; someone—more than one person?—had clearly lost a considerable amount of blood in the accident. There were bloody fingerprints on and around the door handles. Given the state of the vehicle, it was strange that no one had been seriously hurt, although of course they had only fru Åkesson's word for that. She made a mental note to check it out, but right now Embla wasn't really looking for blood-stains. Slowly she allowed the beam of the flashlight to play around the interior of the car.

And there it was, on the floor.

Could she reach it? Maybe, if she was careful and knocked out all the glass. She looked around for something she could use as a tool.

"What the hell do you think you're doing?" came a deep voice from behind her.

She turned and saw a man scrambling up the bank. He wasn't particularly tall, but his physique was compact and solid. Presumably he'd rushed out of the house, because he was wearing only a checked flannel shirt and baggy jeans. His hair was cropped short, and there was stubble on his chin and cheeks. He plowed through the tracks left by Embla and her two- and four-footed companions. Tore might not be a police dog yet, but given what Embla had just found, he was going to be a very good one.

The man who looked like a moving storm cloud must be John Åkesson. He was clenching and unclenching his fists in a way that didn't bode well. "Furious" was the word that best described his expression.

"Police work," she replied tersely.

"That car has nothing to do with fucking police work," Åkesson yelled. His face was bright red and he was breathing heavily after his exertions.

"I need to ask you to back off." Embla adopted her most authoritative tone, and at the same time she took out her phone and called Olle. He answered right away.

"Hi, Embla."

"Tore was right. Come up here."

A fraction of a second later she heard the sound of a car door closing, which made her feel a little better; Åkesson was unpleasant and aggressive. His eyes narrowed and he clenched his jaw so tightly that his puffy cheeks looked rock-hard.

"You have no right to trespass on my land!" he hissed.

"We're investigating a homicide. We have the right to examine anything that might be connected to that investigation."

"Homicide! This has nothing to do with your fucking homicide!"

Åkesson spat out the words, gesticulating toward the car. Embla could see Olle making his way up the bank of snow behind him, although Åkesson seemed unaware of his presence; all his attention was focused on Embla.

When he suddenly clenched his fist and moved to attack her, she registered a brief flash of surprise before reacting reflexively. She leaned back so that he struck thin air, missing her by several centimeters. John Åkesson might be a tough guy, but he was slow and lacked technique. She hunched her shoulders to gather strength, then straightened up and delivered a series of hard jabs to his face; nose-eyebrow-nose-eyebrow. With a roar he raised his hands to protect himself, but Embla had already achieved her goal. Blood was pouring from his nose and from a cut in his eyebrow. There would be no lasting scars; his nose wasn't broken, and eyebrows heal quickly. She knew this because she herself had weak brows; the left one had a slight zigzag shape due to all the times her opponents had split it open.

Åkesson made a few clumsy swipes in midair before Olle reached him and grabbed his arms.

"I'm going to fucking report you!"

"Assaulting a police officer is a serious offense," Olle informed him calmly as blood dripped onto the snow, staining it red.

"Okay, let's take it easy. If you behave yourself, we'll

come back to the house with you. And I'll tape up that cut," Embla offered.

"So now you're a fucking nurse as well, are you?" he snapped, glaring at her through the blood trickling down over his eye.

"Actually, I'm a boxer. I've taped up my own eyebrow plenty of times."

"Shit," he muttered, but the fight had gone out of him and he allowed himself to be led down to the yard. They set off toward the house; now that she was walking beside him, Embla could smell the booze on him.

His wife was on the steps, anxiously shuffling her feet. Embla glanced down at Åkesson's feet; he was wearing heavy Graninge boots. His little wife wouldn't have gotten too far in those.

"What's happened? What . . . ?" she stammered in horror when she saw that her husband was bleeding.

"He slipped. It's pretty treacherous up there," Olle replied before Embla could speak. To her surprise, Åkesson didn't protest.

"I've promised to tape up his eyebrow," Embla said with a reassuring smile. Fru Åkesson's only response was a terrified glance before she turned to her husband.

"The sooner we let the fuckers in, the sooner we'll be rid of them," he said wearily.

Hesitantly, she opened the door, then stepped aside.

The impression of excellent workmanship continued in the house, which was light and airy. The pale oak closet doors and wide oak floorboards made a good impression. The hallway led into a spacious living room, with the kitchen through a wide doorway on the left. It was the size of an old-fashioned farmhouse kitchen, but the décor was ultra-modern. The generous oak table with matching chairs looked new, and there was a Poul Henningsen lamp above. A fire was crackling away in a small soapstone stove in the corner; Nisse had one, too. He always said it was useful in case of a power outage since it provided both heat and a hot stone surface on which to cook. This was useful, because you never knew when the power would be restored out in the country.

They sat John Åkesson on a kitchen chair.

"Lilian, fetch me a bottle of vodka," he ordered his wife.

"But . . . I've got antiseptic . . ." she protested.

"I'm not putting it ON my face!" he snapped. She cowered instinctively and looked at the two police officers. Embla came to her rescue.

"I agree with you, Lilian. I think we'll leave the vodka for now and start with the antiseptic. Do you have a first aid kit?"

An expression of relief came over her thin face as she nodded. She went back into the hallway and returned with one. Embla gently wiped the split eyebrow with antiseptic, then instructed Olle to hold the edges together while she taped it up. The nosebleed had stopped, so all she had to do was clean up his face.

"There you go. Leave the tape in place for at least four days before you change it—preferably a week."

The Åkessons nodded. Olle looked searchingly at Lilian.

"You told us that John and Anton had gone off to fetch something, but obviously John is here. So now we'd like to speak to Anton," he said firmly.

Both parents stiffened.

"He's not home—honestly he's not!" Lilian exclaimed. She glanced at her husband. "I thought they'd both gone, but I guess Anton went on his own."

John nodded in agreement, his expression grim. They had clearly decided on a united front.

"Okay, in that case I'll come back at ten o'clock tomorrow morning, as I said earlier. If Anton isn't here, he'll be required to go to the police station in Trollhättan for a formal interview. And if he doesn't turn up there, I would be suspicious to say the least, and I'll send a squad car to collect him."

John glared at them from beneath his taped eyebrow, and Lilian looked as if she was about to faint, but neither of them said a word.

"We'll see ourselves out," Olle said with a stylish farewell salute. He was good at it; Embla assumed he'd practiced in front of the mirror. Once they reached the hallway she grabbed his arm.

"Go back to the Toyota and pick up the joint that's on the floor under the driver's seat," she whispered.

"A joint? So that's what Tore—"

"Yes. Do you need to borrow my flashlight?"

"No, I've got one of my own. What are you going to do?"

"Ask a few questions," she said quietly, letting go of his arm. He slipped out the door and Embla turned to go back to the kitchen. Lilian appeared in the doorway, and seemed to deflate when she saw that Embla was still there.

"We've decided to optimize tomorrow's interview with Anton by asking you and John one or two questions now," Embla informed her in a pleasant tone of voice.

"Oh . . ." Lilian's shoulders slumped. Her husband

hadn't moved, but his expression darkened when Embla walked in. Neither of them asked her to take a seat.

Embla smiled. No response.

"First of all, do you have any other children?"

"Only Anton," John snapped.

"And how old is he?"

"Eighteen."

Talk about getting blood out of a stone . . . Embla kept her cool. She'd learned a few things during her years at drama school in Gothenburg.

"What time did he get home after the party?"

Lilian and John exchanged a glance.

"We were asleep," John said, and his wife nodded in agreement.

"So you have no idea?"

"No."

Now.

"Whose car is hidden behind the storage shed?"

John clenched his fist and slammed it down on the table. "That's none of your fucking business!"

Embla's expression changed from pleasant to unmoved.

"I'm afraid it is. The car will be examined thoroughly because we've found drugs in it. It's now a crime scene and can't be touched by anyone except the police."

Silently Lilian Åkesson fainted and slipped off her chair.

BEFORE LEAVING, EMBLA and Olle checked out the car once more. They took Tore with them, and the dog reacted in exactly the same way as before.

"There could be more drugs, or he's still picking up the smell," Olle said.

"Okay, let's cordon it off," Embla decided. They

wound police tape around the section of the vehicle that was visible above the snow.

"I've called the CSIs, but they weren't sure if they'd make it out here today," Olle said.

Embla checked her phone.

"Before we go for lunch, let's speak to the woman who heard something."

THE CONTRAST BETWEEN the Åkessons' well-cared-for property and May-Liz Ström's cottage couldn't have been greater. Apparently the place was called Solängen—Sunny Meadow—which sounded idyllic, but it was more or less falling apart. Smoke rose from the dilapidated chimney, and there were large snow-free patches on the roof where the heat from the house had leaked out. Long icicles dangled from the eaves. The paint on the window frames and the front door had almost completely flaked off. The road beyond the hedge marking the boundary had been cleared, but no attempt had been made to shovel the snow in the yard. There were plenty of footprints and pawprints, however. An outhouse next to the main building was at the point of collapse and only appeared to be standing because it hadn't decided which way to fall. Something resembling a dog kennel with a flat roof had been built inside an enclosure beside the outhouse. There was no sign of any dogs out there at the moment, probably due to the cold.

They didn't need to knock. As soon as they started trudging across the yard, they heard a chorus of barking coming from inside the house, along with someone instructing the residents to be quiet. Embla decided that Olle could go first, as he was a dog person.

The barking abated and the door opened. A sturdy woman in her fifties welcomed them with a smile. Two gray-blonde braids hung down beneath her colorful cro-cheted beret; she was also wearing a pair of worn-out thermal pants and a moth-eaten gray sweater that looked like it had been knitted for a man originally. A pair of thick socks and worn-down wooden clogs completed her outfit.

"Hello—come on in!" she said warmly.

"We heard the welcoming committee," Olle replied, gesturing toward a closed door.

"Yes, I have to keep them all indoors when it's this cold," May-Liz said apologetically. There were obviously several dogs, judging by the scratching and snuffling and yelping.

The walls were adorned with miniature paintings of birds and flowers. It struck Embla that May-Liz had prob-ably painted the picture of the bird in the bedroom where Milo Stavic had been murdered.

"What do you breed?" Olle asked.

"Wire-haired dachshunds. I've got four bitches at the moment; Sascha's due to whelp in two weeks. Would you like one? The pedigree is excellent. The sire is a Swedish and Norwegian champion, and Sascha is a Swedish champion. The hunting lines couldn't be better."

Her round face broke into a smile once more. *A proud grandmother boasting about her wonderful grandchildren*, Embla thought. *Why have I never thought of getting a hunt-ing dog of my own? Because I don't have time for a dog*, she quickly answered her own question. *And Nisse has Seppo, who's outstanding when it comes to tracking game*.

"Thanks, but I already have a dog," Olle said. Then, before May-Liz could ask the obvious question, he added: "A Belgian shepherd."

"Of course, you're a police officer." The smile faded slightly, then she said: "Come on in—I'll make some coffee."

Embla didn't really want to spend any longer than necessary in this cold house with the barking dogs.

"Thanks, but we've just had a cup," she said quickly before Olle could accept the invitation. He looked a little disappointed, then nodded in agreement.

"That's a shame. Come and sit by the fire anyway," May-Liz insisted, leading the way into a cozy room.

There was an unmade sofa bed and a kitchen table surrounded by four wooden chairs that didn't match. On the table was a tray of watercolors, a jar of grayish water, and a small pad with something sketched on it in shades of blue. In the corner nearest the sofa, a fire burned cheerily in an antique iron stove. Below the window, a portable electric heater was working hard; there were no fixed radiators. An old-fashioned TV was perched on top of a rickety table, and the walls were covered with small paintings.

"It's hard to keep the place warm when it's so cold outside," May-Liz said. "The girls and I usually cuddle up in here."

As if the dogs understood that she was talking about them, they started barking again.

"Do you mind if I let them out? It's pretty chilly in the bedroom."

"Fine by me," Olle said.

"Me too," Embla hastily agreed; she managed to sound more confident than she felt.

May-Liz opened the door and tried to calm the excited dogs as they poured into the room.

"There we go, be good now. Say hello nicely. No, Natalia! Bad girl! No growling!"

Natalia didn't seem to care what her mistress said, and she carried on growling and glaring at Olle.

"Oh, I think I know what's going on here—is your dog male?" May-Liz asked.

Olle nodded, looking confused.

"In that case she's picking up the male smell—she hates males! Both humans and dogs, but the dogs are the biggest problem. It's impossible to mate her; she either fights or goes off and sulks until they lose interest. I don't have the heart to get rid of her, though, so she'll just have to be a companion for the other three."

Embla was beginning to get a little tired of all this doggy talk. She cleared her throat discreetly to attract the attention of both her colleague and May-Liz.

"Could you tell us what you heard or saw in the early hours of Saturday morning?"

"Oh . . . yes, of course." May-Liz sighed; clearly the pleasant chat was over. "Natalia had an upset tummy during the evening. When we went outside at some point between twelve-fifteen and twelve-thirty, it must have been the fifth or sixth time since dinner. I took her out on her own because she wasn't well; the others went crazy, wanting to come with us, so it was kind of noisy. Just as I opened the door I thought I heard a dull thud. It sounded as if . . ."

She fell silent and thought for a moment.

"It sounded as if someone had struck a big bass drum. Or . . . no, it was more of a metallic clang. But muffled."

Neither Embla nor Olle interrupted her.

"I stopped on the top step and tried to listen, but I didn't hear anything else. Then I thought maybe it was my imagination; the girls were making so much noise, and—"

"Was it this dull metallic thud that you wanted to report?" Embla asked.

"Yes, I thought it might be important. It was pretty loud. I wondered if it was a crash."

The pregnant dog waddled over to her mistress and whimpered. May-Liz bent down and lifted her onto her lap.

"Where did the sound come from?" Olle asked.

"From the direction of the field, I'd say. The far field, I mean."

"Can you show us?"

"Of course."

May-Liz put down the dog and went over to the window. She scraped off a patch of frost until she'd cleared a space big enough for two people to look through at the same time. She stepped aside and beckoned them over.

"There you go," she said with satisfaction.

They stood close together and peered out.

The cottage was on a hill, which meant there was an excellent view of the surrounding area. The property boundary was delineated by a low hedge, which was currently covered in snow with just the odd branch sticking out. On the other side of the road lay a huge field, the virgin snow unmarked. It was at least two hundred meters across, and beyond it Embla saw the tall pine trees that showed where the Klevskog nature reserve began. She could also make out Harald's three cottages; from this distance they looked like tiny Lego houses.

"I didn't realize this place was in sight of the cottages," she said quietly to Olle.

He turned to May-Liz. "Did it sound as if the dull thud came from those cottages?"

"No. There's a field about the same size on the other side of the road leading to the nature reserve. I think that's where it came from."

Both this cottage and Harald's were on minor roads, but people drove fast on the main road. May-Liz had mentioned the possibility of a crash; a theory came into Embla's head, and she decided it was worth testing.

She turned away from the window and smiled at May-Liz.

"I think we've seen all we need to. Thank you so much for getting in touch." She picked her way through the dogs and made for the door, with Olle right behind her.

IT WAS PRETTY chilly inside the car, but before Olle started the engine, he ran a check to see if Anton Åkesson was the registered owner of a vehicle. In seconds he had the answer: Anton owned a 2014 red Toyota Auris.

"I think we know what happened to the car we found at the Åkessons' place," Embla said, raising her eyebrows.

"I think you're right."

"It's worth pursuing, anyway. If Anton crashed and called Daddy, then John could have picked up both him and the car. He's got a tow truck."

"And it would explain why they were both behaving so oddly; they didn't want us to find out about the crash."

"Exactly. And Wille and Ida's father had a strange attitude, too."

"To say the least," Olle agreed.

"But where's Anton? Given the amount of blood in the car, we know he was injured. Do you think he might be in a hospital?"

"We'll check that out as soon as possible. But I just thought of something else . . ."

He paused for effect and gave her a sideways glance. "Both airbags had deployed. Anton wasn't alone."

OLLE SLOWED DOWN after they'd passed the turnoff for Klevskog. Blue lights flashing, they crawled along the main road. Embla peered out across the expanse of snow.

"There!" she shouted.

Olle stopped the car but left the blue lights on. They got out and began to examine the area that had caught Embla's attention.

Two wide parallel tracks left by a heavy vehicle cut across the otherwise smooth surface. Around thirty meters into the field the ground was churned up over a fairly wide area.

"About twenty centimeters of snow have fallen onto the tracks, so I'd guess they were made at the height of the storm," Olle said. "Sometime between two and three in the morning."

Embla nodded and took out her phone. "Let's take pictures."

Methodically they worked their way along the tracks, the rhythmic clicking of their cell phones the only sound breaking the silence. A pale sun battled to penetrate the cloud cover, and the wind had dropped completely. It was still chilly, but not quite as bitterly cold.

As they headed back to the car, a Nissan Navara passed them. Embla recognized it because her hunting companion Tobias had one. It slowed down, and they could just make out two people watching them through the tinted windows. Before they were close enough to see who it might be or to make a note of the registration number, the driver put his foot down and sped away.

Embla and Olle got back in the car.

"So now John Åkesson will know we've found the spot where the accident took place," Embla said.

"Definitely."

Olle glanced at the clock on the dashboard. "Almost one o'clock. Shall we have lunch before we speak to Robin's girlfriend, Mikaela Malm?"

BEFORE THEY WENT into the guesthouse restaurant for lunch, Olle took Tore for a long walk. When Harald spotted the dog through the window, he immediately offered to keep him behind the reception desk so that he wouldn't have to stay in the cold car. The only stipulation was that he had to be tied up, in case any of the guests were frightened of dogs. That was no problem; Olle brought in Tore's teddy bear blanket from the bottom of his cage and looped his leash around the radiator valve. Harald provided a bowl of water and a dish of chopped-up sausages and vegetables, and Tore was more than happy. He gobbled up the food, had a drink, then settled down on his blanket with a sigh of contentment.

Embla and Olle enjoyed a Sunday lunch of wild boar cutlets with a potato gratin, followed by chocolate cake and coffee, then headed back to the car. They felt ready to tackle Mikaela Malm now. She was the same age as Ida; they were classmates. According to what Mikaela had said immediately after the murder, Robin Pettersson had dumped Ida to be with her. And also according to Mikaela, this gave Ida a motive for repeatedly sticking a knife in her ex-boyfriend's body.

"The statistics don't support that theory," Embla said

when they began to discuss the girl they were about to question.

"Oh?" Olle's tone made it clear that he wasn't convinced.

"Sixteen-year-old girls don't murder their boyfriends when a relationship ends. They scream and fight and post horrible things on Facebook and other social media, but murder . . . no."

"Are you sure?"

"Absolutely."

"How about teenage boys?"

"That's different. Knives are pretty common in acts of violence between older teenage boys, although these days they're shooting at one another as well, so that's one of the most common causes of death among men from age sixteen to twenty-five. Girls are killed, too, although that's unusual, and it tends to be because they were in the wrong place at the wrong time. Thanks to guys like Milo Stavic, there are plenty of illegal guns in circulation."

"I'm well aware of that. I saw plenty when I was working in Stockholm," Olle said with a grimace.

The comment gave Embla the opportunity to ask a question that had been on her mind.

"Were you unhappy in Stockholm? Was that why you relocated to Åmål?"

He didn't answer immediately; he seemed to be considering his response.

"It's a good place in many ways, but it's tough. And I wanted to be a dog handler. Tore didn't really like the city, and two posts came up in Dalsland. I never expected to get one of them, but I did. I started in Åmål on January first."

"Congratulations on your promotion. As your mother and sister live in Åmål, I'm assuming your roots are here in Dalsland?"

"That's right, and my father lives in Mellerud. They divorced a few years ago."

He fell silent and Embla decided it was probably time to stop interrogating him. Instead she shared her own story.

"My uncle Nisse is a retiree. He lost his wife a year or so before he gave up work. It was such a tragedy. He and Aunt Ann-Sofi never had children, but I try to come up as often as I can. We go hunting together; sometimes it's just the two of us, but we also hunt with other members of the club."

"So hunting is your main hobby?"

"I guess so, but I spend a lot of time training, too. Mainly boxing."

A smile played around the corners of Olle's mouth. "I know, I googled you. Nordic light welterweight champion. I'd better behave myself."

"If you know what's good for you," Embla replied in her deepest voice.

Olle laughed and glanced at her. "That's when I understood what Göran Krantz meant when he said I hadn't realized how dangerous it could have been when I . . . drew my gun on you." He sounded uncomfortable. "You could easily have disarmed me, couldn't you?"

"Yes."

She had no intention of telling him how close she'd come to directing a roundhouse kick at his wrist.

He swallowed hard. "I'd like to apologize for that. It was dumb. But I was kind of shaken up, and you didn't have any ID . . ."

It was nice of him to say sorry.

"I can understand that. It's forgotten," she assured him with a smile.

They sat in companionable silence for a while, then he asked: "Do you compete much?"

She hesitated before answering, even though it was a perfectly reasonable question.

"I suffered a concussion back in the fall, and now I'm not allowed to compete. The doctors say the risk of permanent brain damage is too great. But I train as much as I can, and I can't help hoping that one day I'll fully recover and be able to start competing again."

She had no intention of going into detail about the incident that had cost her so much almost six months ago. The truth was that she still suffered occasional headaches and bouts of dizziness, especially if she was tired and stressed.

Olle pulled in front of a gray two-story property with white eaves and window frames and parked the car. Together they walked up to the dark-blue front door and rang the bell. They heard the sound of running footsteps, and the door was opened by a boy around the age of eight.

"Can I sit in your car?" he asked.

"I'm afraid not. That's only allowed when we visit schools to give talks," Olle explained.

Disappointment was written all over the child's face.

"Pigs!" he yelled and ran back into the house.

"Don't say that, darling," a female voice remonstrated gently. High heels came tip-tapping across the floor, and Mikaela's mother held out a hand with long scarlet nails; diamond rings sparkled on several fingers. Embla and Olle introduced themselves.

"Siri Malm." Her bright red lipstick emphasized the whiteness of her teeth. She was tall and slim, probably in her early forties, but she was trying hard—not without success—to look ten years younger. Her black dress clung to her slim figure and ended just above the knee. She was also wearing a short cream wool jacket. Her makeup was impeccable, and her thick, shiny bleached-blonde hair was beautifully cut and styled. No comfortable slippers for Siri Malm, but black pumps with a low heel. The way she moved suggested that she might have been a model.

"Come on in. I guess you're here to speak to Mikaela. She's sleeping at the moment, but it's time I woke her. Would you like coffee? There's a pot already made," she said with a warm smile.

The smile was directed only at Olle; Embla might as well have been invisible.

In order to make her presence known, Embla quickly said: "No thanks, we've just had lunch." It came out a little more brusquely than she'd intended.

Siri Malm's eyes flicked toward her for a second, as if she'd heard something but wasn't quite sure what it was and didn't really care. Then she turned the full beam of her smile on Olle once more.

"I can offer you fresh pastries, too."

Somehow she made it sound like a sexual proposition.

If he accepts I'm going outside, Embla thought. This woman was a parody of the classic vamp. Was it deliberate, or did she just need affirmation from every man who crossed her path? Embla had to admit that Olle was good-looking, but he was at least fifteen years younger than Siri, who was now giving him a teasing look from beneath lowered eyelashes.

"Thank you, but no," Olle said. "We'd like to speak to Mikaela now, and of course you're welcome to sit in, as she's underage." He didn't respond in any way to Siri's body language; he didn't glance at her décolletage or give the slightest wink to show that he was interested. Embla let out a long breath.

"Please take a seat," Siri said.

They each chose a gray leather armchair. Between them and a dark-gray sectional sofa there was an oval glass coffee table with a vase of drooping white tulips. A wool rug in gray, white, and red provided the only pop of color in the room. There was an enormous home theater screen on the wall opposite the sofa, with tall speakers on either side. A corner bookcase contained a surprising number of books, and photographs of the children at different ages were displayed on one wall.

Embla turned her head at the sound of approaching footsteps.

Mikaela was neither as tall nor as slim as her mother. To Embla's surprise, she was wearing makeup. Hadn't Siri said she was sleeping? She wore her thick blonde hair loose; it almost reached her waist. She reminded Embla of the pictures in a book of fairy tales illustrated by John Bauer that she'd had when she was a child. The princesses had had beautiful hair, just like Mikaela. Embla, too, had had long, thick, curly hair, but none of the lovely heroines had ever had her bright chestnut-red color. One of the little trolls, maybe.

The girl also had long nails, but hers were painted black. She was wearing tight jeans, a black scoop-neck T-shirt, and a gray hoodie. Embla could see a tattoo of a red rose just above the neckline of the T-shirt, along with the upper part of a red heart. On her feet she wore neon-pink fluffy socks. She slumped down on the sofa and looked morosely at the two police officers.

"Hi, Mikaela. My name's Olle Tillman, and this is my colleague Embla Nyström." Olle held out his hand, but Mikaela didn't seem to see it; her eyes filled with tears.

"Do we have to talk about . . . Robin?" she whispered in a shaky voice.

"Only as much as you feel up to," Olle reassured her with an encouraging smile.

Mikaela leaned back and gazed up at the ceiling. She rubbed her index finger gently under each eye; when she sat up and focused on him, her mascara was still perfect.

"Could you tell us what happened at the party on Friday?" Olle began.

She nodded, her expression filled with sorrow, then sighed deeply. "I mean . . . it's all so *terrible*. I just want to, like, forget the whole thing. We got there shortly after eight and everyone had already started eating. There was, like, a taco buffet. It was nice, but these old guys kept giving speeches. It was some kind of anniversary, I think. Me and Robin sat together."

"Sorry to interrupt, but weren't he and Ida together?" Olle interjected.

Something glinted in Mikaela's eyes. Only when she began speaking again did Embla realize what she'd seen: contempt.

"He dumped her a week ago, but she refused to accept it. She was furious when he ignored her. She's such a fucking loser!"

Olle ignored her scornful tone.

"So you and Robin were together before the party?"

"Yes. Not many people knew about it, but it became clear during the evening. We made it pretty obvious, if you know what I mean. And when the music started, we danced together and had a great time while Ida was in a corner sulking."

She made no attempt to hide her smug satisfaction.

"So she didn't take it well, the fact that Robin had dumped her?"

"Nope! She was *really upset*! And then that idiot Anton came along and tried to persuade her to go to Gothenburg with him. *Let's go to Gothenburg*. What a waste of space. Anyway, she went in the end—she probably thought Robin would be jealous because Anton's got a cool car."

"A red Toyota," Olle said.

"Yes—his dad bought it for him when he turned eighteen, but it doesn't make anyone like Anton. Not even Ida."

The thin smile Mikaela unexpectedly directed at Embla sent an icy shiver down Embla's spine as her own memories from school rose to the surface.

"Did Robin hear Anton ask her to leave with him?"

"Oh yes—we just laughed at them! Robin couldn't have cared less. He even waved to them when they left. Like, *bye-bye, losers!*"

The smile still lingered on her lips and in her tone of voice.

"So this was before he went outside to pee," Olle said, managing to look genuinely interested.

"Yes, at least a quarter of an hour before."

"So they left before Robin was stabbed," Olle stated calmly.

To Embla's great satisfaction, that wiped the smile off Mikaela's face. The girl was smart enough to realize that she'd just provided Ida and Anton with an alibi.

Without giving the slightest hint that he'd noticed her reaction, Olle continued. "So what time did Robin go outside?"

"I'm not sure . . . after twelve. I know that because the DJ made everyone give a cheer for Herremarks indoor bandy club at the stroke of midnight. It was maybe fifteen minutes after that, maybe a little more, when Robin said he was going . . ."

She fell silent and stared into space, then suddenly she buried her face in her hands and cried out, "That was the last time I saw him!"

Siri placed a protective arm around her daughter's shoulders. "This is very difficult for Mikaela," she said quietly.

Olle nodded sympathetically. "I understand that. I think she's been very strong."

Embla was impressed. *This guy has potential.* Her intention was to stay in the background. This was Olle's investigation, not hers.

Without removing her hands from her face, Mikaela said in a trembling voice, "After about ten minutes I got worried, so I went outside to look for him. It was such a *shock . . .* I *tripped over him!*" She slowly lowered her hands and gazed at Olle, her eyes brimming with tears. "I screamed . . . I just remember *screaming.* I ran inside to get some help."

"Do you remember if you saw anything suspicious? Anyone behaving strangely, that kind of thing?"

"No, I . . . I'm not sure."

Olle kept his gaze fixed on her, wondering whether he ought to rephrase the question. Embla understood perfectly; right now they were talking to the person who was most likely to have seen the killer.

"Was anyone near Robin when you found him?"

"I don't remember—" She broke off and looked him straight in the eye. "Yes, there was someone . . . near the barn, over by the wall. I didn't look, because I assumed one of the boys was peeing."

"Any idea who it was?"

She shook her head.

"What happened next?" Olle asked after a brief silence.

Mikaela's eyes filled with tears again. "I just remember screaming. Some people came running out from the kitchen, then I ran inside. I wasn't thinking, I was just like *screaming*. Suddenly there were people everywhere, it was chaos."

She rested her head on her mother's shoulder. The neckline of her T-shirt slipped to the side, revealing the tattoos of the red rose and the heart. There were two large Ms between them, one upside down. Embla had only three small tattoos and was no expert, but she thought Mikaela's were amateurish and clumsily executed. The upside-down M in particular looked crooked. It was a shame on such a young girl, and it would be difficult if she changed her mind and wanted it removed, because it was quite big.

Olle changed tack.

"How did you get home?"

"One of the trainers, Petter Lewinsson, was really kind. He drove several of us home."

"I've already thanked Petter; it was so good of him. I had some of the neighbors over, and we'd had wine with dinner, so none of us could drive," Siri explained.

"It was like a farewell party. We're moving to Åmål," Mikaela said, sounding much more cheerful.

Siri smiled and stroked her daughter's hair. "I've got a new job, starting at the beginning of next month."

Olle smiled. "Congratulations. May I ask what the job is?"

Both he and Embla were trying not to show how curious they were.

"Chair of the Dalsland community council. I chair the local council up here at the moment, so my jurisdiction will increase significantly."

Embla wasn't surprised, but now it was time to ask the question that was her reason for being here. With what she hoped was a sympathetic smile, she leaned toward Mikaela. "Do you remember seeing anything when you were on your way home from the Lodge? A car you didn't recognize, or a person wandering along the road?"

Mikaela thought for a moment, then shook her head. "No, everything was just chaotic. And it had started snowing. I couldn't see a thing."

"Talk about a drama queen!" Olle said with a laugh. Embla managed a somewhat strained smile in return; she had no intention of telling him she'd gone to drama school in Gothenburg. The sound of her phone ringing made them both jump. She checked the display.

"Hi, Göran."

"Hi—any luck?"

"Not really—no one seems to have seen anything."

"I haven't got much to report either. Of course it's Sunday today; the Audi will be examined tomorrow. I have meetings all morning, then I'm conducting interviews after lunch, until about three. After that I'd like you to come with me to take a look at Milo's and Luca's apartments. We're short-staffed—no one else can get there before Wednesday at the earliest."

"That suits me fine. I've promised to interview someone in Nuntorp just outside Brålanda tomorrow, so I can do that on my way down."

She smiled at Olle, who gave her the thumbs-up.

"I've been in touch with the chief of police in Split; he's going to update me on Kador Stavic's disappearance," Göran said.

"Do you know anything else about his family?"

"No, but I'm sure my Croatian colleague will be able to help with that."

"In that case I'll see you about three o'clock."

"Excellent—we'll have time for coffee before we leave."

EMBLA AND OLLE managed to track down Petter Lewinsson in the afternoon. He was nineteen, and explained that he was taking a year off before starting a teacher training course in Gothenburg. He played for the Herremark indoor bandy club and trained the junior girls, from ages thirteen to sixteen. He was also a member of the Swedish Christian Missionary Society and was a teetotaler. It would have been hard to find a more reliable witness to the events of Friday night.

Like most of the others, he'd been on the dance floor when Mikaela started screaming. Because the music was so loud, he hadn't heard her until she came rushing in. She was completely hysterical, and it took a while before he realized someone was badly hurt.

He and his girlfriend, Malin, ran outside. It was dark behind the Lodge because the external light was broken. They could just make out Robin lying on the ground; he was in the fetal position with his hands pressed to his belly. Before Petter and Malin reached him, they saw Wille Andersson and a boy named Gustav trying to turn him onto his back. Malin shouted to them not to touch him. She was in her final year of nursing school and knew quite a bit about first aid and dealing with emergencies.

Wille, who was clearly drunk, had insisted on administering CPR, and had started pressing down on Robin's bloodstained chest. Malin had yelled at him to stop. Gustav had struggled to his feet at that point, but Wille had continued his violent attempt at resuscitation.

Together Petter and Malin had dragged Wille away, then Wille and Gustav had staggered off toward the open kitchen door. As the light spilling out from the kitchen was the only source of illumination in the yard, it was hard to see exactly how Robin was.

"We checked for a pulse, but I couldn't find anything. Malin said she thought there was a flutter in the carotid artery, but I'm not sure . . ." He fell silent and swallowed hard.

"Was it you who called an ambulance and the police?" Olle asked.

Petter shook his head. "No, that was Malin. While we were waiting we covered Robin with a curtain and a tarp that someone found. We didn't dare move him . . . He was bleeding so heavily."

"Did he regain consciousness at all?"

"No. He was completely out of it."

It was clear that Petter had been deeply affected by the experience. He and his girlfriend had done everything they could.

"Did you notice anything strange? I mean, before and after you found Robin," Olle clarified.

Petter pursed his lips before answering. "To be honest, most of the people who were there were behaving strangely. A lot of them were very drunk, like Wille and Gustav. That wasn't the kind of party we'd had in mind; it all got completely out of hand."

The bitterness in his voice was unmistakable.

"Okay, but has anything occurred to you since? Something someone said, someone acting out of character?"

Once again Petter shook his head.

"Things were pretty chaotic. The ambulance came and took Robin away, then the police arrived. They made a note of names and addresses, asked a few questions, then we were allowed to leave. Mikaela and Malin were already waiting in my car. They wanted to go home; Mikaela was beside herself. Then Wille and Gustav insisted on squeezing themselves in, too."

"You must have been covered in blood, all of you," Olle said.

"Yes, although Wille was the worst—he'd spent quite some time kneading Robin's chest. Fortunately Malin had spread a blanket over the backseat to protect the upholstery."

Embla cleared her throat discreetly. "When you were driving the kids home, did you see anyone? A car or a person that caught your attention?"

Petter frowned. "I saw lots of cars and lots of people. Some of the kids had called their parents to come and pick them up, and those who had a ride tried to get away as quickly as possible. As I said, it was chaotic."

"I understand that. I'm thinking more along the road," Embla clarified.

"No, it was snowing. I had my hands full keeping the car under control."

Sitting in on Olle's interviews had proved pointless so far. Nobody seemed to have seen anything that could be linked to Milo's murder. *Let's hope the others have more luck, if they even remember to ask,* Embla thought morosely.

Wille Andersson's friend Gustav wasn't on Olle's list; one of the officers from Trollhättan was due to contact him the next day. The same applied to Petter's girlfriend, Malin.

Olle and Embla spoke to two more girls and a boy during the afternoon. The girls had the same surname and turned out to be fifteen-year-old twins who lived twenty kilometers from the party venue. The interviews were conducted over speakerphone, so the girls' mother could listen in, as they were minors. She had picked them up just before midnight, so they didn't have much to contribute, although one twin said she'd seen Ida Andersson crying shortly before they left the Lodge. Anton Åkesson had gone up to her and put his arm around her shoulders, but the girl didn't know what had happened next.

The last person on Olle's list was Kevin Malm, age eighteen. They had to call him as well, because he worked in a diner in Halden. Olle's first question surprised Embla.

"Malm—are you related to Mikaela?"

"We're cousins. My uncle is Mikaela's dad, but we don't see each other very often," Kevin said warily.

Olle didn't pursue that line of inquiry; it had nothing to do with the investigation. Instead he focused on the evening itself. Kevin insisted he'd been on the dance floor, and hadn't heard or seen anything that had happened behind the Lodge. After Mikaela ran in screaming, he'd stayed where he was. When he found out what had happened, he left as quickly as possible.

"I got a ride with someone and jumped out when they turned to go to Bengtsfors. Then it started snowing, so I had to walk home in a blizzard, like two or three kilometers. Fortunately I was wearing my padded jacket."

"Did you see anyone along the road—a person, or a car?" Olle asked, glancing at Embla.

Kevin didn't answer right away; he was obviously thinking back. "There was something, now that you mention it. When I was almost home I heard a truck engine—or maybe a snowplow, something big. It was driving at full speed."

"Could it have been a tow truck?"

A brief silence, then Kevin said, "Yes, it could have been."

"How far away was it?"

"I don't know. It was pretty faint."

"What time was this?"

There was no hesitation. "Almost two o'clock."

Olle thanked Kevin and ended the call. He and Embla looked at each other.

"So John Åkesson got there fast and picked up the Toyota around two," Embla said.

"Looks that way. The question is, where's his son now?"

There was only one thing to do.

"He must have been injured in the crash. We need to call the hospital."

"I tried earlier, but couldn't get a hold of a doctor who was willing to speak to me," Olle said. "The nurse cited patient confidentiality."

"In that case we need to apply for permission—or see if we can persuade his parents to talk."

They decided that was enough for one day. It was time to head back to the guesthouse; Tore needed a walk and something to eat, and both Olle and Embla were hungry, too.

THEY SOON DISCOVERED there was no need to worry about Tore's dinner. He was fast asleep on his blanket; Monika had given him a bowl of meat and vegetables.

"I think we're friends for life; he let me stroke him when I picked up the bowl," Monika said with a smile.

"I'm not surprised; I'd roll over on my back for a meal like that," Olle replied.

At the sound of his master's voice, Tore woke up. He leaped to his feet, barking happily.

"You'll stay for dinner?" Monika said with an inquiring glance at Olle.

He hesitated for only a fraction of a second before accepting her invitation.

Tore was already by the door, quivering with anticipation.

"How long does he need to be out?" Embla asked.

"No more than half an hour—it's only about six degrees out there. He doesn't care, but it's too cold for me."

"In that case I'll go up to my room—see you back here in half an hour."

Immediately Olle straightened his shoulders and executed one of his perfect salutes. *He* must *have practiced in front of the mirror*, Embla thought. As the door closed behind man and dog, Monika turned to her.

"So you're having dinner with the best-looking cop in Dalsland—congratulations!" she said with a laugh.

"I thought it was the other way around," Embla countered, shaking out her long red hair in a glorious cascade.

Monika raised her eyebrows. "You're a very attractive couple," she said.

"We're not a couple. We're colleagues."

"The two aren't mutually exclusive, you know." Monika lowered her voice. "Berit, our cook, is related to Olle's mother. According to her, one of the reasons why he decided to leave Stockholm was that he split up with his girlfriend. His mother was delighted—apparently she was a real city girl and refused to consider moving."

Interesting. So the dog hadn't been his only reason for applying to Åmål. Embla had tried to run away from more than one relationship herself. She had no wish to share those memories with anyone, not even her closest friends. And no one else knew about them. It was best if it stayed that way.

She decided to change the subject.

"Could you do me a favor and check if Jan Müller was here at any point between the fourteenth and twenty-fourth of October last year? He had a meal at the Thai restaurant in Mellerud, then drove south. I wonder if he might have come to Herremark to take a look around. He might not have rented a cottage, but there is a chance he ate in the restaurant."

"I'm happy to help, but I won't have time this evening—can it wait until tomorrow morning?"

"Absolutely—thank you so much," Embla said, smiling gratefully at her. "I'll be leaving after lunch tomorrow," she added.

"Okay, but I'll keep the room for you for a few days, in case you come back."

Come back? As far as Embla was concerned, her inquiries in Dalsland were complete. It was time to concentrate on the murders of the Stavic brothers, and that investigation was based in Gothenburg.

AFTER A QUICK shower, a dab of mascara, a spritz of Clean Warm Cotton and a change of clothes—she chose a blue top that matched her eyes—Embla felt ready to have dinner with the best-looking cop in Dalsland.

Tore was once again parked behind the reception desk and settled down on his blanket by the radiator. Olle was waiting when Embla came down the stairs, and she thought she saw a glint of appreciation in his eyes.

"It's a good thing a uniform is always appropriate," he said with a smile.

Embla wasn't sure that applied to his dark-blue winter sweater, even if it was adorned with the police logo. However, it didn't really matter; he looked good. His hair had been ruffled by his cap, and she had to quell the impulse to smooth it down with her fingers. Resolutely she tucked her arm under his and led him into the restaurant, where Monika had reserved the same table Embla and Göran had occupied the previous evening.

They chose a celery salad with walnuts and a mayonnaise dressing to start, followed by venison cutlets with cherry sauce and potato croquettes. The small cutlets were crisp on the outside and pink inside, and their delicate flavor was perfectly complemented by the slightly sharp sauce. They both drank mineral water.

During the meal they chatted about anything and everything except the ongoing case. Olle enjoyed his dessert—a fruit gratin with mixed berries and white chocolate, but Embla was too full for something so sweet.

Olle pushed away his empty plate and gave her a long

look. "So what are your thoughts on Robin's murder after today's interviews?" he asked.

Embla gave herself a little time by taking a sip of her mineral water.

"I want to speak to Wille Andersson tomorrow before I say anything. The fact that he wasn't home today could mean that he's trying to stay out of our way, or maybe he's worried that his drunken attempt at CPR made Robin's injuries worse. However, my gut says he's involved somehow."

Olle nodded slowly. "What makes you think that?"

"Wille was the first on the scene after Mikaela Malm ran back inside. His friend Gustav might have been with him, or he might have arrived later—we don't know yet. It was Wille who decided to do CPR; was that to hide the blood on his hands and clothes? The stab wounds were deep, so the murderer must have been covered in blood. And I remember what he said to you: that it was Robin's own fault he'd been stabbed because he was so cocky."

"So *fucking* cocky," Olle quickly corrected her.

Embla rolled her eyes. "Noted. 'So fucking cocky' isn't exactly the kind of thing you say about a dying friend who's just been taken away in an ambulance. Particularly if you're standing there with the victim's blood all over you."

Olle nodded again, his expression serious. "Absolutely. We need to take a closer look at Wille."

"I'll make a start tomorrow. *Skål!*"

They clinked glasses to toast their decision. They chatted for a while, but eventually Olle said, "I guess it's time for me to get going. It's quite far from here to Åmål."

Once again, Monika refused to let them pay for their meal.

"We're so grateful that you're here, trying to solve these terrible murders. You seem like such a good team," she said. Her eyes filled with tears as she took Olle's right hand between her own trembling hands and squeezed it warmly. Then she turned to Embla and gave her a big hug.

EMBLA ACCOMPANIED OLLE and Tore onto the steps, choosing to remain in the doorway so that she could at least feel the warmth of the fire on her back.

"I've really enjoyed this evening," Olle said.

"Me too. And we've had some constructive discussions on the case as well."

"See you at eight-thirty."

"I'll be ready."

This time Embla was determined to be first; her arm came up and she managed a pretty decent salute.

OLLE DROVE INTO the courtyard at exactly eight-thirty. Embla was waiting for him. It had been several years since she'd driven a squad car, and she had no desire to go back to those days. The morning was cold and clear; a few stars still twinkled in the dark sky, but there was a hint of light in the east. The weather forecast predicted snow in the afternoon, with a slight rise in the temperature.

When the car pulled up, a couple of children in the lobby pressed their noses to the window, shouting out with delight. *They're still young enough to find cops and their cars exciting,* Embla thought as she made her way down the steps. She opened the passenger door and got in.

"Morning. Did you sleep well?" Olle asked with a grin.

"I did—how about you?"

"Very well, but I still have a problem with Tore. My sister and her family are no better, and my mom won't be home until Friday. I don't have anyone else to take care of him."

"You're wrong there—you're among friends. I'm sure Monika and Harald will be pleased to see him again, and he seemed pretty happy with them yesterday."

"Of course he was—the way to a guy's heart is through his stomach!"

Tore's tail drooped slightly when he realized he wasn't accompanying his master, but he soon settled on his blanket behind the reception desk.

THE WHITE VAN with ANDERSSON ELECTRICAL SER-VICES on the side was gone. Olle rang the doorbell. The woman who opened the door looked haggard. Her complexion was sallow, and the dark rings under her eyes revealed that she hadn't slept much. She was small and slim, with a blonde bob that was badly in need of a wash. A long black cardigan hung shapelessly over a pale-blue T-shirt and a pair of leggings. Her bare feet were pushed into a pair of blue fluffy slippers. Her bloodshot eyes darted from side to side, filled with both anxiety and exhaustion.

Olle produced his warmest reassuring smile.

"Good morning. This is my colleague, Detective Inspector Embla Nyström from Gothenburg, and I'm Olle Tillman, a detective from Åmål. I assume you're Wille and Ida's mom?"

"That's right. Marie. Marie Andersson."

"We'd like a word with Ida," Olle continued breezily.

The thin figure in the doorway seemed to shrink, and the answer was almost inaudible. "That's not possible. She's really sick."

"I'm sure she can manage a little chat," Olle insisted, the smile still firmly in place.

Marie Andersson simply shook her head. In the silence, all three of them could hear sobbing. Marie cleared her throat.

"She's . . . she's very upset. Grieving . . . Robin was her boyfriend, and now he's dead," she said without looking at either of them.

Enough already—this was a homicide investigation. Embla took over.

"We know that Robin ended things with her a couple of days before the party on Friday."

Marie gave a start; this was clearly news to her.

"We heard that Ida left the party before the murder. She went off with Anton Åkesson in his car," Embla continued.

"She did not! She would never have gone anywhere with Anton!"

Marie straightened up and glared at Embla, who was suddenly struck by her resemblance to Lilian Åkesson, Anton's mother, who had fainted after they'd questioned her. This woman seemed to be made of tougher stuff, but could they be related? Sisters, even? It wasn't impossible; here in northern Dalsland everyone was related to everyone. She knew that from her own experience.

Before either of the police officers could say anything, Marie snapped.

"Robin had promised to drive Ida and Wille home, but then he was stabbed and she and Wille got separated. She had to walk home all by herself through the blizzard—almost two kilometers. She tripped and fell, banged her head. Just imagine, if she'd been knocked out, she would have frozen to death! And now she's sick."

Her body was trembling. Embla and Olle exchanged a quick glance.

"Our orders are to speak to Ida. Today. It can't wait any longer. And our instructions are to bring anyone who refuses to cooperate down to Trollhättan for a formal interview," Olle stated firmly. It was a flat lie, but Embla didn't contradict him. He paused, keeping his eyes fixed on Marie. "This is a homicide investigation."

Marie's anger gave way to resignation. Without a word she stepped aside to let them in. They took off their shoes, then she led the way up a staircase that opened into a light and airy living room. A generous black leather sofa was positioned in front of a large TV on the wall. On the screen a cheerful young man was whisking something in a bowl while chatting to the show's female host. The remains of breakfast were still on the coffee table—coffee, eggs, and porridge.

Marie went over to a door that was slightly ajar and knocked gently. "Ida. There are two police officers here who want to talk to you."

She pushed open the door, and they were met by the acrid smell of sweat with an undertone of honey. The sweat was clearly coming from Ida, and the honey from the untouched cup of tea on the nightstand next to her king-size bed. The black-and-white patterned duvet cover was crumpled; the room definitely needed a good airing.

The first they saw of Ida was a thin back dressed in a baggy black T-shirt. The sharp angles of her shoulder blades and the outlines of her vertebrae were clearly visible beneath the cotton fabric. The sobs continued with undiminished strength; her whole body was shaking.

"Darling, you have to speak to them," Marie said in the same soft tone.

The narrow back stiffened, and after a lengthy pause, the girl slowly turned and looked at them.

According to the information they'd received, Ida was sixteen years old, but she looked no more than fourteen, partly due to the state she was in. Her eyes were puffy from all the crying, and her right cheek was swollen and discolored; an angry reddish-purple bruise extended all the way from her eye to her forehead. She had a large bandage over one temple.

Olle introduced himself and Embla, but there was no response. The tears continued, and occasionally Ida's body convulsed with a sob. Her gaze was fixed on a point beside the two officers.

"She's been given painkillers—only Alvedon though. The swelling has actually started to go down a little," Marie said.

It didn't look good. "Has she seen a doctor?" Olle asked.

"No. She didn't want to."

"Why not? It must be very painful, and I wouldn't be surprised if she'd suffered a concussion. She really ought to be examined by a doctor," Olle said firmly.

Ida turned around and clutched her pillow. She didn't seem to be aware they were talking about her. Embla could see that she was in shock. Because of her parents' misguided attempt to protect her, she had been allowed to retreat into herself and brood about Robin's death, which was not good; she needed to come out of the darkness.

"Ida, can you tell us what happened at the party?" Embla prompted the girl. Ida gave a start, then shook her head.

"Do you remember anything before the accident when you banged your head?"

"No," she whispered.

Had Ida really lost her memory, or was she reluctant to say anything while her mother was listening?

"Do you remember what happened afterward?"

A shuddering sob. Ida looked at Embla for the first time, but only for a second.

"I was freezing cold. It hurt . . . I wanted to get home . . . I didn't feel well."

"I can see how painful it must have been," Embla said, her voice overflowing with empathy. She glanced at Olle, who didn't seem inclined to step in. Ida was suffering, both mentally and physically, and there was a real risk that she might collapse. Maybe it was best to ask the key question now, rather than waiting. She tried to make it sound like a routine inquiry, nothing special.

"I know there was a blizzard and it was hard to see, but did you notice anyone along the road as you were walking home—a car or a person you didn't recognize?"

A barely perceptible nod, then Ida let out a scream and clasped the back of her neck with both hands.

"Does your neck hurt?"

Embla immediately realized how ridiculous the question was. Ida didn't answer; she simply continued to whimper. Olle turned to her mother, his expression deadly serious.

"She could have injured one of the cervical vertebrae or have sustained whiplash. She needs to see a doctor."

Marie's anxiety was clear. "Maybe you're right," she said hesitantly.

"I have to tell you that she didn't fall and bang her head," Olle continued calmly. "She was involved in a car accident. Witnesses saw her leave in Anton Åkesson's car, which we've found hidden on the Åkesson property. It's been in a crash and is badly damaged. The accident happened in a field between the guesthouse and the road leading to the nature reserve."

"And as you may be aware, a man has been murdered in one of the cottages along that road. The murder took place on the same night, and probably around the same time as the crash. That's why it's vital that Ida tells us—" Embla was interrupted by a hysterical scream. Ida began to rock back and forth, tears pouring down her face. Embla wondered how many liters of liquid she'd lost from her tear ducts so far.

Marie sank down on the bed beside her daughter, trying in vain to calm her down. She looked up helplessly at Olle and Embla. "Patrick . . . my husband . . . didn't think there was any point in taking her to the hospital, but you're right—she needs to see a doctor. Although I have a problem—my car's in the shop."

"We'll drive you to the primary-care center in Dals-Ed. If you help Ida get dressed, I'll call ahead," Olle said.

It would only take an extra fifteen minutes to drop them off.

During the drive Embla managed to persuade Marie to give her Wille's cell phone number, although it was a struggle. Once again she was surprised at the reluctance of both the teenagers and their parents to help the police investigate the events of the night in question. Was it just a general distrust of the police, or did they know that the murderer was among them?

WHEN THEY ARRIVED at the Åkesson property, they saw that the pile of snow by the barn had been cleared, and the Toyota was in the process of being secured on the back of a transporter. The Volvo belonging to the CSIs from Trollhättan was parked a short distance away. One of them was talking to a grim-faced John Åkesson, whose expression didn't change much when Olle and Embla got out of their car. If anything, he looked even angrier. The only sign of the previous day's confrontation was the white tape over his eyebrow. Olle greeted the CSIs, who had also been at the crime scene at the Lodge after the stabbing. When he introduced Embla, the guy on the transporter looked down at her. His winter cap, complete with ear flaps, hid part of his face.

"Hi—Ulf Berg. We met during the moose hunt case back in the fall," he said quietly. Embla merely nodded; she couldn't think of a suitable answer.

"The moose hunt case?" Olle said.

It was too complicated to explain; Embla chose to pretend she hadn't heard his question. John Åkesson made no comment on Berg's remark; instead he stared first at Embla, then at Olle.

"Just so you know: Anton's in the hospital. Severe concussion and damage to several vertebrae. But it was me who dug out the car for your colleagues. Lilian and I just want this sorted," he said brusquely. It was obvious how much it cost him to utter those words. Embla noted that he seemed entirely sober; there wasn't even a hint of stale booze or a hangover.

Olle glanced at her, understandably taken aback by the change in Åkesson's attitude. She felt the same way but quickly pulled herself together.

"Good," Embla said in a pleasant tone. "In that case maybe you'd like to tell us why you brought the car here."

His eyes slid away, and for a moment she thought he wasn't going to answer. "We wanted to protect the boy. We didn't want him to be accused of . . . anything."

His reluctance was palpable, and he clearly wasn't telling the whole truth. Embla decided to move on and circle back when he didn't have his guard up.

"How did you find out that Anton was hurt?"

Åkesson swallowed audibly, still refusing to meet her gaze. "Ida Andersson called after the car went off the road. It was in the field, and Anton couldn't move. Ida managed to get out and called me. I drove her home, but she asked me to let her out a short distance from the house. I brought Anton here, but . . ."

He fell silent, his cheeks flushed red.

"We could see that he was in bad shape, so Lilian drove him to the hospital in the Volvo. It's a V70, so there was room to lay him down in the back. It was quicker than waiting for an ambulance."

He stopped speaking abruptly, as if he had no intention of saying any more.

"If he was admitted that night, I'm sure he was tested for alcohol," Embla said calmly. "In which case there will be evidence that he'd been driving while under the influence."

There was no mistaking the anger in Åkesson's eyes as he looked at her, but he didn't attempt to contradict her. The CSIs didn't hide the fact that they were listening with interest; maybe that was why Olle felt the need to join in.

"And that's why you picked up the car—so that no one would start asking questions."

"Fucking smartass." Åkesson turned on his heel and marched toward the house.

"We can't get along with everyone in this world," Ulf Berg said dryly.

A call to the hospital confirmed that Anton Åkesson was in intensive care. The doctor Embla spoke to thought he would probably be moved to an ordinary ward the following day; there was no chance the police would be able to speak to the boy before then.

"The boy? He's eighteen years old, for fuck's sake," she snapped when she ended the call. "He's old enough to vote, and he can marry whoever he likes without his parents' permission. Why do we mollycoddle adults?"

Olle gave her a disingenuous smile. "Boys mature later than girls."

"At least you're self-aware," she replied sourly, making him laugh.

They drove back to the guesthouse. On the way they discussed the case and the interviews they'd conducted so far.

"Speak to Ida again—she might remember more when she's feeling better. And you need to talk to Anton as soon as he's out of intensive care."

"And you're seeing Wille on the way down?"

"Yes—I'll do my best to get a hold of him."

Olle parked the police car next to Embla's Kia. It was almost lunchtime, and several families were heading into the restaurant.

"I guess I'll pick up a hot dog in Dals-Ed," Olle said.

Embla thought about the Thai restaurant in Mellerud and decided it was time for another visit.

Tore was ecstatic to see his master again.

"I'll take him for a quick walk," Olle said, clipping on his leash.

"Okay—I'll go and fetch my stuff."

She'd already packed most of her things. She sat down in the comfortable armchair and keyed in Wille's number. He answered almost right away, his voice deep and mature.

"Wille."

"Hi, Wille. This is Embla Nyström; I'm a police officer, and I'd like to talk to you about the events during the party on Friday night. Where can we meet—I believe you're at college?"

There was a long silence; she wondered whether he was about to cut her off.

"We're in the shop today," he said eventually.

"Okay, where are you? I'll come and see you," she replied implacably.

Another long silence.

"I'll be eating in Burger King in Brålanda."

"Good—can you be there in an hour?"

"Okay."

Before Embla had time to confirm the arrangement, Wille was gone. So lunch would be a burger in Brålanda instead of Thai food in Mellerud. *Oh well*.

When she got back down to the lobby, Olle was already there. He thanked Monika and Harald for taking such good care of Tore, and for the excellent food and hospitality. Embla gave them a hug and expressed her own warm thanks.

"I'm afraid I couldn't find a reservation in the name of Jan Müller for last October," Monika said.

"It was just an idea—thanks for checking."

Olle gave his trademark salute as they said their final goodbyes.

"I'll call you after I've spoken to Wille," Embla said.

"Great—thanks for making time to see him."

They waved to each other as they climbed into their respective cars and set off in different directions.

AS EMBLA WALKED toward the entrance of Burger King, a sticker in the back window of an old Saab caught her attention. The slogan was very familiar to her: THE SWEDISH ASSOCIATION FOR HUNTING—SWEDEN'S MOST IMPORTANT HUNTING CLUB. She'd had the same one on her old Volvo 245. The metallic-blue Saab was well cared for. A smaller sticker bore the word BAR; something told her she'd found Wille's car.

The restaurant was packed, and the majority of the customers were children. The noise level was high, and the kids who'd finished eating were running around playing. Several were wearing the paper crowns they'd received with their meal.

A boy who stood a head taller than everyone else was waiting in line to order. Broad-shouldered and powerfully built, he was a younger version of his father. Large tattoos—mainly tribal motifs, monsters, and skulls—covered his bare arms. On his head was a baseball cap that had seen better days; obviously he chose to wear it backwards. He was in a T-shirt and a sleeveless hunting vest in spite of the freezing temperature outside. *Talk about the need to play macho*, Embla thought. She went and joined him.

"Hi, Wille."

He looked at her, surprised at first, but then his expression darkened when he realized who she was. A brief nod was his only attempt at a greeting.

Embla smiled, handed him a hundred-kronor note, and said, "Get me a veggie burger, will you—I'll go and sit over there."

She pointed to a small table at the back of the room. There were only two chairs, which was probably why it was free. Wille muttered something in response. Embla went and sat down; she watched him order and pay. He was given two huge cardboard cups, but before he picked them up, he pulled up his jeans by the waistband with a well-practiced grip. He filled the cups with Coca-Cola from an automatic dispenser, and Embla groaned to herself; she hated Coke. She should have told him, but all she could do now was accept it with good grace. The most important thing was to get Wille talking.

He put the cups on the table without a word. His whole attitude was sullen and uncooperative. She had to soften him up somehow before his lunch break was over.

"I'm starving," she said with a smile.

He grunted, refusing to meet her eye. One of the

young assistants came over with their plastic baskets containing burgers and fries. Wille dug several packets of ketchup out of his pocket, nodding to Embla to help herself. It was a toss-up as to which she hated most: the burger, the Coke, or the ketchup. She kept the smile firmly in place. "Thank you." Once again, those years at drama school hadn't been a complete waste of time.

Judging by the mound of fries in Wille's basket, he'd ordered a double portion. He also had a double burger with extra everything. He began to open the ketchups one after another, giving his full concentration to the task of dousing his entire meal. It made Embla think of blood. She was going to have to approach this conversation with care, but first she wanted to confirm something that could be significant. She picked up a couple of fries and put them in her mouth. They were limp and slimy, like worms. She licked the grease from the corners of her mouth, then asked:

"The Saab 99 out there—is it yours?"

He looked up from his food in surprise. "What?"

"The sticker in the back window—the Swedish Association for Hunting. Are you a member?"

"Mmmhmm," he mumbled, nodding faintly.

She could hear the defensiveness in his voice. Of course he was wondering why she'd mentioned the Association, but she didn't explain. From the beginning, she'd suspected that the weapon used to murder Robin had been a hunting knife—very sharp, and with a long blade. Things were beginning to make sense.

"Tell me what happened at the party. When did you go around to the back of the Lodge?"

Wille removed the plug of snuff from beneath his

upper lip and placed it next to the pile of fries. He took a big bite of his burger and chewed noisily, then swilled it down with a slug of Coke. He obviously wanted time to consider his answer.

"Twelve-thirty. Maybe later. I was drunk, so . . ." He shrugged, his expression reflecting his uncertainty.

"Did you go out alone?"

"Yes. I needed to pee."

He took another huge bite, so Embla thought she might as well try her veggie burger. It was pretty dry and tasteless, but she'd had worse. To her surprise, Wille had something else to say.

"The light was broken. So I didn't have to go far."

Several witnesses had said that the light above the kitchen door wasn't working. It had been pretty dark out there.

"Did you hear anything? Any groaning, or someone talking?"

"No."

"And where were you when Mikaela started yelling?"

He stared at his fries for a long time, then said, "I was just about to go back inside."

"But you changed your mind?"

"Yes."

"What did you do?"

"Went to where Mikaela had come from."

"Was that when you found Robin?"

He nodded, slurping his Coke.

"And what did you do then?" Embla prompted him. *Patience.*

He wiped his mouth with the back of his hand and belched loudly. Embla steeled herself; she didn't even blink.

"Tried to stop the bleeding."

Without looking at her, he grabbed a fistful of fries and shoved them into his mouth. Embla waited until the chewing subsided.

"Why did you start CPR?"

He gaped at her in surprise. "Did I?"

"Yes, according to two sober witnesses."

"Fuck's sake. Petter and his fucking bitch . . . girl-friend." His expression was one of disdain.

"The question remains. Why did you try to give him CPR when you didn't know how to do it?"

Slowly he raised his shoulders and spread his hands wide. "It was Gustav's idea."

"But you were the one who actually did it."

"Maybe."

"So Gustav was with you when you went out to pee?"

He recoiled slightly, thought for a moment, then shook his head. "I don't think so. I can't remember."

"Do you remember when he appeared?"

"No."

He let out another belch in order to underline his lack of interest. *Charming boy.*

Embla realized he was pretending to be unmoved. She leaned forward and said softly, "Was it you rather than Gustav who came up with the idea of CPR?"

Another fistful of fries. Chomp chomp chomp. Slurp slurp. "Can't remember," he said when he couldn't put it off any longer.

Time to shake things up. Embla sat back and fixed him with her patented no-more-bullshit stare. She'd had plenty of practice, and it usually worked—particularly on those who weren't used to being questioned by the police.

"Why did you tell my colleague that it was Robin's own fault he'd been stabbed?"

Wille swallowed hard; now he looked worried. He picked up the burger and opened his mouth to take a bite.

"Put that down!" Embla snapped.

He sat there with the burger halfway to his mouth, but didn't put it back in the basket.

"Answer the question," she said icily. It wasn't easy to switch from good cop to bad cop in a second, but it had the advantage of surprise.

Wille's eyes darted around the room as if seeking support from one of the families enjoying their lunch, but there was no help to be found. The children were playing, the parents were trying to eat while keeping an eye on them. The noise level was high; no one was eavesdropping on their conversation.

"Like I said, I was drunk," he mumbled eventually.

"But you told a uniformed police officer that it was Robin's own fault he'd been stabbed because he was so fucking cocky. Do you not have a sense of what is and isn't appropriate?"

His upper body jerked, and the look in his eyes changed from uncertainty to aggression.

Short fuse, easily offended, Embla thought.

"If you make a comment like that to a police officer immediately after a homicide, then you need to be prepared to answer questions. Particularly if you're covered in blood, as you were. So why did you say it was his own fault he'd been stabbed?" she repeated implacably.

He threw down the burger and sat back on his plastic chair, then folded his arms to show off his muscles and tattoos. There was menace in his eyes when he spoke. "He had a fucking high opinion of himself—thought he was so good-looking. He was always bragging about all the girls he'd fucked." His arms tightened.

"And that's why you think he deserved to die?"

He sat in silence for some time, staring at his rapidly cooling food. Without looking up, he ground out: "He treated Ida like shit."

"In what way?"

A quick glance at her, then he lowered his eyes again. "He dumped her."

"He deserved to die because he dumped Ida?"

"I didn't kill him." He unfolded his arms and picked up his drink.

Embla caught a glimpse of a tattoo on the inside of his upper arm that she hadn't noticed before; her pulse rate increased when she realized what it was. *Could it really be possible?*

He finished the Coke, put down the cup, and looked her straight in the eye for the first time. "Ida was heart-broken. I was drunk—I don't remember what I said."

With those words he got to his feet, grabbed his burger and the remaining ketchups, and walked out.

The movement of his arm was enough for Embla to see the tattoo clearly. With a contented smile, she took out her phone to call Olle.

SHE'D JUST PASSED Partille when her phone rang. She switched to hands-free before she answered.

"Embla Nyström."

"It's Marie . . . Marie Andersson. Wille and Ida's mother."

Embla was taken aback; she hadn't expected to hear from Marie so soon. With warmth and interest in her voice, she replied, "Hi, Marie. How's Ida?"

"Much better, thank you. We're at the hospital now. They're keeping her for observation, and I think they might want to do a head scan."

"I'm glad to hear she's being taken care of."

"Thank you for driving us to Primary Care."

"Of course. It was on our way."

"It was still kind of you. I've tried to contact your colleague, but he's not answering. I left a message, but . . . I think this might be important, and you did give me your card."

"No problem—what is it?"

Marie didn't answer right away; Embla could hear her breathing heavily on the other end of the line. What did she want? Just as Embla began to wonder if she'd changed her mind, Marie cleared her throat.

"Ida told me how the accident happened. She and Anton left just before midnight. He suggested they go to Gothenburg, but she just wanted to go home. He promised to drive her, but instead he parked at the bus stop just past the guesthouse . . . heading south, I mean . . . and he started trying to . . . make out with her. Ida wasn't interested, and they had a quarrel. Ida was crying, and he got really mad. He pulled out onto the road, and a car quickly came up behind them. Ida says it came from the turnoff for Klevskog—the nature reserve."

Marie paused and took a deep breath before continuing.

"The other car didn't have time to slow down; it passed Anton, but skidded. They almost collided. Anton slammed his foot on the brake, but he skidded, too, and drove off the road. Ida thinks the Toyota might have turned over, but she's not sure. She probably lost consciousness for a while."

At last—something useful from one of the people who'd been at the party. Ida and Anton had left before Robin was killed, so they had nothing to contribute in terms of that investigation, but it seemed highly likely that they'd encountered Milo's murderer.

"Did she see what make of car it was? Did she recognize it?"

"I asked her, but she said it all happened so fast. All she remembers is that it was a big, dark-colored vehicle. She said it reminded her of a large Jeep."

"Did she notice anything about the driver? Or if there were any passengers?"

"No. Again, I asked her—I wondered if it was someone we knew, but she didn't think so. And she didn't see how many people were in the car."

That was disappointing, but at least they'd reduced the time frame for Milo's murder; it must have happened by 12:10 A.M. at the latest. And the perpetrator had been driving a large dark car that resembled a Jeep.

She thanked Marie for calling and passing on such important information.

As she passed Ullevi and the police station came into view, she tried Olle's number again.

THE JOB INTERVIEWS Göran was conducting went long, delaying him by almost two hours, so he and Embla didn't leave Police HQ until five o'clock. Under normal circumstances, the drive to Terrassgatan took only a few minutes, but now it was rush hour. It had also started snowing, leading to even more problems. One advantage of being stuck in traffic was that it gave them time to update each other.

"I've spoken to Tommy Persson and he's happy for you and me to continue with this investigation, since we started it in Dalsland. I went along to morning prayers to pass on what we've found out so far," Göran said.

A great deal of information would need to be exchanged between the Technical Department and Violent Crimes in a case like this, and Embla didn't want that responsibility. Chief Inspector Persson preferred her to be in her normal post, where he was her boss these days. He often made barbed comments about the fact that she couldn't stay away from VGM, "the unit that no longer existed."

"Are you going to liaise with Tommy?" she asked tentatively.

"Yes."

She felt as if someone had released an iron grip on the back of her neck.

"I've also been in touch with the chief of police in Split, Boris Cetinski. His English isn't great, but we managed to understand each other. Kador Stavic disappeared two weeks ago after having a drink with some friends in a bar. He left at about eleven, which was early for him. He said he had an important meeting early the next morning and wanted to be well rested. The others stayed out. The bar is no more than three hundred meters from his house, but he never arrived home."

Embla had never visited Split, but her parents had been there on vacation a couple of years ago.

"Split is a pretty big city, and eleven o'clock isn't very late. Did nobody see him?" she asked.

"Well, nobody's come forward. I asked the same question, and Boris said it was a cold, rainy night, so not many people were out and about. Plus there are very few tourists there in February, if any."

A Nissan King Cab in the lane next to them started signaling and pushed its way in ahead of them. As she slowed to let it in, Embla wondered crossly why people drove such huge gas-guzzling cars in a city. Only then did she realize they were sitting in VGM's Volvo XC90. They'd taken it because all the forensic equipment necessary for examining a crime scene was in the trunk. Göran muttered something about the "inconsiderate bastard" before he continued.

"Kador's wife called one of his friends shortly after midnight to ask if her husband was still at the bar. When she found out he'd left over an hour earlier, she got worried. The other guys didn't think anything of it; they assumed he'd decided to visit one of his girlfriends. According to Boris, he's definitely a ladies' man."

Slowly the line of traffic edged along Södra vägen. They had plenty of time before they got to Milo Stavic's apartment.

"Does his wife know?"

"Presumably, since the chief of police knew."

A militant cyclist quickly zigzagged between the cars and was almost knocked over by the King Cab. The driver leaned on the horn and the cyclist gave him the finger before whizzing off through the slush toward Berzeliigatan.

"Nice to see someone doing their part for the environment," Göran said with a laugh. Embla thought of her colleague, Irene Huss, who cycled all the way home to Guldheden every day. It was a steep, three-kilometer uphill climb. On the other hand, she hardly needed to pedal at all on her way down to Police HQ at the beginning of the day. Irene wasn't exactly a morning person, so that probably suited her.

"Back to Kador. He didn't show up for the meeting the next morning; apparently it had something to do with the sale of a bar. An Englishman was very keen to buy it, and according to Kador's lawyer . . . now, what was his name . . ."

Göran began checking his pockets, frowning and muttering to himself. Eventually he found his little notebook. As usual he licked his index finger before leafing through the pages.

"That's it—Stefan Fabris. He and the Englishman waited for an hour before they gave up. Fabris called Kador's home number several times, as well as his cell, but no one answered. He got worried then; Kador might be a little slapdash in some ways, but never when it comes to business. He drove to Kador's house, but there was no one there."

"So the whole family's missing?"

"Yes. Fabris reported it to the police. According to Boris, they found a witness, a neighbor who lives opposite. He was woken at about three in the morning by the sound of a car, and he got up and looked out. He saw Mirja Stavic and all three children getting into a large dark-colored vehicle. The driver wasn't Kador, but a bald man whom the neighbor didn't recognize."

A pensive silence filled the car. Embla was considering what Göran had told her while trying to concentrate on the heavy traffic. She finally managed to turn off toward Götaplatsen without any mishaps, and drove past the statue of Poseidon, standing there in all his naked glory. As usual she couldn't help glancing at his undersized sexual organs. What had the sculptor been thinking of? Although it was cold out, so maybe the penis was the right size for once. Her musings were interrupted by Göran.

"Boris and I exchanged a few ideas. One theory is that Kador fled with his family. Or maybe he left first. Or they were kidnapped. No one knows."

"And what's the connection between Kador's disappearance and the murders of his brothers?" Embla said.

A heavy sigh. "You tell me."

A few minutes later, they reached Viktor Rydbergsgatan and took the next turn up the hill to Terrassgatan. There were no spaces available, so they parked outside the apartment block. Göran flipped down the sun visor to display the sign VÄSTRA GÖTALAND POLICE. It was a relic of the time before the major reorganization and was no longer valid.

"I hope none of our colleagues lives here," Embla said with a nod at the sign.

"There are no cops living here," Göran said with conviction.

He was probably right. Not even one of the top brass. The tall, impressive dark-red brick building afforded views over large parts of the city center, even from the ground floor. There were several exclusive stores along the street, as well as a hair salon and a nail salon. The doorways were richly decorated stone arches, and the doors themselves were made of the finest wood, each with a highly polished pane of glass.

Göran heaved one of the bags out of the Volvo's trunk. "Can you bring the other?" he said.

The equipment was heavy, but Embla had no problem lifting it. She knew she was stronger than Göran, who grunted with the effort as he staggered across the sidewalk before putting the bag down with a sigh of relief. Embla joined him and checked out the list of residents' names. She read it several times, but there was no Stavic.

"We're in the wrong place," she said.

"No, we're not."

Without hesitation, Göran pressed the intercom button next to the top name, A. Acika. After a few seconds, a male voice answered.

"Yes?"

Göran leaned forward and articulated clearly.

"Superintendent Göran Krantz."

There was a buzzing sound, and the lock clicked open.

"Did Milo call himself Acika?"

Göran looked at Embla with a glint of amusement in his eyes.

"No. Acika is Acika. You'll see."

The floor in the foyer and the stairs themselves were made of marble in various shades of green, and the vaulted ceiling was supported by bronze pillars in the shape of the female form. The center of the stairs was some kind of dark-red stone, presumably meant to imitate a carpet. The walls were painted white, with art deco patterns. The style was echoed by the ceiling lights, which had the same pattern etched on the glass surfaces. Embla and Göran hauled their kit into the elevator. Embla couldn't help feeling slightly claustrophobic in the small space after the steel doors slid shut. Silently they were sucked up to the fifth floor. When the doors opened, a man was waiting for them. In one hand he was holding a slim attaché case in Bordeaux-colored leather. The light from a large crystal chandelier was reflected in his dark, slicked-back hair when he nodded to them. His navy-blue suit hung perfectly over his shoulders. He was elegant and expensively dressed in a crisp white shirt, discreetly patterned blue tie, and shiny black shoes. He was a handsome man, with clearly defined cheekbones and eyebrows and piercing blue eyes.

For one horrible moment, Embla thought Luca Stavic was standing there waiting for them. He stepped forward, holding out his hand with a smile.

"Andreas Acika. Welcome."

He was approximately the same height as Embla, but the way he held himself made him seem taller.

"My condolences. I believe you're the person who worked most closely with Milo," Göran said.

"One of the people. I'm the director of finance."

He spoke without an accent, and his voice was deep and pleasant, but his eyes were hard to read.

"Someone told me you're related?" Göran asked, keeping his tone casual.

"We're cousins."

"So you were born in Croatia, too?"

There was a slight change in the atmosphere, but only for a fraction of a second.

"No. Gothenburg."

Interesting guy, Embla thought, but of course Göran couldn't carry on interrogating Acika. They weren't here to investigate him.

Andreas Acika unzipped the attaché case and fished out a bunch of keys.

"The other elevator," he said, turning on his heel. Only then did Embla see that there was just one apartment door on the floor. Opposite that door was another elevator; there was no call button, just a lock. Andreas inserted one of the keys, and the elevator opened with a hum. The sliding doors inside remained closed until he pressed a teardrop-shaped piece of plastic against a small glass panel. There was a beep, and the doors opened. Embla and Göran carried their bags inside; it was cramped, but bearable. Embla picked up the scent of an expensive male fragrance; it was nowhere near as cloying as Milo's had been. When Andreas reached out to press his card against another panel inside the elevator, she noticed that he was wearing a wide gold ring. Something else glinted in the light, catching her attention. When she realized what it was, she had to make a huge effort to hide her reaction. The sleeve of his jacket rode up, revealing a gold watch the size of an American cupcake. She couldn't tell whether Göran had noticed as well; his expression didn't change.

"Does anyone else have keys to Milo's apartment?" he asked.

"Luca."

"No one else? Kador, for example?"

"What would be the point of that? Kador lives in Split."

The surprise in Andreas's voice was unmistakable, but there was something else—contempt, maybe? Presumably he thought they were stupid.

The elevator stopped, the doors slid open, and they stepped out into a large hallway. An alarm started beeping; Andreas used his card once again to silence it. Then he switched on an even bigger crystal chandelier than the one downstairs.

On the floor lay a beautiful Persian rug in glowing shades of blue and gold. Instinctively Embla avoided stepping on it; in her eyes it looked like a work of art that should be hanging on a wall. Then again, the walls were already crowded with paintings—old and gloomy, in heavy gold frames. A curved rococo chest of drawers with a matching mirror stood along one wall. The mirror frame was highly embellished and gilded, as were the two candelabra on the marble top of the chest, which was flanked by two Gustavian armchairs upholstered in gold brocade.

Embla felt as if she'd walked straight into a museum. Or maybe an antiques store.

To the right of the elevator was a door; the lock suggested it was probably a bathroom. She peered inside and saw a generous guest toilet with a shower, the tiles shimmering turquoise and gold. The faucets and towel hooks were gilded, and there were thick white hand towels.

Meanwhile, Andreas opened the closet in the hallway and took out two hangers.

"You might like to take off your jackets. You can leave your shoes here, too."

"First of all I'd like to check out the closet," Göran said, pulling on a pair of blue latex gloves. He slipped off his boots and put on blue protective overshoes, puffing and panting. One big toe was protruding through a hole in his sock; Embla noticed a faint expression of distaste cross Andreas's face. *So now we're not just stupid, we're also hicks with neither class nor style*, Embla thought as she, too, put on gloves and overshoes.

Göran straightened up and gave Andreas a sharp glance. "How many square meters is this apartment?"

"Two hundred and ten, I think."

His tone suggested that he couldn't see what this had to do with the police.

"When did Milo move in here?"

"At the same time as Kristina and I moved into our apartment—five years ago."

"Who lived here before that?"

"No one. Milo bought the penthouse and fixed it up himself."

"Did he pay to have the elevator installed?"

"Of course."

"It's a big place. I assume Milo did the cleaning himself?" Göran said with a hint of sarcasm.

Andreas stiffened. It was a barely perceptible reaction, but Embla was watching him closely.

"No. My wife, Kristina, is . . . was Milo's housekeeper."

"In which case I assume she also has access to a set of keys."

For a moment Embla was convinced that Andreas was going to punch her former boss, but he managed to control himself. He clenched and opened his left fist several times; he was still holding the attaché case in his right hand.

"The keys are kept in our safe," he snapped.

Göran stared at him for a long time. "We didn't find any keys in the cottage where Milo was murdered. Which means the killer must have taken them with him."

The corner of Andreas's mouth twitched. "A locksmith will be here tomorrow. The insurance company insisted that we change the security system immediately."

He couldn't hide his satisfaction at having dealt with the problem already.

"That's pretty quick. There's no guarantee we'll finish today."

"Kristina can let you in. She's always home."

Göran nodded and said with a polite smile, "In that case we're ready to start. We'll let you know when we're done."

The smile didn't fool Andreas; he knew the dumb cop was telling him to fuck off. Embla saw his face turn to stone. He was clearly reluctant to leave the apartment, knew it would look strange if he insisted on staying.

With a brief nod he stepped back into the elevator. Neither Embla nor Göran spoke until they heard it stop on the floor below.

"Alone at last," Göran said with a cheeky grin. He took out his powerful flashlight and shined it into the closet. Apart from a few hangers made of the same dark wood as the sliding doors, it was empty. He opened the mirrored middle door; Embla could see a row of men's coats and several pairs of well-polished shoes.

"Nothing here." The third and final door revealed a high wooden shelf with different-sized drawers beneath it. There were four hats on the shelf: one forest green, one navy blue, one brown, and one black. Embla had seen pictures of Al Capone in which he often wore hats with a tall crown and a wide brim, as fashion dictated in 1930s Chicago. Milo Stavic's hats reminded her of the notorious gangster's; had he consciously copied Capone's style? Or had he chosen the hats, knowing they would add several centimeters to his height?

The drawers contained soft cashmere scarves, leather gloves, and thick socks. The bottom two were completely empty.

Embla checked out the chest of drawers: three boxes of matches and a box of candles, nothing else. This ornate piece of furniture served no real purpose.

Before they continued into the living room, Göran decided they should put on their crime-scene coveralls.

"We don't know if the murderer has been here, but given that Milo's keys are missing, it's not impossible," he said.

"In which case the murderer must have known how to switch off the alarm," Embla pointed out.

"True, but there would have been one of those plastic tags on Milo's key ring; it's not hard to work out how to use it."

Embla wasn't a fan of the tight, rustling coveralls. She always started sweating within minutes, but she just had to put up with it; it was important not to contaminate the scene.

The apartment was spotlessly clean; Kristina Acika seemed to be an excellent housekeeper. They moved into the living room, with its heavy leather furniture and Persian rugs. Embla had never been in an English gentleman's club, but that was the association that came to mind. Next to one of the sofas was a gilded drinks cart, well stocked with bottles of spirits and crystal decanters sparkling in the light from yet another chandelier. A large tiled stove in one corner looked old but was probably brand-new. On the walls, there were some paintings depicting people who were partly or completely naked. They seemed dark and depressing to Embla. Old-fashioned, but no doubt worth a fortune.

"Do you think he's robbed a museum?" she said with a giggle.

To her surprise, Göran didn't take it as a joke. "It's not impossible," he said. "I'll make sure the CSIs go over the whole place with a fine-tooth comb, and photograph all the paintings."

He nodded in the direction of a picture of a group of voluptuous naked women dancing around a sleeping youth, his upper body bare. A flock of sheep stood in the background, gazing at the scene before them. Embla's interpretation was pretty straightforward: a young shepherd having a wet dream.

It was surprising that Milo Stavic, the gangster who'd worked his way up from simple beginnings, had turned out to be an art connoisseur. Or a collector, at least.

As if he'd read her mind, Göran continued, "I find it hard to imagine that Milo knew much about art. I have a feeling he might have bought an entire collection. Or someone helped him acquire these pieces."

He spent a little while gazing around the walls of the living room, then he strode back into the hallway. Embla heard him talking on his cell, but he was too far away for her to make out the conversation. She left him to it and went into the kitchen.

It was super-modern, with a black stone floor, brushed steel appliances, and a large island housing the stove. Some of the cupboards had glass doors. When Embla pressed the switch, lights came on inside those cupboards as well as the spotlights in the ceiling, making the crystal glasses sparkle. A tall cupboard next to the refrigerator was full of wine bottles; it was the kind of wine cooler you'd find in a small bar. Was Milo a wine connoisseur, too?

A massive oak table with six chairs stood by the window, which offered a spectacular view over the eastern part of the city center, with the three Gothia Towers and Liseberg clearly visible.

There was a large steel fan hanging above the island. The kitchen was so clean that Embla got the feeling it was hardly ever used. When she opened the refrigerator she found five bottles of Champagne, several bottles of a Czech beer, a box of eggs, a variety of cheeses, and a pack of extra-salted butter. No sign of any meat, fruit, or vegetables.

A door in one wall led into a large pantry. A *walk-in pantry*, Embla thought with a smile. The shelves in here were also strikingly empty, apart from bottles of Slivovitz and whisky. There were empty bottles on the floor, along with a case of the Czech beer.

Finally she checked under the sink to see if there was any garbage. There wasn't; the various receptacles for recycling and the landfill were clean and empty.

She met Göran on her way out of the kitchen.

"Anything of interest?" he asked.

"Not as far as I can see."

"Okay. My team will be here on Wednesday morning, so we'll see what they can find."

They went back through the living room and into a hallway with several doors. A quick check revealed a study, a home gym, three bedrooms, and two bathrooms.

"We'll start with the study," Göran decided.

Not surprisingly, the room was decorated in the same style: a huge desk, a black leather office chair that was more like an armchair, paintings on the wall, and tall bookcases filled with leather-bound volumes that appeared to have been bought in sets. The gold lettering on the spines caught the light, but like everything else these were accessories aimed at creating the illusion that the owner of this apartment was a cultured and well-educated person.

There was no sign of any files or folders. However, there were a couple of bottles of fine single malt whisky on one of the shelves. This room also boasted an attractive tiled stove, with two leather armchairs and a small round brass table strategically placed in front of it. The Persian rug on the floor reminded Embla of the one in the hallway.

Göran went straight over to the desk. On its uncluttered surface was a free-standing computer monitor, a laser printer, a mouse, and a brass lamp with a green glass shade, plus a neatly coiled cable for a laptop.

"No computer."

He quickly opened the drawers one by one, unable to hide his irritation as he slammed the last one shut.

"Nothing!"

He stood there motionless, his gaze fixed on the lamp. Only his eyes were visible above his mask, but Embla could see that he was thinking hard.

"Everything must be on the laptop," he said at last.

"And it wasn't in the cottage."

"No, but he could have put it in another room here in the apartment. Or hidden it. Then again, it would be just as easy to take it with him."

He contemplated the paintings on the wall.

"Help me take them down," he said, heading for the nearest one, a naked woman lying with her back to the observer. Her ass was disproportionately large, and she was busy making it even bigger. Her head was tipped back, and she was eating from a bunch of grapes with her full red lips. A shadowy male figure was holding the stalk, his evil grin and the horns on his forehead clearly visible. *Weird,* Embla thought.

She and Göran lifted down the painting. It wasn't particularly heavy, but they didn't want to damage it in any way.

"Bingo!" Göran said as a safe was revealed. They both stared at the combination lock.

"The laptop could be in there. We'll have a word with Acika—he might know the combination," Göran decided. He marched out of the room, his body language showing how disappointed he was. "Let's take Milo's bedroom first, then the guest rooms."

He pushed open the door and walked into a

surprisingly airy space, which wasn't as over-furnished as the other rooms. However, the décor was much as expected, with a king-size bed in dark polished wood, a shiny emerald-green-and-gold quilt, and matching silk cushions. There were nightstands on either side of the bed, with lamps similar to the one in the study. On the wall opposite was a huge TV screen with impressive speakers.

A door led into a bathroom, with a jacuzzi instead of an ordinary bathtub. A frosted glass wall concealed a shower, sink, and toilet. The tiles on the walls were navy blue with a dusting of gold, while the floor was black. Thick white towels were draped over a rack. This was the first room that appealed to Embla. It must be wonderful to sink into a warm jacuzzi at the end of a long day. A day like today.

Göran opened another door and stepped into a walk-in closet. Embla joined him and saw rows of shirts and suits neatly displayed on hangers. The closet was as big as a small bedroom, and was beautifully laid out with clothes racks, cupboards, drawers, and shoe racks. She did a quick calculation; adding in the shoes in the hall-way, Milo must have owned at least forty pairs.

Methodically, Göran began to go through everything. Embla asked if she could help.

"Yes—you can check the drawers."

She knew he had problems with his knees and didn't like crouching. The top two drawers contained sunglasses, cufflinks, and other bits and pieces. The next three were full of neatly folded underwear and socks. In the bottom drawer lay silk handkerchiefs and bow ties in different colors and patterns. Just as she was about to close this last drawer, she noticed that the base was slightly tilted. When she pressed hard on the lower side, the whole thing lifted. Carefully she removed the contents, then took out the false bottom.

The space that was revealed was divided into sections and covered in royal-blue velvet. In each compartment lay three spare magazines with ammunition, fifteen cartridges in each magazine. A significantly larger compartment was empty, but the contours of a pistol could be seen clearly.

"Göran."

"Exactly what we were looking for," he said contentedly when he joined her. He decided they should take the three magazines with them, because it would be a while before the CSIs could document the scene.

"I'm guessing that a Beretta M9 would sit nicely in that space. The ammunition is 9 x 19 Parabellum, which fits the Beretta. I wonder how many cartridges are missing from the magazine in the gun Milo was holding to his breast," Embla said.

"Two shots, one to the head and one to the heart, so at least two should be missing. It's a shame we couldn't check while we were there, but of course we couldn't contaminate the scene. We'll just have to wait."

He paused briefly. "Okay, let's do this."

They went back into the hallway and started to get out their equipment. Göran was the best when it came to handling the camera, a Canon with a round flash. He also took out a small folding floodlight. Embla's area of expertise was guns, and she quickly gave her former boss a crash course on the Beretta M9. It's loaded with a 15-cartridge magazine of exactly the type found in the cottage in Herremark, and in Milo's secret hiding place in the closet. It's a short-distance weapon; at close range, as in the murders of the Stavic brothers, no one can survive a shot to the head or the heart.

They photographed the cache from every possible angle. When Göran was satisfied, he carefully placed the three magazines in separate evidence bags. Once again Embla thought about the pistol tucked beneath Milo's hands.

"We've got the murder weapon, but I'm sure the killer wiped it clean," she said.

"You're right, but there could be prints or DNA traces on both the magazine and the cartridges. We'll be test-firing the gun as well. And Embla . . ."

He paused, looking intently at her over his mask.

". . . when we speak to Andreas Acika, not a word about what we've found in here."

WHEN ANDREAS ACIKA opened the door, he immediately said it was a bad time because he and his wife were busy putting the children to bed. Göran offered to drive him down to Police HQ instead, but he didn't seem too keen on that suggestion and reluctantly let them in.

"Is this apartment as big as Milo's?" Göran asked.

"No, less than half the size," Andreas answered curtly.

Göran tripped over a pair of small plastic skis, but managed to regain his balance. Beside them was a sled, propped up against the wall. It wasn't hard to work out why there was a large rubber mat just inside the door, protecting the red-and-white floral-patterned carpet from pools of melted slush. Two snowsuits and two pairs of children's boots had been dumped on the floor.

"The boys went to Slottsskogen Park while in day care," Andreas explained.

"How old are they?" Embla asked.

"Four and two."

He'd taken off his jacket and tie, and his slim-fitting white shirt revealed a slender, toned body.

They could hear a woman's voice from another room; it sounded as if she was reading aloud.

A boy called out: "Daddy!" Immediately another eager voice joined in: "Daddy, story!"

Andreas turned to them with a forced smile. "Perhaps you'd like to wait in my study while I put the boys to bed."

He led them through a modern kitchen and into a compact room that likely would have provided accommodation for a maid in the past. Andreas nodded in the direction of a small sofa bed along one wall.

"Please sit down. I'll be back soon."

They obediently did as they were told, but as soon as his footsteps had faded away, they both stood up. Silently and efficiently they searched the room. If you don't have the necessary warrant from the prosecutor, it's important not to get caught. The study had been furnished cleverly, making it functional even though it wasn't large. The style was as far from Milo's passion for Olde England as it was possible to get. A black desk stood below the window, with a two-drawer filing cabinet on wheels tucked beneath it. On the desk itself was a laptop connected to a larger monitor and a laser printer. A modern LED lamp provided the lighting; it was designed to resemble an inverted L resting on a base. The desk chair was ergonomic. The window overlooked the courtyard, and on the sill were several thriving potted plants and a colorful glass paperweight. Simple shelving covered one wall, housing books and folders. The books seemed to be mainly related to economics and law, which made Embla yawn. Then again, maybe she was yawning because it had been a long day.

There was nothing out of the ordinary; they were in a practical home office. They heard footsteps approaching; time to sit down again.

"The boys have been out all day; they're having trouble winding down," Andreas said apologetically when he reappeared. He wheeled the desk chair over to the sofa and sat down opposite them. "How can I help?" His thin smile didn't reach his eyes.

Göran smiled back and said pleasantly, "We realize things must be difficult for you at the moment, with the death of your cousins and the implications for Milo's business affairs. I assume you'll be dealing with most matters from now on?"

Andreas grimaced slightly and shrugged.

"Yes, there's a great deal to do, and some confusion, but I'm doing my best to keep things on track. And of course there are managers, boards, and legal advisers who can step in until . . . until we know what's going to happen."

Both Göran and Embla noticed the brief pause, but the superintendent simply nodded to show that he understood the situation and sympathized.

"First of all, can I ask if you have the code for the safe in Milo's apartment?"

"No, that's his personal safe."

"Okay—maybe you have some of his papers down here? You mentioned that you also have a safe."

"It's in our walk-in closet, and it contains only our personal effects."

Sharpening his tone, Göran said: "But there must be a safe containing Milo's business papers?"

"Some documentation will be at the office in Gårda, but Milo deposited his paperwork in various locations—with his lawyers, with the banks, and so on. And I can assure you that everything is above board. We've never had any problems with our tax filings," Acika said firmly, unmoved by the change in Göran's attitude.

They clearly weren't going to get any further, so Göran tried another tack.

"Did Milo tell you why he was going to northern Dalsland?"

Andreas shook his head. "No, he just said he'd be away for the weekend. Sometimes he could be a little secretive, and it wasn't my place to ask. Actually I thought he was traveling down to Split. I'm sure you're aware that Kador and his family disappeared two weeks ago."

"We are. So Milo told you nothing about his plans?"

"No."

The response was firm and emphatic. Göran shifted position on the sofa, and Embla knew that meant a change of direction in his questioning.

"How long have you worked for Milo?"

"Ten years."

Göran looked at the other man appraisingly. "So you must have been very young when you started."

For a second a weary expression came over Andreas's face, but he quickly pulled himself together. "It was my first job after I graduated from the School of Business at Gothenburg University."

"So you're a Business Administration and Economics graduate?"

"Yes. It wasn't easy to find a job, so when Milo made an offer I had to say yes."

"Was your apartment a part of the package?"

Andreas hesitated briefly. "No, I wasn't married back then. When Kristina and I got together, we bought a two-room apartment in Guldheden. Milo acquired this place at the same time, but then he changed his mind. He felt it was too small and decided to sell it before he'd even moved in. Luca didn't want it. Then Milo found out that the housing committee were intending to put the whole of the top floor on the market; all the permits were in place. So he made them an offer and built exactly the apartment he wanted."

"And does he still own this apartment?"

"In a way. It actually belongs to one of our property companies, and I rent it from them. As Milo does . . . did with his."

Göran nodded once again.

"You said earlier that you and Milo are cousins, but you also said you were born in Gothenburg. Milo was born in Croatia—what's the family setup, if you don't mind my asking?"

"Kador and Luca are my cousins. My mother and their father, Ivan Stavic, were brother and sister. Which means my uncle Ivan was Milo's stepfather."

"So you and Milo don't share any blood ties."

Andreas merely shrugged once more, as if to say that this was irrelevant.

"I need to ask about your gold watch. Where did you get it?"

Andreas pulled up his shirt sleeve so that they could see the watch more clearly. There was a sparkling diamond at each digit, and the hands were studded with tiny diamonds. There was a lot of gold, not least in the bracelet. It looked heavy and very expensive.

"It was a gift from Milo for my thirtieth birthday. It's a limited edition; there are only four like this. He gave one to Kador, one to Luca, one to me, and he kept one for himself. I don't usually wear it, but I wanted to . . . honor him." He quickly pulled down his sleeve, as if to indicate that the conversation about the watch was over.

"I'm asking because we know that Milo was wearing his watch when he checked into the guesthouse. The owners noticed it, because it's so striking."

"Exactly. That's why I usually save it for special occasions."

Göran tilted his head to one side, his eyes fixed on Andreas.

"What family do you have here in Gothenburg?"

"What's that got to do with Milo?" Andreas's eyes narrowed, and he frowned. "I have my wife and my two sons."

"No siblings?"

An innocent question, but Embla had a feeling that Göran already knew the answer. It took a while, but eventually Andreas spoke.

"Jiri."

Göran raised his eyebrows.

"Jiri Acika? I recognize that name. Is he still in Gothenburg?"

Andreas's jaw tightened.

"No. He moved to Croatia after . . . after he got out of jail."

"I see. And when was this?"

Göran sounded as if he had no idea, but neither Embla nor Andreas were under any illusions.

"Five years ago."

Göran leaned back and contemplated the man opposite, who was clearly not happy with the turn the conversation had taken. "If I remember correctly, he was sent down for homicide."

Andreas swallowed several times before he was able to answer.

"Yes. He was attacked and shot his assailant in self-defense." He took a deep breath. "It was an altercation between two youth gangs," he added.

"But he was convicted of murder," Göran pointed out calmly.

"Yes," Andreas conceded, pressing his lips together in a thin line.

"How is he now?" Göran looked genuinely interested.

Andreas shifted uncomfortably on his chair and gave Embla a quick glance. "Okay, Jiri took a wrong turn. But he came to realize a number of things while he was behind bars, so as soon as he was released he went down to Split and started work in a relative's restaurant. He's done really well. He's married now, with a three-year-old daughter."

"This relative—was it Kador?"

Andreas looked genuinely surprised.

"Kador? No, it was another uncle—my mother's older brother. He and his wife have no children of their own, so he's kind of taken Jiri under his wing."

"And where's your father?"

A shadow passed across Andreas's handsome face. "He died in the civil war."

"Did he go back to Croatia to fight?"

A deep sigh. "No. My parents divorced several years before the war broke out. He stayed in Split and she came over here to join her brother Ivan. Jiri was only little; I was born a few months later."

"So she left her husband even though she was pregnant."

"Yes. My father was a violent man."

"Did you ever meet him?"

"No. My mother couldn't go back. He'd threatened to kill both her and us if he got the chance."

He stopped speaking and looked over toward the door. Footsteps approached from the kitchen, and a beautiful woman with long dark hair appeared. She gazed at them warily without saying a word. A dark red-dress clung to her body; she was heavily pregnant.

SNOWFLAKES WERE STILL drifting down when they emerged onto the street, but not heavily enough to envelop Gothenburg in a white winter blanket. The flakes would simply merge with the mush already lying on the streets. The temperature had begun to rise, and according to the weather forecast it would be even warmer tomorrow. The inner city squares and sidewalks would be covered in slush and water. At least there had been enough snow to allow the kids to go sledding in Slottsskogen Park for a few days. The winter had been unusually mild until the first week in February, just in time for the spring break.

Dalsland, however, had had a proper winter, and Embla was glad that Elliot had been able to experience it. There was a danger that the memory of the fox hunt would overshadow all the fun things they'd done, but she suspected he'd turn the story of the hunt into a real adventure when he saw his friends again.

They plodded to the car, congratulating themselves on having parked right in front of the building. They got in and Embla turned to Göran. She knew him well, and was sure he'd acquainted himself with all the available facts in advance, just to see how honest Andreas Acika was.

"Did he lie about anything?" she asked.

"Not exactly, but I thought he was evasive when it came to who's going to take over Milo's various business interests. Milo must have chosen a crown prince; his work involved considerable risks and a high mortality rate. I'd have expected it to be one or both of his brothers, given that he didn't have any children."

"But now Luca's dead and Kador is missing."

The ensuing silence was interrupted by the loud rumbling of a stomach; Embla realized it was hers.

"It's after eight; we need something to eat before we head over to Luca's apartment," Göran decided.

"Have you got keys?"

He rummaged around in his pockets, dug out a bunch of keys, and shook them. Embla saw a tag like the one that had opened the elevator door to Milo's apartment.

"Indeed I have. Luca's keys were in his coat pocket."

"Are there any spares?"

"Yes. When the staff at the nightclub were questioned, Luca's assistant said that Luca had put a couple of spare keys in the safe in case he lost his own—apparently that had happened once. They checked, and the spare bunch was there."

"So he had his own keys on him. Has his phone been found?"

"No."

Milo's cell had also been missing from the cottage after his death.

"Something tells me we're not going to find Luca's phone or his computer in his apartment."

"Something tells me you're right," Göran agreed with a sigh.

They'd reached the T-junction at Läraregatan. He pointed to the right.

"Head down to Södra vägen. There are some decent Italian places there."

AFTER THEY'D EACH eaten a filling plate of pasta—with frutti di mare sauce for Embla, Bolognese for Göran—they drove over Älvsborg Bridge and on toward Eriksberg. They found a parking space on Östra Eriksbergsgatan, right outside Luca's apartment. The block was pretty new, like most of the other buildings in the area. The façade was red brick, with large windows and generous balconies overlooking the Göta River.

They hauled their bags over to the door. Göran tried all three keys before finding the right one. In the elevator they discovered there was a lock instead of a button for the top floor. Göran frowned.

"I wonder if Milo was responsible for the security locks, or if they were here from the start," he said. He inserted the right key in the lock and the elevator whisked them up to the penthouse. The heavy steel doors didn't open until he pressed the tag against a plate to the side.

"Looks like Milo's signature to me," Embla said.

As she stepped out of the elevator, all the lights came on. An alarm began to beep, but Göran pressed the tag against the symbol above the rows of buttons, and the beeping stopped.

The apartment was open plan, with an ultramodern kitchen to one side: dark-gray cupboards, white marble counter tops, a white oval table with thin steel legs, white wooden chairs with black leather seats. Beyond the

kitchen lay the living room, with an inviting sofa upholstered in red and four black leather Jetson armchairs. On
the floor was a rug that looked like a gigantic zebra skin,
which was exactly what it turned out to be; several skins
had been stitched together. The art on the walls was
modern. Glass sliding doors led onto a roof terrace, with
two abstract bronze statues on granite plinths on either
side of the doors. Embla had no idea what they were supposed to represent.

They could see all this from their position just inside
the front door. The hallway consisted only of a black
coconut mat and a black coatrack on a white marble
base, plus a closet with three mirrored sliding doors. They
put on their protective clothing, ready to start work.

To the left was a closed door, to the right two open
doors. Göran signaled that he would take the right.

Embla opened the left-hand door and found herself in
a bedroom. A large round bed stood in the middle of the
floor with black silk sheets and pillowcases. A white silk
duvet was neatly folded at the foot. Just as in Milo's bedroom, there was a huge TV screen on the wall opposite.

Glass double doors led out onto the terrace. The view
was spectacular; Embla could see the lights of Majorna
and Masthugget reflected in the Göta River. A Stena
Line ferry was on its way to the quayside and tooted its
horn several times as it passed beneath the Älvsborg
Bridge.

No one could see into the apartment; it was high
above the surrounding buildings.

Over by the glass doors was an attractive reading
chair made of black leather and natural-colored canvas,
along with a floor lamp resembling a UFO that had

crash-landed and a small white marble table with a pile of books on top. Everything was very smart and elegant. What caught Embla's attention were three drawings displayed on one wall.

All three featured muscular young men. One was in motorcycle leathers, one was leaning on a car lighting a cigarette while being serviced by a sailor on his knees. The third was looking at the observer from beneath half-closed eyelids. All three had their pants unzipped, and were equipped with unnaturally large sexual organs. *Approximately the size of a baguette*, Embla thought. She recognized the style; her brother Frej had a very similar picture. It had been a gift from an ex-boyfriend, and he loved it. He'd told her all about it once when she'd visited him in Stockholm. The artist had called himself Tom of Finland because that was where he came from. He didn't dare reveal his real name for fear of ending up in jail or in a mental institution for "spreading homosexual perversion." His art became a significant influence within gay culture. His major breakthrough came in the USA in the late 1970s. He died many years ago, but his art lives on and has achieved cult status.

If these drawings were originals, they were worth a fortune.

Embla crossed the room to the opposite wall. One door led to a bathroom, the other to a walk-in closet.

The design and layout of the bedroom reminded her strongly of Milo's on Terrassgatan. Had he had a hand in this apartment, too?

The bathroom provided even more evidence of Milo's involvement, or at least that of his interior designer. In one corner stood a large jacuzzi, screened from the shower and toilet by frosted glass. Black tiles on the floor, white tiles with a dusting of silver on the walls.

She moved on to the walk-in closet; again, it was almost identical to the one on Terrassgatan, although the wood was darker. The clothes, however, were as far from Milo's formal suits and shirts as it was possible to get. Admittedly there were a number of suits, but in a range of styles and colors. Luca must have had at least as many shoes as his half-brother; they were exclusive brands, a perfect match for his clothing.

There was a safe with a combination lock in one corner; it measured approximately seventy centimeters by fifty centimeters. She tried the door, but as she expected, it was locked. Above the safe was a tall mirror; there was another on the inside of the closet door, which meant it was possible to see oneself from the back. Smart and well-planned, just like everything else in this apartment.

She decided to start with the bottom drawer. It was filled with sports socks; she spent a long time pressing and tapping on the base, but to her disappointment there was no hidden compartment. Methodically, she searched the other drawers but found nothing of interest. There were a few sex toys, but they weren't particularly noteworthy.

She went back into the bedroom, convinced she'd missed something. She gazed at the drawings. She'd seen nothing to indicate that more than one person lived there. That didn't mean Luca never had company, but there was no evidence of anyone else's presence.

Göran appeared in the doorway. "Any luck?"

"No, but there's no doubt about Luca's sexual preferences," Embla said, pointing to the drawings.

Göran came over to join her. "Hmm—you're right. No straight guy would have something like this in his bedroom."

Embla was about to say *Why not?* but stopped herself just in time. The stereotypical images could be interpreted as an ironic comment on the male ideal, with the ever-potent giant cock at the ready, but there was no doubt that men were the objects of these erotic fantasies.

Once again Lollo came to her mind. Luca was the guy she'd fallen madly in love with. Had he already been living as a gay man back then and had simply pretended to be in love with her in order to lure her into . . . what? Prostitution, trafficking, drug smuggling . . . there were so many criminal activities that a young girl could be drawn into. It was a horrible thought, and she pushed it away.

Göran glanced around the room. "Any sign of a computer?"

"No, but there's a safe in the closet. Locked, of course."

Göran went to take a look. He stared at the safe for a moment, then he leaned forward and gently moved the mirror to one side. There was a small piece of paper stuck to the wall with a series of numbers on it: 1-1-9-8-5-6-1.

"Bingo!" he exclaimed for the second time that evening.

Why didn't I think of looking behind the mirror? Embla thought crossly.

"People always do this; they keep their codes and passwords close to the thing that's supposed to be protected. Dumb, but human," he said as he began to key in the digits. The door opened with a loud click.

Embla couldn't see what was inside because Göran's broad back was in the way. Impatiently, she waited for him to move, but he remained in the same position, crouching down in front of the safe. Eventually she'd had enough.

"Anything interesting?"

He straightened up with a groan, his knees protesting at the strain.

"See for yourself."

Embla stepped forward and peered curiously into the safe. Nothing on the top shelf apart from a few large envelopes and plastic folders. There were several boxes on the middle shelf; the smaller ones looked as if they contained cufflinks and jewelry, while the four larger ones bore the names of designer watches. She opened the box marked ROLEX and found Luca's cupcake watch. Carefully she lifted it out and turned it over; the letters *LS* were engraved on the back. She replaced it and returned the box to the shelf. As she did so, it felt as if there were something soft behind it. She bent down and took a closer look. She saw three plastic bags containing white powder.

"Coke," she said.

Göran crouched down again with another groan.

"Probably, although it could be amphetamine; the bags are bigger than the usual portions of cocaine. We'll test the contents. But the bottom shelf is even more interesting."

Embla realized what he meant. On top of a thin blue velvet cushion lay two spare magazines of the same type as they'd found in Milo's drawer. There was no sign of a gun.

IT WAS ALMOST midnight by the time Embla crawled into her own bed after a quick shower. She was so exhausted that her whole body was aching. Göran had been tired, too, but excited at the discovery of the ammunition. He was going to check out the weapon ID on the Beretta they'd found in the cottage where Milo was shot, and he was also going to see if Luca had been issued a firearms license. Then the gun from Herremark would be tested and the cartridges compared with those that had killed the Stavic brothers. Tomorrow would be a busy day for Göran.

"Why don't you sleep in?" he'd said. "You've worked all weekend, and you weren't even supposed to be on duty."

With a clear conscience, Embla decided not to set the alarm. She began to relax. Her arms and legs felt heavy, her eyelids closed. Slowly sleep crept up on her.

Then her phone rang.

She grabbed it from the nightstand and looked at the display: Olle Tillman. Should she ignore it? Best not; it might be something important.

"Hi, Olle. I need my beauty sleep, you know," she said in a weary attempt at a joke.

"Hi—oh, I'm sorry, I didn't realize it was so late. Tore

and I just got home." At least he had the sense to sound apologetic. "And no, you don't need your beauty sleep—you already look pretty good to me," he added with a laugh.

Flattery is always welcome, she thought with satisfaction. He must have had a good day.

"I'll keep it short. After you called me, Tore and I went to the Lodge. Just as you'd suggested, we searched for an area behind the building where someone could have hidden a knife. And I found it. The knife had been pushed behind an electricity meter box on the wall. It's a large hunting knife, like you said."

This was good news. It wasn't surprising that the police dogs hadn't sniffed it out earlier, because there had been so much blood at the scene, plus the scents of all the people wandering around in the snow after the murder. A weapon halfway up a wall behind a metal box could hardly be expected to compete with all those other smells.

"Was it Tore who found it?" she asked.

"No, it was me. It was about two and a half meters off the ground. And before you ask, yes, I did remember to put on my latex gloves, and I managed to get it into an evidence bag without smudging any prints."

Had she been too hard on him at the crime scene in the cottage?

"Great," she said lamely.

"I know. Then I went to see Mikaela, and you were right again—she and Wille have identical tattoos. Hers is just below the collarbone, and his is on the underside of his upper right arm."

"A heart and a rose with a circle in the center. There

are two letters inside the circle—not two Ms with one upside down, as I first thought, but *MW*," Embla said. She was beginning to feel more awake now; this was good news, and it was always satisfying to be right.

"Exactly. They were together for almost a year. They got the tattoos last summer, when they were crazy about each other. But something went wrong over Christmas and Mikaela broke it off. Wille was *like totally devastated*, of course."

Olle's imitation of Mikaela's dramatic tone was spot-on, and Embla couldn't help laughing out loud. Then she pulled herself together and tried to sound serious.

"Has anyone spoken to Wille yet?"

"No, but we'll be bringing him into the station tomorrow. One of the inspectors from Trollhättan is going to interview him. Her name's Paula Nilsson—she said she knows you."

"Yes, we met in Strömstad a few weeks ago. She and Göran Krantz are an item, although they haven't been together long. She's good at talking to kids and teenagers—she has three of her own."

"A police mom. Wille doesn't stand a chance."

Embla laughed, then grew serious again. "Did Mikaela realize she was dumping her ex-boyfriend in the shit?"

"No, she's far too self-absorbed. She was perfectly happy to show me the tattoo. And a little more besides."

Why did she feel a pang of . . . what? Jealousy? The fact that a curvaceous young girl had taken the opportunity to flash her breasts at the best-looking cop in Dalsland shouldn't bother her at all. But it did, she realized.

"I have to say, well done, Olle!"

"Thank you. I'll call you tomorrow evening and let you know how the interview with Wille goes."

"Do that. Good night!"

"Sleep well, Embla."

With a contented smile on her lips, she put her phone back on the nightstand. It seemed likely that the investigation into Robin Pettersson's murder had reached its conclusion, and she had made a valuable contribution.

Well done, Nyström.

Now she was wide awake, of course.

THE OPENING BARS of the original 1977 *Star Wars* soundtrack woke her. It took her a few seconds to locate her phone.

"Embla," she said, still only half-awake.

"Good morning. I hope you've slept well and are raring to go. I need you here."

Göran sounded as if he'd had the weekend off and had slept for at least ten hours the previous night, while Embla felt as if she'd been fed through an old-fashioned mangle. It had taken her over an hour to nod off after her conversation with Olle. He was sweet and funny, and there was definitely chemistry between them. She'd felt it during their dinner at the guesthouse, which had been more like a successful date than anything else.

Her thoughts had gone around and around, keeping her awake, but eventually her sleep had been deep and dreamless, with no nightmares to torment her. She had to admit that ever since Milo Stavic's murder, she'd slept better than she had for many years. Fourteen and a half years, to be precise.

Gradually, she began to come to life. She made a brave attempt to sound more alert than she actually was.

"Has something happened?"

"Yes, it has to do with Kador. I have a Skype call booked with Boris Cetinski at nine. He has interesting news that could have a bearing on our investigation."

Embla was wide awake now. "I'm on my way!"

THE TEMPERATURE HAD definitely risen, and the snow had already melted. A bitterly cold wind came off the sea and howled through the streets. Embla jumped into the Kia, which obligingly started immediately. She'd been in luck last night and had found a parking space right outside the door of her apartment building, which was unusual. Her mother, Sonja, an active member of the Green Party, always said that fit and healthy people who live in cities shouldn't have cars, but with Embla's job it was essential.

SHE WASN'T SURPRISED to find Göran by the coffee machine. He offered her a cup of tea, but she declined. She'd eaten a sandwich in the car and washed it down with a bottle of tepid Ramlösa mineral water she'd found in the pantry.

Göran might have sounded bright and breezy on the phone, but the bags under his eyes gave him away—he hadn't slept much either. After leaving Luca's apartment, he'd gone straight to the lab to check the spare magazines for fingerprints. He hadn't found any on the Beretta that had been used to shoot Milo, but he was still hoping for something on the cartridges in the gun—DNA in the best-case scenario. To reduce the risk of any errors, he'd asked one of their forensic technicians, a specialist in DNA samples, to carry out the tests. She'd promised to get it done the following day if she possibly could.

Göran had already prepared his office for the Skype call by placing a chair next to his own shabby desk chair. He sat down in front of the computer and signaled to Embla to join him.

The screen flickered, and they were able to make out a man removing a large captain's hat. The images on Skype are always slightly distorted, but Embla could see that Chief of Police Boris Cetinski didn't look at all as she'd expected. Unconsciously she'd pictured a man not unlike Milo Stavic, but instead she was confronted with sharp gray-blue eyes behind a pair of horn-rimmed glasses. Cetinski was about sixty, with well-defined features and a long, narrow face. His hair was thick and almost white, as was his small mustache. Embla thought he looked more like a philosophy professor than a police officer. There was so much gold braid on his collar that it was impossible to see the fabric of his uniform jacket.

Göran greeted his Croatian colleague and introduced himself in English. His reference to Embla as "Detective Inspector Embla Nyström, one of my closest men," made Cetinski raise one eyebrow, but he refrained from commenting. Instead he began to go through the new information that had emerged during the search for Kador Stavic and his family.

Early the previous day, a very agitated member of the public had contacted the police to say that the house he'd grown up in had burned down. It was in a remote area in the mountains to the north of Split, and there were no other properties nearby. The owner was very angry because he'd renovated the old place and turned it into a luxury summer cottage, and it seemed as if the fire had been started deliberately. He'd found several empty gas cans not far away. However, the main cause of his distress was that he'd also found the charred remains of a human body in the ruins.

The CSIs had gathered up what was left of the corpse, a blackened skeleton, and transported it to the lab in Zagreb. The police had contacted Kador's dentist in Split; apparently Kador had undergone extensive dental work a few years ago, and his dentist had been able to supply a number of X-rays.

In a few days they would know whether they'd found Kador Stavic; he was the only person who'd been reported missing over the past two weeks.

There was still no trace of his family. The police had gone through every list of people who'd left the area by train, boat, or plane. There was no record of a family with three children of the right ages having crossed the border. If they weren't in hiding in Croatia, they had probably left the country using false passports. The children could have been distributed between two or three adults. It would be nearly impossible to find them if they were traveling under false identities.

The Stavic house had been searched; Cetinski promised to scan and send over some photographs of Kador's wife and children. It was possible that the family would turn up in Sweden, particularly Gothenburg, since Kador's brothers had lived there. The police in Finland had already been contacted because Mirja Stavic, née Hervonen, had said that she came from Helsinki. Her family were allegedly Finland-Swedes who spoke Swedish. She'd told her neighbors that both parents had died in a car accident, and that she had no siblings. The

Helsinki police would contact Boris Cetinski if they managed to track down any of Mirja's living relatives.

On the subject of relatives, Milo had called Cetinski every single day to ask if there was any news on Kador and his family.

When Cetinski had finished, Göran took over and told him about the murders of Milo and Luca. Once again Cetinski raised an eyebrow. Göran filled him in on what the police knew so far; it was early days, but the two of them agreed to keep in touch. It couldn't be a coincidence that Kador and his family had disappeared just before his two brothers were murdered.

"Did you find a computer or cell phone in Kador's house?" Göran asked.

"No. We looked for those especially, but found nothing. Not even the kids' phones or laptops."

"It seems as if the computers are important."

"Yes—they must hold a lot of interesting information. I'll get those photographs to you right away. Goodbye."

"Thank you—we'll speak again soon. Bye."

In spite of the shaky picture, Embla thought she could see the hint of a smile lurking at the corners of Cetinski's mouth. When she turned and looked at her colleague, she could see why. With his uncombed hair standing on end, no tie, and the top two buttons of his shirt undone, Göran was as far from his smartly dressed and richly decorated counterpart as it was possible to get. She herself was wearing no makeup, her hair was piled in a messy bun, and she'd pulled on a faded green T-shirt that didn't exactly flatter her winter-pale skin. Boris Cetinski must have wondered about the dress code for the Swedish police service. The truth was there were strict guidelines in place; full uniform must always be worn in official situations. Maybe a Skype call could be classed as informal, but Embla wasn't convinced.

Göran couldn't have cared less, as he was rubbing his hands with glee. "Things are happening! But if the body in the summer cottage turns out to be Kador, that's the end of one of my theories. I thought Kador might have come to Sweden and killed his brothers."

"An internal power struggle."

"Exactly. But if he was murdered almost two weeks before Milo and Luca, that doesn't work."

Embla nodded. There was something nagging at her subconscious; suddenly she realized what it was, and that it could be important.

"Do you think the murder of the doorman and the attempt on Luca's life four years ago could be related?"

Göran looked as if he was about to answer, but he changed his mind. He thought for a moment, then nodded. "It might be worth taking another look at that shooting. We found a guy in the river a few weeks later; he was supposed to have been a hit man. I'll have a word with Violent Crimes and see what they know about him and if they can find any connection to Croatia and the Stavic brothers."

"I can do that," Embla offered. She had an ulterior motive; it would give her the chance to swing by her locker and change into a cornflower-blue top that suited her much better. She would also have time to brush her hair and put on some mascara. Even if you feel like a wrung-out dishrag, there's no need to look like one, as her mother used to say.

SHE QUICKLY CHANGED and freshened up with a quick spray of Clean Warm Cotton perfume. Feeling considerably more alert than when she'd entered the building an hour earlier, she swiped her card and headed down the hall to the Violent Crimes Unit, cheerfully greeting several colleagues on the way to her boss's door. She hesitated for a moment with her fist clenched in the air before knocking. Chief Inspector Tommy Persson was a good boss, but he had a hard time accepting that she was sometimes drawn into investigations that fell under the jurisdiction of her previous role with VGM. However, her involvement with the Stavic case was purely coincidental, she told herself firmly.

A voice yelled something that might have been "come in." She opened the door and Tommy peered at her over the top of his reading glasses. His desk was covered in piles of papers.

"Embla! We haven't seen much of you lately."

The tone was friendly, but there was no mistaking the underlying message. She pasted on a warm smile.

"Hi. Göran Krantz has asked me to pass on some new information that's come up in the Stavic brothers' homicides. It's possible that Kador, the third brother, is dead, too."

Tommy looked surprised. He waved a hand in the direction of the visitor's chair, inviting her to sit down.

Göran had already provided Violent Crimes with a full report on the murder of Milo Stavic, so she didn't need to go over old ground, and Tommy himself had led the investigation into Luca's death from the start. She began with the discovery of the narcotics during the search of Luca's apartment, then told him about the spare magazines they'd found in both apartments. She summarized the conversation with Boris Cetinski in Split, and finally brought up the possibility of a link between the attack on the doorman and Luca Stavic four years ago, and the current situation.

Tommy didn't interrupt her once. When she'd finished, he gazed thoughtfully at her for a long time.

"We'll definitely take another look at the shooting. I remember the guy we pulled out of the river turned out to be a well-known hit man; I don't recall his name, but we'll dig it out. He was from Yugoslavia."

Yugoslavia hadn't existed since the end of the Balkan War, but Embla didn't think Tommy would appreciate being corrected. She got to her feet, assuming he'd finished.

"Tell Göran I'd like a meeting with him later—after three suits me best. I'll text him," Tommy went on.

"I'll let him know." She headed for the door, but before she reached it, she heard his voice behind her.

"See you soon."

She half-turned and delivered a beaming knockout smile over her shoulder. Her psychologist friend Nicke would have described it as passive-aggressive, or something along those lines. Tommy was completely unprepared, and didn't know what to do with his face. He responded with a rather sheepish smile. It wasn't only in the boxing ring that her opponents went down for the count when Embla decided to go for it.

IF GÖRAN WASN'T at the coffee machine, he'd be sitting in front of his computer, and that was where she found him. She passed on Chief Inspector Persson's request for a meeting. He grunted something in response, but she had the feeling he wasn't really listening. It would probably be best to remind him later, even if Tommy had said he'd send a text.

"The photographs have arrived," Göran said, looking up from the screen and inviting her to join him.

She saw a dark-haired young man smiling at the camera. Clean, handsome features, white teeth, blue eyes framed by long eyelashes. She'd seen that face before—and yet she hadn't. The explanation lay in the text beneath: *Kador Stavic, age 27.* The picture was ten years old. It was the first time she'd seen a professional photograph of Kador. He was very like his younger brother, Luca, which was why he seemed so familiar.

The next picture was from a big wedding. It had been taken outdoors; the sun was shining and the bride's veil was fluttering in the breeze. Presumably Kador was the groom, but it was hard to tell because the happy couple was standing with their backs to the camera, sharing a toast with their guests. There were at least fifty people in attendance. The text was in English: *The wedding with Ms. Mirja Hervonen.* The date revealed that the event had taken place almost fifteen years ago, which meant that Kador had been twenty-two when he got married. According to the information they'd received from the police in Split, Mirja had just turned eighteen. A very young couple.

The third picture was a recently taken photo of the three children; it looked as if it might have been the family's Christmas card to friends and relatives. Miranda was twelve years old, Adam ten, and Julian six. The girl had her father's coloring, with long, straight hair and blue eyes. The studio lights made her dark hair shine like a soft mink coat. Her smile was a little restrained, as if she were trying to live up to the formality of the occasion. She was going to be a real beauty.

Adam was grinning at the camera, revealing several gaps where his baby teeth had fallen out. Blue eyes like his sister, but his dark-brown hair was curly and a little messy.

Julian also had blue eyes, but unlike his siblings, he was blond. His hair was curly, like his brother's. He was laughing at the photographer, showing the gap where two front teeth were missing on his lower jaw.

Where do you hide with three children of school age? Or had the murderer already found them and killed them? It was a terrible thought, because the children bore no responsibility for what their father and his brothers had done.

The last picture was of Kador and Mirja. A stylish bridegroom looking very proud. Mirja's head was tilted slightly, her Mona Lisa smile just like her daughter's. Restrained, dignified, a little mysterious.

The realization hit Embla hard, as if a horse had kicked her in the solar plexus. Breathe! She couldn't breathe! Her chest hurt, she could hear the pounding of her heartbeat in her ears. She heard Göran's voice in the distance, felt him touch her arm.

Then everything went black.

BLURRED FIGURES WERE bending over her. Was she in the hospital? Had she had surgery? Why was someone pressing a paper tissue to her forehead? It hurt. Had her eyebrow split open again? A blow . . . someone must have hit her hard. Out for the count. Or . . . ?

"Embla? Are you okay?"

She recognized the voice, but couldn't remember the guy's name. And why was she lying on the floor? It was cold against her back.

The faces became clearer. Göran. It was his voice she'd heard. His deputy, Sabina Amir. The two CSIs, Linda and Bengan. Why were they here? Instinctively she tried to push away the hand pressing the tissue against her eyebrow, but another hand gently seized her wrist.

"No, Embla. You hit your head on the corner of the desk when you fainted. It's bleeding quite badly."

Göran. What was he talking about? Had she fainted? Why? Slowly the memory of the wedding photograph came back to her.

She felt so dizzy that she had to concentrate hard in order to focus on Göran's eyes. Her lips were stiff and dry;

she licked them several times and finally managed to utter a few comprehensible words.

"The bride . . . it's not Mirja. It's Lollo. Louise Lindqvist. My friend who . . . disappeared."

He looked confused, then realized what she was trying to say.

"The girl in the picture is *Lollo*?"

"Yes."

He let out a low whistle. "I'm not surprised you fainted!"

Embla saw the other three exchange puzzled glances. Presumably Göran noticed, too, but he made no attempt to explain. Instead he took charge.

"Sabina, fetch the first aid kit—you know where it is. Linda, keep the pressure on that eyebrow. I'll call an ambulance."

"There's no need," Embla protested.

"There is—you've got a nasty gash."

Embla made a clumsy attempt to get to her feet, but the dizziness was too much for her and she sank back down.

"There's some surgical tape in my locker. My eyebrows are weak, especially the left one, because it's taken a lot of punishment. I've taped it up myself dozens of times," she said, trying to sound brighter than she felt.

Sabina Amir raised a perfectly shaped eyebrow.

"That explains a great deal," she said with the hint of a smile.

WITH SABINA'S HELP, Linda managed to clean and tape up the wound, which was smaller than expected given the amount of blood. However, when Embla tentatively touched the area around it, she knew it would swell significantly. Meanwhile Bengan had brought her a cup of tea from the machine. She took it gratefully; it was more or less tasteless, but at least it was hot and got her circulation going again.

Göran turned to the others. "Thanks for your help. Embla was shocked because a completely unexpected individual has turned up in our investigation with the Stavic brothers."

With a dramatic flourish he moved the screen and brought up the wedding picture.

"Kador's bride is not in fact Mirja Hervonen, a Finland-Swede. Her name is Louise Lindqvist, and she disappeared almost fifteen years ago. She and Embla grew up together. They lived in the same apartment block and were friends. Some time ago Embla told me about the trauma she still carries, all the unanswered questions about what really happened when Louise went missing."

He paused for effect before continuing.

"And now we have the answer to those questions. Louise ran away to Croatia with Kador Stavic and married him."

At first Embla almost panicked when Göran began to talk about her and Lollo, but her feelings changed to gratitude when she heard the version of her story he'd chosen to tell. Of course it was necessary for their colleagues to know about the relationship between her and Lollo; it would play a key role in the continuing investigation, and Embla wanted to make sure she was a part of that investigation.

Sabina looked at her, wide-eyed. "What a shock for you!"

As always, her makeup was flawless. She was wearing an emerald-green scarf around her neck, bringing out the green flecks in her honey-brown eyes. She had always reminded Embla of the famous bust of Queen Nefertiti. She was thirty-six, but looked younger. Many of their male colleagues had asked her out over the years, but she had always said no, pleasantly but firmly. As is the way with men who are frustrated, certain people began to spread the rumor that she was a lesbian, but there was nothing to suggest that this was the case. She was extremely competent and often worked overtime. You could say she was married to the job.

She and Linda and Bengan left Göran's office to resume the tasks that had been interrupted by Embla's collapse.

Embla sat down on the chair again and stared at the screen, hypnotized by the wedding photo. So many suppressed emotions came rushing to the surface—shame and guilt at not having been brave enough to tell the truth, at having let Lollo down. All the years of nightmares about what might have happened to Lollo, each scenario worse than the one before.

The reality was that Lollo had married only a few months later. She was due to turn fifteen a few weeks after she disappeared, which meant she was fifteen in the picture. Not eighteen, as the personal details held by the police in Split claimed. If you looked closely you could see that she looked very young, but of course many eighteen-year-olds can seem much younger than they are. Had she willingly gone with him and married him? Or did she not have a choice? Embla really wanted answers to all her questions. All she could see was that her childhood friend appeared to be blissfully happy.

"So she ran away with Kador."

The sound of her own voice brought her back to the moment. Had she said that out loud? Apparently she had because Göran was nodding.

"Possibly, but it's not so strange that you thought she was in love with Luca. He was closer in age to her."

Embla nodded toward the screen and swallowed hard a couple of times before she dared to trust her shaky voice.

"It was always Milo and Luca who were seen around. I never even thought about Kador. No one mentioned him. I didn't connect Lollo with . . ." Her voice failed her, and she tried to fight back the tears.

"We have to find her and the children—they could be in mortal danger," Göran said energetically. "And I need to contact Boris Cetinski again. This information puts things in a completely different light."

Embla glanced at him but couldn't speak.

"I think this is a classic gangster war, Embla. A take-over, clearing out the old guard. The Stavic brothers have been removed from the scene and the new gang is now running their well-established business empire. It's essential that we find Louise before they do. She might know who killed the brothers," Göran continued. He got to his feet and paced up and down the room, then stopped and stared at her, his expression grave.

"So that's why all the computers and cell phones are missing. They wanted to access secret information."

"What . . . What do you mean?"

"Coded email traffic. The dark net."

Of course she knew what the dark net was. The place where most criminal activity takes place these days, the place where child pornography is traded, along with other types of illegal sexual activity, drugs, passports, false documents, and even murder. Everything is for sale on the dark net, and communications are virtually impossible to trace.

"Why is it so hard to penetrate the dark net?" she asked.

The world of IT was one of Göran's areas of expertise, and she knew he'd explain it clearly.

"Ordinary search engines can't reach the encrypted network. You have to use a special piece of software, which is usually called Tor; this allows you to surf the net anonymously. You keep moving between different accessible servers until you reach the one you want to communicate with."

He paused to see if she was keeping up. No problems so far—she nodded to show that she understood.

"The really clever part is that each individual server knows only the latest link in the relay, a so-called node. The server also knows which node you're sending to, but that's it. No one knows the origin or final destination of the message. The trail can end anywhere. A year or so ago there was a retired couple in Varberg whose son had given them a secondhand computer so he could email them and vice versa, but they hardly ever used it. The operating system was old-fashioned and all the firewalls were out of date. Both necrophilia porn and several kilos of cocaine had been ordered via that computer." He sighed and shook his head.

"Were you able to find the person behind it?"

"No. It's impossible to find the original sender via logs or network surveillance unless they make an error along the way. All you can do is use Tor yourself to see if you can find that error."

The fact that the murderer, or murderers, had taken all the IT equipment but no valuables suddenly made sense. Although they might have helped themselves to Milo's eye-catching watch and Luca's pistol. The computers could contain damning evidence against one or more of the Stavic brothers' contacts, and of course if someone was planning to take over their empire, having access to their contact network would be extremely useful. Or maybe they already had that information and wanted to make sure it didn't end up in the hands of the police. "By the way, I've heard back about that call you got from Louise. It was made from a burner phone and can't be traced, but we know it came from central Gothenburg."

Embla felt her heart rate increase. "That means she's here. Maybe she needed protection? Why else would she contact me? If she wasn't in the country, I'm sure she wouldn't have bothered."

Göran nodded and began to scroll down his screen. Suddenly he stopped and pointed at the numbers.

"There. The night Kador disappeared there was a call from Mirja Stavic in Split to Milo in Gothenburg at one-fifteen. We don't know what she said because we didn't have a tap on his phone at the time. The conversation was short—only forty-three seconds. Immediately afterward there was a call from a burner phone in Gothenburg to a burner in the area around Split. An hour and a half later Kador's family left their home and went underground."

"So Milo organized the whole thing."

"I think so, yes."

A thought struck Embla. "Do we know if the children speak Swedish?"

"We have no information on that."

Since the Stavic brothers had been involved in trafficking for many years, Milo was probably familiar with various routes across European borders, and he'd also know how to provide Lollo and the children with new passports. The biggest challenge would be finding a place where they would feel safe. Where do you hide a woman with three children of school age who probably don't speak Swedish very well? The most logical thing would be to choose an area where they could blend in—a place where there are plenty of people from different ethnic backgrounds. If the children could speak Swedish, it would make it easier for them to start school. If not, things would be trickier.

Gothenburg is a segregated city, like most big cities these days. The family would stick out like a sore thumb in certain districts, while in others they wouldn't attract any attention at all.

"I think she's in one of the suburbs where there's a high density of immigrants," Embla said.

"You're right—if she's still in Gothenburg, that's the most-likely scenario. I'll speak to Tommy about it this afternoon, see if he can get someone to check recent school applications. The two eldest will have to be registered."

"And the six-year-old."

Embla knew this because she was the one who'd accompanied Elliot on his first day in the reception class, the obligatory year that's meant to prepare children for Year One.

"Oh really? My boys didn't start until they were seven."

Quite a lot has happened within the Swedish education system over the past eighteen years, Embla thought.

AFTER LUNCH EMBLA decided she'd fully recovered from the shock. There was a vague feeling inside
her, and it took her a while to identify it: relief. She was
so relieved that Lollo was alive and that she hadn't been
forced into prostitution or addiction. Judging by the photographs, she seemed to have had a good life with her
family in the beautiful city on the shore of the Adriatic.

Embla was basing her view of Split on what her parents had told her; they'd taken a bus trip around Croatia
four of five years earlier, and couldn't stop talking about
all the wonderful sights they'd seen. Her father had been
particularly enthusiastic about a national park called
Plitvice, with its spectacular waterfalls and emerald-
green lakes—and they'd walked straight into a brown
bear! This was always the highlight of his account, and
every time he was delighted when people gasped in horror. Embla's mother would whisper out of the corner of
her mouth that in fact it was the bear who'd been most
frightened, and gone lumbering off into the undergrowth.

Göran had spoken to Tommy Persson and passed on
the information that Kador's wife, Mirja, was in fact Louise Lindqvist, who had vanished fourteen and a half years
ago. He explained that they'd made this discovery by

pure chance because Embla had recognized her old friend in the wedding photo they'd received from the police in Split. Tommy immediately promised to give someone the task of digging out everything they had from the investigation into Louise's disappearance. Another officer would go through all recent applications to schools across the city and would check on new residents in various districts.

Finally Göran had told Tommy that he would contact Boris Cetinski again to discuss Mirja's real identity. He'd also arranged to meet Embla later for coffee and a debrief.

Embla glanced at her phone; two hours to go. She had received a text message from Elliot, excitedly telling her that he'd been picked for the football team and that his first training session was that afternoon. His friend Love's mom was giving them a ride, and he was looking forward to wearing the cleats Embla had given him for Christmas.

She'd also missed a call from Harald in Herremark; she'd had her phone on silent during the Skype call with Boris Cetinski, and had forgotten to switch it back on. She went into the office she shared with Irene Huss; as usual, her colleague was out and about. It had been almost two hours since Harald had called; he must be wondering why she hadn't been in touch. He answered almost immediately.

"Embla! I've found something in the cottage where that man was murdered, although I don't know if it's important."

Since the cottage had been thoroughly examined by the CSIs, it seemed highly unlikely that anything significant could have been missed, but she didn't want to rain on Harald's parade.

"Sounds exciting—tell me more."

"I went down to make sure the place had been cleaned properly, and I noticed that the cleaner had put the pack of tourist information in the wrong place. When I picked it up to move it, I realized that one of the maps hadn't been folded correctly. I took it out to fix it, and that's when I made the discovery."

He fell silent, unsure whether he was simply wasting police time.

"Go on," Embla said encouragingly.

"An area about twenty kilometers from here was clearly marked on the map—heading west toward the Norwegian border. It's in the middle of nowhere. Monika and I have gone out there to pick lingonberries a few times, so I know it's more or less a wilderness."

Weird. Why would Milo mark a place like that?

"Are you sure it was Milo who made the mark?"

"It must have been. The day he called up to make the reservation I put brand-new maps in the pack."

This could be interesting. No other guest had had access to the new maps. It was certainly worth following up, even if it might not be top priority right now.

"Could you scan the map, or fax it to me?"

"We got rid of the fax a few years ago. Out here in the sticks we have to keep up with the latest developments, you know—I'll scan it and send it to you," he said, clearly amused by her preconceptions.

"Fantastic!"

She gave him her email address, ended the call, and waited by the printer. After a couple of minutes the map arrived, split over two sheets. The first was the flyleaf, with a yellow map on a blue background showing the whole of Dalsland. The northern section was in a darker yellow. The text read: *Welcome to northern Dalsland and the municipalities of Dals-Ed and Bengtsfors*. On the second sheet was an enlarged map of that area; she studied it closely.

Ed lies at the southern end of Lake Stora Le, while Bengtsfors is at the southern end of Lake Lelång. The two lakes are long and narrow, running north to south, almost parallel until they meet at the northern end. In the summer it's sheer paradise for canoeists. The area between the lakes is very sparsely populated, as is the region to the west of Stora Le. The first real settlement is Halden, thirty kilometers across the border in Norway.

Milo had made a mark high up on the western side of Stora Le, no more than a kilometer from the border, and about six kilometers south of a place called Strand. Between the mark and Strand there was a small lake, Ulvsjön.

Embla went into Google Maps and zoomed in. All she could see was a narrow dirt road that cut through the spot that appeared to be marked, then continued into Norway. There are countless similar roads along the Swedish–Norwegian border; why had Milo picked that one in particular? It came off the road that runs all the way down the western side of Stora Le. She could see a small house with several outbuildings, but Milo's mark was nearer the dirt road than the house.

Time to contact Uncle Nisse.

As always he sounded happy to hear from her. He probably got lonely sometimes, even though he insisted he never wanted to move. When Embla explained why she was calling, he asked her to wait while he fetched his own map from the Land Registration Authority.

"The fact is, that place doesn't actually have a name," he said when he returned. "People probably just call it 'the dirt road south of Ulvsjön.' As you can see, it continues into Norway; it could have been used during the war to smuggle people and essential goods, but those who live on either side of the border have been using these little roads and tracks for hundreds of years. Of course, these days it's easier to drive up to Strand, then follow the main road to Halden."

Which didn't explain why Milo had marked it on the map. Or had he? Maybe he'd just dropped his pen while he was looking at the map? It wasn't a proper cross, after all. They carried on chatting for a while, then Embla said she had to get back to work. It was almost time for her meeting with Göran.

THE SUPERINTENDENT WAS already at his desk with a cup of coffee and a Mazarin cake. Embla put down her hot water and dropped in a bag of lemon-scented green tea. As usual Göran wrinkled his nose as he watched the contents of her mug turn yellowish-green and couldn't help asking if she'd like something to go with it.

"My treat," he offered.

As always, she replied, "No thanks."

With a resigned shrug of his broad shoulders, he began to unwrap the Mazarin. He demolished half of it in one bite, chomping contentedly before washing it down with a swig of sweet black coffee. While he was eating, Embla took the opportunity to tell him about Harald's discovery. Nods and small grunts told her that he was interested, but he didn't speak until he'd polished off the whole cake.

"I think you should have a chat with your cop in Åmål. What was his name again . . . Olle?"

Your cop? She nearly objected to the choice of words, but Göran had already moved onto something else.

"We have another Skype call booked with Boris Cetinski in twenty minutes. He emailed me after lunch to say he has new information."

So it was time to communicate with the operetta-general again. Although that wasn't entirely fair; his attitude had been friendly and entirely appropriate. It was just his blinged-out uniform that had been slightly over the top.

No one could accuse Göran of such a thing. A critical appraisal confirmed her impression that he'd neither combed his hair nor changed his shirt since the previous day. His face had a grayish tone in the harsh lighting, which also revealed a significant growth of stubble.

"Do you have a uniform jacket in your locker?"

Her question took him by surprise. "Probably . . ."

"Me too. In which case I suggest we smarten ourselves up. Make ourselves look a little more official. Wash our faces, comb our hair, put on our uniform shirts and jackets."

At first he looked as if he was about to protest, but then he got to his feet.

"To the locker room! Reconvene in fifteen minutes!"

Embla stood up and executed an almost perfect salute. Maybe Olle was having more of an influence than she'd thought.

IT SEEMED THAT Göran also kept his shaving gear and deodorant in his locker. He reappeared after fifteen minutes, freshly shaved, hair neatly combed, wearing a clean shirt and uniform jacket. Embla was impressed. He'd even dug out a slightly wrinkled tie.

He pointed to his non-uniform pants. "Unfortunately my uniform pants appear to have shrunk in my locker," he said apologetically. "But the jacket's fine. As long as I don't button it."

The top button of his shirt wasn't done up either, but his tie hid it pretty well.

Embla had neatly braided her hair and applied a little mascara and lip gloss. She was still wearing jeans, but her shirt, tie, and jacket were immaculate. She knew she looked good in uniform. She thought about the surgical tape on her eyebrow. There wasn't much she could do about that. She would just have to try to keep the left side of her face off camera, which shouldn't be too difficult since she was already sitting on Göran's left. She moved the right side of her chair forward a bit.

"No one can see our pants on Skype," she said, and they exchanged a smile of mutual understanding.

They settled down just as the call came through. Boris Cetinski looked exactly the same as he had earlier. They all said hello, then Cetinski began.

"A few hours after we spoke this morning, I got an email from the police in Helsinki. They've found Mirja Hervonen—the personal ID number fits. Unfortunately little Mirja died of leukemia twenty-nine years ago, at the age of three."

Embla thought her green tea was going to come back up again, but with a huge effort of will, she managed to suppress the nausea. She had been living with the trauma for so long. However, she was now struggling with something new: a sense of betrayal. Her so-called best friend had deliberately gotten her to play along, while she had been planning to disappear with Kador all along. Why? Wouldn't it have been easier if she'd simply slipped away? But that hadn't been Lollo's style. She'd always been a drama queen who liked an audience.

"Embla?"

Göran's whisper brought her back to the moment. She mumbled "sorry" and tried to concentrate. He glanced at her, but said nothing. Instead he continued his conversation with Cetinski.

"It's good to have confirmation that she's been living under a false identity. In fact, through pure coincidence, we've found out that Mirja Stavic is in fact Louise Lindqvist, who went missing in Gothenburg almost fifteen years ago. Someone recognized her from the wedding photo you sent."

Cetinski raised a bushy eyebrow, but to Embla's relief he didn't ask for more details. Instead he cleared his throat and continued.

"Good work. And I can tell you that the skeleton found in the remains of the fire is definitely that of Kador Stavic. The height matches, plus he broke his right forearm in a fall eleven years ago, and the healed fracture is clearly visible. He broke three teeth in his upper jaw and two in his lower jaw on the same occasion, and his dentist here in Split made two ceramic bridges, which were still in place. Apparently ceramic dentistry withstands heat pretty well."

So there was no doubt that Kador had died in the fire.

Or was he already dead when someone set fire to the cottage?

After promising to keep each other updated on any progress in the investigation, they ended the call.

Göran leaned back and loosened his tie.

"As I said, there goes my theory that Kador was behind the deaths of his brothers. Time for a rethink."

Embla was lost in thought again. Lollo was now a widow with three school-age children. The most natural thing for a woman in her situation would be to turn to her family, but she had no family left in Sweden now that her brothers-in-law, Milo and Luca, were gone. On the other hand, Milo had been rich and influential and had probably helped her and the children to flee. But didn't the brothers have any relatives left in Croatia?

"Why didn't Lollo stay in Split and seek refuge with Kador's relations?" she said.

Göran gazed at her, drumming his fingers on the desk. "The only explanation I can come up with is that she knew the family was under threat. Maybe she wasn't sure who she could trust."

"You're probably right."

"Anything else on your mind?"

"Mmm. According to Cetinski, Kador was a ladies' man, and guys like that tend to stay out late—often well into the night. Why would she be worried if he didn't get home on time?"

She didn't mention her own experience of living with a Casanova. Jason had frequently stayed out all night.

"That's true, and yet she reacted right away. She contacted Milo within an hour of the time Kador should have been back," Göran agreed.

"Which suggests she was expecting something to happen to him."

Göran nodded, his expression serious. "Yes—and she knew exactly what to do. I wonder if she'd had some indication of what was going on."

The silence that descended on the room felt heavy. Embla thought the air was throbbing, then she realized it was her own heartbeat pulsating in her ears. She took a few deep breaths in an effort to calm down, which helped a little. She tried to focus on the facts. After a while, Göran spoke.

"If she was involved in Kador's murder in any way, she would hardly have asked Milo for his help."

That sounded reasonable; once again Embla was relieved. She was about to leave, then remembered a key question.

"Any news on the pistol?"

Göran's face broke into a satisfied smile. "Luca had a license for a Beretta M9. I've checked the gun that was tucked beneath Milo's hands, and it's Luca's Beretta. It's also the murder weapon in both homicides."

"Luca's pistol? Both homicides?" Embla repeated, completely taken aback.

"That's right—it's entirely logical when you think about it. Luca was shot first, between eight and ten on Friday evening according to the medical examiner. Unfortunately the body wasn't discovered until the following morning because it was hidden behind the car."

It was all a bit of a mess, but when Embla considered the course of events, no doubt Göran was right.

"Didn't anyone hear the shots?"

He shook his head. "No witnesses have come forward.

The parking garage is at least a hundred meters from the nearest house, plus there's a busy street in between. The weather was terrible, sleet and a cold wind. No one was around."

Embla's brain was hurting.

"But why did the killer leave Luca's pistol with Milo? It's hot, it's been used in two homicides!"

Göran shrugged. "Maybe for that very reason—to get rid of the murder weapon. Although I agree it sounds crazy. And another thing—he must have had access to keys. My theory is that our perp visited Luca's apartment before the murder and took the computer and the Beretta. I assume he took the phone from Luca's dead body."

Embla made a huge effort to think clearly.

"But if the murderer was in the apartment *before* the murder, then he must have had a set of spare keys, because Luca's keys were still in his pocket when he was found. Is there another set, apart from the ones in the safe at La Dolce Vita?"

"Not as far as we know, unless they're in Milo's private safe in his apartment."

"And when will that be opened?"

"Soon, I hope."

It was all very confusing. They didn't seem to be getting anywhere with the keys, so Embla decided to focus on the gun.

"So once again—why didn't he get rid of Luca's Beretta after murdering Milo? And why take Milo's gun with him rather than leaving it behind?"

Göran spread his hands wide. "I can't give you an answer. It's going to be at least two days before we hear about any possible DNA on the magazines or the gun itself. Lena has her hands full. There have been two new shootings, an internal dispute between two gangs of youths in Biskopsgården. Totally unrelated to the Stavic brothers."

Embla's head was spinning. They could certainly be looking at the same murderer, but his schedule was pretty tight. He must have had help.

"So after he'd killed Luca, he headed straight up to Herremark and shot Milo?"

"Yes. Same MO, same murder weapon, so we have to assume it's the same murderer. But he must have had a hell of a job getting back down to Gothenburg, even if he had a big car. The snow caused chaos overnight, and the E45 across the Dalsland plain was completely blocked."

"Okay, so the killer had probably gotten hold of Luca's pistol before Luca was murdered—but maybe he went into the apartments *after* the murders to take the computers?" Embla suggested.

Göran leaned back even farther, ignoring the protests of his chair.

"That's not impossible. No guard was stationed at either apartment after the murders; we assumed they were as secure as Fort Knox. Everyone was involved in other ongoing investigations. Linda and Bengan had to travel up to Herremark, and spent the whole of Saturday there. When they got back they went straight to Biskopsgården to help out at the crime scenes following the gang shootings. And you and I didn't get to the apartments until yesterday evening—three whole days after Luca and Milo were killed."

Embla nodded.

"If someone had access to keys, he or she could have gone to Luca's place first and taken all his IT equipment and the Beretta, then handed the gun over to the killer. It doesn't have to be the same person who entered the apartments and carried out the murders. And if we're looking at a Mafia-style killing, then it's not unreasonable to assume that several people were involved. Someone could have gone into Milo's apartment after the murder up in Herremark," Göran continued.

"So now we have to find out who might have had access to those keys—although in Milo's case we already know it was Andreas Acika," Embla said slowly.

"Exactly, but he claims he doesn't know the combination for Milo's safe, which could contain Luca's spare keys. Then again, we didn't have any trouble finding the combination for Luca's safe," he said, raising his eyebrows meaningfully.

This meant that the murderer had had no need to struggle back down to Gothenburg in a snowstorm. His only job had been to kill the brothers. His sidekick—or sidekicks—had taken care of the apartments.

"So where did the killer go after he'd shot Milo?" Embla wondered.

"Maybe that's something you and Olle could look into. Why don't you go back up to Herremark and see if you can find his hiding place?"

"I think we should also take a closer look at the area Milo had marked on the map."

"Good idea. We don't know if it was a deliberate mark; it might mean nothing, but it's worth checking out, just to be on the safe side."

At that moment, Göran's phone rang.

"Hi, Tommy. Yes, she's here."

Embla got to her feet, but he signaled to her to stay put. She didn't sit down again, but waited by the chair.

"I'm sure she can . . . Hold on, I'll ask her."

He covered the mouthpiece and looked up at her.

"Tommy's asking if you can go over to La Dolce Vita and have a chat with the executive assistant, which is apparently his proper title. He called Violent Crimes to say he has important information, but no one has time to go over there today. Could you fit it in?"

The very thought of going to that place made her stomach turn over. She hadn't set foot inside since the night Lollo disappeared. She had been too afraid of bumping into the Stavic brothers, and she was anxious about confronting the spot where her nightmare had begun.

She had no intention of admitting any of that to Göran, though.

"No problem," she heard herself say.

"Great. Tommy? That's fine. By the way, what's the guy's name?" He listened for a moment, then said, "Okay, I'll pass that on," and ended the call.

"The executive assistant is Stephen Walker. Age thirty-two, English, but he's also held Swedish citizenship for the past three years. He's worked in various bars and restaurants as a waiter and then a maître d', but for the past three years he's been Luca's assistant. According to Tommy, rumor has it their relationship wasn't just professional."

"But they didn't live together."

"No, Luca lived alone."

Embla glanced at the clock on the wall; it was almost four-thirty.

"Is he at La Dolce Vita now?"

"Yes, he's waiting for someone from Violent Crimes. The restaurant doesn't open until five."

"Okay, I'll go right away."

As she turned and headed for the door, she felt as if she had a burning cannonball in her stomach.

FOR ONCE EMBLA had no problem parking in the area around the Avenue. There were several empty spaces behind the Concert Hall. Typical. She would have been happy to cruise around for a little longer in order to try to summon up at least a semblance of inner calm.

It was already dark, and the temperature had dropped below freezing. The slush and water had frozen, turning roads and sidewalks into ice rinks. To be on the safe side she held on to the railing as she went down the steps from the parking garage. She was no more than five minutes from La Dolce Vita. If she blamed the treacherous conditions and took tiny, tiny steps, maybe she could stretch it to seven. But there were heating pipes beneath the sidewalk on the Avenue, and her plan was soon foiled. Not a trace of ice.

As usual there were plenty of people around: groups of noisy schoolchildren who'd finished for the day, shoppers, commuters on their way home from work. However, it wasn't really crowded. That would change in the spring and summer, when visitors from all over the world poured in and were inexorably drawn into the tourist traps. That evening it was mostly the English and Scots who were hanging out in bars like The Dubliner and The

Bishop's Arms, trying to soak in the "genuine atmosphere." There were a number of restaurants and clubs in the area, and Gothenburg was known as Little London

The closer Embla got to the nightclub, the more hesitant her footsteps became. Outside the double doors made of reinforced glass—according to Göran—she stopped. Her heart dropped like a stone and settled beside the burning cannonball in her stomach. A faint hope that she might not be able to get in was crushed when she saw a man waiting inside, peering down the street. As soon as he saw her he opened the door.

"Good evening—who are you looking for?" he asked politely.

She almost burst out laughing, and some of her nervousness subsided. He spoke and looked like a younger version of Tony Irving, one of the judges on the TV show *Let's Dance*—although he was more muscular and significantly taller.

"Hi. Detective Inspector Embla Nyström. I'm looking for Stephen Walker—something tells me that might be you."

He pushed the door open wide and stepped aside. "That's correct. Please come in."

With more assurance than she was feeling, Embla walked up the steps and went in. From the door, she could see straight into the restaurant.

Her memories from the evening when Lollo disappeared were extremely vague, but she'd always thought of the décor as black—walls, floor, ceiling, all painted black. Even the bar had been black. Either she was wrong, or the whole of the interior had been redone. Now the walls were covered in eggshell-colored wallpaper, the floors were pale-gray marble, and the bar, tables, and chairs were made of cherry wood. Heavy white silk curtains framed the tall windows, while lush green plants created a pleasant atmosphere and prevented anyone outside from seeing in. The lower part of the bar was made of mirrored glass, while the counter itself was sparkling white marble. The wall behind the optics and shelves of bottles was also mirrored, as was the ceiling above.

At the far end of the foyer was the staircase leading down to the nightclub.

"This way," Stephen Walker said.

She followed him down the stairs. This was where it had all happened. Strangely enough, she didn't remember ever going downstairs with Lollo.

In the basement the lighting was muted. The wallpaper was silver-gray; the floor was marble, but in a darker shade. The atmosphere was sophisticated and international. The bar was the same as the one in the restaurant, but the counter was twice as long. There was a DJ booth in one corner of the large dance floor.

Next to the booth, Embla could see a door, the door that had etched itself on her mind. It was painted the same silver-gray shade as the walls, so that it blended in and was almost invisible. The sign was gone, and there was a keypad beside it.

Stephen Walker quickly entered the code, the lock clicked, and the door swung open. For a moment Embla felt the rising panic from her nightmares, but she managed to pull herself together. She followed him along the hall.

The eggshell wallpaper had been used again here, and

there were plenty of brightly colored paintings on display. Pale-gray wall-to-wall carpet completed the décor. They went past several closed doors, each with a keypad. Embla had no memory whatsoever of the doors. In her nightmare there was only a long, dark hallway with a single bulb dangling from the ceiling at the end. That couldn't possibly have been the case, she realized now. There was nothing claustrophobic about this light space. Or had it been so different on that fateful night?

Stephen stopped at the final door and entered the code.

"Is there a back door?" Embla asked as innocently as she could manage.

"In here," he replied, politely holding the door open.

In there? That must mean that the far end of the hall had been closed off and converted into a room. She recalled her last sight of Lollo, a small figure lying on the floor in something that resembled a hallway inside the back door. Three men looming over her: Milo, Kador, and Luca. Terrified and drunk, Embla had assumed that they'd drugged her friend, or knocked her down. She had obviously misinterpreted the situation, since Lollo had run away with Kador. Or had she been taken against her will? That possibility still existed.

With the burning cannonball spinning around in her stomach, Embla entered the room. The first thing she saw was the back door—it was covered in steel. The windows up by the ceiling had been replaced with glass tiles. They allowed the light to pass through, but no one could see in or out. Windowless rooms often make people feel uncomfortable. Embla didn't usually suffer from claustrophobia, but it was creeping up on her now.

The décor was pleasant; the carpet continued from the hall. The office chair was white leather, and on the desk stood a Mac monitor, keyboard, and laser printer, all white. A white sofa and two armchairs were arranged around a glass coffee table. On two of the walls hung large oil paintings in bright colors, one in tones of red, the other blue. Abstract, but attractive. Embla could imagine having one of them in her apartment—if she'd had a wall that was big enough.

"Please take a seat," Stephen said, gesturing toward an armchair.

Very polite.

He sat down opposite her and leaned back. The light fell on his medium-length blond hair and revealed lines etched by weariness around his mouth. His eyes were bloodshot—was he just tired, or had he been crying? Or both? He didn't look as if he'd slept much over the past few days.

"Can I offer you something to drink?"

His voice was deep and warm, his gaze steady. However, his hands moved constantly. He rubbed his face, tucked a strand of hair behind his ear, clasped his hands on his lap, then immediately unclasped them and grabbed the armrests. This guy was anything but relaxed.

"No thanks—I had a coffee a little while ago."

"Okay."

Embla decided to make a cautious start, ask a question to which she already knew the answer. It was also a way of finding out how truthful he intended to be.

"How long have you lived in Sweden?"

"Ten years."

"Have you always been in Gothenburg?"

"No. Seven years in Stockholm and three in Gothen-burg."

"And how long have you worked here?"

She followed the question with a vague gesture around the room, accompanied by a friendly smile.

"It will be three years in April."

"So you moved to Gothenburg to work at La Dolce Vita, as Luca's assistant."

A brief nod. He picked nervously at his pants, then clasped his hands again.

"My boss asked me to come here—he said you had something to tell us," Embla continued.

Stephen stood up and went over to a tall cupboard, divided in two across the middle. He pressed the upper door and it swung open to reveal a refrigerator. Embla saw a couple dozen Champagne bottles and pale-blue bottles of mineral water. Stephen took out two of them. The lower cupboard contained a wide range of glasses. He chose two medium-sized tumblers, then closed both doors. He returned to his armchair, placed one bottle and glass in front of Embla, and poured himself a drink. After a few sips of the chilled water, he took a deep breath.

"Luca and I saw a great deal of each other. Privately. We were together."

For a moment his hands stopped moving. When he looked at her with his blue-green eyes, she merely nodded.

"Okay, in that case maybe you'll understand why I did . . . what I did," he said quietly, lowering his gaze. There was no point in stressing him; she gave him time to compose himself.

"Luca and I liked to relax on Friday evenings," he

continued after a few moments. "That was our time. We would eat well, drink some wine—cozy Friday, we used to call it." A tear trickled slowly down his cheek, and he dashed it away with the back of his hand.

"Last Friday we were planning to do the same as always, but just as we were about to leave here, his phone rang. I didn't hear exactly what he said, but he kept nodding and saying 'hm-hm.' Then he told me he had to go and meet someone."

Embla could hardly breathe. "Did he tell you who it was?"

"No. I asked, but he just said it was business. Confidential matters. Milo was away, so he had to deal with it."

Confidential matters. Like most of the Stavic brothers' affairs. The hope of finding out the name of the man Luca was meeting faded away. Embla made one final attempt.

"He didn't say what kind of business?"

"No." His fingers started plucking at his impeccable suit once more. He straightened his tie for what must have been the twentieth time. "He walked out. Luca's never done that before—just left me like that. I wanted to see who he was meeting."

Embla nodded encouragingly.

"I know Luca. He always wants to freshen up before he sees someone important. As it was business, I was sure he'd go home first, so I drove out to Eriksberg." He let out a half-sob; he was wringing his hands now. The poor guy was completely devastated. Embla reached into her pocket for a pack of tissues and passed them over. He mumbled his thanks, wiped his eyes and blew his nose, then took a deep breath.

"I got there at about eight. It was sleeting, and of course it was dark, so there was no one around. I parked outside the parking garage; I was waiting to see if he'd come back to pick up his car to drive to his meeting, or if someone was coming to him. In the apartment," he said, clearly distressed.

"You suspected he was seeing another man," Embla clarified.

"Yes—what else was I supposed to think?"

That he was heading off to a last-minute business meeting because Milo wasn't available, she thought.

"Have you had any reason to suspect that Luca was seeing other men?"

He shook his head emphatically.

"No, never. But something didn't feel right." He ran his fingers through his hair and adjusted his tie yet again. "I'd been sitting there for five minutes at most when a guy emerged from the parking garage. At first I didn't really pay any attention to him, because he looked nothing like Luca. The way he was dressed."

"How was he dressed?"

"Gangster style. You know—a short black leather jacket over a hoodie, blue jeans. Luca would never dress like that. The guy had his hood up, but there was something about the way he moved . . . He was walking straight toward me. I sat perfectly still; I don't think he saw me. He went over to a black Range Rover that was parked a few meters away. He tossed a bag into the backseat, then pushed back his hood. I had a hell of a shock!"

Stephen broke off and looked Embla directly in the eye.

"At first I thought it was Luca. It was hard to see in the

dark and the sleet, although there was a streetlamp nearby. Then I realized it wasn't him. The face was very similar, but the eyebrows were bushier. And his hairstyle was the same as mine."

Slicked back, Embla thought.

"He was also shorter than Luca," Stephen added. He drank deeply from his glass of water. "I've been ashamed to tell anyone that I was spying on Luca. When I found out he was lying dead inside the parking garage while I was sitting outside . . . But I think the fact that I saw the man could be important. I think I know who he is."

The little flame of hope was rekindled in Embla's breast. Would he really be able to give her the name of the killer? He spoke slowly, emphasizing every word.

"It must have been his brother, Kador. I've never met him, but the age fits, and Luca always said they were very much alike."

The flame went out. Kador was already dead by the time Luca and Milo were murdered. Embla did her best to hide her disappointment. She was suddenly struck by a thought, and glanced over at the desk. Monitor, keyboard, printer—no computer.

"Do you know if Luca took his laptop home from here?"

Stephen nodded. "Always. He often worked at home in the evenings."

So the murderer had taken it. Presumably it had been in the bag he tossed in the back of the car—along with his phone.

"Thank you so much for telling me this; it could be really important. We'll be in touch, probably tomorrow.

I'm sure my boss will want you to come into the station to work on a police sketch."

They both got to their feet at the same time. Stephen accompanied her down the hall, through the nightclub, and up the stairs. Faint music was coming from the restaurant; some early diners had arrived. Embla's stomach contracted with hunger.

Another question occurred to her.

"Were you aware that Luca owned a pistol, a Beretta?"

"Yes, he showed it to me once. He kept it in his safe in the apartment."

"Did he often practice with it? Was he a good shot?"

Stephen looked surprised.

"Practice? No, I don't think so. As far as I know, he never fired it once during the years we were together." He couldn't help smiling; it was obvious that he found the idea of Luca as a crack shot amusing, in spite of the circumstances.

After brief consideration, Embla decided not to ask him if he'd known about the drugs they'd found in the safe. That could wait until the contents of the bags had been analyzed, and any investigation would be up to Narcotics.

"Call me if you think of anything else," she said, handing him her card.

"Thanks, I will."

After a quick meal of whole-wheat pasta with tomato sauce, Embla began to feel more human. She went into the living room with a steaming mug of green tea, curled up on the sofa, and called Göran's phone.

"Hi, Embla. What did Luca's executive assistant have to say for himself?"

He was trying to sound alert, but Embla could tell how much of an effort it was. She briefly summarized her meeting with Stephen Walker.

Göran remained silent for a while, then said, "I'm pretty sure it was our murderer that Stephen saw."

"Me too."

"We can definitely rule out Kador, but clearly it was a man who reminded Stephen of him and Luca."

The penny dropped.

"Andreas Acika!"

"That's exactly what I was thinking. Okay, so I'm seeing Tommy Persson at eight o'clock tomorrow morning; I'll pass on what you've just told me. And I'll have Acika brought in for questioning; I want to know where he was and what he was doing on Friday evening and during the night. I'd like you to go to Dalsland and check out the area that Milo had marked on the map—take your good-looking colleague from Åmål with you. If there's a problem with his boss, just let me know and I'll have a word."

"He's not *mine* and his name is Olle. Detective Inspector Olle Tillman. Nothing else," Embla retorted.

She heard laughter on the other end of the line.

"Whatever you say. But I don't want you going up there on your own."

THE FIRST THING Olle said when she called him was that Wille Andersson had confessed to the murder of Robin Pettersson.

"He kept on denying it until he was confronted with the evidence from the knife. We found two of his fingerprints in the blood on the shaft, plus we tracked down the maker. It's signed by a well-known smith in Årjäng who keeps a record of every knife he sells. This one was a Christmas present to Wille from his parents."

"Congratulations! You did it!" Embla said, genuinely pleased for him.

"Well . . . with a little help from a friend."

"You were the one who found the knife."

It was important not to diminish Olle's achievement; he had solved the case very quickly.

"Yes, but it was you who told me to look for it at the scene. Wille must have hidden it before he started pretending to give Robin CPR; in fact he was just making sure there was a reason for having blood all over his clothes."

Wille must have thought surprisingly quickly; he gave the impression of being slow and not very bright, but maybe he was cleverer than he looked.

"Smart kid. But not smart enough," she said.

"Exactly. Not smart enough to get away with murder. His first mistake was using his own knife. His second was to wear a T-shirt on a cold winter's day. If he'd kept the MW tattoo hidden, you might not have worked out his motive."

She had to admit he was right. She obviously had more experience in investigating serious crimes than Olle did, but he was sharp and persistent, which were important qualities in a cop.

"Are you sure you want to be a dog handler? I think you've got the potential to be a colleague of mine," she said, keeping her tone light.

His response showed that he was giving serious consideration to what she'd just said.

"Taking an active role in this case has been interesting, but I still feel dog handling is the path that appeals to me the most. I'm going to do the training, anyway; if I change my mind I can apply to Crime later."

It was a sensible approach, and he was still young. Although he was only two years younger than her. That fact popped into her mind every time she thought of him. Why? Irritating.

"Absolutely. Anyway, what did your charming boss Chief Inspector Johnzén have to say?"

Olle let out a laugh so loud that Embla had to move the phone away from her ear.

"Nothing—he's furious! He kept muttering about the refugees until Paula Nilsson showed him the bloody prints on the knife and told him they were Wille's prints but Robin's blood."

Embla shook her head, even though Olle couldn't see

her. "That guy has a problem. Do you think he'll object if I ask you to help me tomorrow? I have to check out something connected to the murders of the Stavic brothers, and Göran Krantz suggested you come along."

"If he knew, I'm sure he'd refuse to let me go, but it's my day off tomorrow, so I don't need to ask. I'd love to come!"

Embla explained about the area marked on the map, and they agreed to meet at the harbor in Ed at eleven o'clock the following morning. She ended the call and glanced at the clock. Only nine o'clock. Resolutely she got to her feet. Fifteen minutes later she was heading down the street in her running gear.

A BITTERLY COLD north wind swept in across the lake known as Stora Le, bringing with it tiny snow crystals that felt like pinpricks against her skin. It could hardly be more inhospitable, but Embla wanted to stretch her legs and get a little fresh air, so she walked over to an ice cream kiosk that was closed for the winter. After a minute she gave up and got back in the car. It was only quarter to eleven; she'd reached Ed in good time. A few minutes later a blue Passat station wagon pulled up next to her Kia. Olle was driving, and she could just see Tore's head through the bars of his cage in the back. The dog sat up and looked out the side window, ears pricked and an alert expression in his eyes.

Olle got out and chivalrously opened her car door.

"Good morning," she said as she got out.

"Good morning to you."

Before she knew what was happening, he let go of the door and gave her a big hug. She felt enveloped by his warmth, and an unfamiliar sensation spread through her body; she wanted to stay in his arms. To be safe and secure. She didn't usually allow herself to be drawn into situations where she wasn't in control, but with Olle she was able to lower her guard for some reason. Not completely, but enough to give her pause.

Gently she extricated herself and looked at him. No uniform today; he was wearing a dark-blue padded jacket, gray wool hat, jeans, and sturdy boots. His blue-gray eyes looked clearer than she remembered.

"It's so good to see you again," he said, blushing slightly.

It could be the cold and the snow crystals that had brought color to his face, but she didn't think so. Impulsively she took off one of her mittens and laid her hand on his cheek.

"It's good to see you, too."

What the hell was wrong with her? She was standing here and . . . doing what, exactly? Flirting? Or more than that? Definitely more than that.

But this was neither the time nor the place for romance. For one thing it was freezing cold, and for another they had a job to do. She gently stroked his cheek, then put her mitten back on. She turned away to hide her confusion.

"I'm glad you've brought your top police dog along," she said.

"Absolutely. My sister's family still has the flu, and my mom isn't back from Tenerife yet."

Embla locked the Kia and went around to the passenger side of the Passat. Before getting in she stuck her head in and said: "Hi, Tore!" A brief bark in response made her wonder how much the dog actually understood.

THE TEMPERATURE HAD remained below freezing in northern Dalsland, and the snow was still piled high along the roadsides. To be fair, it had only been two days since Embla had gone down to Gothenburg, but so much had happened that it felt as if it had been much longer. They were heading for an area approximately thirty kilometers from Ed, but the road was narrow and it was impossible to travel fast. This gave them time to discuss what had gone on in their respective investigations.

Olle told Embla they'd had big problems with Wille Andersson's father. He'd stormed into the police station in Trollhättan where Wille had been questioned, yelling that nothing his son had said was admissible because he hadn't had a parent or guardian with him during the interviews. He had been informed that the age of majority in Sweden is eighteen, and since Wille was nineteen, there was no requirement to have an adult present. He had also been provided with a public defense counsel, who would support him throughout the process. Unfortunately this hadn't calmed John Andersson down in any way; quite the reverse, in fact. He'd gone crazy, shouting that he was going to contact the press, his son was innocent, he was going to sue the Åmål police for framing the boy and planting the knife at the scene of the crime. In the end, he had to be physically ejected from the building.

"Thank God I had a decent camera with me; I took lots of pictures before I removed the knife from its hiding place. And as my personal crime-scene tutor taught me, I was wearing latex gloves and was extremely careful when I transferred the knife to an evidence bag," he said with a sly sideways glance.

"So you're not involved with the case anymore?" Embla asked.

"No. Trollhättan took over, and of course the prosecutor's based there, too."

"That means you can help me with a clear conscience."

"Absolutely—but purely on a hobby level, if I can put it that way. Johnzén would shoot me if he knew what I was up to right now."

"Why?"

"Because Göran Krantz put him in his place. That's enough to make Johnzén hate him for the rest of his life."

"He bears a grudge, then."

"Are you kidding me? He still hasn't forgiven the midwife who slapped his ass when he was born!"

Embla laughed.

"On top of that he's petty-minded and bad-tempered—the perfect combination."

It might have been a joke, but there was a hint of unhappiness, even resignation in his voice. There was no doubt that Chief Inspector Johnzén was a difficult boss.

Embla went through everything that had emerged in the Stavic brothers' case. Nothing had leaked to the media yet, so this was all news to Olle. When she told him about Stephen Walker lurking outside Luca's apartment, consumed with jealousy, and about the man Walker had seen, Olle jumped in.

"So this guy looked a bit like Luca."

"And Kador, but we know it couldn't be him because he was dead by the time Luca and Milo were killed. However, their cousin Andreas Acika bears a certain resemblance to the brothers."

"If it's not him, it could be a contract killer they've brought in, maybe from the Balkans. In which case he'll be hard to find."

"You're right. If he's a professional hit man, he's unlikely to be in Sweden at this point."

They hadn't seen a single building for the past few kilometers, though there was probably the odd summer cottage covered in snow down by the lakeside. They met only one car, a black Range Rover. Not an unusual make in an isolated area like that, where a decent vehicle to tow heavy loads and travel over rough terrain was necessary, but what attracted Embla's attention were the two men in the front seat. Both drivers had to slow down in order to pass on the narrow road, so she had plenty of time to get a good look at them.

The driver was heavyset, bordering on fat. He was wearing a camouflage jacket and had a green wool hat pulled down over his ears. He could have been a member of the home guard. His companion was slimmer and bare-headed, but the jacket was the same. His dark hair was sticking out in all directions; maybe he'd just taken off his hat. Both had several days' dark stubble. Something about their appearance made her think they had nothing to do with the home guard after all.

Embla kept an eye open for the turn; according to Google Maps it was so narrow that it would be easy to miss.

To her surprise the snowplow had cleared the dirt road. Olle drove slowly. Eventually they reached a neat red-painted cottage with several outbuildings. The yard was covered in virgin snow, and there was no sign of life.

"Nice place," Olle remarked.

"It was marked on Google Maps."

"Were there any more buildings?"

Embla hesitated. "There's something that looks like a little cabin farther on."

"Someone must be using it. The road's been cleared. How far is it?"

"About a hundred meters."

Olle braked and pulled into a spot where the snoplow had cleared a space to turn. There was enough room for two cars to pass.

"I'll park here and we'll walk," he said.

Embla took out her phone and looked at the screen. Just as she'd feared, there was no coverage.

"Do you have a signal?" she asked.

Olle reached into his pocket. After a glance at the display, he shook his head.

"Nothing."

As soon as they got out of the car, Tore started whimpering and moving around anxiously. Olle sighed and smiled apologetically.

"He needs a comfort break."

They always say you shouldn't work with children or animals, Embla thought.

Olle opened the back door and Tore jumped out. Just like the time when they went to speak to Anton Åkesson's parents, he shot under Olle's arm and raced up onto a bank of snow. And once again he was affected by total deafness, unable to hear his master's command to COME BACK HERE! Tore scampered happily along on top of the hard-packed snow; the last they saw of him was a wagging tail disappearing around the bend up ahead.

"Goddamn dog!" Olle hissed, his face red with anger.

"I'd say he needs a little more training," Embla teased him.

Olle didn't answer, but marched off in pursuit of Tore.

The snow crunched beneath their boots and the cold nipped at their cheeks. As they rounded the bend they stopped. At the end of the dirt road lay a dilapidated cottage. There were grubby net curtains at some of the windows. The paint was flaking off the walls and window frames. Impressive icicles hung from the roof, a clear indication that warmth was leaking from the poorly insulated building. Above the door was a frosted dormer window—*presumably a bathroom*, Embla thought.

Smoke was rising from the chimney.

About twenty meters from the cottage was a red building that looked pretty new; it appeared to be some kind of storage shed. There was a window on the gable end facing the road, but the glass was tinted, making it impossible to see inside. A white Mercedes van was parked outside, with its back doors wide open.

There was no sign of Tore.

Silently they began to move forward. When they were ten meters from the van, they heard someone whistling loudly and tunelessly inside the shed. The noise was accompanied by the faint squeak of wheels that needed oiling. The door flew open with a crash and a man pushing a fully laden cart stepped out. He stopped whistling as soon as he saw the two police officers. With lightning speed, he let go of the handles of the cart and drew a gun from inside his jacket.

"Stop!" he yelled.

"We're from the police and—" Olle began, but he was immediately interrupted.

"You're trespassing on private property!"

The man spoke Swedish with a barely perceptible accent. The hand holding the pistol was steady; he was clearly used to handling guns. He was wearing a gray hoodie underneath his jacket, and the hood was drawn tight around his face to keep out the cold. Embla saw a pair of bushy eyebrows, well-defined cheekbones, and black stubble. He looked to be between thirty and forty with a normal build and was slightly below-average in height.

A faint suspicion began to take shape. This could be the man Stephen Walker had seen leaving the parking garage after Luca's murder. In which case they were standing unarmed in front of a murderer.

Suddenly Embla caught a movement by the corner of the building. Tore. The dog paused for a second, but when Olle muttered "Go! Go!" he reacted instantly. He'd practiced many times: when someone points a gun, neutralize the threat. He flew toward the man, leaped, and sank his teeth into the man's right wrist. This guy wasn't wearing the thick protective pad on his arm that Tore's target usually wore during training, which made it easier for him to get a good grip.

A shot was fired. Embla felt the hot draft as the bullet whizzed past her left cheek, immediately followed by a thud as it hit a tree trunk behind them. The man dropped the gun, yelling in pain and anger. He began hitting Tore with his left hand, which simply made the dog sink his teeth even deeper into the soft, yielding flesh. Olle and Embla rushed forward to rescue Tore. Embla grabbed the gun on the way; one glance told her it was a Beretta M9.

Together Olle and Tore forced the man to the ground. Several times Olle gave the command to let go, but Tore was having none of it and growled menacingly.

In spite of the fact that Olle was considerably taller

than his opponent, he had some difficulty turning the man over onto his stomach because he wouldn't stop writhing around. Embla stepped in to help, and they finally managed to get the handcuffs on—much to Tore's disappointment because then he really did have to let go. However, he carried on growling and barking, just to show that he was still involved.

"Sorry, it's his first real capture."

Embla merely nodded. The dog's contribution had been invaluable; without him they might have been dead by now. She could put up with a little barking from the hero of the hour.

Getting the handcuffs on had also been problematic because the man was wearing an unusually large watch on his left wrist. A gold watch, the size of an American cupcake.

IGNORING THE MAN'S protests, Embla took off his heavy gold watch. It looked exactly the same as the one Andreas Acika had shown them, and the one they'd found in Luca's safe. Holding it by the clasp on the gold bracelet, she turned it over to see M.S. engraved on the back.

Olle went through the man's pockets. He didn't find any ID—just two spare magazines for the Beretta, the keys to the Mercedes, another bunch of keys, a plastic cigarette lighter, and an almost-empty pack of Marlboros. In the back pocket of the man's jeans was a wallet containing a few Swedish notes and coins, plus four 500-Euro notes and a photograph of a little girl in a white lace dress and white knee socks. She was holding a doll wearing a similar dress.

"We'll lock him in the van," Olle decided.

Together they managed to haul him to his feet and bundle him into the back of the van. He was swearing loudly, mostly in Swedish but also in another language. Judging by the tone, it was just as well they didn't understand everything he said.

When Olle had locked the back doors, he took the dog leash out of his pocket. Tore obediently stood still, panting slightly.

"I think I'll put him back in the car and get some evidence bags to—"

Before he had time to clip on the leash, Embla hurled herself at him and sent him crashing to the ground. It was a good thing the door of the storage shed was open, otherwise he'd have banged his head on it.

A bullet whined past over their heads and disappeared into the building.

"I saw someone poke the barrel of a rifle out the bathroom window!" Embla explained.

Clearly the man they'd just locked in the van had one or more associates in the cottage. Encouraged by the shot, he started kicking the doors and bellowing with rage. Without wasting any time, Olle crawled into the shed, closely followed by Embla. They each took one side of the doors and pressed themselves against the wall. Olle was pale and looked very shaken. Tore was barking again, responding to the noise the man was making. Fortunately the van was between the dog and the gunman in the bathroom.

"Tore! Come here!" Olle hissed.

This time the dog obeyed, slinking in through the door just as another shot was fired. It slammed into the doorframe, and Olle and Embla moved away from the opening. It wasn't completely dark inside the shed due to a couple of bare bulbs. Embla positioned herself behind one of the pillars holding up the roof and quickly scanned the room. There was a pile of wooden boxes over by the far windowless wall, and to the right of the door there was a window with heavily tinted glass. She was able to see the gable end of the cottage, but not the bathroom window. She noticed that it was easier to see out than in through the tinted glass.

Old tools and work clothes hung on nails to the left of the door, and there was a large snowblower in the corner. When Embla spotted a mattock among the tools, she crept over and took it down. Cautiously she edged closer to the door, then dropped to her knees and quietly took a deep breath. She stretched out her arm, hooked the mattock over the side of the door and pulled it shut. A bullet immediately smashed into it, but luckily the door was reinforced with steel on the inside. She sighed with relief. Then she got to her feet and turned off the lights. The small amount of daylight seeping in would have to do.

"Quick—we need to get those boxes open," she said.

Olle, who had sought refuge behind another pillar, looked puzzled.

"Why?"

"They might contain guns."

"But we've got the pistol."

"That's evidence. It's a Beretta M9, and I'm pretty sure it's Milo's."

Olle went a little paler as he absorbed the implication of what she'd just said. The man they'd locked in the Mercedes van had murdered the Stavic brothers.

Embla spotted a short iron bar with a pointed end leaning against the wall below the tools.

"This will do nicely," she said, weighing it in her hand. Without further comment Olle took down a small hammer, and together they went over to the boxes. Tore was sniffing around behind them; the gunfire hadn't bothered him at all. He'd been trained to ignore it and wasn't in the least bit afraid.

He'd also been trained in other aspects of police work.

As they approached the boxes, his head went up. Whimpering with excitement, he ran over to a stack at the far end, then froze.

Olle looked at his dog.

"We can ignore those—they contain drugs," he said.

The text on the boxes was written in the Cyrillic alphabet; the only thing they could understand was the logo, Motor Company Ltd. There were fifteen boxes total—twelve if you ignored the ones Tore found most interesting—and they were heavy. Embla hoped at least some of them contained guns, so they wouldn't have to use the Beretta.

They tackled the first box. Beneath a layer of wood shavings lay a selection of machine parts, then more shavings. They tipped the lot onto the floor to reach the bottom layer, which was covered with a piece of Styrofoam. Olle cautiously lifted it up.

"Fuck!" he said. The bottom of the box was packed with hand grenades, each sitting in its own compartment in a thicker piece of Styrofoam.

"We can use those. How are your throwing skills?"

At first Olle looked like a giant question mark, then his face brightened.

"I was pretty good in school, and I did my military service with the infantry. Hand grenades are not a problem."

"Grab a few and keep an eye on the house in case the guy with the rifle decides to come over here."

"Okay."

He took three, slipped two in his pockets and kept one in his hand as he moved over to the window by the door, which gave him a good view of the cottage.

Embla started on the next box. Wood shavings, machine parts, more hand grenades. Next box.

Suddenly Olle said: "The door's opening! A guy with a pistol . . ."

A second later the window shattered. Embla and Tore were a safe distance away, but if Olle hadn't been quick enough, he could have been injured by flying glass. Or he could have been shot. Fortunately he'd managed to press himself against the wall and was unhurt. They needed backup, but with no cell phone coverage, they had no way of contacting anyone. Embla's heart began to pound, but she forced herself to sound calm and composed.

"Throw."

Without a word Olle removed the pin, counted to three, then tossed the grenade through the empty window frame.

The explosion was deafening and even made Tore whimper. Snow, gravel, and splinters of wood whirled around and hit the walls of the shed with terrifying force. When everything had settled, Olle ventured a quick glance outside.

The Mercedes was no longer white, but was covered in a layer of dirt. There wasn't a sound from inside; presumably the occupant had received a genuine shock, which filled Olle with great satisfaction. However, the sight of the cottage brought him down to earth with a bump.

"Jesus . . . I scored a direct hit on the porch. It's been blown to pieces—and I think the guy with the pistol's gone with it."

Embla couldn't hide her relief.

"Good! Keep watching the house in case there's any-one else in there."

If they were lucky, it was the sniper from upstairs who'd been blown to pieces along with the porch, but they couldn't count on that. With renewed energy she tackled box number three. Wood shavings, machine parts . . . Yes! Two small assault rifles. She picked one up and weighed it in her hand; it was pretty light, some-where between three and a half and four kilos. It was far from new, and former users had carved centimeter-long marks on the stock. She counted fourteen—was that the number of people who'd been killed with this gun? Pos-sibly. Both rifles seemed to be well-oiled and in good condition. She took a closer look and decided the model was probably of Serbian origin, a Kalashnikov 7.62mm, generally known as an AK-47.

She scrabbled around in the wood shavings, but there was no ammunition in the box. She moved on to the next box and was disappointed to find that it contained two guns of the same type but no ammunition. She would just have to keep looking.

She was still a little hard of hearing after the explo-sion, so it took her a moment to realize that Olle was calling quietly to her. She stopped what she was doing and turned to face him.

"What?"

"There's a car."

She listened carefully, and picked up the sound of a powerful engine.

"Could be the Range Rover we met on the way," Olle said. He'd moved over to the window on the gable end, which gave him a clear view of the road. It meant he could no longer watch the house, but then they'd already caused considerable damage there. If anyone else was inside, they would probably lie low for a while.

If the two men in the Range Rover were on their way back, they would no doubt be armed. Olle and Embla were also armed, of course—they had plenty of hand grenades and a growing pile of guns. Resolutely, Embla continued her search for ammunition, sweat pouring down her back as she struggled with the heavy machine parts.

She lifted the bottom layer of wood shavings and let out a whoop.

"Yesss! We have ammunition!"

With a triumphant smile she picked up two full magazines and a box of bullets, but her smile faded when she saw Olle's grim expression.

"Load the guns!"

Only now did she realize that the sound of the engine had stopped. The new arrivals had parked around the bend, behind Olle's car. They were intending to approach on foot. She pulled off her gloves and slammed a magazine into one rifle, then another. Before joining Olle she slipped a hand grenade into each pocket, plus two spare magazines. Each contained thirty bullets; that should be enough. She crouched down and ran across the room, making sure she couldn't be seen from outside.

Olle was busy securing Tore's leash to one of the pillars well away from the windows; his hands were far from steady.

"I don't want him running around if there's shooting," he said.

"Good thinking. He could get hit by mistake if we don't know where he is."

She handed him a rifle and one of the spare magazines. Olle looked unsure of himself but crept back to the window.

"Two men are heading this way. With pistols."

"Are they the ones we saw in the Range Rover?" Embla's mouth was dry, and her voice came out rough.

"I think so."

"Distance?"

"Twenty to thirty meters."

She made a quick decision.

"We can't let them split up. Throw!"

Olle propped the rifle against the wall and took a grenade out of his pocket. Keeping well out of the way, he lifted the hasp, opened the window, removed the pin, counted to three, and hurled the grenade.

They both covered their ears and pressed themselves back against the wall. Even though they were prepared this time, the explosion was equally terrifying. The ground shook as snow, stones, and gravel slammed against the wall; shattered the window; and rained in. Tore raised his head and began to howl; the noise must have hurt his sensitive ears.

After a while—it could have been seconds or minutes—they dared to move. Tore alternated between barking and howling; he'd obviously had enough.

Cautiously they peered out through the space where the window had been. In the middle of the dirt road a man lay motionless on his back, with one leg sticking out at an odd angle. There was a rapidly growing pool of blood around his head, and a pistol a couple of meters away from him. He looked like the guy who'd been driving the Range Rover.

There was no sign of his companion.

"He's thrown himself over the bank of snow," Olle said grimly.

"Exactly. Can you make Tore shut up?"

Without questioning her order, he crawled over to the dog. Apart from the odd faint whimper, Tore fell silent as soon as he heard his master's reassuring voice.

Embla's ears were still ringing, but fortunately it wasn't as bad as it had been after the first explosion; she had to listen hard now. She pressed one ear to the wall, and after a little while she was able to pick up faint sounds from outside, the crunch of approaching footsteps.

The plan would work if she fired first. She had the advantage; she was armed with a semiautomatic rifle, while her opponent had a pistol. She assumed he was trying to reach the window. If he was smart he would try to hit the boxes containing the grenades, but she suspected that he would attempt to kill both her and Olle first. The desire for revenge tends to stop people from thinking logically.

She stepped back and edged over to the corner of the building closest to the pile of snow. She needed every scrap of concentration now. She dropped to her knees, adopted the firing position, and aimed at a point a short distance away from the corner, about a meter above floor level.

She heard a loud crunching noise as the man got closer. It's impossible to move silently across hard-packed snow.

Stillness descended; he was clearly listening, trying to work out where they were. Embla counted to two, then she fired. Thirty bullets went straight through the wall.

The velocity of a semiautomatic rifle is usually just above seven hundred meters per second, and a wooden wall is no hindrance. With lightning speed, she changed the magazine and fired again, aiming slightly lower this time.

If he made a sound when he was hit, she didn't hear it, but as the echoing shots died away, he began to bellow.

Before Embla could stop him, Olle rushed over to the window and stuck his head out.

"No!" she yelled.

At that moment, a shot was fired.

SOMETIMES PEOPLE HAVE a guardian angel watching over them; Olle certainly did on this occasion. As he looked out he placed both hands on the window frame, the left at the bottom and the right on a level with his face. The bullet whizzed past his nose and straight through his right hand, embedding itself in the wood.

Now Embla heard two men screaming with pain. The only consolation was that the man who'd emerged from the house and the driver of the Range Rover were quiet. Dead quiet.

She quickly dragged Olle away from the window and pulled off her scarf. The wound was bleeding profusely, but it would soon ease and hopefully stop. He needed to go to the hospital to have it cleaned and sutured.

"Keep your hand up."

He grimaced as she wrapped the scarf tightly around it. Tore understood that something had happened to his master and started barking again. Without much expectation of success, Embla turned to him and said: "Tore! Quiet!"

To her surprise he fell silent, but remained on full alert with his eyes fixed on her.

"He knows who the boss is," Olle said.

She didn't know how he could joke in a situation like this, but he'd made her smile. She composed herself and turned back to him. "Just keep Tore quiet."

She went back to the window, took out her phone and clicked on the camera icon, then held it so that she could see where the man was.

He was on his back in the snow, less than a meter from the shed. He was bleeding heavily from both legs and possibly from an injury to his midriff. His right forearm was also covered in blood and lay limply by his side, but he was holding the pistol in a firm grip in his left hand. His injuries looked severe enough that he wouldn't be able to move from his spot.

She checked for a signal again; nothing. She sat down beside Olle and whispered: "The guy who shot you has a pistol in his left hand. He's probably right-handed, but we don't know for sure. He's still conscious, which means he's a danger. The guy from the Mercedes isn't going anywhere, but we don't know who else is in the cottage. Any ideas?"

Olle looked her in the eye. "We shoot the bastard holding the gun. One less to worry about."

There it was again, the desire for revenge. It was only human, of course.

"No. We need as many of them alive for questioning as possible."

"Good luck with that. Exactly how are you planning to get us out of here?"

She forced herself to sound positive. "Let's not give up. We've done pretty well so far—we can do this."

Three shots were fired in quick succession, making them both jump.

"Shit! He's shooting through the fucking wall!" Olle exclaimed.

The pistol's velocity was significantly weaker, but it was still dangerous. The bullets hadn't landed anywhere near Olle or Embla, fortunately.

Embla looked around and her gaze fell on the snow-blower. She went to check it out and discovered that it was a Husqvarna and looked brand-new. Uncle Nisse had a similar one, although his was a much older model. This machine was bigger and had several refinements, but its basic function was the same. She pushed it over to where Olle and Tore were sitting and parked it in front of them.

"Okay, so this will shield you. I'll bring some boxes over, too."

Quickly she gathered up the machine parts that were strewn across the floor and threw them back into the boxes that had contained the guns, then stacked the boxes next to the snow blower. She positioned the boxes of hand grenades so that they couldn't be hit by a random bullet fired through the windows or the wooden wall. On the other side of the snow blower she placed the boxes that contained drugs, according to Tore. When she'd finished she'd constructed a protective barrier that was better than nothing.

"I think our police-dog-in-training is right. There might be machine parts in these boxes, but they're a lot lighter than the ones containing weapons," she said.

The next task was to find out if there was anyone left in the house. Sticking her head out the window wasn't an option. If someone was at the bathroom window, they would fire as soon as they saw any sign of movement.

The tools and work clothes hanging on the wall caught her attention.

"I've got an idea."

Before she explained, she again used her phone to check on the man who was bleeding. The snow around him was sodden with blood; he needed medical attention very soon if he was going to survive. The main thing was that he couldn't move or shoot.

She took down a rake, then searched through the clothes until she found a pair of overalls. With some difficulty she managed to dress the rake in the overalls, pushing the shaft down one leg. "Give me your hat," she said quietly to Olle.

With a sigh he took it off and threw it across the floor. There was no point in asking why.

She noticed his resigned expression and tried to jolly him along.

"Showtime," she whispered.

He merely raised an eyebrow.

WITH THE RAKE in one hand and the hat in the other, Embla made her way over to the window. She managed to balance the hat on the tines of the rake, sticking up above the collar. Carefully she turned her creation so that its back was facing the window, then took a firm hold of the shaft and allowed the puppet to appear briefly.

Twang! A direct hit on the tines. She let go of the shaft and the rake fell to the floor. If it had been a real person, the bullet would have hit the back of the neck.

A sharpshooter.

The ricochet sent the bullet flying sideways. It slammed into the pillar Tore was tied to—at least a meter above the heads of both the dog and his master, but it wasn't good.

"Okay, so now we know," she said, trying to sound calmer than she felt.

Their eyes met and Olle nodded. Now they knew. Whoever was inside the house was a crack shot. Fuck. They both realized what that meant. This gang had made it clear from the start that they were ready to kill anyone who got in their way. Somehow Embla and Olle had to put the shooter at the window out of commission, but how?

She looked around but didn't find any inspiration. She pushed one hand into her pocket to warm it up; she didn't dare put on her gloves in case she had to start shooting again. Her fingers touched the grenade; she'd forgotten it was there.

Suddenly she had a strategy.

"Cover your ears," she whispered to Olle. Once again he didn't ask questions, but simply did as he was told.

With the grenade in her right hand, she went to the window overlooking the dirt road. She quickly confirmed with her phone that the man lying on his back hadn't moved. The pistol had fallen from his grasp and was lying next to his limp hand. Was he dead? Possibly.

She removed the pin and flung the grenade as far toward the side of the road as she could. In a second she was at the other window, facing the house. As the explosion shook the ground, she picked up the semiautomatic rifle, aimed at the bathroom window, and fired off a round of thirty shots.

An unnatural stillness followed, except inside her head, where there was a cacophony of ringing noises. War without earplugs is horrific, as poor Tore loudly informed everyone. In spite of Olle's attempts to calm him, he wouldn't stop howling and barking. The brave dog had had enough of shooting and explosions. A glance at his master told Embla that he'd had enough, too.

She hoped it was over now. The question was whether she'd managed to hit the sniper; if not, they still had a major problem. There was also a risk that he wasn't the only one in the house.

She crawled across the floor and picked up the rake. Olle's hat was in tatters; her puppet would have to manage without it. As before, she allowed it to appear briefly at the window. There was no answering shot this time. That didn't necessarily mean the gunman was gone; he might have realized it was a trick and was simply sitting there, biding his time.

She padded back to Olle and Tore. The dog had stopped barking and was whimpering quietly as his master stroked him and attempted to reassure him. She could see that Olle was even paler now, and his hand was obviously causing him pain. He needed medical attention as soon as possible.

She pointed to the window overlooking the road.

"I'm going to climb out and go around the back of the shed; the sniper won't be able to see me. The critical point will be when I cross the yard. Do you think you can throw one more grenade?"

At first she thought he was going to object, but then he nodded. "Okay."

"Good. Throw it through the same window, then there's no risk of any debris hitting me."

"Okay," he answered in a weary monotone.

"Throw it when I knock three times on the wall."

A nod.

With the reloaded gun in her hand and two spare magazines in her pockets, she went to the window and repeated the maneuver with her phone. The man still lay motionless in the red-stained snow. She swung her leg over the sill and jumped down, keeping a close eye on him. She crouched down beside him; he was dead. To be on the safe side she felt for a pulse in his neck, but there was nothing. *Shit!* This wasn't good.

To her surprise, she felt very calm. She recognized this

coolness; it resembled the concentration needed for the hunt. Her ability to keep a clear head had saved her back in the fall.

The pistol beside the dead man was a Sig Sauer, the pistol used by the Swedish police. She picked it up and checked the magazine: three bullets left. Good. With the Sig Sauer in her left hand and the rifle in her right, she went around the back of the shed. When she reached the corner she stopped and listened. There was absolute silence, apart from the ringing in her ears. And that was only going to get worse. She took a deep breath, then knocked three times on the wall with the butt of the pistol.

THE EXPLOSION CAME when she'd counted to seven. She immediately began to run. If the gunman was still at the window, he would automatically look in the direction where the grenade had gone off, not down at the yard. She raced toward the house, every fiber of her being on full alert. A bullet could strike her at any second.

When she reached the house she pressed herself against the wall to catch her breath and send a thank-you to her own guardian angel. She wasn't out of the woods yet; the odds had been against them from the start, but now at least the threat had been significantly reduced.

The house.

She slipped around the corner, heading for the gaping hole where the porch had been. The door had been blown inward, and the floor was covered in splintered wood. She turned her head and looked back at the devastation. A short distance away among the fir trees, she saw a pair of severely mutilated legs sticking up behind a snowdrift. *That must be the guy who stepped out to shoot us before we found the guns*, she thought. *He didn't get far, thanks to Olle's throwing skills.*

She stepped inside. The place was in darkness; she had

to move cautiously through the debris. She pushed open a door on her right with the barrel of the rifle, then crouched down and looked in. It was a small, old-fashioned kitchen that didn't look like it had been renovated since the 1960s, which was probably the last time it had been cleaned. Empty vodka bottles, beer cans, dirty plates, and fast-food boxes covered every available surface. It stank of mold, rotting garbage, and stale cigarette smoke.

She continued through the hallway. Straight ahead was the living room, furnished with a sagging sofa, a badly scratched coffee table, and a camp bed with a torn sleeping bag. There was an old stove in the corner, with an open fire crackling away.

She checked behind two other doors in the hallway and found two closets: one empty and the other one containing a metal bucket and an old broom. That just left upstairs.

Just as she placed her foot on the bottom step, she heard a faint whimpering from above. It sounded like a woman. Was the sniper female? Had she been hit? Or was it a trap? A male sniper could be forcing her to make a noise.

There was only one way to find out. She crept up the stairs as quietly as she could, ignoring the inevitable creaking and moving fast. The sniveling was coming from a room to the right of the stairs. She tried the door, but it was locked. The sound subsided, but Embla could still hear suppressed sobs. She decided that the occupant didn't represent an immediate danger.

Time to focus on the bathroom, which lay straight ahead. That door was also closed, while one to her left was ajar. She kicked it open and glanced inside. Three camp beds, three sleeping bags. Plus more empty bottles, beer cans, and piles of cigarette ends, and there were five bags with the Nike logo. The air was thick with cigarette smoke, and it brought tears to her eyes.

Bathroom. The sniper had to be in there; she had to make sure she didn't get shot through the thin door. Like a crab she sidled along the wall. She assumed the door was locked. She listened hard; not a sound.

She took a step back and kicked the handle as hard as she could. The door flew open as Embla hurled herself sideways, rolled over, and adopted the firing position.

Nothing.

She took out her phone, clicked on the camera icon, and reached into the room.

Blood. Lots of blood. A male body dressed only in underpants, lying on the floor. A rifle with a telescopic sight lay beside him.

If all the blood had come from the man, he was almost certainly dead. Slowly, Embla straightened up and moved to the doorway.

The stench was appalling. *It can't be coming from him; he hasn't been dead that long.* Then she saw the body of a girl in the rusty old bathtub. She had been dead for some time, probably several days. Her skin was white with a faint grayish tinge, and there were green patches on her belly, which looked swollen. She was naked apart from a short T-shirt.

Embla turned her attention back to the man. The right side of his forehead was gone. He'd been dead before he hit the floor. He was of medium height, slim, and muscular. His chest, arms, and legs were covered in dark hair. The hair on his head was cut very short, but that, too, was dark, as was the stubble on his chin and cheeks. She thought he was probably around thirty. Why was he wearing nothing but underpants? It must have been freezing, walking barefoot on the cold floor.

Maybe he'd been asleep and had woken when he heard the fracas between Embla, Olle, and the man locked in the Mercedes, then grabbed his gun and rushed into the bathroom. He would have had a bird's-eye view of the whole yard from the window. That seemed like the most credible scenario.

The woman's sobs had grown louder. Embla turned to face the locked door. She positioned herself to one side before she knocked.

"Police!"

The sobbing stopped for a second, then resumed with renewed strength.

"I'm going to kick open the door!"

She gathered herself, then kicked the handle as hard as she could. She had to repeat the maneuver twice more before the door flew open. With her rifle at the ready, she entered the room.

The occupant was a young girl, not a woman. Fifteen years old at the most. She was sitting on a mattress on the floor, arms wrapped tightly around her knees. Her eyes were wide with terror, and her entire body was shaking with a combination of cold and sobs. She was wearing only a dirty T-shirt with the slogan BEER BUILT THIS BODY. There was a blanket in a heap on the floor, and the room stank of body odor and semen. Embla saw a supermarket paper bag filled with used toilet paper, and there were several rolls beside the mattress. Against the

opposite wall was another filthy mattress that had presumably been used by the dead girl in the bathroom.

This girl had a shackle around her wrist; she was
chained to the radiator.

Embla lowered her gun and tentatively stepped forward. The girl shook even more violently, tears pouring
down her cheeks. Embla stopped and said as gently as she
could: "I'm here to help you."

Although how was she going to free her? She was
clearly in shock, traumatized by multiple rapes and no
doubt other violent acts. Presumably she'd seen the other
girl die, and of course she'd heard the shooting and the
explosions. It was hardly surprising that she'd broken
down.

Embla slowly picked up the blanket and held it out to
the girl, but she shrank away and made no attempt to take
it. With an encouraging nod, Embla put it down within
reach. She had to get the girl out of here as quickly as
possible; the temperature in the house was dropping fast
because there was a gaping hole where the porch and
front door had been, and there was no glass in the bathroom window.

Embla decided to go back to the shed to see if she
could find a tool to break the girl's shackle.

"I'll be back in a minute," she said reassuringly. She
closed the broken door in an attempt to retain what little
warmth there was in the room; *better than nothing*. She
went over to close the bathroom door, too. Just as
she touched the handle, she heard the sound of an
approaching car.

NOT MORE OF *them!* She felt as if every scrap of strength had drained from her body. She went into the blood-soaked bathroom to check, trying to ignore the stench of death.

As she peered out the window, her heart sank like a stone. The Mercedes van that had just arrived was exactly the same as the one parked outside the storage shed. She bent down and picked up the sniper's gun. The stock was covered in blood, but she didn't care. Right now it was a matter of life and death as far as she and Olle were concerned. And Tore. She placed the gun in position; it felt sticky against her cheek and hands. She peered through the sight and saw two men in the front seats. There was no one behind them, thank goodness. Was there anyone in the back? She pushed that thought aside; if that was the case, she and Olle wouldn't stand a chance.

The driver was a big guy and looked to be between twenty-five and thirty. He had close-cropped blond hair and pale-gray—almost colorless—eyes. *Fish eyes,* Embla thought with a shudder. His features were strongly defined, and he had a distinctive underbite. Tattoos wound their way up his neck and chin. Both he and his companion were wearing dark-blue padded jackets with fur-trimmed hoods. They were unzipped, revealing black T-shirts underneath. *Standard uniform for these guys,* she thought. The passenger was much skinnier, and his ratty little face was generously tattooed. He had several eyebrow piercings, a substantial ring through his septum, and a number of short spikes in his lower lip. It was hard to make out his hair color because he wore a black wool hat.

The van stopped at the first grenade crater and the new arrivals stared at the dead man lying on the dirt road. Embla could see them gesticulating and talking over each other, wondering what the hell had happened.

Would they continue toward the shed and the house? If so, she had to stop them from getting out of the van at all costs. If they went into the shed, they would find Olle. And Tore. If they came into the house, there was no guarantee that Embla would be able to deal with them on her own.

She watched as both men took out their pistols. Sig Sauers, probably, but she could be wrong. They appeared to be arguing now; Rat Face shook his head, his piercings glinting in the light. He obviously didn't like his companion's suggestion, but Fish Eyes looked determined to get his own way.

She checked to make sure the gun was loaded; if not, there was plenty of ammunition on the floor by the window. The guy she'd killed had been a professional, judging by his accuracy and the type of weapon he'd used.

When she looked out again, she saw that Fish Eyes was

about to open the door. Suddenly he stopped; something in the side mirror had caught his attention.

Embla lowered the gun. Flashing blue lights behind the Mercedes! How the hell had that happened? A wave of relief flooded her body, and to her surprise, she felt as if she was about to burst into tears. She pulled herself together; the officers who'd just arrived didn't know that the men in the Mercedes were armed. On the other hand, the men in the Mercedes didn't know that she was at the bathroom window, ready to take them out if necessary. She calmly positioned the gun against her shoulder and focused.

Rat Face and Fish Eyes were sitting perfectly still, each staring into their mirror. By slightly moving the rifle sight over, Embla was able to see what they were looking at. Two armed, uniformed officers were approaching the van, one on each side. They must have left their vehicle around the bend. She quickly switched back to Rat Face and Fish Eyes. They were speaking to each other, but without taking their eyes off the cops. Both held their pistols at chest height, ready to fire as soon as they got out. They opened the doors at exactly the same moment. The police officers stopped, guns raised.

As Fish Eyes set foot on the ground, Embla shot him in the right lower leg. He managed to fire at the officer as he went down, but he missed. Before he could take aim again, Embla put a bullet in his right shoulder. He let out a yell and dropped the gun.

Rat Face stood motionless, his left hand resting on the door. Slowly he turned to face the house and raised his gun. Embla shot him in the right shoulder, too. He looked extremely surprised as he fell backward. The gun flew out of his hand.

When she looked for the two officers, she saw them peering out from behind the Mercedes where they'd sought shelter.

She yelled at the top of her voice:

"This is Detective Inspector Embla Nyström from Gothenburg! Detective Inspector Olle Tillman is inside the storage shed to your right. He's injured—we walked straight into a trap, and we've had to fight for our lives!"

This was an unnecessary piece of information; the place looked like a bomb site.

The officer closest to the shed cupped a hand around his mouth and shouted, "Tillman—are you there?"

Embla heard a faint response from inside the building. The officer went over to the window overlooking the road, the one Embla couldn't see from her vantage point. Olle's colleague picked up the pistols belonging to the men she'd shot. Embla could hear voices, but she couldn't make out what was being said; her ears were ringing again.

Slowly she put down the gun. She left the semiautomatic rifle where it was, propped against the wall. There wasn't a sound from the room where the girl was; right now Embla didn't even have the energy to open the door and check on her.

She plodded down the stairs feeling as if her boots were filled with lead. When she reached the bottom she went over to the hole where the door used to be and leaned against the wall. Olle emerged from the shed with Tore. His colleagues patted him on the shoulder and made a fuss over the dog. All three men were smiling, overcome with relief. Then they turned and saw her.

Their smiles disappeared, and suddenly they looked horrified. She couldn't work out why. Weren't they going to come over and congratulate her? Why were they just standing there?

Slowly she realized what the problem was. Both her hands were sticky with blood. She had blood all over her clothes. Blood everywhere. Her light-brown boots were dark red. With blood.

Blood. Blood. Blood . . .

SHE HAD VERY little recollection of what happened after that—only vague images of the journey to the hospital by ambulance. She did remember the lovely feeling of lying on a stretcher and being able to relax. Her body ached from all the tension, and there was a constant ringing in her ears. What annoyed her most was that she wasn't allowed to sleep. The paramedics had told her they suspected she'd taken a blow to the head because she'd collapsed when she emerged from the house. Therefore she had to stay awake so that they could monitor her. She could have protested, told them she'd probably fainted because of the severe concussion she'd suffered back in the fall, but she didn't have the energy.

She was taken into a side room in the emergency department. A health-care assistant named Ali stayed with her. He smiled a lot; his teeth were very white, and his voice was soft and kind. His presence was reassuring. He accompanied her to the bathroom across the hall. As she shuffled along, all activity stopped and everyone stared at her. She assumed it was because seeing someone covered in blood who was still able to move was quite a novelty. Ali advised her not to lock the door; he would wait outside.

Back in the side room he talked nonstop to prevent her from nodding off. Afterward she couldn't recall a word he'd said.

He gently helped her remove her bloodstained clothes, placed them in a black plastic bag, then washed the blood from her face and hands.

Blood. Bloody hands. I've got blood on my hands.

Two nurses and a doctor arrived. The doctor was young, and his hair stuck out in all directions. In one hand he was holding a green paper surgical cap, which he balled up and put in his pocket before introducing himself. Embla immediately forgot his name. They clearly didn't believe her assertion that she was unhurt and examined her carefully. They found no external injuries and decided to send her for an ECG and EEG.

The three of them left, and she was alone with Ali again. Good. At last she could get some sleep. But no, Ali had been instructed to keep her awake until all the tests were completed. He found her some faded hospital clothes; her colleagues would collect her own clothing for forensic analysis.

AFTER WHAT SEEMED like an eternity, the doctor returned. He was only a couple of years older than her, but the expression in his eyes was that of an old man who'd seen the worst of humanity. It struck her that maybe she had the same look. Right now she felt about the same age as her grandmother, who'd been dead for almost twenty years.

"The good news is that we haven't found anything wrong, either on the ECG or the EEG. In fact you have the heart of an elite sportswoman," he informed her with a smile.

I am *an elite sportswoman,* she thought, but she didn't have the strength to answer. She simply nodded.

"I've read your notes from back in the fall. You went through a terrible trauma, both physically and mentally, and I suspect that what you've experienced today was even worse. Like a war zone."

A war zone. The explosions, the gunfire, the dead bodies, the adrenaline pumping. She had feared for her life, but her survival instinct had kept her functioning.

She met the doctor's weary gaze. "You're right. There was blood. A lot of blood."

He nodded. "Exactly. You're suffering from post-traumatic stress right now. It often affects those who've been exposed to severe trauma. It's not uncommon among soldiers who've been—"

"In a war. Yes, I know. I saw a psychologist for a while last year; she talked a lot about post-traumatic stress."

Her eyelids felt so heavy. His voice came from far, far away.

"It's good that you already have that insight. The question is how we can best help you."

"Home. I want to go home. Call my parents. Ask them to come and pick me up."

She was practically asleep before she finished speaking.

Embla was on sick leave for the following week; after that she would be on desk duty until the internal investigation was completed. She was called in to the police station several times to go over her account of the events near Ulvsjön. On each occasion she had to make a real effort not to yell: "Leave me alone! I know I killed two people—but they tried to kill us first!" She realized she had to make a professional and trustworthy impression on her colleagues. It took its toll, but she succeeded in presenting a cool, calm façade.

Deep down she felt anything but calm. The nightmares that had haunted her after the events of the previous year returned. She was surrounded by men, their heads and limbs shot to pieces, while she was frozen to the spot, incapable of getting away. Her own screams usually woke her when the first zombie reached out his bloody hands to grab her.

The only positive aspect was that she no longer dreamed of the night when Lollo had disappeared.

In spite of her poor mental state, she refused all offers of counseling. She just couldn't bear the thought of probing what had gone on. It wasn't the battle she wanted to avoid talking about—because it had been a real battle—but the exchange of fire during the previous fall's moose hunt. She couldn't afford to make a mistake in that context.

Before the initial interviews with the internal investigators, she and Olle had been told not to speak to each other. Once their respective accounts had been documented, there was nothing to stop them. Embla took the initiative and made the first call. To her relief he sounded genuinely pleased to hear her voice. From then on they'd spoken more or less every evening, and it felt good to be back in touch.

Olle was still on sick leave as well. A specialist surgeon had had to remove splinters of bone from the gunshot wound and reposition sinews and bone; the hand was still bandaged. Tore had found it hard to settle for the first few nights, but after a week or so of peace and quiet with his master, he was feeling better.

ON THE MONDAY of the second week, Embla was back at work, on light duties only. She slipped into the conference room where the morning briefing was held and sat in the back, as far as possible from her boss. After a moment, she was joined by Irene Huss, who arrived with a cup of coffee in each hand as usual.

Tommy Persson was standing at the front by the whiteboard, leading so-called morning prayers. He nodded to Embla. "First a quick update to get Embla up to speed."

Everyone turned and looked at her. *So much for sneaking in unnoticed,* she thought.

"Two men were shot dead up by Ulvsjön, and two were blown up with hand grenades," Tommy said. "None of the dead have been identified yet, but we've sent photographs, fingerprints, and DNA samples to our colleagues in Split. Something tells me they'll know who those guys are. The only one we have identified is Jiri Acika; his DNA and prints are in our database from his previous spell in jail. He's the brother of Andreas Acika, Milo Stavic's director of finance. They're both cousins of the Stavic brothers. Jiri is also the only one of the three survivors who's not in the hospital; he's being held on remand. The only medical treatment he's received is a tetanus shot and antibiotics for the dog bite on his wrist. At least the dog who inflicted the injury isn't required to face an internal investigation."

He smiled and gave Embla a meaningful look before continuing.

"The two guys who turned up just before the police arrived are both in Sahlgrenska Hospital. Their bullet wounds aren't life-threatening and obviously they're under armed guard around the clock. They've been identified as . . ."

He clicked on his laptop and Fish Eyes appeared on the whiteboard.

". . . Liam Eklund, age twenty-six. He served four years in Kumla for narcotics offenses and complicity in a homicide. Member of the Red Devils, an offshoot of the Hells Angels. He's mixed up in most of the crap both gangs are involved in."

Another click, and Rat Face's nasty little eyes were staring down at them, overshadowed by the multiple piercings in his eyebrows.

"This is another old acquaintance. Timmy Johansson,

age twenty-five. He's served two sentences, each for two and half years. The first was for serious narcotics offenses and aggravated assault, the second for human trafficking and multiple rapes. He's been out for less than six months, and we think he resumed his career. One theory is that he and Eklund had come to collect the two girls we found in the house—and probably drugs and guns. We can't be sure because neither of them has said a word."

Embla didn't want to draw attention to herself, so she whispered to Irene, "Can you ask what the girl in the bathtub died of?"

Irene nodded and politely raised her hand.

Tommy nodded to her.

"Do we have a cause of death for the girl in the bathroom?"

His expression was grim as he answered. "The preliminary autopsy report suggests an overdose. The other girl is in pretty bad shape, both mentally and physically. They'd pumped all kinds of different drugs into both girls. The one who died is about fifteen years old, the one who survived a year or so younger."

There was a brief silence; several officers shook their heads.

"Three cans of diesel were found in the Range Rover. It could well be that the two gang members in that car were intending to burn down the house in order to get rid of all the evidence, including the dead girl."

"Just like they did with Kador," Embla murmured, so quietly that only Irene could hear.

The image on the whiteboard was replaced with a picture of a pistol. *A Beretta M9*, Embla thought.

Tommy gazed at his audience, and suddenly his face broke into a broad grin.

"I've actually got some good news! This Beretta was under Milo Stavic's hands when his body was found. But as we know, it wasn't his; it belonged to his brother Luca. Göran Krantz has checked all available numbers and registers; he's also carried out test firing. We now have the facts about the brothers' two Berettas."

Another click, and an identical pistol appeared.

"This is Milo's Beretta. Jiri Acika was holding it when he threatened our colleagues Embla Nyström and Olle Tillman. We assume that he swapped the guns after killing Milo because he didn't want to keep a pistol that could be linked to the two murders. He did, however, want a high-quality Beretta for himself, so he kept the one he found in Milo's room, which, of course, was a completely idiotic thing to do. We also know that he took Milo's iPhone and possibly a tablet and a laptop. Those haven't been recovered. Greed overcame Jiri, and he couldn't resist helping himself to Milo's gold watch, which he was wearing when he was arrested. We think he tried to steal a valuable emerald ring, but he couldn't get it off Milo's finger. He also had a bunch of keys in his pocket; Göran has established that they're the keys to Milo's apartment."

He fell silent, pausing for effect.

"Forensics have lifted a right thumbprint from Luca's pistol—the murder weapon—and they found DNA on the magazine. Both from Jiri Acika!"

His face lit up with triumph, and there was a scattering of applause around the room. Human witnesses can be threatened and frightened into silence, but there's no arguing with strong forensic evidence. It's often the key to sending a criminal to jail.

When the hum of conversation subsided, Tommy raised a hand and continued. "So Jiri Acika killed both Milo and Luca, but plenty of questions still remain. We know that Luca had his laptop and iPhone in the car, so it was easy for Jiri Acika to take them. And we know that Luca was shot first, with his own gun. But how did Jiri get a hold of it? Who gained access to Luca's apartment, with its security system and alarm?"

Embla immediately started wondering, then realized her boss was still talking.

" . . . involved in an accident. Jiri's car collided with a motorbike at a junction. No one was seriously hurt, but there was a patrol car on the scene within a minute because the collision happened a stone's throw from the police station in Split. It was in the middle of rush hour, at a quarter to five in the afternoon. This was the day before Kador disappeared. After that we know nothing about Jiri's movements. Presumably he traveled under a false name because we have no record of his arrival in Sweden during the past two weeks. Nor any other suspects. New arrivals from the Balkans are of interest, but we've found nothing so far."

Something was nagging Embla, but she couldn't quite pin it down. Who could have had access to Luca's pistol inside his own personal Fort Knox? Suddenly it all made sense. She really didn't want to draw attention to herself, but this time she had no choice.

Hesitantly she raised her hand. Tommy gave her an encouraging nod.

"I don't think Luca's killer went into his apartment."

"No? So how did Jiri Acika get a hold of the Beretta? He's not a ghost who can walk through locked doors," Tommy said. The accompanying smile didn't reach his eyes. Embla's uncertainty was replaced by a flare of anger, but she couldn't let it show. She took a deep breath.

"Both Milo and Luca knew that their brother Kador had disappeared. They must have realized there was a risk he'd been murdered. Even if they didn't believe they themselves were in danger, they each owned a Beretta. I'm pretty sure Milo would have told Luca to make sure he was armed, and I'm also pretty sure Luca would have done just that, bearing in mind that he'd been shot four years earlier."

Almost everyone was looking at her now. No one tried to interrupt, but she could see that some of her colleagues looked dubious. A couple of people were checking their phones, and one was staring out the rain-streaked window.

"But Luca was no marksman. He rarely if ever practiced, according to his partner, Stephen Walker. Where does a person who's not used to being armed put his gun when he's driving? In the glove compartment, probably. Or on the passenger seat. Then he picks it up when he gets out of the car. The safety is still on, which makes it comparatively easy for an assailant to surprise the owner of the gun and take it. With violence, if necessary, but I suspect there was no need in this case."

She had the attention of the room now, which gave her the confidence to go on.

"So Jiri Acika was waiting inside the parking garage. When Luca got out of his car, Jiri went over to say hi to his cousin. I'm sure Jiri had a gun with him, but when he saw the Beretta in Luca's hand, he got an idea."

She fell silent and looked around the table. Even the guy who'd been staring out the window was with her now. Who would lose patience first and ask the question?

"So what do you think happened?"

Tommy, of course.

"They were cousins. I think Jiri called Luca and said he knew something about Kador. Milo was out of town, so he needed to tell Luca—but not over the phone, they had to meet. In secret—no one was to know that Jiri was in Sweden."

Her throat was dry; she'd gotten out of the habit of talking so much. She drank some water and continued. "So Jiri saw the Beretta, and he overpowered his own cousin and shot him twice."

No one spoke for a moment, then Tommy said thoughtfully, "It sounds plausible, and it explains how Jiri acquired Luca's pistol. And his laptop and cell phone. Then when he found Milo's Beretta in the cottage, he decided to swap them. Maybe he thought one or both guns were unregistered."

He looked at Embla with something that might have been respect.

"Well done, Embla. I think you're right. The simplest explanation is usually the correct one."

He glanced around the room. "Okay, so Jiri will be questioned again today. We still don't know why all three brothers were killed, but it could be some kind of apocalyptic battle between different gangs operating across Europe, with their base in the former Yugoslavia."

He glanced at his notepad before raising his final point.

"The issue of Kador's family remains. I've spoken to Göran Krantz, and he's agreed to coordinate the search because he's in regular contact with our colleagues in Split."

Could Lollo and her children be in Sweden? Göran had said it was possible, because the only people she could turn to were her in-laws in Gothenburg. Imagine seeing Lollo again! The thought made Embla's stomach contract with nerves, and she felt a shiver of anticipation. However, she was increasingly afraid that the killers were also trying to track down Lollo. Jiri Acika might be in custody, but his associates were still out there. Presumably that was why Lollo had fled from Split. She might have important information about the Stavic brothers' various activities. She might even know who was behind the murders. The police had to find Lollo—and soon.

EMBLA HAD BEEN back at work for a few days and Olle was on his second week of sick leave when she decided phone calls weren't enough; she needed to see him. She contacted him on the Wednesday evening, and he immediately asked how she was.

"I saw the doctor again today; she says I'm still suffering from post-traumatic stress. She could be right—I'm having nightmares. Are you?"

He hesitated before answering.

"I did at the beginning, for the first few nights. My hand was really painful, too. It's getting better, but neither Tore nor I are at a hundred percent yet."

He swallowed hard. He sounded unusually serious, and he made no attempt to dismiss what had happened with a joke, which was his usual style.

"Nobody else can understand what we went through up there," Embla said quietly. "If that guy hadn't been driving past along the main road just as one of the grenades exploded, he wouldn't have contacted our colleagues in Bengtsfors . . . and there's no guarantee we'd have made it out of there alive."

Her final words were no more than a whisper. Tears burned behind her eyelids, and she had a lump in her throat. It was Göran who'd told her about the man who'd been passing at exactly the right moment. He'd realized something serious was going on and had been sensible enough to put his foot down until he reached Strand, where he knew there would be a phone signal, and he had called the police.

They sat in silence for a while, each lost in their own thoughts.

Eventually Olle said, "Maybe we should meet. I haven't heard much about how the investigation's going, which is kind of frustrating."

"I can understand that. I think it would be good to meet up. I have some information, but the picture is far from complete. And of course I'm not directly involved in the events at Ulvsjön because of the internal investigation."

It was somehow humiliating that she wasn't allowed to play an active role, when she was the one who'd taken the greatest risks and made sure the Stavic brothers' murderer had been caught.

"I've been given the job of looking for Kador's family. We're not certain they're in Gothenburg, but it seems likely. We also know they're living under a false identity."

The driving force in this depressing task was the hope that she would manage to find some trace of Lollo and her children. The clock was ticking, and the risk of someone else tracking them down first was increasing.

Olle cleared his throat. "Are you doing anything this weekend?"

Embla had arranged to go out for a meal with friends, but she could easily do that another time.

"Nothing I can't rearrange," she said, keeping her tone light.

"Where shall we meet?"

"You decide. You're the one who's still suffering with a sore paw."

I'm suffering with a sore soul, but that doesn't show, she thought.

"I'm not suffering, and it's not too sore," he informed her. He sighed deeply and added: "My sister's family has recovered from the flu, and Mom is back from Tenerife. They've all decided they need to take care of little me, and it's kind of wearing."

Embla giggled; she knew exactly what he meant. Her parents and brothers had made an enormous fuss over her, inviting her over for meals and calling every day to see how she was. Not to mention her friends and colleagues . . . It became exhausting after a while, to say the least. It was good to know that people cared about her, of course, but enough was enough.

"Maybe one of them could watch Tore for the weekend? How is he, by the way?"

There was a lengthy silence. "He's doing okay, but I think it's too early to leave him with someone else. I'll have to do it when I go back to work, but right now . . ." He broke off, and Embla understood. He was torn between wanting to see her and wanting to stay with his courageous dog, so that Tore could make a full recovery and become his old self again. The question was whether any of them would be able to do that. What had happened was etched on their mind forever; they could never erase it completely.

She had carefully thought through her plan before she called him, but she managed to make it sound as if it had just occurred to her.

"Maybe we need to go on a retreat for a couple of days," she suggested casually.

"A retreat? What do you mean?"

"You know the kind of thing—you cut yourself off from the outside world. No phones, no TV, nothing to disturb your inner calm."

"You want us to go camping in the mountains?" he said with a laugh.

"No—I've got a much better idea, and Tore can come, too. I need to check on something, then I'll get back to you."

There was a brief silence, then he said: "Sounds promising. And . . ." He took a deep breath. "It will be good to see you again. The day after tomorrow . . . or on Saturday?"

"Let's aim for Friday evening."

"Fantastic!" There was no mistaking the joy and relief in his voice. Embla thought it was best to let him believe he was the one who'd taken the initiative in arranging to meet up.

WHEN THE ALARM woke her on Thursday morning, Embla felt fully rested. She hadn't had a single nightmare. Presumably it was the thought of the weekend retreat that had made her feel so much better. She'd arranged everything immediately after speaking to Olle; it was all organized.

The rain had stopped at around midnight; the sky cleared and the temperature quickly dropped below freezing. All the water on the roads and sidewalks froze, covering the city in a sheet of ice. It happens almost every winter in Gothenburg, and it always causes total chaos. People can't get into their cars, because the doors are frozen shut. There are lots of broken bones thanks to the treacherous sidewalks, and the hospitals' emergency rooms soon fill up. There are also more road traffic accidents than usual, despite winter tires.

In light of her previous experience, Embla decided to take the tram. She was wearing her thick-soled hunting boots, which were excellent when it was slippery.

As she was taking them off in the changing room, her phone vibrated. It was a text from Göran: *Think I've found something re: Louise.*

Her heart began to beat faster, and once again she felt

a confusing mixture of hope and . . . what? Fear? Anticipation? She kicked off her boots and slipped on the
ballerina pumps she kept in her locker. She decided to
give morning prayers a miss and go straight to Göran's
office. On the way upstairs she sent a text to Tommy
Persson: *New info from GK re: Louise L. Will report back
asap.*

Embla found Göran by the coffee machine talking to
the male technician who'd been with them up in Herremark. All she knew about him was that his name was
Bengan, and he'd been with forensics forever. Small and
skinny with thin gray hair and a lined, sallow face, he
looked kind of dried out.

Both men turned as she approached. Bengan nodded
to her, murmured something to Göran, then disappeared
with a steaming cup of coffee in his hand.

"That guy is worth his weight in gold. He's almost
reached retirement age, but I'm keeping my fingers
crossed that he'll stay on for a while longer," Göran whispered loudly enough for his aging colleague to hear.

If Bengan did hear, there was no reaction; he simply
continued down the hallway, stooping slightly.

Göran offered Embla a cup of tea and she accepted,
just to be sociable. He jerked his head in the direction of
his office.

"I've got freshly baked cinnamon buns."

That was an offer she wouldn't be accepting. Even
though she no longer competed as a boxer, her eating
habits had stayed with her. They'd been hammered home
by her trainer over a period of more than a decade. It was
important to eat a nutritious diet and to avoid things like
processed meats, sugar, and alcohol. According to her

eldest brother, Atle, she was suffering from orthorexia. She'd googled the word and discovered that it was used to define a condition where a person is fixated on a healthy lifestyle and can become obsessed with excessive exercise and a healthy diet. Sometimes it can turn into anorexia. Embla thought Atle was wrong. Besides, he was no expert when it came to nutrition. He was an anesthetist. His patients didn't eat anything. He put them on a drip and sent them to sleep.

Göran refused to tell Embla about the search for Louise until he'd eaten her cinnamon bun as well as his own, and fetched another cup of coffee from the machine.

"Bengan and Linda went through Milo Stavic's Audi yesterday. They didn't get around to it before because we have several ongoing homicide investigations. Anyway, Milo picked it up the week before he drove to Herremark. Ten days before, to be precise. There are only five hundred and sixty kilometers on the odometer. Since it's so new, there aren't many fingerprints or other traces in the car—which makes the ones they did find all the more interesting."

He put on his reading glasses and took a sheet of paper out of his in-tray.

"As expected, the trunk was almost completely clean. They found prints belonging to staff at the Audi dealership, and to Milo himself. However, on the inside of the back door they also found a set of prints from a small right hand. Those same prints occurred again around the front passenger seat. And there were three different sets of children's prints in the backseat."

As Göran was reading, Embla felt an icy chill creep across her scalp, down the back of her neck and her spine. She had to exercise great self-control to stop her teeth from chattering.

He looked up at her.

"We have Louise Lindqvist's prints on record following her disappearance. Need I say the ones in the trunk are a perfect match?"

Embla's tongue was sticking to the roof of her mouth. She ought to say something, but she couldn't do it. She nodded mutely.

Göran peered over the top of his glasses, smiling with satisfaction.

"Louise and her three children have definitely been in that car."

He referred to the sheet of paper once more.

"We also found strands of hair of different lengths and from different people. They've been sent for DNA analysis, which could take some time. However, we do have Louise's DNA, so we should be able to establish her identity, and the fact that the children are related to her."

Embla felt that she was able to breathe normally again. It was true: Lollo really was alive. In a moment of clarity, she realized she hadn't believed it until now. Those years of feeling guilty about her friend had left their mark. As time went by, the fear that Lollo was dead had grown stronger, along with the conviction that it was Embla's fault. The revelation that Lollo had left on her own accord and had been living in Split all along had come as an even greater shock. Realizing that Lollo had lied and dragged Embla into her planned disappearance aroused mixed feelings that she couldn't shake.

GÖRAN WAS A genius when it came to computers, and he was very good at finding people, but right now he was busy with a thousand things at once. Therefore he'd asked Embla to continue searching for Louise and the children. When she said she wasn't sure where to begin, he'd replied: "Use the computer. Contact the authorities. She's bound to show up somewhere sooner or later. It's just a matter of getting a hold of the right loose thread and pulling on it." Then his phone had started ringing and she'd left his office.

After reporting back to Tommy Persson, she'd headed for the office she shared with Irene Huss. Her colleague was at her desk staring out the dirty window. Somehow she managed to balance her long limbs in a half-seated position on her chair without appearing to be uncomfortable. A faint pink flush had begun to find its way between the buildings, giving the façades a golden glow. Maybe there would be a really beautiful sunrise. It had been a while.

"Hi—how's it going?"

Irene turned to look at her and unexpectedly gave her a big smile.

"Great! I'm just sitting here trying to recover from the shock."

Embla raised her eyebrows. "The shock?"

"I'm going to be a grandmother!" Irene flung her arms wide, as if she wanted to embrace the whole world.

It was unexpected, and Embla didn't quite know what to say. It wasn't that Irene's twin daughters were too young to become parents—they were only two years younger than her—but . . .

"A grandmother . . . Wow! I mean, congratulations!"

"Thank you! It's Katarina and Felipe. Katarina emailed me late last night, and I've only just read her message. She's just been to the doctor for her first examination, and she's in her tenth week. It's a little early to start cheering, but I think it'll be fine. She's suffering from morning sickness, but otherwise everything's going well."

"Have they moved back from Brazil?"

The smile faded slightly.

"No, they're still living in São Paulo. Katarina's got a permanent post at the English girls' school, and Felipe's architecture company has plenty of work."

"Will she come home when the baby's due?"

Irene shook her head. "I don't think so. They have good health insurance through Felipe's job. The baby will be born in one of Brazil's best private hospitals."

Embla thought about her friend Agnes. When her contractions had started last summer, there hadn't been a single maternity bed available in the whole of Gothenburg. She'd had to go to Varberg Hospital, where the poor midwives had been running from one room to another, trying to be there for all the women at different stages of labor. According to Agnes, one mom had had to give birth in an ordinary examination room. That didn't sound safe to Embla; maybe it was better for Katarina to have her baby in São Paulo.

"So what are you working on at the moment?" Irene asked, giving her a searching look.

"I'm trying to track down my childhood friend Louise Lindqvist, also known as Mirja Stavic, and her three children. All we know is that she and the kids have entered Sweden under false names, and that they've been in Gothenburg. If we're lucky, they're still here."

Embla filled Irene in on the forensic evidence from Milo's new Audi.

"So now I have a big problem—I don't really know where to start."

Irene nodded thoughtfully, then said, "Start where you know she's been—with the car."

"Okay—thanks."

Embla sat down and logged into her computer with her ID card. She stared at the screen for a long time. Computers weren't her thing, but she wasn't completely useless; no one under forty-five is these days.

She went into the vehicle database first and entered all the information Göran had given her about the Audi. It was registered with a company called STAV Property Ltd. A quick check told her that all three Stavic brothers were listed as owners.

The homepage showed a solid building that dated back to the beginning of the previous century. The copper roof had acquired an attractive blue-green patina and was adorned with several pinnacles and turrets. The balconies had white marble balustrades, and bay windows studded the reddish-brown façade. Around the windows, faces and floral garlands had been carved into the stone. It was charming and beautiful, and appeared to be well cared for.

The text below was full of breathless enthusiasm.

> *This is your chance to realize your dream of an apartment in the heart of Gothenburg! We are pleased to announce the sale of Phase Two in the Vasastan district of the city. The first apartments should be ready to move in to by the end of September at the latest! The next batch will be finished by the end of December, the remainder in May next year. By then the entire building will have been renovated, and we are taking great pains to maintain the period charm of the early twentieth century. Forty-five apartments are available in total, with between two and five bedrooms. They are light and airy, with large windows. The ceiling height is no less than three meters!*

Embla worked her way through lyrical descriptions of parquet flooring, modern kitchens with a retro style, and generous entertaining spaces. Out of sheer curiosity she clicked on "More information" and scrolled down to the prices of the apartments. At first she couldn't believe her eyes, but there it was on the screen. A place the same size as the one she rented in Krokslätt would cost 4.4 million, with a monthly service charge of 5,350.

The service charge might be okay, but who the hell can afford 4.4 million for an apartment measuring fifty-two square meters? Not someone earning a police officer's salary, that was for sure.

Down at the bottom was a number to call between

9:00 A.M. and 4:00 P.M. if you were interested. On impulse Embla made the call. It took a while for someone to answer.

"Good morning, STAV Property Ltd. How can I help you?" said a cheerful female voice.

Embla felt a faint tremor of recognition, but couldn't quite work out why.

"Good morning—who am I speaking to?"

"Anna in the main office."

Then Embla knew exactly who it was. She tried to disguise her voice. "Sorry, wrong number," she croaked.

"No problem. Have a good day."

Embla's heart was pounding. She immediately called Göran, and before he could speak she said:

"I've found her!"

FINDING THE ADDRESS wasn't a problem because the phone number on the homepage belonged to a landline.

"She's in Milo's office block in Gårda—the tall glass complex," Embla said.

Göran was studying the website she'd found.

"So we know where she is at the moment, but not where she lives." He looked up at Embla. "Are you sure she didn't recognize your voice?"

"Absolutely—I disguised it."

Göran nodded to himself and turned his attention back to the screen. After a while Embla couldn't keep quiet any longer.

"Listen, I've got an idea of how we can approach this."

"Go on."

She decided to come straight out with it; if he didn't

like her plan, they'd have to try to come up with something else.

"I can't contact her again—she'd recognize my voice, and she'd disappear in no time. I suggest we put the building under surveillance, then follow her home."

He glanced up at her and nodded, which encouraged her to continue.

"On the other hand, you could call her, say you're interested in an apartment. Book an appointment."

He thought it over.

"That could work. I can say that my wife and I are selling our enormous mansion in Hovås and are looking for a suitable apartment in the center of town," he said with an ironic smile.

"Perfect! That sounds like a typical client."

"I'm sure you're right. The only thing is, I can't understand why they don't have a real estate agent dealing with sales." He read through the text again. "It sounds kind of unprofessional to me. 'The next batch . . .' That's not the terminology I'd expect. And those exclamation marks . . ."

"Asking who the agent is might be a good opening question," Embla suggested.

They talked over their tactics for a little longer, then Göran went off to the lab to pick up a burner phone. Before making the call, he set the phone to record, then switched on the speaker so that Embla could follow the conversation.

"Good morning, STAV Property Ltd. How can I help you?"

It was the same woman, and it was definitely Lollo's voice. Embla gave the thumbs-up to show that he'd rung the right person.

"Good morning. My name is Gunnar Karlsson. I see from your website that you're about to start selling apartments in Vasastan. My wife and I would like to know more."

"That's right, you can sign up right now to get more information and register your interest. There will be three releases of fifteen apartments each. You can see the plans by clicking on the tab at the bottom of the homepage. Were you thinking of the first batch in September?"

"We were. Is there an agent I can contact?"

A sharp intake of breath.

"I'm afraid the agent who dealt with Phase One isn't able to take care of Phase Two because it clashed with another project. The owners are currently negotiating with another agent who will take over sales at a later stage."

The owners are currently negotiating . . . The Stavic brothers are dead. Sounds suspicious. Well, of course it does—we're talking about Milo Stavic's business affairs. So who's running the show now? Embla wondered, exchanging a glance with Göran, who raised his eyebrows in mutual understanding. Lollo—or Anna—had just told him a straight lie.

"So it's not possible to view any of the apartments at this stage?" he asked in a pleasant tone of voice.

"Not yet, I'm afraid. The renovation work is in full swing. Plumbing and . . . that kind of thing. We will have a show apartment ready at the beginning of April, then each apartment will be available to view as soon as it's finished."

Lollo was doing a sterling job. She'd always been good at taking the lead, while Embla had been the admiring friend, providing backup. In hindsight, their roles in the relationship had been very clear. Embla had always gone along with her suggestions, acted as the approving audience who never questioned Lollo's ideas. She'd always seen Lollo as her best friend, her only real friend, and she'd been terrified of losing her, which was exactly what had happened.

One advantage of Lollo's disappearance from her life was that she'd been forced to find new friends. Through boxing and hunting she'd gotten to know like-minded individuals, but she'd also connected to people she'd met in different contexts. Over the years she'd acquired a wide circle of friends and acquaintances whose company she enjoyed.

"So should I register my interest now, or wait until the new agent takes over?" Göran asked, following the strategy they'd discussed earlier.

"You can register right now."

He winked at Embla.

"I think I need to speak to my wife first; we'd better take a look at the plans on your website before we make our decision. I'll get back to you," he said hesitantly.

"No problem. You have a nice day," Anna/Lollo said, still cheerful and friendly.

"Thanks—you too."

He ended the call and looked at Embla.

"You're absolutely certain that's Louise Lindqvist?"

"One hundred percent."

"Okay. Let's find out where she lives."

THE GLASS COMPLEX in Gårda was large and had several entrances, plus two access points to the underground parking lot, so they needed at least four cars to mount a surveillance operation. It was difficult to release so many officers on such short notice, but within an hour there were five of them in the Violent Crimes Unit's conference room. Göran was leading the briefing, but Tommy Persson was there, too.

"So we now know that Louise and the children are in Gothenburg, and we know where she's working," Göran began.

Detective Inspector Fredrik Stridh raised his hand.

"Is there anything to suggest that their lives are in danger? I can understand that they fled from Split when Kador Stavic went missing, but surely they're safe here?"

Göran's expression was serious.

"We can't rule out the possibility that they're still in danger. Thanks to our colleagues in Split, the four men who were killed up in Dalsland have been identified as members of a rival gang from the Zagreb area. Apparently they're a powerful group with plans to expand across the Balkans and throughout Europe, but in Split the Stavic brothers, represented by Kador, were too strong. Jiri Acika has lived there for the past five years, ever since he was released from Tidaholm prison. We've been questioning him for almost two weeks, and we've gotten precisely nowhere. He's been remanded in custody on suspicion of murdering both Milo and Luca Stavic. We have evidence linking him to both homicides, and we also know he'd been recruited to the Zagreb gang because he was with them at the house in Dalsland."

"How about his brother?" Irene Huss asked.

"We haven't found anything to indicate that he was involved. Andreas Acika was Milo Stavic's right-hand man—but was Milo nurturing a snake in his bosom? It is possible that both brothers had links to the gang in Zagreb."

He looked around the room; Fredrik was waving his hand again.

"So what does Andreas Acika say? I presume you've questioned him, too."

"We've given him a real grilling, but he maintains he's innocent. He insists he had no idea that his brother was in Sweden, or that Jiri had anything to do with the Zagreb gang. Then again, we don't know exactly where Andreas's loyalty lies. Milo was the spider at the center of a huge international criminal web. How many of his men have gone over to the other side? And how many of them are in Gothenburg?"

Tommy Persson cleared his throat. "It does seem as if Milo thought the family wasn't safe in Split since he took steps to get them out of the country just hours after Kador's disappearance. He also provided Louise and the children with false identities, and he must have had a place to live ready for them. There's no evidence that they've been in his apartment—only in the Audi," he pointed out.

Göran agreed. "I'm sure you're right; he was ready to implement his plan if it became necessary. And a part of that plan was to give Louise a job at STAV Property's head office."

He then went through the surveillance notes. Louise was probably in one of the offices on the top story, where Milo's parent company, MISTAV Ltd., occupied the whole floor. MISTAV was also part-owner of the building, along with another major construction firm.

"No night shift, thank goodness," Fredrik said to Embla as they left the room, firing off a flirtatious smile. He always did that when they met. As usual she merely gave a faint smile and nodded. *Sorry, but I don't date married men,* she thought. Nadir's handsome face flashed through her mind. He still made her heart turn over, but she knew she'd done the right thing in ending things with him. It had been a brief, passionate fling, and she was never going to get involved with a married man again.

SURVEILLANCE BEGAN AT exactly 11:00 that same day. Half an hour earlier Irene Huss had called STAV Property Ltd. to express an interest in the apartments in Vasastan. As before, Lollo/Louise/Mirja Stavic/Anna Something-or-other had answered.

In spite of the morning's promising sunrise, the weather had changed. It was bitterly cold and raining hard, and pedestrians hunched their shoulders against the icy wind. In other words, it was a return to the usual late-winter conditions in Gothenburg.

A major problem was that the last picture they had of Louise was her wedding photo, which was taken almost fifteen years ago. Embla was pretty sure she wouldn't have dyed her hair because she'd always been proud of her thick pale-blonde locks. Apart from that, they had no idea what she looked like. Strangely enough, it seemed that Mirja Stavic had never been issued a passport, so the police in Split were unable to supply a current passport photograph.

At lunchtime, employees came pouring out of the building; there were several blonde women among them, but none who resembled Louise. Maybe she was eating in the in-house cafeteria.

Fredrik Stridh had made his way down to the underground parking lot, dressed as an employee of the firm responsible for the parking facilities in and around the building. Göran had told him to look for a new Audi A6. He'd found two, but when he checked the owners, only one was really interesting. A brand-new white A6 was registered as a company car with STAV Property. It had been supplied by the same company that had sold the big Audi to Milo, and both cars had been collected at the same time, the week before Milo drove up to Herremark.

Fredrik quickly returned to the unmarked police car waiting by the ramp that led down to the parking lot. He changed into his own jacket; now it was just a matter of waiting for Louise to leave work.

Göran and Embla were in a black Volvo XC40, a recent acquisition by the Gothenburg police. The new-car smell was so strong that it made Embla feel nauseated, and she had to open the window in spite of the cold. Her mouth was dry, her stomach churning. She didn't need her psychologist friend to tell her that she was nervous at the prospect of seeing Lollo again.

They had a long wait; the Audi didn't emerge until 4:15 P.M.

Fredrik informed his colleagues who were dotted around the building in their cars: "The white Audi just left. Female driver, no passengers. Turning onto Levgrensvägen."

The other unmarked cars set off in the same direction; Embla made sure the Volvo was last in the line. Louise mustn't catch sight of her under any circumstances, otherwise the whole operation would fail.

They traveled north, out onto the E20. Through

Partille, past Lerum and Floda. When the convoy left Västra Bodarna behind, Göran spoke for the first time since they'd set off. "She's heading for Alingsås."

He seemed to be right; they drove into Alingsås, coming off a large roundabout and weaving their way through a network of narrow streets. Many of the low wooden houses were pretty old, but they were well-maintained and gave the place a certain charm. There were also some newer areas, which brought a modern dimension to the town. Embla thought it was attractive and realized, to her surprise, that this was the first time she'd been to Alingsås, even though it was only thirty-five kilometers from Gothenburg.

They eventually reached a smaller roundabout; the Audi signaled and took the road leading to a district called Nolhaga. They continued down a hill with new houses on one side and a park on the other. They passed a series of apartment blocks by a river, then turned right.

Because there wasn't much traffic, only Fredrik Stridh and Irene Huss followed in their cars. Embla pulled into a parking lot, turned the car around, and waited with the engine idling. There was a swimming pool opposite, and a group of middle-aged ladies walked in through the doors, chatting away. For a moment Embla envied them. She would have loved to go for a swim, then relax in the sauna.

Göran's voice brought her back to reality. "I'll call Fredrik, find out where they are."

Fredrik answered right away, and Göran switched to hands-free so Embla could hear.

"She stopped at a daycare center and picked up a little boy. It didn't take long; he was waiting. Now she's parking the car in a designated spot. I'll park illegally farther down. Irene's driven past; there's a parking lot up ahead."

He ended the call before they could say anything. Embla pulled out onto the road again. On the left-hand side there was a forest, the trees bare. No doubt it was lovely in the spring and summer, but now it looked gloomy. Rain dripped from the branches and rotting, gray-brown leaves covered the ground.

It's March; in a month it will be spring. The thought gave Embla a burst of positive energy, which was exactly what she needed.

Fredrik called again. "Can you see those yellow apartment blocks straight ahead?"

"Yes," Göran and Embla chorused in unison.

"The street is called Lövskogsstigen. Louise Lindqvist has just gone inside. If you go into the courtyard and around the corner, the entrance is there. I suggest you drive to the ICA store and park there, then walk back. It's around a hundred and fifty meters. Irene and I are waiting on the corner."

Just as before, he ended the call before they could respond.

They drove past the apartment blocks, saw their colleagues on the corner, and continued to the ICA store. The weather was appalling. Embla pulled up her hood as soon as they got out of the car and heard Göran mutter: "A hundred and fifty meters . . . Surely that has to count as exercise . . ."

He glanced at her sideways and gave her a sly smile.

IRENE AND FREDRIK looked relieved when Göran and Embla joined them; it was no fun standing in the wind and rain.

Göran took charge. "Fredrik, keep an eye on the

entrance from the outside. Irene, you come with us, but I'd like you to stay on the landing and monitor the court-yard through one of the windows," he said.

Fredrik didn't look particularly happy with his assign-ment. The only consolation was that there was a low building in the courtyard, possibly some kind of storage facility. It had a decent porch; he would have a good view of the door while being sheltered from the rain.

They trooped along to the main door and looked at the list of residents' names. The only possibility was A. Leko on the fifth floor. A *for Anna,* Embla thought. Maybe Leko was a Croatian surname. There was an A. Sjöström on the same floor, but that sounded too Swed-ish, given that the children were unlikely to be able to speak the language without an accent. They concluded that A. Leko was their best bet.

While Göran was deliberating, Irene pressed the but-ton for A. Sjöström. After a moment a woman's voice said:

"Yes? Who is it?"

A. Sjöström was clearly an elderly lady. Irene thought fast.

"I'm so sorry. I must have pressed the wrong button. My name is Irene Huss and I'm here to see Anna Leko about her children's home language tuition."

Her colleagues exchanged appreciative glances, impressed by Irene's quick thinking.

"Could you possibly let me in?" she went on.

"Of course."

The lock buzzed, and Fredrik politely opened the door for them. When they were all inside, he took up his post in the porch across the way.

Embla, Göran, and Irene crowded together in the tiny elevator, which sped up to the top floor.

Embla's heart was racing, and she couldn't seem to slow down her breathing. *Göran thinks I'm going to go in with him and speak to Lollo, but I can't do it!* Her stomach was churning and she felt sick again. And yet she knew she had to do it; she needed answers to all her questions.

A large window on the landing overlooked the generous inner courtyard. It had a broad marble sill where several potted plants were displayed. Irene moved a wilting weeping fig and sat down.

"This is perfect," she said with a smile.

There were three doors: A. Leko, A. Sjöström, and O. Carlson. Göran pressed the bell for A. Leko, and Embla noticed that the door had extra security locks. They heard the sound of running feet. A woman's voice called out, but the feet were already there. Someone fumbled with the catch, the woman's voice shouted "No!" followed by what sounded like a reprimand in a language they didn't understand.

The door opened and a little boy with curly blond hair gazed up at them with big blue eyes that were inquiring at first, then filled with fear. Embla recognized Julian, the six-year-old from the Christmas photograph.

When she looked over his head, she met a pair of equally blue eyes. Lollo's.

She knew who Embla was right away and stood there as if she'd turned to stone. The boy didn't say anything; he simply stared at the tall man and the red-haired woman.

All the tension and anxiety left Embla's body.

"Hi, Lollo. Good to see you again," she said without

taking her eyes off the other woman. As soon as she said it, she knew how true it was. She felt as if an enormous weight had been lifted from her shoulders. All the guilt, fear, shame, and sorrow disappeared, and she was filled with an inner calm.

The boy backed away until he felt his mother's leg behind him. She placed a hand on his shoulder but didn't speak.

Göran took over. "Superintendent Göran Krantz. I know you and Embla were close friends when you were growing up, although she used the name Åsa back then. We'd like to ask you a few questions. As I'm sure you realize, this is linked to the investigation into the murders of your husband, Kador, and your brothers-in-law, Milo and Luca."

Every scrap of color drained from Louise's face and she swayed, but she managed to remain upright by tightening her grip on her son's shoulder. He winced and twisted free.

"Kador's . . . Is Kador . . . ?" she whispered almost inaudibly.

Only then did they realize she didn't know her husband was dead.

Offering no resistance, Louise allowed herself to be steered into the kitchen by the superintendent's gentle hand beneath her elbow. He pulled out a chair and she sank down onto it. Julian repeated something in Croatian several times. When Göran asked her what the boy was saying, she slowly turned her head and looked at him, as if she'd just become aware of her son's presence.

"He's asking . . . if Daddy's coming soon. And he wants a sandwich."

The table and chairs were in the bay window of the large kitchen. Embla didn't know who the designer was, but she recognized the white oval table with thin steel legs. There had been an identical one in Luca's apartment. She thought they might be Myran chairs or something like that.

"Is it okay if Embla fixes a drink and a snack?" Göran asked.

Louise gave a barely perceptible nod.

Embla immediately set to work making tea and coffee. Julian pointed to the box of chocolate milk above the exhaust fan. All the crockery in the cupboards was part of the same Rörstrand design—twelve of everything. The same with the Kosta glasses—a full set of every kind of glass you could think off. There wasn't a single thing that didn't match. The refrigerator was full of food; someone had clearly been shopping.

She set out cups, glasses, bread, milk, butter, and various toppings, keeping an eye on Louise the whole time. Would she have recognized her childhood friend if they'd passed in the street? Hardly. Maybe if their eyes had met because Louise's eyes were still that same intense shade of blue. The aura of an ethereal elf that had surrounded her as a teenager was completely gone. The long pale-blonde hair that had curled around her fine-featured face and tumbled down over her shoulders was nothing more than a memory. It had been cut to medium length, and those curls had been carefully styled. The platinum-blonde color had come out of a bottle; the roots were considerably darker. She had put on weight; her body could best be described as plump, although she hid it well in a pair of dark-blue jeans and a loose white silk blouse beneath a denim jacket. She was also wearing an intricate pendant on a gold chain, with a large blue stone in the center. Given how the stone sparkled when the light caught it, Embla assumed it was a sapphire. It matched both Louise's eyes and the stones in the ring on the third finger of her left hand. In fact she had several rings on both hands, all with different stones. Gold and sapphire earrings completed the look. *Slightly over the top,* Embla thought, *but typical of the friend I remember. Always too much of everything. Never just the right amount.*

The same applied to her makeup. She'd been generous with her eyeliner, and her lashes were thick with mascara. Her full lips shone with glossy pink lipstick. She was still beautiful. As a teenager she'd hardly suffered from acne at all, while Embla had battled away with different soaps and ointments. Now Louise's skin was concealed beneath a layer of foundation, but Embla could still see how pale she was.

Julian said something and tugged at his mother's sleeve.

"He wants cold chocolate milk," Louise translated, her voice devoid of any emotion.

Embla poured a glass of milk and added the chocolate powder according to the directions on the box. Then she looked at Julian, raised her eyebrows, and pointed to the different sandwich toppings on the table. He caught on immediately and pointed first to a packet of salami, then to a block of cheese. *Okay, two sandwiches*. She made up his order, placed the sandwiches on a plate, and put it in front of the boy. He dug in without looking at the adults around the table.

"Tea or coffee, Lollo?" she asked.

Louise gave a start and looked at her in confusion. She swallowed several times before she was able to answer.

"Coffee."

Embla poured her a cup. She didn't even bother asking Göran; she simply poured him a coffee, too. There was a small bowl with a lid on the shelf next to the cups; she picked it up, assuming it was sugar. When she took off the lid, she saw that the bowl was full of little packets of white powder. She glanced at the table and was relieved to see that Lollo was facing away from her. Without saying a word, she replaced the bowl. She found a box of sugar lumps in the cupboard and handed it to Göran.

Gently Embla touched her shoulder; the woman jumped as if she'd received an electric shock.

"Can I make you a sandwich, too?"

Louise didn't turn around; she simply said in the same expressionless voice, "Yes, please. Cheese."

While Embla busied herself with the sandwich, Göran reached out and picked up a slice of bread. Then he paused and looked at Louise.

"Is it okay if we have something to eat?"

Embla was surprised, but she realized why he was asking. He thought they were going to be here for quite some time.

Louise nodded without taking her eyes off her son, who'd started on his second sandwich. "Of course."

"We have a colleague on the landing—could we take her a coffee?"

Another nod.

Embla poured a large cup of black coffee because that was how Irene took her elixir. Taking care not to spill a drop, she made her way into the hallway and managed to get the door open. Irene took the hot drink with a smile. She refused the offer of a sandwich and settled down on the windowsill once more.

As Embla headed back to the kitchen, she heard Göran say:

"I'm so sorry. I assumed you knew that Kador was dead. That you'd heard from the police in Split."

His apology was met by silence.

After what seemed like an eternity, Louise said, "How . . . How did he die?"

"Before I tell you any more, I have to ask how much Swedish the boy knows."

"None at all. Miranda and Adam understand the odd word."

"But not whole sentences?"

"No."

"By the way, where are the two older children? It's almost five-thirty," Göran pointed out.

"They're at the pool. They're both keen swimmers, and they've joined the Alingsås swimming club."

Embla remembered the parking lot where she and Göran had pulled in; it was some distance away. Göran must have had the same thought.

"Will they be walking home?"

"No. The mother of one of Adam's classmates will bring them back." Louise looked down at her hands. "How did he die?" she asked again.

"According to our colleagues in Split, he was found in a cottage up in the mountains. The place had been burned to the ground. His teeth were X-rayed and the results were compared to dental records."

The blue eyes were huge in her pale face. "His teeth . . . Was there . . . nothing else left?"

Göran swallowed. "Not much."

Still no tears, but Embla could see that Lollo's hands were shaking with the shock. She picked up her cup but had to put it down again. She hadn't touched her sandwich.

After several attempts, Göran managed to reestablish eye contact with her. "Do you feel up to telling us what happened? Why you and the children left in such a hurry?"

The shimmering pink lips were compressed into a thin line, and she looked down at her coffee. After taking a moment to compose herself, she met his gaze once more. "I had no choice. For the safety of my children . . . and myself," she said, speaking a little more loudly now.

Göran gave her an encouraging nod. Meanwhile, Embla took out her phone and pretended to read a message. Discreetly she pressed the record button and placed the phone next to her cup.

"Did Kador feel threatened?"

"Yes."

"How long had he felt that way?"

"Ever since Luca was shot outside the club. And since his . . . friend died."

"We know about that, but that happened four years ago. Are you telling me Kador hasn't felt safe since then?"

"Yes."

"What did he say to you about the situation?"

Before she could answer, Julian said something. Louise nodded and he slid off his chair and ran out of the room.

"His favorite show is on TV," she explained as the high-pitched chatter of a cartoon started. A door closed, and the sound was muffled.

"The kids have televisions in their rooms. A present from Milo."

For the first time, Embla saw tears in Lollo's eyes. Maybe the initial shock was wearing off.

"What did Kador say to you about the situation?" Göran repeated.

With the back of her hand, Louise wiped away the tears rolling down her cheeks. "Milo contacted Kador when Luca and the doorman got shot. He called several times. Then Kador told me we weren't safe either, that we needed to establish a security system."

She got up, went over to the counter, and tore off a piece of paper towel. She dried her eyes, blew her nose, threw the paper away, and tore off a fresh piece, unconsciously balling it up in her hand as she returned to the table.

"So you and the children were in danger four years ago?"

Louise shrugged. "I don't know, but I guess Kador and Milo thought so."

Göran gave Embla a quick sideways glance. It was hard to interpret, but she assumed he wanted her to listen carefully to decide if Louise was telling the truth.

"Tell me about this security system."

For the first time Louise looked at him steadily, the tears in her eyes sparkling along with the sapphires she was wearing. "Everyone needed to be on alert so that we could react fast if something happened."

"So you were a part of this system, too?"

"I had to be because of the children. I was still at home with Julian and Adam and was about to go back to work at the hotel, but then Kador decided I should stay home. We've always had a nanny, but the girl we had at the time couldn't drive. I had to take Miranda to school and pick her up, and if the children were seeing friends, I gave them a ride, too."

She paused to catch her breath and take a sip of coffee.

"So you and the nanny were responsible for protecting the family?"

She put down the cup carefully, her hands still trembling.

"Not just us. Kador had one of his security guards drive past the house once an hour, around the clock. Then he came up with the idea of the blue butterfly."

"The blue butterfly?"

A faint smile passed across Louise's face. "It's an emoji,

but 'my little blue butterfly' was his nickname for me. We were to send each other that emoji at exactly midnight every night, and if we didn't get a butterfly in return, we had to get ready to . . . run."

Her voice almost gave way on the last word.

Embla and Göran exchanged a glance. It seemed like a very simple device.

"And did it work?"

"Yes. Until the evening when he . . ."

She couldn't quite suppress a sob. She paused and drank a little more coffee, then she picked up the sandwich and took a small bite.

Göran let her finish, then said, "Tell us about the evening when Kador disappeared."

Louise nodded and took a deep breath. "It was a month ago. He was due to sign a contract on the sale of a bar the following day. The buyer was an Englishman who had a flight to catch, so they'd arranged to meet at seven in the morning. Kador had promised to be home early—before eleven, he said. But he didn't come. I was worried and sent the blue butterfly at midnight. Nothing came back, so I sent another. Still nothing. Then I knew, so I called Milo."

"What did he say?"

"As the crow flies. That was our code. I knew exactly what to do because Kador and I had gone over it. Everything was ready; I always kept two suitcases packed with clothes and essentials for me and the kids."

"Did you have fake passports?"

The question clearly took her by surprise. She pursed her lips before replying in the affirmative.

"Did you drive the car?"

The tension around her mouth eased, and she gazed into his eyes. "No. We took a cab."

The first lie they could be sure of. Göran and Embla knew that the neighbor who'd seen them leave had said they were picked up by a big black car, not a cab.

"Where did you go?"

"To an airport."

"Which one?"

"I've no idea. The children and I were asleep."

Another lie. Nobody arrives at an airport, checks in, and goes through security without knowing where they are. Embla was getting irritated.

"So you flew to Sweden?" Göran continued.

"Yes. To Landvetter."

Hardly. Every passenger list for incoming flights during the relevant period had been meticulously checked. A woman with three children the same age as hers had not been found. Lie number three.

"Did you travel under the name Leko?"

She hesitated. "No, we changed our identity again when we got here."

"So what name did you use for the flight?"

She looked wary. Her eyes were her best feature, but they also gave her away.

"I . . . I don't remember."

Nonsense. The reason why she was lying was obvious; she didn't want to give away the methods Milo and his gang used for human trafficking.

Embla knew that Göran must be thinking the same thing, but he kept his tone neutral.

"When did you arrive in Gothenburg? Or rather Alingsås."

This time the answer came without hesitation.

"Four weeks ago."

Which confirmed that Louise and the children had been in Sweden when she called Embla on that Friday evening and called her Åsa.

Embla became aware of voices outside the door. She could hear two children, as well as Irene's calm voice. She realized that whatever Irene said, she wouldn't be able to explain why a strange woman had parked herself outside their door; according to Louise, they understood only odd words in Swedish.

Embla quickly interjected, "Sorry, but I think the children are home."

Louise gave a start. "Don't tell them Kador's dead! Say you're here to inform me that he hasn't been found yet. Please! They won't be able to handle it. Leaving Croatia, a new language, a new school, new . . . everything. And we can't go to their father's funeral—we'd be killed, too," she said, sheer panic in her eyes.

Göran nodded.

The sound of a key in the door put an end to the conversation. Julian was still watching television in his room; judging by all the *swish-swosh* and *boooms*, there seemed to be an intergalactic war going on. The two older children took off their coats and shoes in the hallway, chattering the whole time. They appeared in the kitchen doorway together and stopped dead, confused by the sight of two strangers. They fired off a series of questions at their mother. She pointed to Embla and Göran in turn, her voice calm and reassuring. It was clear from the children's expressions that they'd taken in her explanation that their father hadn't yet been found; they were upset, but there was also an element of relief.

Miranda was prettier in person than in the Christmas photo. She had her father's features and coloring. Adam was also an attractive child. He had Kador's dark hair, but his mother's curls. And little Julian was more like Lollo. She had three lovely children; it was perfectly understandable that she was worried about them and was prepared to do anything to keep them safe, much like the millions of parents around the world seeking refuge.

Miranda stepped into the kitchen and nodded stiffly to the two police officers. "How do you do?" she said politely; her English was good.

"Fine, thank you," Göran replied.

"Hi," Embla said with a smile.

Adam went and stood next to Louise. When she gave him a gentle nudge, he mumbled hi.

Louise said something, and the children made themselves a cup of chocolate milk and a sandwich, then disappeared into their bedrooms.

"Great kids," Göran said.

"Yes. They're my life," Louise said proudly.

The children. Embla was struck by a thought. Presumably Lollo would inherit Kador's personal effects and money—but what about Milo's and Luca's estates? Neither of them had children. There were cousins, Jiri and Andreas Acika, for example, but in Sweden cousins don't inherit when there are closer relatives. As far as she could work out, Kador's three children were the heirs to the Stavic brothers' empire of hotels, restaurants, bars, casinos, properties, and goodness knows what else. Then there was the dark side of their business: human trafficking, prostitution, money laundering, arms and drugs smuggling, plus more lucrative crimes, like murder and extortion.

Who would take over now that all three brothers were dead? In most criminal organizations one or more individuals are primed to step in if the leader is seriously injured or killed. Presumably the Stavic brothers had designated one another as their successors, but what now? Kador's children were too young to be seen as an option. It would be at least ten years before Adam had a chance to claim his inheritance, if then. What was going to happen in the meantime? Embla realized there was a serious risk of a gang war. Or were they already in the middle of that war?

"Let's go back to where we were. So you arrived in Gothenburg a month ago—did you come straight to Alingsås?" Göran asked.

"Yes."

"How did you get here?"

"Milo drove us."

True. That fit with the DNA found in the Audi.

"Was this apartment ready and waiting for you?"

"Yes."

"When did you buy it?"

"We didn't—Milo did."

"When?"

Louise thought for a moment. "It must have been two years ago."

"So he bought this large apartment, had it decorated and furnished, then left it standing empty for two years?"

"Yes, but he sent brochures so I could pick out what I wanted, then he ordered everything."

So no one had actually walked into a store to choose the contents of this apartment.

"Why did he go for this particular place?"

Louise took a sip of her coffee and another small bite of her sandwich before she answered. "There are good schools nearby—preschool, junior high, and a high school. There are plenty of stores, a medical center, and a hospital. You don't have to go into Gothenburg for anything if you don't want to. And it's a big apartment—six rooms on two floors." She spread her arms wide, gesturing toward the window with its fantastic view of the city lights.

"I understand that this meets your family's needs, but did something in particular happen two years ago to make Milo and his brothers step up their security arrangements? And buy this apartment?" Göran asked.

Louise bit her lower lip as she considered her response and ended up with pink lipstick on her front teeth.

"Things . . . were difficult. In Croatia."

"Go on."

She looked away and swallowed hard. "A guy who worked in one of our bars was murdered. Shot dead. A bomb went off in one of our restaurants in the middle of the night. No one was killed, but some of the people who lived in the building were injured. And I know both Kador and Milo received threats. They were angry and worried things were going to get worse."

"Who was behind all this?"

Once again she hesitated. "They never mentioned a name, but there was a guy who wanted to take over Kador and Milo's business empire—by terrorizing us."

"Do you know where this guy came from?"

Another long pause.

"Zagreb, I think."

There it was again. The body recovered from the Göta River a month after the shooting incident involving Luca and his friend the doorman had been identified as Damian Pacić, a known criminal who'd worked for a major gangster in Zagreb. That was more or less all they'd managed to find out; it had proved impossible to trace him back any further than five years. His true identity remained a mystery.

"So the threat from Zagreb led to Kador and Milo preparing an escape route to Sweden for your whole family," Göran clarified.

"Yes. Kador still had his Swedish citizenship."

"But it's been four years since Luca and the doorman at La Dolce Vita were shot. You're talking about two years ago—were things quiet until then?"

"Not really, but I didn't pay much attention to what was going on—I had my hands full with the house and the kids."

Could that really be true? If your husband and his brothers are feuding with another gangster, with violence as an inevitable consequence of that feud, how can you *not* know the other guy's name? It sounded unconvincing, but then again Embla knew that with some mafia families, the man is in charge, while the woman takes care of the home and the children. She might know a lot about her husband's activities, but she pretends not to. If he ends up in jail, there has to be someone on the outside while he's serving his sentence. These loyal wives always maintain that their husbands are innocent and never tell the cops anything. That's the role a mafia wife takes on.

Lollo was a good gangster wife, Embla realized. She would never tell the truth about the gang war that had led to the brothers' deaths. However, they did have Milo and Luca's killer, Jiri Acika, in custody. Fortunately his name hadn't yet been leaked to the media.

An impulse made Embla lean across the table and ask her first question. "What do you know about Jiri Acika?"

The effect was as powerful as if she'd slapped her childhood friend across the face. Louise let out a gasp and her eyes opened wide. She clearly hadn't expected them to know anything about Jiri.

"Jiri . . . Why?"

Then she fell silent and stared down at her coffee.

Why the strong reaction? Embla wondered.

Göran looked searchingly at Louise, but when she didn't say anything, he stepped in. "How well do you know Jiri Acika?"

She took a deep breath and looked up at him, eyelashes quivering. When she spoke her voice was weak. "He and Kador are cousins. He lives in Split, too."

"Do you know him well?" Göran wasn't giving up.

A slight shrug. "Not really."

She's lying. Why?

Julian came rushing in and said something to his mother. Louise gave him a brief answer. The boy didn't look happy and stomped off back to his room.

"He wants to know when we're having dinner. We usually eat between seven and eight, so . . ." She rubbed her forehead wearily. "I'm sorry, I can't do this anymore." She got to her feet and began to clear the table. Embla stood up to help her.

"In that case I suggest we meet at the police station tomorrow morning. And that Embla stays here with you."

Louise spun around. "There's no need."

"It's routine, I'm afraid. You've just found out that your husband has been murdered, and you have no relatives or friends here to support you. Therefore Embla will stay with you in the capacity of family liaison officer."

Embla was about to protest, then she realized what he was up to. As an old friend, she might be able to get Louise to reveal information that she wouldn't give while he was there. Clever, and worth a shot. And besides, she had some questions that needed answers.

WHEN GÖRAN AND Irene had left, Embla stood in the hallway with Louise. Julian was clinging to his mother's leg.

In order to break the silence, Embla said, "I noticed a pizzeria across the street. How about pizza for dinner? My treat."

Louise was too tired to argue. She shouted to the other two children and asked them a question. Embla picked up *calzone* and *Hawaiian* when they answered; pizza names are pretty much global.

Louise phoned the order through, and Embla asked for extra salad. A hoarse male voice informed them that delivery would arrive in fifteen minutes.

Julian raced back to his room, singing: "Pizza! Piiizza! Pizzaaa!"

Embla was reminded of Elliot warbling variations of "hunting" not so long ago. She felt a pang of guilt; she hadn't called him. They'd met up a couple of times during the week she was on sick leave and had talked about what they'd done during spring break. They'd discussed the fox hunt as well, and just as Embla had hoped, he'd managed to convince himself and everyone he spoke to that hunting was the most exciting adventure imaginable.

Louise and Embla returned to the kitchen to set the table.

"We don't need plates," Louise decided.

Embla was used to eating pizza straight out of the box when she was working, but she thought it was nicer to put the food on a plate when she had the chance. She didn't say anything though. She found knives and forks while Louise set out glasses—including two generous wine glasses. Of course, it was understandable if Louise felt she needed a drink given the news she'd just received. She did seem to have recovered pretty well, though it could have been because she was trying to maintain a calm façade for the children or because she'd already suspected that Kador was dead. Or maybe she was a good actress.

The conversation centered on the children and how they were acclimating. None of them had visited Sweden before. Louise hadn't wanted to return to her hometown because of the risk that someone would recognize her—a former classmate or a neighbor. The children were her responsibility, so they'd stayed with her in Split when Kador went to Sweden once a year or so. And Milo had gone to Croatia every spring and fall. Luca rarely visited his brother—once every couple of years at most.

"But now I feel able to come back. As you can see, my appearance has changed quite a lot," she said with an ironic smile.

No doubt she was expecting a contradiction, but Embla could have easily passed Louise on the street without reacting. She recognized her old friend now that they'd spent some time together. Some things hadn't changed: her voice, her expressions, her body language.

But her appearance was a long way from the young girl she remembered.

The best she could come up with was: "Your eyes are just the same."

Louise looked pleased. "And my hair—although of course it's shorter," she said, patting it coquettishly.

It was nothing like the thick, pale-blonde locks she used to have, but Embla simply nodded. "Absolutely."

The doorbell rang. Embla peered through the peephole and saw a skinny teenage boy in a New York baseball cap, his face covered in angry red spots. He was balancing a pile of pizza boxes. She opened the door and paid him.

The bottom box was hot, so she hurried back to the kitchen. Louise called the children, who came rushing in. The pizzas were passed out. Miranda didn't take her eyes off Embla, nor did she make any attempt to hide her curiosity.

She's suspicious. She can probably smell a cop—it's in the genes, Embla thought. She realized she was shuffling uncomfortably on her chair.

Without a word the girl took her pizza and a can of Coke and went back to her room. The door slammed shut.

The boys stayed at the table, eating their pizzas and drinking Coke. Louise opened a bottle of red wine, but Embla made the excuse that red wine gave her a headache. The truth was that she didn't drink much wine at all and certainly not when she was working. This wasn't a fun reunion party.

"White?"

"Same problem. I'll stick to water."

Louise grimaced and demonstratively filled her own glass almost to the brim. Then she took a small carafe out of the cupboard, filled it from the faucet, and slammed it down on the table next to Embla's glass with such force that some of the contents spilled out.

She and the children chatted noisily in Croatian, while Embla sat quietly watching them. When they'd finished their pizzas, the boys went back to their rooms.

Louise rolled her eyes and let out a long breath. "Peace at last. Sure you won't have a glass of wine?" she said, tilting her head.

"Positive."

Louise frowned, then refilled her own glass and took a big gulp with obvious pleasure.

It was time to start asking questions, but Embla had to proceed carefully; she didn't want to make Louise clam up.

"I didn't know you had a boyfriend before you . . . went away. When did you and Kador get together?"

Tears sprang to Louise's eyes. "I didn't tell anybody—although I did say I was in love with a boy I'd met during the summer, if you remember. You weren't around much. I hung out with some of my classmates, and I met Kador in a bar. We clicked right away; we just knew we were going to be together for the rest of our lives. But we agreed that we couldn't talk about our relationship." She fell silent and filled her glass yet again; there wasn't much left in the bottle now.

"Why not?"

Louise leaned forward and said in a confidential tone, "He was engaged. Well, not exactly engaged, but he was with a girl. Her father was some big shot in the transportation industry, and a friend of Milo's. They'd decided that Kador and his daughter should get married, but then along came little me." A smug smile passed across her face.

"Did this girl live in Sweden or Croatia?"

"In Gothenburg, but her family was from Zagreb."

Zagreb and Split. Those two cities kept coming up.

"So that was why you decided to run away?"

Those blue eyes darted around the room. "Kind of . . . It was Kador who said we had to go. I was a bit unsure; I didn't really feel I was old enough to . . . but then he proposed and gave me a fantastic engagement ring and showed me pictures of the house we were going to live in outside Split. So I said yes. But I didn't know what I was getting into." She paused and looked down at the remains of her pizza.

"Did you tell Milo you were going?"

"Yes. He went crazy at first, but then he helped us organize everything. He sorted out passports and plane tickets; we took the morning flight to Zagreb and we were there by lunchtime. Then we drove down to Split. I felt sick the whole time; you and I had drunk a lot of wine the night before," Louise said with a laugh.

So Milo had been the one who provided fake passports and booked plane tickets under fake names.

It was time to find out more about the events that had haunted Embla's nightmares ever since Louise disappeared.

"To be honest, I can't remember much."

"No, you were completely wrecked. That was a key part of our plan."

Louise hiccupped, then started coughing. She couldn't

speak for a long time, but Embla resisted the impulse to thump her on the back. Instead she considered her next question, the one that had been burning inside her for so long.

"Lollo, why did you want me to go with you that evening?"

There was no mistaking the surprise in those blue eyes.

"Why? Because it worked out perfectly. I knew my mom was going to be away for a couple of days, and we'd told your parents we were going to the school disco. No one would miss me if I disappeared—not until after the weekend. So you had to come with me—I couldn't tell you I was leaving. But you had to be drunk, otherwise you'd have realized what was going on."

"So you and Kador had already decided to go?"

"Yes. When Mom was invited to a fortieth birthday party in Kungälv, I knew she'd stay over. Those women always drank way too much."

Bitterness seeped through her words.

Embla felt a surge of rage. "How could you just take off like that? Did you never think about me? Or your mom? Or your dad, who came here . . ."

She'd crossed a line. There was pure hostility in Louise's eyes.

"Think about you . . . you and your wonderful family! They all made such a fuss of you, and your uncle Nisse and his wife adored you. My mom just drank and felt sorry for herself. My dad fucked Ellen and got her pregnant and went off to live in England. Nobody cared about me! Nobody!"

She slammed her fist down on the table, making the glasses and silverware jump in the air.

An oppressive silence filled the kitchen. Embla had no idea what to say; her brain was empty. Her memories didn't match what Louise had said at all. *She* was the one who'd been lonely; no one in her family had had any time for her, the little afterthought who was seven years younger than the youngest brother. The only person who'd been there for her was her best friend, Lollo.

A door opened and after a few seconds Miranda appeared in the doorway and looked inquiringly at her mother. Embla noticed that the girl's eyes registered the almost-empty bottle, the glass of wine, and Embla's water. She asked a question; Louise answered briefly with a dismissive wave of her hand. As Miranda turned away, Embla caught the sadness on her face. *She's experienced this before*, she thought with a pang of sympathy.

She wanted Louise to tell her more about the actual journey from Gothenburg to Split rather than the reasons behind her departure; it was clearly a traumatic experience that she hadn't worked through. She sat up a little straighter, determined not to show how upsetting she found what she was about to say.

"I have a vague memory of following you through a door in the nightclub, then trying to run after you along a dark hall. I saw you lying on the floor, with Milo and his brothers bending over you. Milo spotted me and grabbed me by the throat. He threatened to kill me if I said anything, then you all disappeared through the back door. What happened in that hall, Lollo?"

"What happened was you got scared shitless. And it worked, because you didn't talk. Milo's been keeping an eye on you, so I knew you'd become a cop. But I didn't know you'd changed your name. Embla. You said that was your middle name."

"It's actually my first name. But I'm still wondering what happened in that hallway. Did they drug you?"

Louise threw back her head and laughed. She almost knocked over the bottle. "Drug me? You're so funny! Drug me . . ."

She used her hands to wipe away the tears of laughter, messing up her mascara in the process.

"They didn't need to drug me—I was already drunk. And I hadn't eaten all day because of the excitement. So I fainted in the hall. I never even saw you, but Milo told me about it later. He was good at . . . showing his claws, you might say."

She picked up her glass and spilled wine on her white blouse. It was obviously an expensive item of clothing, but she didn't seem to care. Red wine, white silk—that was never coming out.

"Tell me what happened when you arrived in Split," Embla said with an encouraging smile.

Louise dabbed half-heartedly at the wine stain with her fingertips, then looked up. Her gaze lacked focus, but there was a glint of wariness.

"We moved into a house outside the city center. It was already furnished, but we bought quite a lot of things to put our own stamp on it. And we had to get married—Kador's relatives and the neighbors didn't like the fact that we were living together without being married."

Even though she'd already seen the photographs, Embla asked, "Was it a big wedding?"

For a second Louise looked blissfully happy.

"It was huge—a hundred and fifty guests. The party went on for three days. I felt like a princess in a fairy-tale."

You'd just turned fifteen. You were a child. Of course you felt like a princess in your long white dress, veil, and bridal crown. You were the center of a huge celebration that marked the end of your childhood, and you had no idea, Embla thought.

"It sounds amazing," she said.

Louise pulled a face that was hard to interpret and took another swig of her wine.

"Did you get a job?"

"Yes, I worked at our biggest hotel, the Imperial. Obviously I couldn't work at reception in case any Swedish guests arrived, so I was in the office. I learned bookkeeping and studied Croatian at the same time. It's not an easy language!"

"How old were you when Miranda was born?" Embla asked, even though she knew the answer.

"Eighteen. Just barely."

Louise picked up the wine bottle and peered at the label, but she seemed to be having difficulty focusing. She put it down impatiently with a bang.

"And then your boys came along."

"Yes."

A curt response. Time to change the subject.

"Tell me more about Kador—all I know is that he's the middle brother."

Louise's eyes filled with tears once more.

"He was gorgeous . . . so good-looking."

Her voice gave way. She raised the glass to her lips with shaking hands. Before Embla could think of what to say next, Louise continued.

"Other girls thought so, too." She stared into her glass.

It was heartbreaking to see her old friend in this state. Life clearly hadn't turned out the way she'd expected; she'd paid a high price for her childish romantic dreams. Too high.

The silence became uncomfortable, but Embla still couldn't work out what to say. Suddenly Louise continued.

"Milo always supported me because he realized that neither he nor Luca were going to have children of their own. He was sterile, and Luca didn't want kids, so they started to formulate a plan in case something happened."

With those words she knocked back the contents of the glass. *A whole bottle in less than an hour!* That didn't bode well for the rest of their conversation. Louise was already slurring her words, and her head was beginning to droop. Had she also taken something? Her eyelids were fluttering, and it was high time to ask the key question that was bothering Embla.

"Why did you call me when you arrived in Sweden? I realized it was you, and I was so pleased," she said, putting as much warmth as possible into her voice.

Louise glanced up at her, a tremulous smile on her lips. "Were you?"

"Absolutely. But I still don't understand why you called me."

Fat tears rolled down Louise's cheeks. "Because I don't have anyone else. Anyone else to call. I'm so lonely."

Embla's heart beat faster and her throat contracted; Lollo was telling the truth now. She might have plenty of friends in Croatia, but she probably didn't know who she could really trust. Gang wars are always violent, and people are often happy to change sides for the right incentive. An old friend can suddenly turn out to be the one who kills you. Here in Sweden, both her brothers-in-law had been murdered, and she and the children were still under threat.

"Maybe you should go to bed. It's been a tough day," Embla said gently.

"Too fucking right it has! I want you to leave—get out!"

Louise covered her face with her hands and began to sob. Instinctively Embla recoiled at her outburst; what the hell was that about? Should she go? Göran had asked her to stay with the family.

"Lollo, I . . ."

"Anna! My name is Anna," she mumbled into her hands.

Poor Lollo. Or Anna. It was understandable that things had suddenly gotten to be too much for her. Not only had she been confronted by her childhood friend, who along with her colleagues had blown her cover, she'd also been told that Kador was dead. It was enough to break the strongest person.

"Okay. Anna. I'll go home, but call me if you change your mind. I'm only thirty minutes away. And if you suspect you might be in danger, call me—I'll have the police here in no time."

Embla stood up, resisting the impulse to give her old friend a hug. Instead she patted her gently on the shoulder.

"If you only knew how happy I am that you're alive. And it's good to hear about your life over these past fourteen years—and to meet your kids. Do you want me to check on them before I leave?"

Louise slowly shook her head. "No. I always put them to bed myself."

In that moment, Embla realized how lonely her friend really was.

"Okay. I'll see you tomorrow."

As she set off toward the door, Louise made a movement to get to her feet but fell back onto the chair with a thud. She looked up at Embla, her face stained with tears, and whispered almost inaudibly, "Yes. See you."

When Embla reached the front door, Miranda emerged from her room. Embla stepped out onto the landing, then turned to say goodbye. Without so much as a nod, Miranda closed the door. Embla heard a click, then the rattle of the nine-cylinder lock.

The girl couldn't have made it any clearer. Embla wasn't welcome.

ON THE WAY back to Gothenburg, Embla called Göran and played the conversation with Louise to him. When it was over she said she suspected that Louise was a heavy drinker and possibly a drug user. She told him about the little bags of powder in the bowl in the kitchen cupboard.

"I didn't take one—she probably would have noticed, and I don't want to make her think she can't trust me. But I'm pretty sure it was cocaine."

"No doubt she's had easy access to drugs during all those years in Split. Kador could have supplied her with what she wanted. Or one of the other members of the gang," Göran said.

"Jiri, maybe? She reacted oddly when we mentioned his name."

"Exactly. And speaking of our friend Jiri, we've had confirmation that footprints from his boots were found in the cottage where Milo was murdered. The pattern on the sole is distinctive since there is damage to the right heel. He was wearing the same boots when we arrested him."

Embla laughed out loud.

"He's made every mistake in the book! First of all he

didn't get rid of the murder weapon, and he left finger-prints on the magazine and a bullet. Then he took Milo's keys and watch. And now the boots. He's going down!"

"Absolutely. The guy's an idiot—but a dangerous idiot. He was definitely involved in Kador's murder, then he traveled to Sweden as quickly as possible, before Milo and Luca found out their brother was dead. As far as they knew, he was missing. The question is whether Jiri had help when he killed Milo and Luca. Stephen Walker's witness testimony suggests that Jiri was alone when Luca was shot, but we don't know about the cottage in Her-remark; he could have had one or more of his associates with him, probably the guys in the Range Rover. Maybe they drove Jiri up to Ulvsjön after the murder. God knows why he stayed there."

Embla thought about what he'd said. "It's in the mid-dle of nowhere—perhaps he felt safe there. Or he might have gotten stuck because of the blizzard."

"Good point."

"I've been wondering how Jiri knew about all three brothers' movements leading up to their murders," Embla went on.

"What do you mean?"

She paused, working out how to explain something that she'd been mulling over for a while. "The evening Kador was kidnapped and killed—Jiri must have known that he was planning to go home earlier than usual and that he'd be alone."

"True—someone must have tipped off his murderers. I'm assuming there were at least two of them since they managed to overpower Kador and drive him up to the cottage in the mountains."

"Jiri also knew that Luca was going straight home from work. Milo wasn't in town, so Luca needed to take the meeting. That call was a trap, and as I said before, I think it came from Jiri. Then all he had to do was wait inside the parking lot."

"Once again, I agree. Presumably Jiri simply suggested that they meet in Luca's apartment."

Encouraged by Göran's positive reaction, Embla continued. "As far as Milo's concerned, Jiri must have known that Milo was going up to Herremark and that he'd rented a cottage there. Someone must have tipped off Jiri or his associates in each case, or they couldn't have possibly known where the brothers would be at those specific times."

"I'm guessing the guys up at Ulvsjön were expecting Milo." He fell silent and thought for a while. "Both Milo and Luca were lured to a particular place," he continued. "My theory is that Milo went up to northern Dalsland to meet someone important—or so he thought. It must have involved big business for him to go personally. And given all the drugs and guns we found at Ulvsjön, it's hardly surprising that he was interested, although we don't know if he was buying or selling. Selling, I'd guess—we know the two Swedish guys were buyers. However, I'm convinced that the Zagreb gang set a trap for him. They might have intended to kill him at Ulvsjön, but for some reason they changed their minds and shot him in the cottage instead. Maybe they didn't want to draw attention to the house at Ulvsjön, because they were planning to burn it down. The fact that one of the girls died was a fly in the ointment, of course."

Too many guesses and not enough evidence.

"This is such a complicated case," Embla said with a sigh.

"It is. So I think you should go home and get some sleep. You've had a long day."

So have you. But if I know you as well as I think I do, you won't be going home anytime soon, Embla thought.

WHEN SHE GOT home she wandered restlessly around the apartment, unable to settle in front of the TV and take it easy. She realized what she needed: a hard training session.

She picked up her sports bag and her car keys and headed to the boxing gym where she'd trained from the beginning. It always stayed open late, and her former trainer, Sten "Sluggo" Olsson, was bound to be there. He would find her a good sparring partner. She needed some-one tough; she had a lot to get out of her system. Her career as a competitor might be over, but she would never stop training. That was her therapy.

WHEN EMBLA WOKE up on Friday morning, her entire body was aching. Wonderful. She smiled to herself. The training session had been perfect. After a thorough warm-up, she'd had to work really hard against her sparring partner. He was only eighteen and still had a lot to learn when it came to technique, but he was fast and had lightning reactions. A lithe, supple panther with the mentality of a pit bull—the ideal combination. Just like Embla herself, in fact. Hassan showed great promise for the future; he had the right attitude to the sport.

She swung her legs over the edge of the bed with a low groan and got up. She felt full of confidence. There was still a lot to do, but things were beginning to fall into place in this complex case.

And later that night she was meeting Olle, and the whole weekend was theirs.

SHE WALKED INTO Göran's office and found him sitting at the computer as usual. As far as she could see, he was wearing the same clothes as the previous evening.

"Morning. Have you been here all night?" she asked, keeping her tone light.

The weary look he gave her said it all. He rubbed his eyes and said, "I got a couple of hours' sleep."

There was a small windowless room with a narrow bed, a hard pillow, and a cotton blanket for the occasional use of staff, but it wasn't conducive to a good sleep.

"Have you had breakfast?"

"No. The place I've been has kind of taken away my appetite," he replied cryptically.

Embla didn't bother asking what he meant; an emergency intervention was needed here. It was eight o'clock and Göran hadn't had breakfast. She headed for the canteen and bought a cup of herbal tea, a large coffee with two sugars, and two ham and cheese sandwiches. The tea was hers, the rest was for him.

When she put the tray down on his desk, he managed a wan smile. He thanked her and dug in.

Embla sipped her tea and waited for him to finish. As he pushed his plate away, she asked, "So where's this place that took away your appetite?"

He grimaced. "The dark net."

"But we haven't found any of the brothers' cell phones or laptops. Or iPads, if they had any," she objected.

"No, but I took a look around anyway. I found a few leads, but the problem is that everything is in Croatian, and I'm sure it's encrypted as well. There are chat rooms in English, but it's hard to know if I'm on the right track. I really need their laptops!"

Once again he rubbed his bloodshot eyes, then he sighed and looked at her.

"I spoke to Tommy Persson a little while ago. He and I both agree that it would be better if someone who isn't too close to Louise Lindqvist conducts any future interviews with her. Irene Huss and Fredrik Stridh will be talking to her from now on; they'll be contacting her today."

Her first reaction was disappointment, but then she realized that Tommy and Göran were right. It was best if someone who could remain objective took over.

SHE SPENT THE rest of the morning in her own department, Violent Crimes, for once. She went through the interviews with Jiri Acika, which didn't take very long, as he hadn't said a word. There were, however, a couple of longer interviews with his brother, Andreas, that proved interesting.

According to Andreas, he'd had no idea that Jiri was in Gothenburg. Nor had he known where Milo was going on that Friday; Milo had simply said that he'd be away for the weekend.

Needless to say, Andreas had a watertight alibi for the Friday evening. Between six and eleven he'd been with around a hundred people at the opening of a new bar in town. It was actually Milo who'd been invited, but he'd asked Andreas to go in his place. Kristina hadn't been well enough to accompany him, due to pelvic pain in the late stages of her pregnancy.

Embla pictured the good-looking man who'd spoken to her and Göran in his compact study. He'd taken off his tailored jacket to reveal his equally tailored shirt, which had fit his muscular upper body like a glove. The big gold watch had glinted on his wrist. Was he a father of three by now? The apartment was in a fashionable building, but maybe it was a little small for his growing family. Did Mr. Fitness want to break free, in more ways than one?

Become his own boss? Buy a house? Or maybe just move up to the penthouse?

Could he have been involved in the murders? Been bribed by the rival gang in Zagreb? In which case he would have known that Jiri was in Sweden when the brothers were killed. Embla wasn't convinced that Milo hadn't told him where he was going; maybe Milo had said he was treating himself to a night at the guesthouse in Herremark. Given the state of the accommodation at Ulvsjön, it wasn't hard to see why a comfortable cottage was considerably more appealing. And then there was the excellent restaurant, of course.

It would explain a great deal if it transpired that Andreas was involved in the deaths of the Stavic brothers, not least the feeling both she and Göran shared: that the murders were well planned, and that the killer or killers had known exactly where the victims were.

Andreas Acika was across everything when it came to the brothers' business affairs and private lives. He knew all three of them well, knew their habits and vices.

Unfortunately there wasn't a shred of incriminating evidence against him. Only a cop's gut instinct, as Irene Huss would say.

Embla gathered up the printouts of the interviews with Andreas, put them in a folder, and headed back to Göran's office.

He didn't interrupt her once; he merely nodded in agreement a couple of times. The bags under his eyes bore witness to the lack of sleep, but he began to brighten up as Embla expounded on her theory.

"Andreas could well have been involved," he said when she'd finished. "I don't mean he was actually holding the gun, but he could have passed on information."

"Do we have anything at all that points to him?" she asked hopefully.

He sighed and shook his head. "No. But when we got a warrant to open Milo's safe, it was suspiciously clean. Eleven thousand kronor in cash. No drugs, no guns, no compromising documents. There were contracts, share certificates—exactly what you'd expect of a serious businessman."

"Someone got there before us."

"Looks that way. And who would have the code to Milo's safe if not his right-hand man?"

They both fell silent, thinking things over.

"We need evidence of contact between Andreas and the gang in Zagreb," Göran said eventually.

"What do you know about them?"

He didn't even try to hide an enormous yawn.

"Not much. The boss is named Mikael Vlasic. He's fifty-two and notorious for his brutality. He was an officer during the Balkan Wars in the nineties, but he'd already started building up his business before that. He has adult twin sons who also work within the organization, which is a mirror image of the Stavic brothers' criminal activities, hence the rivalry. It's understandable that Vlasic thinks it would be a good idea to take over the Stavic brothers' flourishing empire. No doubt he sees his boys running a highly lucrative network in the future."

Embla considered how they could gather more information about Vlasic's gang and try to find a possible link to Andreas Acika.

"So Vlasic must have someone who can run things here in Gothenburg," she said.

"Definitely."

"And who better than Andreas Acika?"

One corner of Göran's mouth twitched in a faint smile. "No one."

"Could the contact we're looking for be between Jiri Acika and Mikael Vlasic?"

Göran raised his eyebrows. "Why didn't I think of that?"

He leafed through the printouts of the interviews with Andreas, then triumphantly held up a sheet of paper. "That's it! This is the only information we have about Jiri's life in Split over the past five years. According to Andreas, he's married with a three-year-old daughter. And he doesn't work for Kador, but for a relative. Their mother's older brother. Time to contact Boris Cetinski again, I think. But not on Skype," he added with a weary smile. "I haven't got the energy to smarten myself up today."

EMBLA HAD A quiet afternoon. She'd arranged to leave at four o'clock—on the dot. She was going straight from work to meet Olle. Her bag was already packed and in the trunk of her car. Her heart flipped when she thought of him. Over the past few days they'd spent hours talking on the phone, and she felt they'd been able to open up to each other in a way that was very rare for her. He was funny and easygoing, but he was also capable of discussing difficult issues, like the events up at Ulvsjön. At the same time she could tell he was also interested in her because he was flirtatious—without going too far.

And she was definitely interested in him! She couldn't wait to see the best-looking cop in Dalsland again.

The sun was shining in, even though the windows were grubby from the long winter, and it was just possible to see the first green shoots coming up in the flower beds in the park. March had arrived, and maybe everyone could start looking forward to the spring. There was a while to go yet, though. In the meantime, perhaps something was beginning to grow between her and Olle.

Her romantic thoughts were interrupted by the sound of her phone. Göran, asking her to come back to his office. She glanced at the clock: two-thirty. Only an hour and a half to go. She smiled and ran down the stairs, her footsteps as light as air.

HE LOOKED LIKE an exhausted giant panda and smelled like a man who hadn't showered or changed his shirt in almost forty-eight hours, but his eyes were alert and he was smiling.

"Boris Cetinski is a diamond. He already had most of the information I was asking for, and what he told me is sensational!" he exclaimed. He leaned back in his chair with a triumphant expression. "Jiri Acika is married to a woman named Gabriela, and as we know they have a three-year-old daughter. Gabriela's maiden name was Pavic, but her mother's maiden name was Vlasic—in fact, her mother is Mikael Vlasic's sister! So Jiri's wife is the niece of the gang leader."

A crystal-clear link to the Stavic brothers' rivals in Zagreb. Embla felt her pulse increase.

"That could give us an opening with Jiri. It might even

help us find some evidence of contact between Andreas and Vlasic," she said.

Göran's face split into a broad grin, which made him look like a contented bulldog. "We already have that evidence. The link is Andreas's wife—what was her name again?" He leafed through the papers in front of him. Embla had just gone over the interviews with Andreas, so she knew the answer.

"Kristina."

"That's it, thank you. Now listen to this"—he started tapping his index finger on the desk, emphasizing every word he said—"Jiri's wife, Gabriela, and Andreas's wife, Kristina, are sisters!"

"Wow!"

It wasn't the best response, but she was so surprised she couldn't think of anything sensible to say. Göran didn't seem to mind. "So Kristina's maiden name was Pavic," he continued. "The Acika brothers each married a sister, and Mikael Vlasic is their uncle."

"Do you think Milo knew that?"

"He did."

"And surely Kador must have known that the Pavic sisters were related to the gangster in Zagreb."

"He did. Just like Milo. According to Boris Cetinski, it seems to have been Mikael Vlasic and Milo Stavic who arranged the marriages between their nieces and the Acika brothers. It's been six years since Andreas and Kristina got married. Apparently the two gang leaders were good friends back then, and the marriages were presumably supposed to cement the peaceful relationship between the gangs—and provide the opportunity for both men to expand their activities."

The chair protested as he leaned back and clasped his hands behind his head, then stretched both straight out in front of him and yawned. Presumably that was his exercise for the day.

"Jiri and Gabriela got married as soon as he got out of jail—that was five years ago. But then Milo and Mikael had a big falling-out. They were two roosters who both wanted the spot on top of the dung heap; it was never going to work in the long run. There were a lot of violent incidents down in Croatia, but the only thing that came to our attention was the shooting of Luca and his friend the doorman—and the professional hit man we fished out of the river."

"But nothing happened after that," Embla pointed out.

"Not in Gothenburg, but according to Boris Cetinski, there was plenty going on in Zagreb and Split, culminating in Kador's disappearance. It's not surprising that Kador and Milo had everything in place to get Louise and the children to safety at a moment's notice."

A possible way to solve the murders had opened up: the Acika brothers. Not only Jiri, but super-smooth Andreas.

However, it was going to take lengthy interviews, surveillance, and cooperation with the police in Croatia. There was no rush; the important thing was to nail as many people as possible who were involved in the tangled mess. The dream scenario would be to shut down the entire organization the brothers had built, but that was an unlikely outcome. The cracks in the network were probably already being sealed. Lawyers and board members in the various companies would make it as difficult as possible for prosecutors to work out what was normal business practice and what was criminal activity. The statute of limitations for economic crimes is relatively short, so prosecutors often don't have enough time to investigate complex issues. Embla was glad she wasn't involved in that part of the case.

"What about Louise and the kids? Do you think they're safe in Alingsås?" she asked.

"Yes. I've spoken to Maina Sahlén in Witness Protection, and she thinks their new identities are good. Milo didn't half-ass anything. We're not putting their location in writing, not even the fact that they're in Sweden."

A weight lifted from Embla's heart. It felt good to know that Lollo's family was no longer in danger, even though the woman she'd met yesterday wasn't the person she'd known when she was growing up. To be fair, Lollo had been in shock after learning of Kador's death.

A discreet glance at the clock above Göran's head told her it was exactly four o'clock.

"I've arranged to leave early today, so I'm going home now," she said, doing her best to sound casual.

"Home? You're not heading up to Dalsland, then?" he said with a teasing smile.

Shit! He knew her too well.

"Well, yes, actually. I'm going to Nisse's, then I'm going to Herremark to see Monika and Harald."

She couldn't help blushing, but it was the truth. She might have left out one or two details, but that was her business.

FOR THE FIRST few kilometers there was no sign of snow. The low afternoon sun shone out of an almost cloudless sky, dazzling her with its reflection on the surface of the damp road. For the first time that year there was a hint of spring in the air, and huge flocks of Canada geese grazed on the open fields of the Dalsland plain, picking up everything edible that they could find.

As agreed Embla drove past the turnoff for Uncle Nisse's place—she would visit on the way home—and continued toward Herremark and the guesthouse. The midday thaw had reduced the depth of the snow on the ground, but there were still a few centimeters left. The beauty of the scene took her breath away as the last of the sun's rays colored the snow among the trees pale pink and the underside of the few clouds bright cerise. As the sun went down, the pink shifted into shades of blue. The car's thermometer showed that the temperature was dropping fast; no doubt it would be below freezing overnight.

She turned into the guesthouse yard and parked. The little Kia was a good, reliable car. She gave the dashboard an appreciative pat before she got out.

Nothing had changed. Harald was at the reception

desk entering something into the computer. His face lit up as soon as he saw her.

"Embla! Welcome!" He hurried around the desk and gave her a great big bear hug. "It's so good to have you here again."

He laughed and went back behind the desk. He put on his reading glasses, which he wore on a cord around his neck, and peered at the screen. "Let's see . . . Your boyfriend and his dog have already arrived—number fifteen. Dinner in half an hour—Monika's reserved a table for you. The same one as last time," he added with a meaningful wink.

Boyfriend, indeed. However, she didn't protest; she simply smiled and took the key. After all, she and Olle had only booked one cottage.

The twilight was deepening as she made her way across the yard. She couldn't see any light from inside the cottage; was this the right one? Yes, it said 15 on the door. She looked around. There were lights on in several of the other cottages, but the two closest to theirs were also dark. She'd chosen the best spot, right by the lake. No neighbors in front or to the sides. Peace and quiet.

She smiled as she went up to the door and put her bag down on the step. She was about to insert her key in the lock when she caught a movement out of the corner of her eye. A second later she was on the ground.

"Tore! Stop that!" Olle called, sounding amused.

She couldn't analyze him too closely because Tore was standing over her, licking her face.

"Yuck!" she said, wiping away the saliva with the sleeve of her jacket. Tore scampered back to his master.

"Sorry—he beat me to it!" Olle said with a laugh.

Keeping a firm grip on Tore's collar, he held out his other hand and helped her up. "Are you okay?" he asked with a hint of anxiety.

"I'm fine, apart from my self-esteem; my reflexes aren't what they should be!"

She shook her head, but couldn't help smiling. He was even better looking than she remembered, and she realized he was still holding her hand. He gave her a hug that was more than a friendly hug. And the kiss that followed was more than a friendly kiss. A lot more. A wonderful warm feeling surged through her body. Reluctantly she freed herself from his embrace and unlocked the door. They went in and took off their outdoor clothes. Olle switched on the light in the living room and had a good look around.

"This is bigger than the one where we found Milo Stavic," he said.

"It is. Two bedrooms, slightly larger living room, and it's the only cottage with a sauna and jacuzzi."

She didn't mention that it was usually known as the bridal suite.

"And look at the view over the lake—fantastic!"

Olle was clearly delighted. Tore seemed happy, too, having sniffed his way around every single millimeter.

Olle produced a bottle of Champagne from a cooler and managed to find two suitable glasses in one of the kitchen cupboards. Embla decided she could allow herself a glass of bubbly; she felt as if they had a lot to celebrate. When Olle popped the cork, Tore stiffened. Maybe he wasn't entirely over the events up at Ulvsjön.

"Harald said dinner will be served in"—she glanced at her phone—"fifteen minutes."

"In that case we'd better drink fast!"

His eyes sparkled as he raised his glass to her. It took a second for her to realize they were sparkling with tears, and she could hear the emotion in his voice when he added:

"Thank you for saving me and Tore."

"Oh, come on—we both played our part."

"We did, but without your knowledge of guns and the fact that you stayed calm under pressure, we'd have been dead meat."

Without me you wouldn't have been up there in the first place.

Olle cleared his throat and smiled shyly. "Here's to you."

They sipped the cold, delicious drink. Their eyes met, and now it was Embla's turn to smile and propose a toast of her own. "Here's to us!"

The warmth in Olle's eyes could have melted a glacier in seconds. "To us!" he echoed.

Embla moved closer to him and touched his sweater. Slowly she slid her hand up to his cheek, cupped it gently, and drew his face down to hers. With her lips almost touching his, she whispered, "I booked this cottage because I thought Tore would need his own bedroom."

It's quarter past two and I can't sleep. It's dark and so fucking quiet everywhere. The silence . . . It's driving me crazy! My head is spinning. Maybe I've had a little too much to drink . . . I need someone to talk to, but there's no one . . . That's why I'm recording this. Then I'll delete the recording. I could have died when Julian opened the door and Åsa—no, it's Embla now—was standing there with that detective. Shit! I was really shaken up by the fact that they'd found me—Milo had promised the plan was watertight. No one would be able to track us down, he said. For fuck's sake—it only took the cops a month. How did they do it? At least they promised that nothing would be put in writing about me and the kids. Our new identities mustn't get out. And now we're under police protection . . . Ha! What a joke! If only they knew! Actually I thought I did pretty well, pretending to be grief-stricken over that asshole Kador. I certainly won't miss the little shit. Nor Milo. He might have been there for our family, but he was always all over me when he'd had a few drinks. Wanted me to "play nice." Fucking pig! No risk of anything like that with Luca, of course, but I hardly ever saw him. Anyway, I managed to hide my shock when Embla and the other cop turned up, then I pretended to be grief-stricken when they told me my husband was dead. I had another shock when they asked me about Jiri . . . How the fuck do they know about him? And do they know anything about the two of us? It's fortunate that he and Kador are cousins; you always come into contact with relatives whether you want to or not. That's what I'll say if they ask me any more questions. Although I've got a bad feeling . . . I read something in the papers about a gang war up in Dalsland, and it was on the news, too. Four Croatians killed, two Swedes injured. They said a man had been arrested for the murders of Milo and Luca, but they didn't give his nationality. There was a lot of other stuff about smuggling guns and drugs, but Jiri talked about a big deal going down out in the middle of nowhere—Croatians, a Swede, and some Norwegian gang were involved. I'm beginning to worry that this was the deal he meant. He knew Milo was spending the night at a place with a really good restaurant, and he knew the name of the place because Milo had been there before and talked about it. Jiri was going to fix him. And he did. And he fixed Luca, too . . . Mikael will reward Jiri. He knows nothing about me and Jiri; he wouldn't like it if he found out. Jiri's going to fix Gabriela, too—sour-faced whining bitch. They'll have to get a divorce, though—killing her would be too risky, even if that's what I'd prefer.

My darling Jiri was heading back to Split as soon as he'd fixed Milo and Luca—a quick in-and-out job, as he put it. Did he manage to get away? There was a blizzard . . . Did he stay in Dalsland? Please, God, don't let him be dead! Please let him be safe in Split! I can't find any concrete information about what's happening. They're not giving any names online . . . What will I do if Jiri's dead? What if he's the one they've arrested for the murders of Milo and Luca? Can they link him to Kador's murder? I hope not—Croatian prisons are awful.

I'm intending to stay here for six months, then go back. Jiri and I have agreed that we won't contact each other during that period. I hope by the time I get back his divorce will have gone through. Or if he is the one who's been arrested and he ends up in jail in Sweden, I'll wait for him.

I won't dare see Embla again. I'd really like to—I've missed her so much, especially in those first few years. We always had so much fun together. But she's a cop—I must never forget that. She sat in my kitchen sipping water, the hypocritical bitch, just waiting to see if I'd start babbling. I know I drank quite a lot of wine. That wasn't smart, but all those . . . shocks were too much for me. Oh—my other cell phone's ringing. Shit, where did I put it? There it is!

IF YOU LISTENED carefully, you could hear another phone ringing in the background, before the recording ended. Embla stared at the phone lying in the middle of

Göran's desk. She realized she wasn't breathing and was beginning to feel faint. With a huge effort she took in a shuddering breath. It couldn't be true, but deep down she knew she'd just heard Lollo's own words and feelings. Her old friend might have been slurring her words, but this was no drunken ramble, it was an honest admission that she loved Jiri and had hated Kador. She hadn't said so, but there was a strong possibility that she could have been involved in her husband's murder. If so, she was the one who'd tipped off Jiri, told him that Kador was going home alone at an earlier time than usual the night he disappeared.

She'd thought Embla was a hypocrite, and yet she'd said she missed her. It was loneliness, alcohol, and maybe some other drug that had made her call Embla that Friday evening.

Göran was looking at her, and Embla could see sympathy in his eyes.

"We found the phone when we searched the apartment on Saturday. It had slipped down between the cushions on the sofa; presumably she dropped it and then forgot about it."

There was a long pause before Embla managed to force out the question that was burning inside her.

"Did you find anything else?"

"No. No sign of a struggle. The wine glass and the empty bottle had been left on the coffee table, but there was no IT equipment—only this burner phone. And there were no ID documents in the name of Leko or any other name. The bowl containing the little packets was still in the kitchen cupboard; we tested the powder, and it is cocaine. The new Audi is still in the parking lot."

Embla took another deep breath.

"No trace of any of them?"

Slowly he shook his head. "No. Both Louise and the children are gone. Vanished without a trace."

"Do you know when they went missing?"

"Early on Saturday morning, we think. Irene and Fredrik went to the office and spoke to her during her lunch break on Friday. She didn't have time to see them after work, because she had to go and pick up Julian, then give the children a ride to their swimming lessons. Apparently the mothers take turns driving, and it was her turn. She promised to come into the station for questioning at eleven o'clock on Saturday, but she didn't show up. We entered the apartment in the afternoon to find them gone."

She could feel the scalding tears behind her eyelids. She swallowed hard several times, but she couldn't make a sound. It had been such a huge relief to know that Lollo was alive, and that her disappearance hadn't been Embla's fault.

After listening to the recording, her feelings were mixed to say the least. A little time passed before she became aware of the empty space that had opened up inside her. She recognized it only too well, and she knew why it was there.

She had lost Lollo again.

Acknowledgments

FIRSTLY I WANT to give a special thank-you to my Swedish publisher, Erika Degard, and my editor, Sofia Hannar, for all their help and support while I've been working on this book. A big thank-you to everyone at Massolit for their brilliant efforts and achievements.

The characters in my books are always fictitious. All resemblance to any person, living or dead, is coincidental and not the intention of the author. As usual I have taken considerable liberties with geographical facts. I do not adapt my narrative to suit the existing geography; reality is adapted to fit the story instead.

Helene Tursten

Other Titles in the Soho Crime Series

STEPHANIE BARRON
(Jane Austen's England)
Jane and the Twelve Days
   of Christmas
Jane and the Waterloo Map

F.H. BATACAN
(Philippines)
Smaller and Smaller Circles

JAMES R. BENN
(World War II Europe)
Billy Boyle
The First Wave
Blood Alone
Evil for Evil
Rag & Bone
A Mortal Terror
Death's Door
A Blind Goddess
The Rest Is Silence
The White Ghost
Blue Madonna
The Devouring
Solemn Graves
When Hell Struck Twelve
The Red Horse

CARA BLACK
(Paris, France)
Murder in the Marais
Murder in Belleville
Murder in the Sentier
Murder in the Bastille
Murder in Clichy
Murder in Montmartre
Murder on the Ile Saint-Louis
Murder in the Rue de Paradis
Murder in the Latin Quarter
Murder in the Palais Royal
Murder in Passy
Murder at the Lanterne Rouge
Murder Below Montparnasse
Murder in Pigalle
Murder on the Champ de Mars
Murder on the Quai
Murder in Saint-Germain

CARA BLACK CONT.
Murder on the Left Bank
Murder in Bel-Air

Three Hours in Paris

LISA BRACKMANN
(China)
Rock Paper Tiger
Hour of the Rat
Dragon Day
Getaway
Go-Between

HENRY CHANG
(Chinatown)
Chinatown Beat
Year of the Dog
Red Jade
Death Money
Lucky

BARBARA CLEVERLY
(England)
The Last Kashmiri Rose
Strange Images of Death
The Blood Royal
Not My Blood
A Spider in the Cup
Enter Pale Death
Diana's Altar

Fall of Angels
Invitation to Die

COLIN COTTERILL
(Laos)
The Coroner's Lunch
Thirty-Three Teeth
Disco for the Departed
Anarchy and Old Dogs
Curse of the Pogo Stick
The Merry Misogynist
Love Songs from a Shallow Grave
Slash and Burn
The Woman Who Wouldn't Die
Six and a Half Deadly Sins
I Shot the Buddha
The Rat Catchers' Olympics

COLIN COTTERILL CONT.
Don't Eat Me
The Second Biggest Nothing
The Delightful Life of
   a Suicide Pilot

GARRY DISHER
(Australia)
The Dragon Man
Kittyhawk Down
Snapshot
Chain of Evidence
Blood Moon
Whispering Death
Signal Loss

Wyatt
Port Vila Blues
Fallout

Bitter Wash Road
Under the Cold Bright Lights

TERESA DOVALPAGE
(Cuba)
Death Comes in through
   the Kitchen
Queen of Bones

Death of a Telenovela Star
   (A Novella)

DAVID DOWNING
(World War II Germany)
Zoo Station
Silesian Station
Stettin Station
Potsdam Station
Lehrter Station
Masaryk Station
Wedding Station

(World War I)
Jack of Spies
One Man's Flag
Lenin's Roller Coaster
The Dark Clouds Shining

Diary of a Dead Man on Leave

AGNETE FRIIS
(Denmark)
What My Body Remembers
The Summer of Ellen

TIMOTHY HALLINAN
(Thailand)
The Fear Artist
For the Dead
The Hot Countries
Fools' River
Street Music

(Los Angeles)
Crashed
Little Elvises
The Fame Thief
Herbie's Game
King Maybe
Fields Where They Lay
Nighttown

METTE IVIE HARRISON
(Mormon Utah)
The Bishop's Wife
His Right Hand
For Time and All Eternities
Not of This Fold

MICK HERRON
(England)
Slow Horses
Dead Lions
The List (A Novella)
Real Tigers
Spook Street
London Rules
The Marylebone Drop (A Novella)
Joe Country
The Catch (A Novella)
Slough House

Down Cemetery Road
The Last Voice You Hear
Why We Die
Smoke and Whispers

Reconstruction
Nobody Walks
This Is What Happened

STAN JONES
(Alaska)
White Sky, Black Ice
Shaman Pass
Frozen Sun
Village of the Ghost Bears
Tundra Kill
The Big Empty

STEVEN MACK JONES
(Detroit)
August Snow
Lives Laid Away
Dead of Winter

LENE KAABERBØL & AGNETE FRIIS
(Denmark)
The Boy in the Suitcase
Invisible Murder
Death of a Nightingale
The Considerate Killer

MARTIN LIMÓN
(South Korea)
Jade Lady Burning
Slicky Boys
Buddha's Money
The Door to Bitterness
The Wandering Ghost
G.I. Bones
Mr. Kill
The Joy Brigade
Nightmare Range
The Iron Sickle
The Ville Rat
Ping-Pong Heart
The Nine-Tailed Fox
The Line
GI Confidential

ED LIN
(Taiwan)
Ghost Month
Incensed
99 Ways to Die

PETER LOVESEY
(England)
The Circle
The Headhunters

PETER LOVESEY CONT.
False Inspector Dew
Rough Cider
On the Edge
The Reaper

(Bath, England)
The Last Detective
Diamond Solitaire
The Summons
Bloodhounds
Upon a Dark Night
The Vault
Diamond Dust
The House Sitter
The Secret Hangman
Skeleton Hill
Stagestruck
Cop to Corpse
The Tooth Tattoo
The Stone Wife
Down Among the Dead Men
Another One Goes Tonight
Beau Death
Killing with Confetti
The Finisher

(London, England)
Wobble to Death
The Detective Wore
Silk Drawers
Abracadaver
Mad Hatter's Holiday
The Tick of Death
A Case of Spirits
Swing, Swing Together
Waxwork

Bertie and the Tinman
Bertie and the Seven Bodies
Bertie and the Crime of Passion

SUJATA MASSEY
(1920s Bombay)
The Widows of Malabar Hill
The Satapur Moonstone
The Bombay Prince

FRANCINE MATHEWS
(Nantucket)
Death in the Off-Season
Death in Rough Water
Death in a Mood Indigo
Death in a Cold Hard Light
Death on Nantucket
Death on Tuckernuck

SEICHŌ MATSUMOTO
(Japan)
Inspector Imanishi Investigates

MAGDALEN NABB
(Italy)
Death of an Englishman
Death of a Dutchman
Death in Springtime
Death in Autumn
The Marshal and the Murderer
The Marshal and the Madwoman
The Marshal's Own Case
The Marshal Makes His Report
The Marshal at the Villa Torrini
Property of Blood
Some Bitter Taste
The Innocent
Vita Nuova
The Monster of Florence

FUMINORI NAKAMURA
(Japan)
The Thief
Evil and the Mask
Last Winter, We Parted
The Kingdom
The Boy in the Earth
Cult X

STUART NEVILLE
(Northern Ireland)
The Ghosts of Belfast
Collusion
Stolen Souls
The Final Silence
Those We Left Behind
So Say the Fallen
The Traveller & Other Stories

(Dublin)
Ratlines

REBECCA PAWEL
(1930s Spain)
Death of a Nationalist
Law of Return
The Watcher in the Pine
The Summer Snow

KWEI QUARTEY
(Ghana)
Murder at Cape Three Points
Gold of Our Fathers
Death by His Grace
The Missing American
Sleep Well, My Lady

QIU XIAOLONG
(China)
Death of a Red Heroine
A Loyal Character Dancer
When Red Is Black

JAMES SALLIS
(New Orleans)
The Long-Legged Fly
Moth
Black Hornet
Eye of the Cricket
Bluebottle
Ghost of a Flea

Sarah Jane

JOHN STRALEY
(Sitka, Alaska)
The Woman Who Married a Bear
The Curious Eat Themselves
The Music of What Happens
Death and the Language
  of Happiness
The Angels Will Not Care
Cold Water Burning
Baby's First Felony

(Cold Storage, Alaska)
The Big Both Ways
Cold Storage, Alaska
What Is Time to a Pig?

AKIMITSU TAKAGI
(Japan)
The Tattoo Murder Case
Honeymoon to Nowhere

AKIMITSU TAKAGI CONT.
The Informer

HELENE TURSTEN
(Sweden)
Detective Inspector Huss
The Torso
The Glass Devil
Night Rounds
The Golden Calf
The Fire Dance
The Beige Man
The Treacherous Net
Who Watcheth
Protected by the Shadows

Hunting Game
Winter Grave
Snowdrift

An Elderly Lady Is Up
  to No Good

ILARIA TUTI
(Italy)
Flowers over the Inferno
The Sleeping Nymph

JANWILLEM VAN DE WETERING
(Holland)
Outsider in Amsterdam
Tumbleweed
The Corpse on the Dike
Death of a Hawker
The Japanese Corpse
The Blond Baboon
The Maine Massacre
The Mind-Murders
The Streetbird
The Rattle-Rat
Hard Rain
Just a Corpse at Twilight
Hollow-Eyed Angel
The Perfidious Parrot
The Sergeant's Cat:
  Collected Stories

JACQUELINE WINSPEAR
(1920s England)
Maisie Dobbs
Birds of a Feather